A MURDERER'S MESSAGE

She had left the lights on for herself downstairs, but their bedroom was dark. Ken was asleep, so she pulled her Honda into the driveway next to Ken's big dark green Saab 9000 and closed the door as quietly as she could.

She locked the car and walked along the brightly lit path to the back door when she stopped in her tracks. Beyond the pool of light she heard a rustle in the rhododendron bushes.

She listened for a while. She heard nothing more. It had probably been her imagination anyway, so she continued toward the house.

The rustling again! This time louder and closer.

She stopped, her heart pounding in fear, all senses on full alert. A deep, loud, menacing warning, more like an animal's growl than a human voice, came from the rhododendron:

"Death will come soon!"

Scalpel's Edge

Margot J. Fromer

DIAMOND BOOKS, NEW YORK

SCALPEL'S EDGE

A Diamond Book / published by arrangement with
the author

PRINTING HISTORY
Diamond edition / September 1991

ISBN: 1-55773-580-8

Diamond Books are published by The Berkley Publishing Group,
200 Madison Avenue, New York, New York 10016.
The name "DIAMOND" and its logo
are trademarks belonging to Charter Communications, Inc.

PRINTED IN THE UNITED STATES OF AMERICA

10 9 8 7 6 5 4 3 2 1

**Dedicated to the memory of
Beatrice Neuman Fromer**

1

AMANDA KNIGHT TURNED into the driveway of the large brick Georgian house, got out of the car, and stood for a few minutes breathing in the crisp October air that was such a relief after the particularly hot and humid Washington summer. She unlocked the door, threw herself down on the big sofa, kicked off her shoes, and groaned with fatigue and relief at being home.

It had been a ghastly day at the hospital. The nurse she'd had to fire—the second one this month—slammed the door of Amanda's office so hard that a diploma jumped off the wall. Then her secretary had let her in on a juicy piece of hospital gossip—that she, Amanda, was having an affair with Eddie Silverman. Amanda grinned at that, but she was puzzled, too. She and Eddie had been best buddies for years, but they had barely seen each other in the past six months. Why was the story weaving its way through the grapevine *now*?

But Amanda shrugged that off for the moment because to top off what was turning into a thoroughly rotten week, that bastard Leo McBride had gone and gotten himself murdered.

Murder at J.F.K. Memorial Hospital. Amanda shivered at the thought of someone killing McBride, but at the same time she realized that she would never have to tolerate insults from him again. Nor would he ever put his sneaky hands on her behind again. He'd never again chew out and humiliate the medical residents. And she'd never have to listen to stories about how he, of all the physicians at the hospital, never saw patients who could not afford to pay his full fee.

Still, the thought of a cold-blooded killing, practically right under her nose, was sobering. Frightening. "He was an odious bastard," Amanda told the big gray cat that had jumped onto the sofa and was now purring in her lap as she stroked the soft fur. "But no one, not even Leo McBride, deserves to have his trachea slit open with a scalpel."

But the truth was that many of the people she had talked to thought that Leo McBride had gotten exactly what he deserved, and as she had told the police that afternoon when they questioned her and everyone else in the administrative office wing, they could suspect half the hospital staff. The homicide detective to whom she made the remark, Bender or Bonder or something like that, had widened his eyes and looked at her strangely.

"That's an odd thing to say about a highly respected doctor, the chief of medicine in an important hospital like this."

Amanda had looked him straight in the eye and said, "He was an excellent doctor, a brilliant diagnostician, but a greedy, mean, spiteful tyrant."

"I take it you didn't like him, either," said Bender/Bonder dryly. "Did you kill him?"

"I respected him as a doctor."

"But did you like him?"

"No."

"Did you kill him?"

"No."

"Do you have any idea who might have?"

"No, I don't."

Amanda knew she wasn't being helpful. She was in shock and frightened, but she also knew that she did not appear to the police as grief stricken as perhaps she should have. She had spoken more tartly than she usually would have responded to people, especially the few policemen she had come in contact with. But Bender/Bonder and his partner, a woman who in a million years Amanda wouldn't have thought a police detective, would not let her get on with her work. They had questioned her for a half hour about McBride and the killing. The woman didn't say much, maybe she was new on the job or was the junior partner, Amanda didn't know how these things worked, but Bender/Bonder had pressed on, always polite, always soft spoken, but never letting up until she had answered all his questions. And when he was finished, he had made it clear that he would probably be back for more.

He reminded her a little of Colombo, the television detective that Peter Falk had played so perfectly. Colombo was more rumpled than this guy, and he appeared a little more bumbly-fumbly, but there was that same hard, intuitive intelligence behind the casual facade. Amanda was willing to bet that Bender/Bonder had the same success rate as Colombo.

Now, sitting on the couch, telling Shadow what had happened, she wished that Ken, her husband of only a little more than a year, was sitting there too instead of off on a business trip to Japan. But at least he'd be home tomorrow. She also wished she hadn't snapped at the detective. And she *did* care who had killed McBride.

She wondered who had the guts to do it, who had finally gotten fed up enough to have gone into his office and neatly sliced open his windpipe.

And it *was* a neat job. Amanda had been one of the first to see it. She had just left her office to dash across the street to the Italian grocery for a sandwich when she heard the piercing shriek from McBride's office not ten paces from where she stood. The scream was like nothing Amanda had ever heard, and she knew instinctively, as surely as she had ever known anything, that it heralded very bad news indeed.

It was lunchtime, so not many people were about, but those who were followed Amanda as she ran toward the screaming woman and through McBride's outer office, where his secretary Ina worked, and into the spacious, elaborately decorated office of the chief of medicine, who lay reclining in his high-backed chair with a stainless steel scalpel embedded in his throat.

Amanda's mind took a snapshot of the scene, as effective and detailed as any crime reporter's, and she looked at it now as she sprawled on the couch in the peace and quiet of her living room.

McBride had insisted on having his office decorated professionally and had bamboozled hospital administration into paying for it. No one else had an office with original oil paintings on the walls and $150-a-yard fabric on the uphol-stered chairs and sofa—not even the medical director, and certainly not Jonathan Bernstein, the chief of surgery and McBride's counterpart and arch rival for the medical director's job, which would be available in a little more than a year.

McBride had insisted on having built-in bookshelves while everyone else had to make do with functional but boring bookcases from hospital stores. Amanda had to admit that the effect was impressive: an entire wall of books with a large antique desk in front of it sitting on a huge spectacular Aubusson carpet.

It was against this wall of books that McBride had come to his final rest. Amanda saw him now in her mind's eye, with his chair tilted back, the front two legs lifted off the ground, the edge of the high back resting against a shelf of medical reference works, some of which the victim himself had written.

McBride was leaning back, as he often did when he had a visitor, especially when he wanted to exert power over who-ever was sitting in the chair on the other side of the desk. His chin was tilted up, as it often was, but he wasn't in his usual position of ease and comfort. This time, the last time he would sit in that chair, his body was twisted at an awkward angle, but his clothes were not in disarray and more than anything else, his face seemed surprised.

The crease in his trousers was as sharp as ever, and even his tie was still neatly knotted, although the small, drying trickle of blood staining his collar—aside from that shining steel sticking out of his throat—was the only discordant note in a scene that could otherwise be photographed for *Architectural Digest*.

Whoever slipped the scalpel into that arrogant throat had had easy access to it. Amanda knew that you didn't have to go to detective school (or wherever it was that people learned how to detect) to see that McBride had been killed by someone he knew. "But that, soft kitty cat," she said to Shadow as she set off to the kitchen to get something to eat for both of them, "could include half the population of Washington."

Later, after finishing the cold leftover pasta with shrimp and lobster and soggy salad and forcing herself to eat an apple instead of a chunk of cake, she took a shower, washed her hair, and cuddled up in bed with a novel she'd started the night before. But there was no way she could concentrate; not tonight, with McBride barely cold in the morgue.

Amanda tried to feel guilty about being relieved that he was dead, but she couldn't manage it. No, that was wrong. It wasn't his *death* that she had wished for. It was just getting him out of her life. "Should I feel guilty about feeling free of him?" she asked Shadow, who pricked up her ears and purred at the sound of Amanda's voice.

Amanda wanted Ken. He would have told her it was silly to worry so much about her feelings. "You feel what you feel," he'd say. "Why do you always worry about having the right or wrong feelings?"

He was right, of course. Ken rarely worried about his emotions. He would just get on with his life and keep crawling steadily up the corporate ladder. He was one rung away from the top now, and Amanda knew how much he wanted to be named chief executive officer of Naylor-Noyes, the largest computer manufacturer in the world. If one of *his* fellow executives had been found murdered, and if Ken had hated him as much as Amanda had hated Leo McBride, he would have put on a sad face for the public, sent flowers to the widow, and secretly rejoiced at his good fortune. But in a million years he wouldn't have behaved snippily to the police. He would have fully cooperated in their investigation.

Ken's practicality and emotional cool was a source of both inspiration and frustration for Amanda. She loved and admired his steadiness and ability to keep his head in any situation, but his inability to display his feelings made her nervous. But he never bored her, and she knew that he appreciated the laughter, openness, and spontaneity that she had brought into his life. She missed him now and longed to see his deep blue eyes open wide as he watched her reaction to his lovemaking.

"Stop that now," she said aloud. "This time tomorrow you'll be doing exactly what you want to be doing now."

I shouldn't have shot my mouth off to that detective, she thought. Now he'll think I murdered McBride—not that the thought hasn't crossed my mind a few times.

She squirmed a little as she realized how she must have sounded to Bender or Bonder or whatever. Everyone else probably carried on about McBride as though he were the greatest thing since sliced bread—now that he was dead, now that the fear was gone, now that the oppressive, malignant weight was lifted from the department of medicine at John F. Kennedy Memorial Hospital.

God, he was a sleazy little shit, she thought as she remembered one of their last conversations. Amanda had gone to a regional meeting of directors of nursing and had practically broken her jaw trying not to yawn through budget discussions and speeches about motivational methods. She had brought with her a pile of application letters and was making notations on all of them so that Louise, her secretary, would know which form letter to send in response.

The meeting lasted far longer than the pile of letters, and when it was over she refused an invitation to lunch with a group of directors. She'd rather have her arteries clogged at McDonald's than suffer through more nurse talk—although there might have been some juicy gossip, and she always hated to miss that.

She passed no McDonald's on the way back to the hospital, and the only appealing restaurant had a parking lot so crowded that she didn't even bother to go in. By the time she got back to the hospital, she was ravenous and the cafeteria was almost empty. She settled down at a corner table, crumbled some saltines into the bowl of chili, and took the bookmark out of her novel.

Just as Amanda was losing herself in the story, Leo McBride sat down opposite her. With all the dozens of empty tables in the cafeteria, why did he have to bother her? But that was typical McBride; no one else's comfort or needs were as important as his own.

"Not disturbing you, am I?" he asked.

"You are, but you're here now," she replied, "so you might as well stay. What's new?"

The trouble with asking McBride what was new was that he'd describe something he'd bought. He had only two topics of conversation: medicine and money, and the former he reserved for doctors, who he believed were the only people who understood the ins and outs of health care. But he was willing to discuss money and his possessions with anyone who would stay still for a few minutes. And now she was trapped.

He droned on for a while about a new conference table—he was the only person she'd ever met who bragged about his office furniture—and then started a story about how cleverly he'd bilked another patient.

"I don't think I want to hear this," said Amanda.

"Oh, come on, sure you do. It's a great story.

"You know, all doctors have set fees that we are very happy to discuss with patients beforehand. So I had this guy, an auto mechanic who had no health insurance. Can you imagine that in this day and age?"

Amanda could easily imagine it. There were close to 40 million Americans, most of them with jobs, who had no health insurance. The problem was becoming a national emergency. But she said nothing, hoping this would be over soon.

"Anyway," he continued, "he needed some diagnostic tests, and that ran the bill up higher than my girl had originally estimated. Then the guy squawked that he couldn't afford the fee and asked if he could pay it off a little at a time. Of course I said no." McBride was still outraged at the memory.

"So I called his boss—it was an independent garage that works only on foreign cars—and asked to have his wages garnished. The guy told me to shove the bill up my ass! Can you imagine the nerve of someone like that?"

Amanda cheered silently for the auto mechanic. "That was kind of a chintzy thing to do, Leo. You make a bundle, and your wife wasn't exactly selling matches on the street when you married her. Why do you need to screw some poor guy out of an extra few hundred dollars?"

McBride thought she was joking. "Oh, come on," he said. "Everyone does it. You don't approve because you have a job with good health insurance, and now you've got a rich husband who can afford to buy any kind of care that either of you need."

Amanda chose to ignore the crack about her rich husband. "Having insurance or enough money has nothing to do with it," she said. "The way you treated that man is small and mean—way beneath your dignity."

Actually, it wasn't beneath his dignity. McBride *had* no real dignity except when it came to the way he practiced medicine, but they dropped the subject then, and Amanda finished her chili as fast as she could and went back to her office not knowing whether to laugh or cry over McBride's greed.

Now, lying in bed with Shadow pressed close to her, she thought about that conversation and how typical it was of McBride's philosophy. Who knows? she thought. Maybe the patient killed him. People have done worse things out of anger and humiliation.

The phone rang.

"Hi!" said a voice in that familiar two-tone fashion after Amanda had answered.

"Oh, Glen, am I glad you called. Do I have big news for you. All hell has broken loose at the hospital. Guess what happened," said Amanda, all in a rush.

"Your favorite medicine man got knocked off," said Glencora Rodman, Amanda's best friend and absolute confidante.

"How did you find out about it already?" asked Amanda. Glencora was the editor of *Style and Sense*, a local magazine that was beginning to gain national attention. She knew everything that was going on in Washington, but how had she found out about this already?

"It's all over the news. Weren't you tripping over the TV cameras at the hospital?"

"I guess there were some, now that you mention it," said Amanda. "But I didn't stick around to be interviewed. I have enough problems with the nurses without shooting my mouth off on TV. I had to fire another one today; she let a patient go into electrolyte shock, and he died."

"Eee gad," said Glencora, who sometimes talked as though she were living in East Hampton in 1918 and didn't know electrolyte shock from electrolysis.

"Tell me everything," demanded Glencora. "Who do you think did it? Did you see the body? Was it gross?"

Amanda began to cry.

"Amanda, I didn't know you cared about the guy. I thought you didn't like him."

"I didn't," she said stifling a sob. "I hated him. He was a shit. I don't know why I'm crying.

"Yes, I do," she said, and cried even harder. "Everything's falling apart at the hospital. The nurses seem to be doing their best to knock off all the patients through sheer stupidity, and of course it's my responsibility and I'm going to get fired—and now someone's killed the chief of medicine."

"You're not going to get fired," said Glen. "It's not your fault the nurses are idiots."

"Fault, shmalt," said Amanda, who had calmed down to an occasional hiccupping sniffle. "That's not the point. I'm *responsible*, and if I don't get fired, I'm going to get sued. You know how people are when they sue hospital workers. *Everyone* gets caught up in the net. Even McBride's been sued, and he *never* made mistakes."

"Do you want me to come over?" asked Glen. "You sound like you shouldn't be alone right now."

"Oh, I wish you would," said Amanda, suddenly realizing how alone she felt and how much she wanted cheering up. "How soon can you get here?"

"I'll leave now, so I'll see you in a few minutes," said Glen happily. She *did* love a scandal, and McBride's murder would probably shape up to be one of the best of the year. Amanda went downstairs to open a bottle of the burgundy Ken had bought before leaving and rummaged through the cupboards to find some tidbits for them to munch on. As she was deciding if the cheese was still edible, she thought about calling Cicely McBride. As much as she avoided the woman's company—over the phone or in person—she had to offer her condolences.

She may be a silly twit, but her husband just got killed, and I should say something, thought Amanda. But then again . . . maybe it's too soon for her to deal with anyone but family. So she took her hand off the phone.

A half hour later Amanda heard the tires of Glen's car crunching on the driveway stones, and she opened the door before her friend had a chance to ring the bell. Glen, carrying a white bakery box, looked lovely.

"I thought we needed a little sugar to discuss a murder!" she said, and they talked the night away. They started out in the living room in front of the fire and then moved upstairs to sit cross-legged on Amanda and Ken's big bed to watch the eleven-o'clock news report of McBride's death.

Glen was still dressed in her work clothes, still as beautifully turned out late in the evening as she had been when she started out in the morning. Her makeup was fresh, her silk blouse remained neatly tucked into the soft wool skirt, and her shiny hair was softly curved under precisely at the ends of her earlobes. Amanda knew from the several European vacations they'd taken together (during one of which they had met Ken) that Glencora even slept and woke up neatly, with her hair tousled a little and her nightgown barely wrinkled. It was damned irritating!

"So who dunnit?" asked Glen.

"Oh, God, it could have been anyone in the hospital, and if he was regarded the same way outside of work as he was at J.F.K., then it could have been almost anyone in the entire D.C. metropolitan area. Leo McBride was not a warm and fuzzy person," replied Amanda. Then she thought for a moment. "But killing someone seems a little excessive, don't you think? True, he was a pain in the ass, a son of a bitch actually, but half the world is like that. It's not a reason to *kill* someone."

"It is, if it's *you* he's directing his meanness at," said Glen. "Look at it this way: If you eliminate all the murders committed by strangers, like an escaped convict knocking off an entire incredibly wholesome Iowa farm family just for the hell of it, and if you eliminate all the true loonies like that Hinckley creep who tried to assassinate President Reagan, and if you eliminate all the people who go into a McDonald's and spray the place with machine-gun fire, what have you got left? You've got people who detest other people and who kill them just because they detest them—or for their insurance money or an inheritance or something like that. People want other people out of the way, Amanda. And while it *is* a little drastic, it happens."

Amanda shuddered. "You've got a point," she admitted. "If you could have seen him . . ."

"Did it look like a deliberate killing," asked Glen, "or was it some madman looking for drugs or God knows what he expected to find in a doctor's office?"

Amanda consulted her mental photograph again. "It was deliberate, all right. It was precise, neat—there was hardly any blood. It was absolutely cold-blooded murder. It was one person who wanted Leo McBride dead. Not just anyone who happened to be in the office. And not just any doctor. It was McBride he wanted."

"How do you know that?" asked Glen.

"I don't know. I just do. You would too if you'd seen it."

"Okay, I believe you," said Glen in a placating voice because she could see that Amanda was near tears again. "But why do you care so much? What difference does it make who killed him as long as he's gone? Why are you so bent out of shape about it?"

"For God's sake, Glen. It's a *murder*! If you can't get upset about murder, that's pretty jaded."

"Jaded, shmaded—as you would say," said Glen. "People get murdered every day and you don't bat an eyelash. You don't even read about it in the paper. None of us does. People are slaughtered by the thousands in all those disgusting little Middle East countries, and it barely registers on our conscience. And now one shithead, who you just happened to know, gets his throat cut, and you're carrying on like it was the end of the world. I don't buy it. What's really wrong?"

Amanda burst into tears again and Glen hugged her and handed her tissues until the storm was over.

"It's not so much McBride, I guess," she admitted. "But that patient today . . . he went into cardiac arrest because a nurse that *I* hired was too stupid or too lazy to watch his fluids, so his electrolytes went all out of whack, and he went into V-fib, and the respiratory therapist—the *respiratory therapist* for God's sake!—found him. They worked on him for ages, but they couldn't defibrillate him. We're going to get sued up the kazoo."

"So you fired her?" asked Glencora. "Isn't that a little much for one mistake?"

Amanda looked at her friend in amazement. She had no idea what it was like to run the nursing department of a 650-bed teaching hospital. They'd been friends for years, but Glen still didn't truly understand how much of a patient's care was in the hands of nurses, how they could make or break a recovery from illness or surgery, how much damage they could do just by not paying attention. Doctors did the surgery and prescribed the medicine, but it was the nurses who took care of the patients; they were the ones who got them better—or sent them to the morgue. Amanda had always thought that if the public knew how much total power a nurse had over a hospital patient—and what absolute numbskulls most of them were—they'd rather have their surgery on the kitchen table at home.

"Look," she said to Glen, "if one of your staff writers libeled some politician just because he was too stupid or lazy to check facts or go to other sources or whatever, and if the guy sued you, wouldn't you kick the writer's butt out the door? Wouldn't you consider it journalistic malpractice?"

"I guess so," admitted Glen. "As long as you put it like that."

"Well, what this dip-squirt nurse did was a thousand times worse than libel a politician. She ended someone's *life*." The two women stared at each other in unhappy silence. Shadow jumped up onto the bed, rolled onto her back, and asked to have her belly scratched. Amanda stroked the cat's soft fur to stay the fresh flood of tears that threatened to roll down her cheeks, and she felt some of the tension ebb.

"Are you *really* in danger of getting fired?" asked Glen.

"Not right this minute," replied Amanda. "But if these things don't stop happening, I will be. If something else bad happens, I'll have to be the sacrificial lamb. David Townsend won't have any choice. I understand that."

"So what can you do to straighten things out?" asked Glen. "To whip the nurses into shape?"

"Well, for starters, I could single-handedly make nursing a more attractive profession so more intelligent women would be interested in it, so not so many of them would want to be doctors, lawyers, and Indian chiefs. I could raise the pay about fifty percent and they wouldn't be so angry and disgruntled all the time. I could revise the state board examinations so that practically any dope off the street wouldn't be able to pass them. I could change the entire structure of nursing education so they learn in school what they really need to know to work in the real world of sick people."

Again, they stared at each other. Amanda's voice had become increasingly impassioned as she voiced her private concerns about the enormity of what was involved, and Glen realized how solid the brick wall was that Amanda had to batter down.

Glan snapped her fingers. "Piece of cake!" she said. "You'll get it done by noon tomorrow."

There was nothing left but to burst into wild laughter, and of the three of them sprawled on the big bed, only Shadow detected the note of hysteria in Amanda's laugh.

2

CICELY MCBRIDE WAS sobbing nicely, she thought. Her face was puckered just enough to demonstrate her grief but not enough to distort her beautifully classic features or smudge her eye makeup.

Lieutenant Paul Bandman of the Metropolitan Police Department sat on the couch opposite her and waited for the flood of tears to subside. He and Detective Lydia Simonowitz had brought the news of her husband's murder, and as he sat across from her and watched the widow cry, Bandman saw nothing but crocodile tears.

This woman is about as grief stricken as a newly elected Congressman, he thought, and as he glanced at Simonowitz, he saw his thoughts reflected in her face.

He'd give Mrs. McBride another two minutes to pull herself together and then he'd start asking questions . . . such as, "Where were you, lady, late this morning, when someone who your husband knew and trusted did a little open-throat surgery on him—without the benefit of anesthesia?"

Bandman wasn't put off for a minute by the elegance of the house, the obvious health of their bank accounts, or the fatness of the family stock portfolio. He'd been a cop far too long for that, and he knew that murder, like disease and natural death, knew no economic or racial boundaries. And by the look of her, he knew that this crisp, rich tootsie of the symphony committee and the charity balls, who was now sniffling quietly into a handkerchief that looked like it cost a day's detective pay, could have stuck it to her husband as easily as anyone else.

And during the time he had spent at the hospital, Bandman learned that the chief nurse was right. Half the world would have been happy to have wielded that scalpel. Not one of the people he or Simonowitz had interviewed registered sorrow at McBride's death. Some even had difficulty concealing their relief—even delight. He must have been one hell of a prick, thought Bandman. Even his wife wasn't bothering to put on much of a show.

"Mrs. McBride, where were you from the time you woke up this morning until we walked in your door?" asked Bandman with no preliminary.

"How can you ask me a question like that at a time like this?" she said, and crumpled her face as if to cry again.

"Look, lady, I'm a homicide detective, a police officer, and I can ask any questions I please. A man—*your husband*—was murdered in cold blood a few hours ago by someone who he knew well and trusted enough to turn his back on. And that someone put an arm lock on him and slashed his windpipe open with an instrument designed to cut through things a lot thicker than a little cartilage and skin."

Bandman had taken a few liberties with the scenario, but the hospital pathologist, who had been summoned from his den of death in the basement to make a preliminary judgment (the final cause of death would not be officially established until the District of Columbia Medical Examiner had finished the autopsy), said that McBride was obviously stabbed from behind, and Bandman himself could see that the killer had stretched the neck, presumably to straighten out the trachea so that he (or she) could get the blade in on the first try. Because there wouldn't be another easy chance. McBride was a strong, healthy fellow who probably didn't take kindly to the sight of a glinting metal blade being pointed at his throat. Therefore, thought Bandman, the killer had to be at least an equal physical match for McBride, either in actual strength or in some other physical way—like a wife or girlfriend coming from behind with a kiss or a caress . . . followed by a knife blade.

But Bandman didn't say any of this to the cool, elegant woman who thought she could patronize him. He went on, "So you'll either answer my questions here, or we can go to the station house and you can answer them there. Take your choice."

But she would not be put off so easily. "I don't have to answer any of your questions, and if you take me away, you can't ask me anything without my lawyer there."

Bandman was getting annoyed. Maybe she wasn't as dumb as she wanted to appear. Either that or she watched too many police shows on TV, and like everyone else in the country, she knew the rules of questioning. "You're right," he said quietly. "You don't *have* to talk to me here. But I want to ask you some questions, and I get what I want, so I'm going to arrest you, read you your rights, and then Simonowitz here will cuff you behind your back. Then I'm going to call for some police backup, and the dispatcher will send six or seven police cars that'll come tearing up the street with their sirens screaming, and the officers will draw their guns and surround the house. By that time all the crime reporters who monitor the police band will have had time to get here.

"Then Simonowitz and I will walk you out to the car *real* slow so the neighbors can get a *real* good look at the show, and, lady, I'll bet you dollars to doughnuts that after we've taken a *real* slow ride to the station, the TV cameras will be out in force. And then we'll walk you past them *real* slow . . . so your neighbors and friends can watch it on the six-o'clock news. And they'll probably tape it so they can look at it over and over—and show it to their friends.

"And then—with your lawyer sitting right there—I'll ask you whatever I please."

Bandman was delighted with his story, although he admitted to himself that it was pretty farfetched. He made it up as he went along and was a little disappointed when he saw all the bluff go out of this pompous woman like air leaking out of a circus balloon. Maybe she *was* as dumb as she seemed. It was hard to tell with women; so much went on under the surface, and they were so damn complex.

Cicely McBride saw Bandman's smile through a haze of fear. She was looking forward to a happy and *very* rich widowhood, and the idea of having it marred at the outset by nasty publicity was intolerable. She didn't know what to do.

She had to tell that tacky little detective (he was wearing a suit that she was positive was polyester and a tie that had gone out of fashion five years ago) something, but she couldn't tell him the truth. She needed time to make up a convincing story because she never thought she would be asked for an alibi.

It was stupid of me not to have a story ready, she reprimanded herself as she watched the detectives stare at her. Why wouldn't I be a suspect. Isn't the grieving widow *always* a suspect? But what jury would believe that Cicely McBride, heiress to the Wilcox telecommunications empire, would murder Leo McBride, the nationally renowned physician to a president of the United States? Would Cicely McBride, who gave some of the best parties in the nation's capital and who was always on Washington's best-dressed list, kill her charming, handsome, smart, and very well connected husband, whose income was close to a million dollars a year?

Well, why not? she asked herself. Cicely McBride was, if she was nothing else, very, very practical, and she was angry at herself for not thinking of everything. But she had to think of something to do now, and serious thinking under stress was not her long suit.

When Bandman saw little beads of sweat appearing on Cicely's upper lip, he knew he had let her squirm long enough.

"Where's your phone, Mrs. McBride?" he asked, getting up from his chair.

"Who are you going to call?" she asked.

"I told you what I'm going to do. You haven't answered my questions, so I'm putting you under arrest," replied Bandman. "I don't have time to fart around. I have a murder to investigate."

Lydia Simonowitz had listened to Bandman bully Mrs. McBride and was alternately amused and amazed, but now she was puzzled. He never used crude language in front of civilians. Even in the station house, about the worst he ever said was "horseballs," and even then he had to be provoked to the point where other people would start throwing punches. She had never heard him say "fart."

They couldn't arrest Mrs. McBride; there wasn't the slightest shred of evidence. And even if they did, they would do it quietly and with as little fanfare as possible. Seven police cars tearing up the street, my ass, thought Simonowitz. And what was he smirking about? What tricks does this guy have up his sleeve?

This was the first murder case Simonowitz was given since she had been promoted to detective, and she felt lucky to be working with Bandman. He was a nice guy, he called her by her name—never the "babe" or "honey" or worse to which she had become inured over the six years she had been on the force. And he was smart. That was the part she liked best.

Even when Bandman dealt with the sleazebags who sold dope to children, punched old ladies in the face for their welfare checks, set fire to their own businesses for the insurance money, and left their dogs out in the freezing cold all night, he was polite. In fact, he was one of the most even-tempered people Lydia Simonowitz had ever met, on or off the force. So what was he up to now? This semibereaved widow could pick up the phone, whimper a little over the death of her husband, and complain directly to the chief of police about how she had been bullied and treated roughly by the very same detective who had come to break the news about her husband's death.

So why was Bandman risking a tongue-lashing from the brass? Did he think this bimbo had actually killed her husband? She didn't look smart enough to find her way downtown, let alone plan a murder. But maybe she didn't plan it. Maybe she was in her husband's office for some other reason, entirely innocent, and they had a fight, and she picked up a scalpel and stuck it in his throat.

Don't be a jerk, Lydia, she told herself. This isn't the movies. Doctors don't have scalpels lying around their offices, especially ones who aren't even surgeons. And this guy, McBride, wasn't killed on the spur of the moment or after a fight.

And she remembered what Bandman had told her a few weeks ago when they were talking to a street-smart stud with two gold front teeth and a poorly concealed switchblade sticking out of his hundred-dollar track shoes: "Don't ever take anyone at face value. People pretend all kinds of things and live out fantasies that in our wildest dreams we couldn't imagine. Always look as deep as you can beneath the surface— and even then sometimes you see no more than people want you to see."

Bandman told her that this lesson could save her life someday. "That guy with the knife is the sweetest thing on two feet. He's been a police snitch for years; he coaches basketball for little ghetto kids who don't have fathers and will turn himself inside out to keep them off drugs."

So Lydia looked at Cicely with fresh eyes as she recalled the crime scene. The whole thing was too neat to be a crime of passion. It was eerily neat, in fact, and remembering the way the office looked, the opulence of it, Lydia too started to dislike McBride.

This is crazy, she thought. The guy's dead, a victim of a premeditated murder. You didn't know him, and already you don't like him. What's going on here?

Lydia trusted her instincts. They were good, and she had learned to respect what they told her. If *I* feel antagonism to McBride—and I didn't even *know* the guy, she thought—he must have had one powerful personality. Powerful enough to drive someone to murder, and who would know him—and hate him—more than his wife?

"Simonowitz, send out the officer-needs-assistance call," said Bandman in his most bored and fed-up tone of voice, snapping Lydia out of her reverie.

"Look, officers," sniffed the weeping widow, who was crying in earnest now as she pictured herself in handcuffs being led down her front steps and into a waiting police car, "I'd like to cooperate with you. I really do want to answer your questions. I can't imagine why I said I wouldn't."

Oh, yes you do, lady, thought Bandman as he said aloud in his most soothing, nonthreatening tone, "Thank you. Please tell us what you did today."

"I got up rather late, I'm ashamed to say," said Cicely with the little-girl voice she assumed when she wanted to turn attention from what she said to the way she said it.

"Then what?" asked Bandman, with more kindly patience than he felt.

"Well, then I had breakfast, of course."

"Then what?"

"What do you mean, 'then what'?" asked the widow, dry eyed now and more in control of herself.

"What did you do after breakfast?" asked Bandman, just the slightest bit less patient.

"Well, I didn't do anything," said Cicely, "unless you call reading some magazines and chatting on the phone *doing* something, Lieutenant. But I don't think a man in your position would think that."

She's lying through her teeth, thought Lydia, and judging from the look that Bandman gave her, he thought so, too. And what's with this lady's sarcasm all of a sudden? she wondered.

Lydia had been on the police force long enough to know when someone was scared, and Cicely McBride was quaking in her designer silk undies.

People got snotty when they had something to hide, and everyone has a dirty little secret or two—or seven. So what was Mrs. McBride doing all morning that she didn't want to admit? She didn't look like the type who'd have a morning quickie with the United Parcel man, but then again, everyone is the type to do just about everything, including murder.

"A *man in my position*, Mrs. McBride, isn't paid to make judgments about what murder suspects do with their time," said Bandman. "Unless, of course, they're using it to stick surgical instruments into their husbands. Did you, Mrs. McBride, kill your husband?"

"No, I didn't, Mr. Smarty-Pants Detective, and I think you'd better leave now."

Bandman's eyebrows went up a little, but other than that he didn't react. He'd been called a lot of names in his lifetime, but never Mr. Smarty-Pants. Never as a child, never as an adult, never as a policeman, and certainly never from a society matron who, it seemed, had the emotional responses of a ten-year-old. Which went along with the intellect of a finishing-school reject. Or, he thought, the cunning of a fox that led Cicely McBride's social compatriots on idiot chases Saturday mornings riding overbred horses for no purpose other than scaring the hell out of the poor fox.

But didn't he always hear that the fox had more fun than the hunters? Was this bimbo leading the police on a chase, only to disappear down a hole? Was she not such a bimbo?

But she was gorgeous, he had to admit, and if the society editors knew what they were talking about, she gave some of the best parties in town, never worrying about the most important Washington party ingredient: VIP guests. The McBrides were on everyone's A list.

Bandman got up, and Lydia did the same. In a quiet voice he said, "I'll need you to identify your husband's body, Mrs. McBride. Will you come with us now, or shall we send another police car for you?"

That cracked her facade a little. "Well, um, I have some calls to make—to family, you know. Why don't I join you in a little while. I'll let you know when I'm ready."

Now Bandman was really angry. "Mrs. McBride, this isn't a tea party, and even if it were, *you're* not pouring. You'll go to the morgue to identify your husband's body at our convenience, not yours. A squad car will be here in an hour. You will accompany the officer. You do not have a choice about it. Detective Simonowitz and I will be back to ask more questions. Please make yourself available at all times. Good day."

Lydia eased the unmarked police car into the gathering afternoon traffic and glanced over at Bandman slouched in the passenger seat. He looked relaxed and pleasant; all traces of that last flash of anger had evaporated, and she felt emboldened to ask, "Well, Mr. Smarty-Pants, what do you think?"

Bandman looked over at his new partner, winked, and said, "Liar, liar, pants on fire!"

They both laughed, and Lydia concentrated on the traffic as she threaded her way through the narrow one-way streets of Georgetown on the way back to the hospital. But she was happy. This was going to be an interesting case, and once again she felt as though she had lucked out getting Bandman as a partner. She wanted him to like her.

"What's your tolerance for driving around looking for a legal parking space?" she asked.

"About ten seconds," Bandman replied. "If we don't find

one directly across the street from the hospital, we'll flash our shields to the security guard and park in the doctors' lot."

They both knew that in the midafternoon there wouldn't be a space anywhere near the hospital, so Lydia drove directly into the emergency entrance.

"Don't hospitals change shifts about now?" asked Lydia. "I wonder if there will be anyone here for us to talk to."

"Right now we don't need the people who change shifts. They can wait till tomorrow. We want the big guns now, the secretary who found him, other people with offices near his, that sort of thing," replied Bandman. "We've seen the chief nurse, so we'll continue with McBride's secretary and go from there. But before we go in, tell me what you think of the grieving widow."

"Grieving, my ass," replied Lydia with a snort. "She may or may not have killed him, but she sure isn't sorry he's dead."

"Do you think she killed him?" asked Bandman.

Lydia hadn't expected to be asked to solve the crime so soon. She blinked and stared at Bandman, who waited patiently for her response.

"I don't know," she admitted. "We don't really have much to go on, do we? She doesn't *look* as if she has what it takes to commit a murder that was obviously carefully planned, but I know what you're thinking," she said as Bandman smiled at her. "All murderers aren't madmen foaming at the mouth!

"But we don't have a motive. McBride didn't seem like a very nice guy, but that's no reason to kill someone. Even if he was the worst shit ever to have drawn breath, murder is a little *excessive*—especially for someone like Cicely."

Lydia saw a slight frown cross Bandman's face and took her cue from that. "No, scratch that," she said. "I know you think everyone's a potential murderer, and I'm sure you're right. But people have to have a *reason* to do something as drastic as killing their husbands—even people like Cicely! And we don't know her reason."

"You're a good thinker, Lydia," said Bandman. "We don't know anything yet. I just wanted to make sure you weren't jumping to conclusions.

"But keep one thing in mind. People—especially people like Cicely—sometimes don't like to do their own dirty work."

"A hit man!" she exclaimed.

Bandman grinned at her. "You watch too much television! Come on, let's go detecting."

Ina Wolfman sat at her desk doing nothing. Her back was ramrod straight and her hands were folded in front of her. She looked for all the world like a recalcitrant schoolchild waiting to be punished. She was neatly dressed in plain navy blue and wore a mousy, apologetic expression. She looked as childish as Cicely McBride had acted. Bandman put this observation into his mental file drawer: the one labeled "hunches." Ina looked surprised and frightened as Bandman and Lydia walked into McBride's outer office, where she was sitting. "I'm Lieutenant Paul Bandman from the Metropolitan Police and this is Detective Lydia Simonowitz," he said, not showing her his shield.

Bandman never flashed his shield to suspects or witnesses unless they asked for identification. It always amused him to see how many people were willing to talk frankly to a total stranger and how happy they were to implicate others.

Out of the corner of his eye he saw Simonowitz reach into her pocket for her shield, but then she noticed that he didn't show his, so she came up empty-handed. She was quick.

Ina immediately burst into tears, and her state of distress threatened to spill over into hysteria. Lydia put her arm around the crying woman and said, "I know how hard this must be for you and how upset you must be, but we need to ask you some questions. If you'll help us now, we'll be able to catch Dr. McBride's killer a lot faster."

She pulled a few Kleenexes out of a box next to the typewriter, handed them to Ina, and said kindly, but with absolute authority, "Now pull yourself together."

Ina obeyed. Sniffling a little, she said, "I'm okay now."

"Good," said Bandman, sending silent thanks to Lydia. "Now, tell us what happened."

"Well, I went out to the little girls' room, and after that I went down to the storage room because we were running out of some supplies. Then, when I got back, I walked into the doctor's office."

Her voice quavered and she nearly began to cry again but controlled herself. "I had some pads of paper and pens for him, so I walked in, and that's when I saw him. Oh God, it was awful. . . ."

She shuddered and gulped and opened and closed her mouth like a fish out of water.

"Go on," said Bandman in his soothing voice. "You're doing fine."

"Well, he was leaning back in his chair, and at first I thought nothing about it because he always leans back like that when he wants to think. But there was something wrong with his eyes, and then I noticed that *thing* in his throat."

She shivered again and said, "Then I guess I screamed because the next thing I knew Ms. Knight and Louise came running in. Then there were a lot of people: Dr. Miller and a security guard and some others that I can't remember. Then Dr. Miller said we should get out of the office and not touch anything until the police got there. So we all waited right here." She reached out to indicate her desk area and the small waiting room. "Then the police came, and I guess you know the rest."

"Who is Dr. Miller?" asked Bandman.

"He's the medical director for the whole hospital. Dr. Alfred Miller. His office is the next one down the hall."

Lydia made a notation in her notebook, and Bandman questioned Ina closely about the position of the body, the condition of McBride's office, whether it looked as though there had been a fight, and if she thought anything was missing. Ina wasn't much help. She must have started screaming only two or three seconds after she walked in the door—as soon as she realized McBride was dead. It was a natural reaction, but still, Bandman wished she had been more observant.

"Think carefully, Ms. Wolfman. Close your eyes if it will help. When you walked into the office did you see *anything* unusual or out of place? Anything missing? Anything new that wasn't there before?"

Bandman knew what the answer would be. He had seen the body and the office and knew immediately that the killer had not come for any purpose other than murder. But he had to ask. He had to be thorough.

"No, I don't think so," replied Ina. "I don't know, really. It was all so frightening and confusing. I'm sorry I can't be of more help."

"You're doing fine," said Bandman. "Tell me, Ms. Wolfman, who do think killed your boss?"

Now she became flustered. "Oh, I don't know. I wouldn't have any idea about that."

"Did Dr. McBride have enemies?" asked Bandman.

"Enemies?"

"Yes, you know . . . people who hated him, who might want to hurt him, to *kill* him."

"Well, I wouldn't know about that," she replied, stammering now, unable to look at the detective.

"Then let me ask in a different way," said Bandman kindly. "Would you say that Dr. McBride was a well-liked man?"

"Oh, he was a wonderful doctor. You couldn't find a better doctor than him." She was relieved to be able to say something positive.

"Yes, but did anybody *like* him?"

Ina said nothing for a while; she seemed to be making a decision, and Bandman pressed his advantage. Softly he said, "Dr. McBride is dead. Nothing can hurt him now, but if you're open and frank with us, we can help him, at least help his memory by catching his killer. Was Dr. McBride well liked?"

Ina took a deep breath. "No, he wasn't liked," she said bitterly. "Why should anyone like him? He was a hateful, evil man."

Her eyes widened in shock at her own outburst. Why hadn't she kept her mouth shut? She'd pay for that mistake.

"Thank you for your honesty, Ms. Wolfman. I know how hard that must have been for you, and you can be assured that we'll keep everything you say entirely confidential." Bandman's voice got softer and softer as he inched up on shakier emotional ground.

"But I'm curious about something," he said, his voice like

velvet. "If Dr. McBride was such a hateful, evil man, why are you carrying on as if you'd just lost your last friend?"

Ina's eyes opened wide and the pupils dilated to their outermost limits. Lydia could see a superficial artery begin to throb in Ina's temple, and her breathing was shallow and irregular.

This woman looks like she's just finished the Boston Marathon, thought Lydia. Don't tell me *she* did it! But neither detective said a word. Ina Wolfman was quiet, too, but her lapse into silence was not the same patient waiting of the police.

"Answer my question, Ms. Wolfman," said Bandman in a gentle voice that demanded a response.

"He wasn't my best friend," said the victim's secretary finally. "But how would you feel if all of a sudden the man you'd worked for for so long got stabbed right in his own office?" Her voice was rising to a screech again. "You should have *seen* him," she said. "It was awful!"

"We did see him," Lydia said. "We're the police, remember?"

"I can understand that you might have been shocked," added Bandman, "but actually we've seen much bloodier murders. This one was pretty neat, as though the murderer knew *exactly* what he—or she—was doing. How long have you worked for Dr. McBride?"

She sighed and tears sprang to her eyes. "Twelve years. Twelve long years."

"I ask you again, Ms. Wolfman, if Dr. McBride was so hateful, why did you keep working for him all that time?"

Now the tears rolled down her cheeks in earnest. "He saved my husband's life. He was the only doctor who wouldn't give up. My Frank was dying, and everyone else said there was nothing they could do. But Dr. McBride wouldn't give up, and he found out what was wrong with Frank, and he saved his life. I was obligated to him."

Lydia was puzzled. McBride was obviously a good doctor in the business of saving lives, but why should the woman feel obligated to work for a doctor, who had probably charged an arm and a leg in the first place, who was simply doing his job?

What kind of hold did he have over this simple woman to impose a twelve-year obligation when none existed? What was going on here?

"And did Dr. McBride cure your husband?" asked Bandman.

"Oh, he did. He saved his life."

"He must have been very ill," said Bandman, who couldn't imagine what was wrong with the guy that only McBride could save him.

Ina started to weep again. "I don't like to talk about it," she said, shuddering.

"I'm sure it must have been very frightening. Cancer is a terrible disease."

"Oh, Frank didn't have cancer."

"Then what was wrong with him?"

There was silence in the room, broken only by Ina's steady crying. Bandman was positive that there was a connection between Frank Wolfman and his wife's dead boss and that it had to do with his mysterious illness. Or maybe there was something else going on here. This woman was not the simple little servant she appeared to be. People never were. Bandman sighed; there was no point in pushing her now. Ina would protect her husband's privacy. He changed his approach.

"Thank you, Ms. Wolfman," he said in his normal voice. "You've been very cooperative, and we appreciate it. If you think of anything else, give us a call." He handed her his card. There was no point now in not volunteering identification. He had gotten about all he thought Ms. Wolfman had to offer, at least for now, and was anxious to get on with the investigation. But just before he and Lydia walked out of the office, he turned as if he had forgotten something.

"What are you going to do now?" he asked. "I mean now that Dr. McBride is dead. Where will you work? With your husband so sick, you must be worried about your income."

"My husband's not sick anymore, Officer. I told you that," she said, a little testy now. She got up from behind her desk and stood up straight. "He works for the government and he makes a good living. I don't *have* to work."

"Well, that's a relief, isn't it?" said Bandman. "I must have misunderstood you before when you said you were obligated to work for Dr. McBride even though you hated him so much. I thought you had to support your husband."

Ina's wifely pride popped out. "My Frank has a good job. He's a GS-15 at the NIH, and he supports us very well," she said more primly than she probably intended.

"The National Institutes of Health. That's an important place," said Bandman. "What does he do there?"

"He's a researcher."

"Is he a doctor?"

"No, he's a molecular biologist, but I don't know exactly what he does. I've never understood those things."

There was another silence as the detectives waited for her to go on. But she finally realized that the conversation was no longer about McBride. "What does my husband have to do with all this?" she asked.

"That's for *you* to tell us," Bandman responded, and didn't elaborate further. "Thank you again," he said. "We'll see you soon again."

Bandman and Lydia stood in the corridor. "Well, what do you think?" he asked.

"I think this is weird as hell," she answered. "Did the obligation to work for a man she obviously detested come from her own masochistic little mind, or did McBride have something on her? Is she just a Passive Polly with an overdeveloped sense of responsibility? Or maybe she and her husband didn't have the money to pay McBride and this was her way of paying off the debt? Or was he forcing her to work off the debt? I'm sure going to check payroll to find out what she was making."

"If he's a government employee, he's loaded with insurance, and even if McBride charged way beyond what the insurance would cover, a GS-15 makes good money, upwards of sixty thousand dollars. So it can't be just money," said Bandman. "And what the hell was *wrong* with the guy if only McBride could cure him?"

"Did she hate him enough to kill him? And if she did, did it have anything to do with her husband?"

"She certainly had free and continual access to him. Maybe she closed the outer office door, went into his private sanctum, and casually stuck a scalpel in his throat instead of going to the storeroom for paper and pencils. Or maybe she was sleeping with McBride," Bandman mused.

"Oh God, you've got to be kidding!" she responded. "The king of the doctors turned on by Miss Mouse? Come on!"

He laughed. "You're probably right, but stranger things have happened. And something strange is going on with Miss Mouse. We're not through with her yet! Let's go see Miller."

3

AMANDA WAS DRIVING to work in the new bright red Honda Accord that Ken had given her for her birthday two months ago. Every time she stopped at a light, she thought her head would fall off and roll under the seat.

She wasn't actually hung over, but the combination of burgundy, banana cake, and only two hours of sleep had taken its toll.

I'm too old for these all-night bull sessions, she thought when a wave of nausea rolled over her after she slammed on the brakes to avoid someone who didn't believe in red lights.

However, she felt a little less tired when she thought about what the evening would bring. Two weeks was a long time. Her lips curved up in a lewd little smile as she thought about what she and Ken would be doing in just a few hours. God, she missed him.

But first she had to get through the day.

As she walked into her office, her secretary Louise said, "Dr. Silverman called three times. He really wants to talk to you."

"Okay, I'll call him right now," said Amanda. "Anything else new?"

"Amazingly, no," said Louise. "It's been like a tomb since I got in. Oh dear," she said with an effort to keep from laughing. "Not the best thing to have said right now."

"Actually, it probably *was* the best thing to have said," replied Amanda. "And there's really no reason for either of us to be in the middle of this—unless you did it," she added with a laugh. "Is there any coffee?"

30

"Unless you consider constant sexual innuendos a capital offense, I didn't have much motive," said Louise. "And yes, the night people left a half pot."

"Oh God, it probably tastes like embalming fluid. I'll make us a fresh pot if you page Dr. Silverman," replied Amanda, who could never bring herself to ask Louise to make coffee.

Dr. Eddie Silverman answered his page almost immediately. "Hi, Amanda," he said breathlessly, as though he had run down the hall in response to his beeper. "Isn't this something? Are you free for lunch? I've *got* to talk to you."

Amanda didn't want to give in to Eddie's last-minute request, especially since she had been planning to eat only a carton of plain yogurt in her office as penance for the excesses of the night before. But something in his voice made Amanda mentally put that aside. "Sure," she said. "In or out?"

"In" meant the hospital cafeteria, which, except for the salad bar, was the same as hospital cafeterias everywhere: depressing food in a depressing atmosphere—but with the compensation of a foot-thick grapevine. "Out" meant Giovanni's, the Italian deli across the street, where at lunchtime the customers were almost entirely hospital staff and the gossip possibilities were almost as good as the cafeteria.

"Neither," replied Eddie. "I want to go someplace where there are no white coats or stethoscopes."

Amanda's curiosity was definitely humming. Perhaps he had heard the rumor that they were having an affair and didn't want to feed the flames. But Eddie usually didn't care a whole lot about what most people thought as long as he did his job well. It was one of the reasons Amanda liked him so much. Or perhaps he was finally going to explain his behavior of the past half year.

"Every place in Georgetown is a madhouse at lunch," said Amanda, who didn't want to make a production out of lunch today. She had piles of work to do and planned to leave early to be at Dulles Airport on time to meet Ken's plane. "Why don't you run to the deli, bring stuff back, and we'll eat in my office with the door closed?"

That ought to set the gossip radar humming at high frequency.

"Okay, what do you want?" he asked.

"A tuna sub, no cheese, no extra mayo, and a diet Coke, no ice," replied Amanda, who always had the same thing at Giovanni's. They made the best tuna salad in the world. "Do you have enough cash for both of us?"

"Yes, Amanda. Residents may be among the lowest order of humans, but we're not ready for the bread line yet!"

Amanda laughed. "See you when you get here."

Amanda and Eddie had known each other for only the five years that Eddie had been a medical resident at J.F.K. Memorial, but she felt as if she had known him her entire life, so comfortable were they together.

She'd met him when her affair with Ken was in one of its several shaky periods. She was a nursing supervisor and he was a green intern, fresh out of medical school, new in Washington, and seemingly friendless and alone. She was eight years older than he and miles ahead of him in her career, but there was something about him that wiped out all those differences and made them contemporaries.

He was not like the dozen or so other interns that had started at the hospital that July. He actually cared about his patients as people, and she never heard him refer to a patient as "the cardiac in room 212" or "the emergency chest case" as did most of the doctors and nurses. He referred to his patients by name, and Amanda liked that. She also liked his asking for help when he didn't know something instead of bumbling through and causing trouble for everyone.

They started having long talks at Giovanni's and in the cafeteria, seeking each other out at lunchtime. Once in a while they had supper together after work, but even after two years of increasing emotional intimacy, there had been no hint of sexual desire—at least not from Eddie. Amanda would have gone to bed with him in a minute if they had not worked at the same hospital—and if she had felt his inclination for a physical relationship. But she never had.

Glen had an explanation for the absence of sexual sparks between Amanda and Eddie. "He's gay," she said.

"Now, how do you know that?" Amanda had demanded, her

heart sinking with disappointment. "You've never even met him."

"Oh, come on, Amanda. A good-looking guy who's smart, eligible, has the requisite number of arms and legs and no disgusting diseases who doesn't make a pass at a good-looking woman that he likes—what would you think? Does he have a girlfriend? Does he talk about women?"

Why did it bother her so much that Glen thought he was gay?

"Oh shit, Glen," she said, when the answer struck. "I'm in love with him, too."

"Well, of course you are. Any fool can see that," replied her friend. "But what are you going to do about it? You could ruin a really nice friendship by trying to seduce him, or you could just go on as you are and consider yourself lucky."

So Amanda did the smart thing, and the friendship had deepened and grown stronger. Their careers had flourished together; he was now chief medical resident, which meant that he was assured a place in the private practice of his choice in Washington—a city where pots of money were to be made as a physician.

But lately the friendship had changed. They didn't eat lunch together as often, and when they did, little of their easy camaraderie was left and there were no more deep talks about how they felt about things. At first Amanda thought that her having gotten married might have made Eddie uncomfortable. Maybe Glen was wrong, after all, and she wondered if she had inadvertently said something to hurt him. After all, she stuck her foot in her mouth all the time.

Eddie denied that. "I can't imagine why you're asking," he replied when she had finally talked about how sad she felt that their friendship seemed to be falling apart. "Nothing's changed."

That was when she knew that everything *had* changed, and that it wouldn't get better. Eddie was a sensitive, intuitive man who didn't miss much, so his claim of not knowing what had happened between them was a lie. And that was when she started to grieve for the loss of the friendship.

It had occurred to her that he might have AIDS. Glen was right, of course, about his being gay. She was always right about those kinds of things. So Amanda watched Eddie carefully for signs of illness, and although some days he looked half-dead from fatigue, so did every other medical resident in the history of the modern hospital system. But other than that, he looked as well as ever. So something else must be going on in his life. Maybe lover troubles, maybe the stress of deciding what to do after residency. Maybe he didn't like her anymore.

Amanda sighed and put the phone back in its cradle just in time to field another call. It was a patient calling from one of the beds upstairs, and she was angry. It seemed that the night nurses wouldn't let her open the window even though she was in a private room. Amanda promised to go up to see her before the end of the day, but now she needed to get back to her paperwork.

But she couldn't concentrate. What the hell was this new complaint about? Why did the nurses have to be so stubborn and rigid? If a patient wanted a window open, what was the big deal? Open the damn window. She'd go up later and soothe the woman's ruffled feathers, grateful that that was all it was.

Tuesday had been far worse. The feathers hadn't been ruffled, they'd been dead. One of her nurses had killed a patient, and Amanda was sure that not only would the family sue the hospital for everything it had—right down to the last piece of gauze—but that criminal-negligence charges would be brought and that Amanda would play a starring role in both legal actions.

She dreaded the thought of spending her days giving depositions and testifying in court (perhaps without a job to go back to—she wouldn't put it past Townsend to fire her for this), but the nurse had done something so appallingly wrong that she deserved to spend the rest of her life in the slammer. And Amanda would personally like to put her there.

About an hour later Louise put her head in the door, roused Amanda from her reverie, and said, "I just went out to the john and you should see what's going on in the corridor. It's crawling with police. They're pestering poor Ina with questions again, and she hardly knows what to do with herself now that her boss is dead. I thought I'd take her someplace off hospital grounds for lunch. Is that okay?"

"It's fine, and don't worry about watching the clock," replied Amanda. "Are the TV cameras still around?"

"Ina says that Mr. Townsend won't let them in the door, so they're all piled up outside. It's a real madhouse out there," said Louise, who looked as though she were enjoying it all.

David Townsend, the hospital administrator, was probably having a good time, too. There was no love lost between him and McBride, and now that hospitals were competing fiercely for patients, he would take advantage of J.F.K. Memorial's position at the top of the news and on the front page of the paper for the next few days. Good publicity opportunities like this didn't last long, and if Amanda knew anything at all about this slick, charming man with the connections in very high places, he had probably spent the night on the phone with the hospital's publicist, trying to figure out a way to get the most out of this murder.

"Poor Leo McBride," said Amanda. "If only he knew how much fun everyone was having over his corpse, he'd be furious."

"Well, that'd be nothing new," snorted Louise. "He was always furious about something, and now if people don't care if he's dead, it's his own fault."

"I guess you're right," sighed Amanda. "How's Ina bearing up under all this?"

"The police grilled her for a long time yesterday afternoon, and she was pretty upset about it. They asked her a lot of questions about Frank," said Louise.

"What's Frank got to do with it?" Amanda wanted to know.

"I don't know," replied Louise. "Ina says she doesn't know, either, but she seems awfully upset. She can't stop crying."

"I'll go in and talk to her after lunch," said Amanda, immediately regretting her offer. She didn't give two hoots about Ina Wolfman, someone she barely knew, and she had enough trouble of her own to deal with.

"By the way," she added, "I'll have to leave even earlier than I'd planned to pick up some groceries on the way to the airport. The only thing to eat in the house is a piece of stale cheese."

The minute Ken left, Amanda had slipped into her single-

woman mentality about food: she thought about it one day at a
time, and although her refrigerator was never this bare, she
didn't do much in the way of meal planning and could live for
weeks on take-out sandwiches, frozen dinners, or chicken
breasts that she picked up on the way home from work.

When she was single she had cleaned the house only when
she expected guests or the dust was so thick that Shadow left
paw prints on the coffee table. Housekeeping was not one of
her strong points.

She and Ken had solved the dust problem by hiring a
cleaning lady, and they shared kitchen chores: She did all the
cooking, and he always cleaned up. It worked out well; she
loved to cook, and he was a neatness nut. But that didn't
solve the present problem of an empty refrigerator.

"Why don't you call a caterer, and give him a real elegant
welcome home?" said Louise.

"What a fabulous idea!" exclaimed Amanda, reaching
immediately for the phone book. In ten minutes she had
arranged for three sinfully decadent courses and a bottle of
Piper Heidseck champagne.

Feeling better, and more than a little horny at the prospect of
the long, sexy night ahead, Amanda turned on her computer
and worked on next year's budget until Louise and Ina poked
their heads in to say they were leaving for lunch.

Not ten minutes later Eddie Silverman came in holding a
large white, leaking paper bag, which he plopped on her desk
and then threw himself lengthwise on the couch.

"Christ, what a morning!" he said. "We had two codes in an
hour but only one survived, and all anyone wants to do is talk
about McBride. Alice Bonner didn't show up for work, so of
course everyone's buzzing about that. They're all speculating
that maybe she did it."

Alice Bonner was the latest in Leo McBride's string of
conquests on the nursing staff. Their affair lasted longer than
anyone had expected, but finally he dumped her uncere-
moniously—and publicly—by calling her an adolescent slut
within earshot of patients and staff on Center Wing 4 right
during the busiest part of an exceptionally busy morning.

Alice responded by punching him in the jaw and locking herself in the nurses' john, which was a scene in itself and a nuisance because it was the only staff bathroom on the unit.

Amanda was summoned as the peacemaker, or at least the bathroom-door opener, and when she had no luck in persuading Alice to unlock the door, she called maintenance and ordered them to take it off its hinges. Alice had come out before the door came off, and Amanda took the nurse to her office to give her holy hell.

Remembering now what Alice had said about Leo McBride and what she would like to do to him, Amanda shivered a little. *This* woman scorned could be a real menace.

"Does anyone seriously think that?" asked Amanda. "Have the police questioned her?"

"I don't think so," said Eddie. "At least not as far as I know. And frankly, I don't give a damn. Anyone stupid enough to sleep with that bastard deserves to be grilled by the cops."

"I'll drink to that," said Amanda as she unpacked their lunch and put it on the conference table at the far end of her office. The aroma of tuna fish, olive oil, oregano, and the meatballs from Eddie's sandwich set her stomach growling, and she said, "Come on, let's eat."

Amanda and Eddie ate in silence for a few minutes as she studied the ever-deepening lines on his craggily good-looking face. It wasn't classically handsome nor did it have the perfection of features that made Ken so pleasant to look at, but it was a nice face and had a sweetness of expression that appealed to Amanda. But now it was a worried, troubled face.

"Eddie, when was the last time you slept for eight hours in a row?" she asked. "You look like hell."

"Actually," he replied, "I was doing pretty well in the sleep department until last night. That damn McBride!"

"But you hated him," she replied, genuinely puzzled that he looked so devastated over McBride's death.

Eddie took a deep breath and said, "Amanda, we're buddies, aren't we? We trust each other totally, don't we?"

"Yes, we do," Amanda replied gravely. This was going to be serious, and as much as she cared about Eddie, she was annoyed that after all these months of freezing her out of his life, he was now going to lay something heavy on her. She had an urge to run out of the room, leave all this ugliness behind, get in her car, and sit in a plastic chair at Dulles Airport until she could wrap her arms around her husband and spend a few days with him under the covers. She did not want to hear what Eddie was going to tell her. But she sat quietly.

"Yes, we do," she repeated. "Talk to me, Eddie."

"You know about me, don't you, Amanda?"

This was the first time he had ever mentioned it, and Amanda thought for a moment about playing coy, but that seemed pointless, and he obviously needed to talk about it now.

"Yes, I've always known." Maybe a little lightness would help. "How do you think I restrained myself from jumping on your bones all those late nights here and in the cafeteria!"

He laughed, relieved that it was okay with her. He knew it would be, but it was a relief all the same.

"Well, McBride hasn't always known. He only found out last year, and he's been blackmailing me ever since."

"Blackmail! Oh, Christ, Eddie, what a complete sleazebag he is—was. You were paying that bastard money to keep him quiet. Why? Why didn't you tell him where he could shove his blackmail threats? How could he blackmail you? Half the single men in Washington are gay. No one cares anymore. Who thinks about things like that? So that's what's been wrong all these months?"

Amanda was angrier than ever at McBride, but she was relieved to know what had been making Eddie seem so removed and aloof. Being blackmailed was enough to turn anyone into a block of stone. Now, when the police caught the murderer, she and Eddie could get back to their old relationship.

"Doctors think about it, Amanda. Patients think about it. The AIDS epidemic has set us back fifty years. How long do you think I'd last as a doctor in this hospital—with VIP patients all over the place—if people knew I was gay? All they'd think about was AIDS. Amanda, every single practice that I've been interviewing with would slam its door in my face. I'd be finished before I started.

"So I paid him his filthy money whenever he asked. It wasn't much. A hundred here, fifty there. It wasn't the money that he cared about. It was seeing me squirm. It was humiliating me. It was keeping me in my place. Amanda, I'm glad he's dead. I *wanted* him dead."

Amanda saw his problem immediately. Eddie had the perfect motive. Amanda didn't think that Eddie had killed McBride, but she could see how the police might think so if there was anyone else who knew about the blackmail.

"You have to assume that even McBride wouldn't brag about blackmailing someone. If you're going to commit a crime and you have any sense at all, you don't broadcast it," she said. "And McBride was no dummy. I doubt that he told anyone."

"What about his wife?"

"Eddie, come on, you've seen them together. I don't think he'd tell her the time of day, let alone confide in her about committing a felony. He treats her like a concubine."

Amanda squeezed his hand. "Eddie, McBride's death is a true liberation for you, so let's put some perspective on it. Your worst fears are that McBride told someone he was blackmailing you, which in this place would mean that he told everyone. Even if the whole hospital knew and if the police find out . . ."

"Oh, they'll find out. How could they not find out?" he asked.

"They won't find out if McBride didn't tell anyone about it. But let's just say the police do learn about it. So you'll be a suspect—along with half the staff. But you didn't do it, and you can prove it. Weren't you upstairs stamping out death and disease when McBride was killed? You've got an airtight alibi with all those people who saw you."

Eddie looked miserable. "I don't have an alibi at all. I wasn't in the hospital."

Amanda felt her stomach clutch uncomfortably. This was getting really unpleasant. She said nothing and waited for him to go on.

"For some reason we weren't busy yesterday morning. I finished rounds in record time and got all the paperwork done.

All the patients were stable, and the second- and third-year residents were there, so I decided to go for a walk outdoors. It was such a nice day. So I told the ward clerk I'd stay in the neighborhood so she could get me on my beeper, and I went out. I didn't do anything except amble around looking at the houses and admiring the gardens. The air felt so fresh and good, and the leaves are just starting to turn.

"I stayed out about two hours—until I got hungry. When I walked back in the hospital, all hell had broken loose, and the minute I found out what had happened, I knew I was in deep shit. Very deep shit."

"Oh, Eddie," said Amanda. There was no need to say more. They both knew the trouble he was in.

When Eddie left, Amanda went to McBride's office to see Ina. She didn't especially want to talk to the wimpy little woman, but it was a good way to temporarily avoid thinking about what Eddie had told her.

The outer office was empty. Ina's desk was painfully neat, the box of tissues arranged just so, the pencils all sharpened to precise points, the little vase of pathetic plastic flowers placed above her blotter. Amanda hated plastic flowers. For some reason they depressed her beyond all rationality, and the sight of them now pushed her over the brink, and she felt tears welling up again.

Christ, all I ever do lately is cry, she thought. As she reached for one of Ina's tissues, she glanced through the open door into McBride's office and saw a man standing by the desk, staring at McBride's chair, now neatly aligned with the desk. Although the man's back was to her, Amanda knew he was unaware of her presence; she could sense the force of his concentration.

"May I help you?" she asked softly, thinking it was someone from the police.

The man spun around, and for the briefest instant, she had the impression of a snake uncoiling to strike. She instantly knew that this was no police officer, but the moment passed even before it could register fully on her mind. He looked at her and said, "I'm looking for my wife."

"Are you Mr. Wolfman?" she asked, relieved.

"Yes," he said pleasantly. "I thought I'd take Ina out to lunch just to get her out of the hospital. This has been very hard on her."

"That's really nice of you," Amanda replied as she wondered briefly whether Ken would do the same for her. "Louise and Ina went out together awhile ago. I think they went to someplace nice in Georgetown, although they didn't say where."

"I'm Amanda Knight, by the way. I'm really sorry Ina had to be the one to find Dr. McBride. She must be very shook up—anyone would be."

"She is," replied Wolfman, "but she'll get over it. I ought to be getting back to work now as long as I know she's okay. It was nice meeting you, Ms. Knight."

He was gone before Amanda had a chance to say anything else. Good, she thought. I'm not in the mood to make small talk with a stranger.

As she walked down the hall back to her own office, she met Louise and Ina returning from lunch. Ina looked much more relaxed than Amanda had ever seen her, even before McBride was killed. "Well, you two look fine," said Amanda with a smile. "Where did you go?"

"To the Third Edition," said Louise, rolling her eyes toward Ina and bringing her hand to her mouth in the classic she's-had-a-few gesture.

To Ina, Amanda said, "You just missed your husband. He came over to take you out to lunch, but I told him you were out with Louise, so he left. That was really nice of him," she added.

Ina finally spoke. "Sure," she said with a trace of bitterness in her voice. "The all-American nice guy."

Oh, Christ, thought Amanda. Just what I need: someone else's marital problems. But she was intrigued. This was the first time she had ever heard anything that resembled emotion from Ina, and it made the woman seem real for the first time.

"Actually, I came by your office to say how sorry I was about McBride. I guess it was no secret that he wasn't the best-liked man at J.F.K., but I'm sorry you had to be the one to find him. You didn't deserve that piece of bad luck," said Amanda. "Come on, I'll walk you back."

"Did Louise tell you about how the police have been asking me all kinds of questions?" asked Ina in her usual, flat, little-girl voice.

"Actually, she said they'd been grilling you," replied Amanda. "How come? Just because you were the one to find the body?"

"I guess so," replied the secretary, who wasn't exactly drunk, but wasn't entirely her usual efficient, alert self. "They wanted to know all about Frank, too."

"No kidding! Why?"

"I don't know." Ina was vague now, her eyes slipping off to somewhere beyond J.F.K. Memorial Hospital.

Amanda, you jerk, said her inner voice, the one that knew how much work was piled on her desk, leave this poor woman alone with her pointy pencils and plastic greenery and go back to your office. What do you care about her husband? He looks just as nerdlike as she does.

"Well, did McBride and your husband know each other?" asked Amanda, ignoring her conscience.

"No!" Ina said quickly. Too quickly.

Why don't I believe her? thought Amanda. And why do I care?

But she pressed on. "So what did the police ask you?"

Ina looked as though she might cry. "They wanted to know everything—you know, did I see anything? Who do I think killed him? Did he have any enemies? That sort of thing."

"What did you tell them?" asked Amanda, who was starting to feel guilty about harassing this sad, confused woman. But she waited expectantly for the reply.

"I didn't tell them anything because I don't know anything. Why would *I* know anything? I was only his secretary. He never told *me* any of his private business. He hardly even noticed me." Her voice was high pitched and querulous now. More emotion. Twice in less than a half hour. Poor Ina would be exhausted this evening!

Why are you being so mean to her? her conscience nagged again. Leave her alone!

But something strange is going on here, Amanda thought. Ina is not herself at all.

Well, of course she's not, you jerk, said the voice. How would you like to walk in on your boss and find a scalpel sticking out of him?

Amanda thought she wouldn't mind. At least she wouldn't have to account to Townsend for one of her nurses killing a patient.

"I have to get back to work," she said to Ina. "But if you want to talk about anything, come on over to see Louise or me. If you get to feeling strange sitting here by yourself, I'm sure Mr. Townsend will let you go home early."

"Oh, I don't mind," said Ina. "I'm glad to be alone for a while."

A few hours later, as she battled rush-hour traffic on the Capitol Beltway, Amanda thought again about Eddie. He was in serious jeopardy. When he had left her office she noticed that his face was more deeply lined than it had been when he came in. Amanda wondered whether he was facing more than a few sleepless nights and some fast talking to the police. Did he face a lifetime behind bars?

Did Eddie kill McBride? The question moved in and set up housekeeping in her mind, and as much as Amanda tried to brush it away, she couldn't. He had the strongest possible motive and no alibi. If this were a movie or a TV show, he'd be taken down to the station house and grilled by detectives. Amanda shuddered as she realized that even though this was no movie, that very thing might happen.

Was Eddie's standoffishness of the past half year more than just anger and fear over being blackmailed? Was he plotting murder? *That* would certainly tend to preoccupy one's mind and make you avoid your friends, she thought grimly.

Amanda had never known Eddie to go strolling through the neighborhood before, especially during the middle of a busy workday. If there was nothing pressing to do, he, like all other residents, would grab an hour's sleep in the on-call room. And he'd never expressed so much as a word of interest in gardening. He and his lover, Donald, lived in a town house, and their entire garden consisted of three pots of wilting impatiens and a geranium or two. His whole story was so out of character that she had a hard time believing it. But, oh how she wanted to. She did *not* want one of her favorite people turning out to be a murderer.

As Amanda negotiated the nightmarish interstate highway that circled the nation's capital, her thoughts ranged from her husband to her friend Eddie, to the funny little scene she had had this afternoon with the patient, a Mrs. Lambrusco, who complained that the night nurses wouldn't let her open the window.

Mrs. Lambrusco was well known to the emergency department staff at J.F.K. Memorial. Four or five times a year she would arrive by ambulance in the throes of an asthma attack. The treatment was always the same. She got a few squirts of a superpotent decongestant, a tankful of oxygen, and a sedative, and in a few hours she was well enough to go home.

But four days previously, the familiar ritual had turned into a near disaster. Mrs. Lambrusco had a cardiac arrest. The staff had gone into well-rehearsed action, and within a half hour her heart had been restarted with an electric defibrillator, and a hole was cut in her windpipe and a plastic tube inserted so that she'd keep breathing.

Now, after spending two days in the intensive care unit, she was in a private room with only two tubes left: an intravenous feeding line and the plastic tube poked into her trachea. When Amanda walked into her room, she was sitting up in bed, wearing a fluffy pink bed jacket, full makeup, and dangly earrings.

Amanda had never met Mrs. Lambrusco, but she had heard about her. She was surprised to see someone so vibrant and alert; she'd always thought of her as a hunched-over bag lady living on the edge of despair. This woman was not on the edge of anything—except outrage.

"At these prices, I ought to be able to do as I damn please about the windows at night," she fumed after Amanda had introduced herself. She put her finger over the hole in her throat to force the exhaled air up around her vocal cords and out her mouth instead of escaping out the hole that had been cut below the larynx.

"Don't tell me your nurses believe that old wives' tale about night air being bad for you. If I want to freeze my buns off at night, I'll do it!"

Amanda felt entirely sympathetic with Mrs. Lambrusco. She wondered how anyone could sleep in closed-up, tight, over-heated rooms. She kept her own windows open even during the winter. Ken hated it.

"There's no reason why you can't sleep as you please as long as your door is closed," said Amanda. "I can't imagine why the nurses were giving you a hard time, and I'll certainly see that they don't do it again. I'll get to the bottom of the problem. I'm glad you called me. I wish more patients were as assertive as you."

Mrs. Lambrusco was taken aback at how quickly she got results from her complaint, and Amanda could see the surprise on her face. It had happened many times before. Hospital patients never thought their complaints would be taken seriously (in most hospitals they weren't), but Amanda had a different attitude. She saw the people who occupied the beds as paying customers as well as patients and thought they should be pleased as well as cared for. And she insisted that her staff agree with this philosophy and treat people accordingly.

The nurse who had given Mrs. Lambrusco a hard time was left a note to appear in Amanda's office when she got off duty in the morning. Amanda would give her very polite but very definite hell and would follow up the verbal reprimand with one in writing so that the nurse would know that this was a serious offense.

As Amanda turned off the beltway onto the Dulles Airport access road and breathed a sigh of relief to be out of the heaviest flow of traffic, she smiled as she remembered the ten-minute chat with Mrs. Lambrusco and how dignified and healthy she looked despite the tracheostomy hole in the middle of her throat.

Suddenly her eyes opened wide and her hands gripped the steering wheel convulsively. "Holy shit!" she said aloud.

Another picture superimposed itself over the one of Mrs. Lambrusco in Amanda's mind: McBride's throat. There he was, leaning back in his chair, with a look of surprise and a scalpel sticking out of him, while a thin trickle of blood dripped onto his shirt collar.

And there was Mrs. Lambrusco, hale and healthy with a hole in *her* trachea at almost precisely the same spot as McBride's.

She was alive; he was dead.

Again she spoke aloud: "Whoever stuck that scalpel into McBride's throat didn't kill him!"

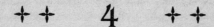

4

JONATHAN BERNSTEIN MET Alfred Miller in the latter's office at about the time that Amanda pulled into a parking space at Dulles International Airport. They sat for a while in silence, uncomfortable with each other and at a loss for words after their initial greetings. Both had been questioned by the police; Bernstein had an alibi, Miller did not.

Bernstein was chief of surgery, McBride's counterpart in one of the most important departments in any hospital. Surgeons brought in the most revenue for a hospital and thus were the darlings of the accounting department, but they also ran up the biggest bills, always wanting some new piece of equipment and always jealous of what other hospitals had.

They also had the greatest number of therapeutic misadventures, which made them the scourge of the legal department. Public relations didn't like it much, either.

"What the hell is a therapeutic misadventure?" Glencora had once asked as Amanda described a particularly ghastly operating-room accident.

"It's what happened to that poor women today: it's when some jerk amputates the wrong breast, and the patient ends up going home—after a side trip to her lawyer's office—completely topless. Therapeutic misadventure is medicalese for a royal fuckup—and it'd make even *your* hair curl if you knew how many times it happens. It's what my darling nurses have been doing more and more often lately."

Jonathan Bernstein had left an instrument or two inside patients in his long surgical career, and he'd had his share of

47

failed operations, but he'd never done anything really big and dumb, and his care and attention had paid off. Now he was apparently next in line, now that McBride was out of the way, for the position of medical director of John F. Kennedy Memorial Hospital, the most prestigious hospital in the nation's capital—one of the hospitals on the White House's list in the event of a presidential emergency.

Amanda wasn't the only one who knew that the scalpel in McBride's trachea didn't kill him. Anyone who knew anything about anatomy would realize it as soon as the shock of the ugly scene had worn off—and after seeing how little blood McBride had lost. But Bernstein hadn't been a witness, and it came to Miller now that the surgeon believed that McBride had died of the scalpel wound. He told him the truth.

"Jesus, Al, I thought he'd had his throat slashed. That's what everyone upstairs said."

"It's ironic," said Miller. "You had the motive but were shut up in the operating room all day. I was right here the whole morning, but I don't have a motive to kill McBride."

Bernstein wasn't so sure about that last statement, and he resented Miller saying that he wanted McBride dead. But there was no point in arguing with the old man; he probably wouldn't remember it in five minutes. Instead he said, "But that's all beside the point, Al. Whoever stabbed McBride flunked anatomy."

Miller, who at the age of seventy-four should have retired five or six years ago because he was beginning to lose his grip on things and spent a good deal of time in an increasingly dense mental fog, said, "This isn't the time for levity, Jonathan. Murder isn't something to laugh at."

"I didn't mean to offend you, Al, " said Bernstein not very contritely, "but you have to admit that no one will miss the guy very much. Not even you."

"Yes, I suppose you're right," said the old doctor with a sigh. "On the other hand, he brought a lot of good business to this hospital, and *you* have to admit that his social connections never hurt us. We'll miss that."

Good grief, thought Bernstein, he sounds like a recruiter for a law firm.

Jonathan Bernstein cared little for the business side of hospital operations. He'd never come out of the operating room if he didn't have to. In fact, he rarely did. He weaseled his way out of staff meetings as often as he could, ate a brown-bag lunch in the OR suite, drinking muddy coffee from the staff pot or soda from the vending machine. He dictated his surgical notes while slouched on a couch in the doctors' lounge and went for days without setting foot in his office in the administrative wing.

When he took off his green operating scrubs, he put on rumpled pants and a sweat shirt and escaped from the hospital as fast as he could, often going down the back stairs from the OR suite to the parking garage.

He was a surgeon, but he thought of McBride as an operator. He didn't like the man, but didn't he hate him, either. He felt contempt for his greed and small-mindedness but respected his remarkable talent as a doctor. Because Bernstein was apolitical and had a different perception of the two men's relationship than did McBride, he didn't need to hate him. He dealt with McBride by ignoring him as much as he could.

Bernstein didn't want to be medical director, but neither did he want McBride to get the top slot. In fact, he was dead set against it, so he let everyone think that he too was in the running.

Aloud he said to Miller, "I suppose you're right, Al. I never thought of it that way. But there are lots of good medicine men in this country. Get another one. Dangle McBride's office in front of him. The hospital paid for all that fancy stuff; you might as well put it to good use."

Bernstein was itching to get out of the hospital and didn't much care who was hired as chief of medicine as long as he was a good doctor. He had a lot of say in the matter, but there was time enough to think about it when the recruiting process got under way. Right now he wanted to go back upstairs, take another look at the cases he did today, and then go home and spread the truckload of mulch that the nursery had dumped in his driveway the day before.

"You and Townsend can handle this," said Bernstein, rising from his chair. "And the police will catch the murderer. That

Bandman fellow looks very competent and so does his assistant. They'll catch the guy, Al, don't worry."

"The guys, you mean," said Miller.

In response to Bernstein's quizzical look he added, "If the scalpel didn't kill McBride, something else must have."

Bernstein knew this; there was no way one could not know it after thinking about it for a minute. But he preferred not to think about it. The idea that *one* person had hated McBride enough to kill him was disgusting enough, but two? It was outrageous.

As Bernstein drove home, he realized that now he'd be in the middle of a murder investigation. No one at the hospital believed that he wasn't interested in Miller's job; McBride had seen to that by creating a competitive atmosphere where none had existed. Now Bernstein was sorry he had ignored it, had not told McBride that the job was all his. But it had amused him to watch the political infighting from what he had thought was the safe distance of the OR suite.

While Jonathan Bernstein was patiently waiting in the line of bumper-to-bumper rush-hour traffic on Military Road, Seth Morgan was sliding his oiled hands along the slim flanks of one of his clients. He had to think for a moment before he could remember which one—most of his clients blended together in his mind to form one nondescript personality.

Seth was a masseur to Washington's VIP wives. He was good with his hands and even better with his mind. Seth had more money in the bank than many of the husbands who paid for his services—because he provided a service that they did not.

Seth massaged more than thighs and backs, and when he left his clients' houses, they were satisfied in ways they chose not to describe to the payers of Seth's bills. He was *very* good with his hands.

But this afternoon he had his hands, not his mind, on Stephanie Lewis's body, and when she began to writhe on the portable massage table in a way that indicated she wanted to get on to the reason why Seth was so popular, he couldn't remember what Stephanie wanted, what he needed to do to satisfy her so that there would be an engraved presidential portrait or two in addition to the check for the massage fee.

This afternoon he had his mind on the McBride murder. Had Cicely actually knocked off her husband? The TV news last night said that McBride was found in his office with his throat cut, and Seth knew that Cicely wasn't strong enough to overpower her husband.

But there had been three frantic messages from her on his answering machine yesterday afternoon, and he was dying to know why she was so desperate to get in touch with him. When he finished with Stephanie, he'd call her.

Seth, who was in a position to know, was certain that Cicely was no bundle of muscles, but how much strength did it take to whip a knife across a man's throat, especially when he had no reason to be on guard?

Almost all of Seth's clients were like Cicely: interested almost exclusively in money and the power it brought, which was one of the reasons he liked to service them but never make love to them. He never took his clothes off, never had intercourse with them, and never permitted them to reciprocate the sexual release he gave them. He was their servant, yet by keeping himself at a physical and emotional remove, he exerted power over them. He liked that. He too enjoyed power, and although his was narrow in scope, it was, for the short time he had his hands on his clients, total.

Most of the clients were content to keep the relationship the way it was. He swore all of them to secrecy and told each one that she was the only exception to his rule of never turning a therapeutic massage sexual. Most believed him, or at least said they did. They were ashamed of the intensity of their sexual needs, mortified that they were not satisfied by their husbands, and afraid of the risk of disease that taking a lover would entail. Thus, he was assured discretion.

Except for Cicely. She always wanted to break the rules and never stopped trying to get him into bed. She plucked at his clothes and rubbed herself against him, reminding Seth of a cat in heat, meowing and purring and pushing its rump into the air in a desperate attempt to respond to the call of its hormones.

Once she showed up at his house at eleven o'clock at night

wrapped in a sable coat with only a transparent negligée underneath. He had mistakenly opened the door without looking through the peephole because he was expecting someone else, and he had a hell of a time getting rid of her. She shrugged off her coat and opened her negligée, as if the sight of her naked body would turn him on. She begged him to make love to her and described how she would return his sexual favors, none of which appealed to him because Seth had very exotic sexual tastes, way beyond what Cicely and his other clients could imagine.

Seth was positive that Cicely had had a snort or two of cocaine, and that made her even more difficult to control. He cursed himself for ever having introduced her to the man in Rockville. Finally he threatened to discontinue the massages if she didn't leave, and that did it. She wept and apologized, and he threw the magnificent fur over her shoulders and hustled her out to her car.

She had behaved herself for about six months afterward, but lately she'd been talking about how nice it would be if she weren't married, how she and Seth could travel together, maybe lie on a beach in the hot sun in the dead of winter. Her fantasies had metamorphosed from the purely sexual to the impossibly romantic, and he practiced ignoring them.

But now her husband had been murdered, and all the talk came back to him in full force. Had she come to believe her fantasies? Was she in love with Seth? Or was she just blinded by the shattering orgasms and believed them to be something more than they were? Had Cicely actually killed her husband so that she and Seth could run off together to some never-never land of perpetual sex? A shiver of fear and rage passed through him, and he couldn't wait to finish with Stephanie so he could find out what that bitch wanted.

Or did the murder have nothing to do with him? Seth knew that Cicely didn't have much physical strength, but she was such a willful and selfish woman, and not nearly as childish as she wanted people to think. She could easily talk herself into believing that killing her husband would bring whatever was lacking in her life. But Seth didn't think she knew what she wanted and needed—and that made him even more nervous.

He forced himself to turn his attention back to the body beneath his hands. Stephanie was coming along nicely. Her lips were parted, her breath was coming in short, shallow gasps, and suddenly he remembered what she expected. He applied himself to his task and was soon rewarded not only with her climax but his: a check and two pictures of Andrew Jackson.

On his way to the next client, Seth stopped at a pay phone and found two more messages from Cicely on his machine. She sounded near tears. He put another quarter in the phone and dialed her number.

"Oh, thank God you've called," said Cicely. She picked up the phone during the first ring. "Why didn't you call me last night? Didn't you get my messages?"

"I *did* call you, but you weren't home," replied Seth in his less-than-warmest voice. "I heard about your husband, and I want to offer my deepest sympathy," he said, this time a little warmer and more friendly.

"Oh God, all hell has broken loose. That's why I called. I have to see you. Can you come over here now?" she asked, close to panic.

Seth didn't like the way she sounded, and he wanted to stay as far away from this as possible. "I can't, Cicely. I'm booked up for the rest of the day. I wish I could. You sound as though you need a nice, relaxing massage—and one of my very special treatments."

Cicely relaxed a little at the mention of what she craved, but still she begged. "Cancel someone, please."

"I can't. How about Saturday morning? I have an hour free."

"I can't wait that long," said Cicely, on the verge of tears. "And anyway, the funeral's Saturday. What about tonight or tomorrow? Maybe I could come over to your house tonight."

At the thought of another visit from Cicely McBride, Seth gave in. "I'll come over after dinner tonight, but it might be very late. Wait for me."

He hung up the phone without waiting for her acknowledgment. She'd be there tonight, pacing the floor from the way she'd sounded, and he decided to let her stew a little. He wouldn't show up until around eleven o'clock—just when she was *really* frantic. Actually, he thought, she sounded pretty frantic already. Why? he wondered. Why would the death of the husband she didn't even like put her into such a spin? She stood to inherit tons of money, which Seth knew she badly needed, but she also had plenty of her own, so greed couldn't have been the motive if she *did* knock off the philandering physician she was married to.

He sat up straighter in the seat of his bright orange Porsche. That could be it! Leo McBride would screw any woman who wasn't locked up—at least he would try. Maybe Cicely had had enough and thought that the only way she could stop him was to kill him.

Nah, he said to himself. All those rich society guys screw around, but the wives don't kill them for it. They get back at them in other ways. They spend money like it's going out of style, they compete with each other with party giving and house decorating. In this town you need to be married, so they put up with a lot of crap.

But Cicely wasn't as discreet as his other clients. She acted as though she had nothing to protect, but Seth knew she had more to lose than any of them.

Damn her trips to Rockville!

He turned the key in the ignition but not before he flipped through the file of index cards he kept on all his clients. On each card were details about the sequence of events that, through careful research and attention to detail, he had discovered would most satisfy the client and produce the biggest tips.

At the end of each session he made three pencil notations on the card: one for the amount of the massage fee, one for the amount of the cash tip, and one on the woman's sexual responses. Then, each evening when he returned home, he entered the data on his computer along with other information: gossip, comments about the stock market or bits of business news, and tidbits of information from women whose husbands held high government posts. Everything was potentially useful, and much of the information stored on his floppy disks had contributed to his fortunes.

Seth let in the clutch on the Porsche and sped off to the last appointment of the day.

Seth *did* hear a frantic note in Cicely's voice. When she put the receiver back in its cradle, she saw the moist imprint of her hand on it.

"I can control this," she said to herself. "I don't need to do it this time."

She sat in a chair in her sumptuous living room and practiced her breathing exercises. Her respirations were slow and even, but her mind flitted and hovered like a hummingbird. She didn't know what to do. She needed what she was going to ask of Seth, but what if he refused? There was no reason for him to provide her with an alibi; she had no power over him. If she threatened to expose him, all she would get would be a denial, derisive laughter from the community that mattered in Washington, and the undying enmity of his other clients, many of whom were her friends.

"The hell with it," she said. "I'll do it just one more time. Once more can't hurt. Then I'll stop. I promise I'll stop," she said to the empty room.

So Cicely McBride got into her new Jaguar XK and drove east from her home in Potomac to the Twinbrook section of Rockville, a few miles north of Washington on the Maryland side of the Potomac River.

She pulled into the parking lot of a 7-Eleven store on Rockville Pike and rummaged through her purse for a quarter for the pay phone outside the store. Immediately she wished she hadn't. A pickup truck pulled up next to the Jaguar, and three men in mesh baseball caps got out and ran their hands over the shiny green surface of the car. Cicely shuddered watching them stroke the car with their hands as they stroked her body with their eyes. There was no mistaking her as the driver of the car, and there was no mistaking the sexual connection in the minds of these men.

As she waited for someone to answer the ringing phone, Cicely tried to think of what to say to the men to make them stop. She recognized the menace, but she had no idea how to handle it. It never occurred to her that all she had to do was get in her car and drive away. Visions of gang rape and bicycle chains flashed through her mind so that by the time the man answered the phone, she was breathless with anxiety.

"This is Dorothy," she said to the man who knew her name wasn't Dorothy and who knew exactly who she was. He had to know who his customers were.

"Would it be all right if I dropped by for a minute now?"

She received an affirmative answer and hung up the phone but stood paralyzed with fear and indecision in front of the three grinning men. Cicely hated it when things like this happened. She knew that other women, the ones who worked downtown and carried briefcases and wore running shoes with their business suits, wouldn't give this predicament a second thought. They wouldn't even think of it as a predicament, and they would know what to do. She didn't.

Her anger and insecurity made her feel impotent when she let inferior people get the better of her. And that impotence was why she needed to run this errand.

The men, sensing her fear, laughed at her, but soon they tired of the game and went into the store. Once safely inside her car, she threw the gearshift into reverse and careened out of the parking lot, hands shaking on the steering wheel, safety belt unfastened, sweat trickling down her armpits.

In ten minutes she turned onto Boiling Brook Parkway and pulled up in front of a small suburban house, neatly covered with aluminum siding and perched behind a waist-high chain-link fence. The house was surrounded by dozens just like it, all on neat lawns, some with children's play equipment scattered about. Several of the houses had lawn ornaments, and one sported two iron deer that looked surprisingly real.

Cicely pulled down the visor and checked her hair and makeup before getting out of the car. Her bowels were still cramping unpleasantly from fright, but her hands had stopped shaking. When she got out of the car, she felt steady on her feet.

She opened the gate and walked up the sidewalk, knowing she was being watched. The door opened before she had a chance to knock, and the man greeted her pleasantly.

"Sit down, please, Dorothy. Would you like a cup of tea?" He was always polite and always offered her refreshment.

"No, thank you. I'm in a bit of a hurry today." She always said the same thing, and she never took the proffered chair.

The man understood her reluctance, her unwillingness to be in his home. Many of his clients felt the same way.

"How much would you like today?" he asked, as if he were a butcher inquiring about the size of the roast.

"This much," said Cicely, holding out an envelope with five thousand dollars in it.

The man counted the money carefully and deliberately, went into another room, and came back with a plastic bag filled with precious white powder. Cicely held out her hand and tried not to appear too needy as she put the cocaine into her purse.

But the man noticed Cicely's anxious expression, her effort to appear casual, and he waited for the request he knew would come.

"Do you mind if I use your bathroom?" asked Cicely in an apologetic voice. "It's a long ride home."

"Please," he said, pointing down a small corridor off the living room. "You know where it is."

The man was both amused and contemptuous. Why did they all pretend to have to go to the bathroom? What did they think he believed about the cocaine he sold them? Didn't they know that he understood their desperation? Why didn't they just take a blow right there in front of him? They all pretended to be so cool, but he knew and they knew that he was all that stood between them and the street dealers who didn't provide tiled bathrooms, fresh hand towels, scented soap, and delicate little spoons of just the right size.

He heard the toilet flush and waited for Cicely to emerge. She looked much better. The anxious pinched look was gone, and she seemed to stand taller and straighter, ready to face the mess that her husband's murder must surely have created. He wished he could offer his condolences, but that was out of the question. "Dorothy's" husband hadn't just been murdered.

He also wished he could offer her some help. The man had plenty of help to give, and he didn't want to lose one of his best customers. Not many of them bought five thousand dollars' worth of cocaine as often as she did, and the man wondered, not for the first time, whether she was cutting it and starting her own little business. Or maybe she was just overly generous with her friends who didn't want to buy their own.

Her habit was getting more expensive by the week, and he knew that her own money wasn't enough to pay for it. She needed lots of cash for these trips to Rockville, but had she murdered her husband to get it?

"Thank you," she said to the man as she walked to the door.

"And thank *you*," he replied. "It's been my pleasure. I trust this will help."

And, he said to himself, I trust that if you *did* stick it to your old man, you'll have sense enough to keep me out of it.

The man was in a position to offer help to "Dorothy," but he was also in a position to hurt her.

It was almost dark when Paul Bandman and Lydia Simon-owitz got back to Second District Police Headquarters on Idaho Avenue, N.W. They had had a frustrating day, and neither one was in a good mood.

Earlier that morning Lydia had called the J.F.K. Memorial Personnel Department to inquire about Ina Wolfman's salary. She had identified herself as a police officer and had gotten the information almost immediately. Ina earned a normal salary.

"I could have been anybody," Lydia said. "She didn't even call back to verify who I was."

"People are gullible," said Bandman, "and they're anxious to comply with authority, even the illusion of authority. Frightening, isn't it?"

They had gone back to the hospital and spoken to everyone who had been in the administrative office suite and had run into McBride's office in response to Ina Wolfman's scream. No one knew or saw anything. Not even Ina.

"When you walked back from the supply room who did you see in the corridor?" asked Bandman.

"No one," replied Ina.

"You mean the corridor was completely empty? Is that usual right around lunchtime?" Bandman pressed her; something about this woman didn't strike him as quite right.

"There's not a lot of traffic here," she responded, and Bandman could see that this was true. Glass doors separated the administrative hall from the main corridor that led to the elevators, gift shop, and all the offices where patients and their families did business. The administrative offices were off the public's beaten path, and a lot of the secretaries and others had already gone to the cafeteria for lunch.

"So you would have noticed a stranger coming down the hall?" he asked.

"Yes, especially if he were coming in here."

Bandman pounced. "Why 'he'? Why do you assume it would be a man?"

Ina was flustered again. "I don't know," she answered. "I just said 'he.' It's natural, isn't it?"

"Is it?" asked Bandman, who knew it was. Everyone spoke in the masculine, but he was stalling for time, wishing this wasn't the end of twentieth-century America. If he could put this woman on the rack—just for a minute or two, just to scare her, really, not to actually pull anything out of joint—he knew he'd hear something good.

But all he could do was sigh and say, "Mrs. Wolfman, I know you're hiding something. I don't know what it is, but I *do* know that you have more information for me, and I intend to get it. How about making my job easier and giving it to me now?"

Her eyes dilated fully, and he noted the thin film of sweat on her upper lip. "I don't know what you mean," she said, making an obvious effort to control her voice. "I've told you everything."

Bandman put on his sad hound-dog expression that Lydia was beginning to recognize as the precursor to a verbal alligator snap. "No, you haven't," he said. "But you're going to. Oh yes, you will. And by the time you do, I'll already know what you're going to say. I'm a *very* good detective, Mrs. Wolfman."

He and Lydia had left her then, her heart pounding in fear.

They had gotten the same story from everyone else. Either they weren't there, or they had been in their offices, heard the scream, and come running. And the ones who were more than three or four doors from McBride's office knew nothing until they either left their offices or were notified.

That's how Alfred Miller found out. "I was on the telephone," he said, "and Ms. Knight came bursting into my office. She didn't even stop at my secretary's desk." Here he pursed his lips a little as if this gaffe were more troublesome than the murder of his colleague.

"Were you surprised?" asked Lydia.

"Surprised?" repeated Miller. "What do you mean 'surprised'? It was a terrible, terrible shock for us all," he said, his voice again registering more disapproval than horror.

"But deep down," said Bandman, continuing what Lydia had started, "didn't you think that someday someone would try to get even with McBride?"

"What do you mean, 'get even'?" asked Miller, looking genuinely puzzled. "Why would anyone want to get even with Dr. McBride? He was a brilliant physician. Patients came to him from all over the world. I don't understand you."

"I think you do," said Bandman. "Think about it a little, and perhaps your memory will be refreshed the next time we talk."

As the detectives walked into the station house, Joe Gingrich, the desk sergeant, said, "The M.E.'s report on McBride is here."

Lydia took the report out of its manilla envelope and within thirty seconds was totally engrossed in what she read. When she was finished she tossed it across the desk to Bandman.

The report was both bizarre and sad. McBride had had liver cancer, was hiding it, and would have bought the farm in another few weeks without anyone hurrying him along.

He had track marks along both arms, and at first the M.E. thought he might be a secret doper, but then he noticed that the skin on McBride's hands and face was discolored. The discoloration turned out to be thick pancake makeup, and when he washed it off he saw the full extent of the jaundice: on the skin and in the whites of his eyes, which McBride hid with scleral contact lenses (the kind that fit over the whole eye, not just the iris).

Then, when the M.E. had made the Virchow incision, the giant slice that extended from throat down through the pubic hair with flaps cut back from maximum exposure, he found the liver cancer. There were also big doses of two or three anti-cancer drugs in McBride's blood and tissue.

Bandman finished reading and he and Lydia looked at each other. "So what did McBride die of?" he asked.

"If it wasn't the cancer, and the scalpel didn't do it, and there are no wounds or other obvious causes of death, that leaves only one thing: poison," replied Lydia.

"If you're right, we run smack into an awfully big coincidence," said Bandman. "He had to have been alive when the stabber went into his office, but he was dead when Ina Wolfman found him. That would mean that the poison had to have taken effect at practically the same time that the scalpel went into his windpipe."

"I see what you mean," said Lydia. "Unless—and I know this is really reaching—the scalpel itself was poisoned. You know, like the Indians used to do to their arrows."

"I thought of that, too," said Bandman. "But why would a murderer with a knife in his hand need poison, too?"

"And," added Lydia, "why would a murderer with a knife in his hand not inflict a fatal wound? If his goal was murder, wouldn't he have slashed as wide and deep as he could? And wouldn't he have used a bigger instrument that would do the job faster, like a carving knife or a switchblade or something? A scalpel is sharp but not very big."

"And what if I wasn't just talking through my hat to Mrs. Wolfman?" said Bandman. "What if it wasn't a he? What if Miss Mouse did it herself?"

"She sure seems to have hated him enough," replied Lydia, "and she had the time and opportunity. All she had to do was close and lock both doors, the one to the corridor and the one to his private office, and do it."

"But *how* did she do it? And *why*?" he asked.

Lydia smiled. "God, you ask hard questions!"

Bandman laughed. "So . . . ?"

Lydia thought for a minute. "How's this? She got a

scalpel—they must be all over the place—and then she smeared it with some kind of poison, it'd have to be really fast-acting stuff, and stuck it into his windpipe and held him down while the poison took effect."

"And the whole time McBride was just sitting there letting her do it," said Bandman.

Lydia saw his point immediately. There had been no sign of a struggle in that immaculate office. She looked chagrined.

"But I like your idea of a poisoned scalpel. That rings true," he said. "The only problem is that the M.E. didn't find anything suspicious in McBride's blood. We'll have to look for something that doesn't leave a trace."

He sighed, knowing how many dozens of chemical compounds fit that description. "First thing tomorrow we'll call the police toxicologist and check out poisons. Then we'll talk to Alice Bonner."

"I could stop over there now. She lives not too far from me," said Lydia. "Unless you want us to go together."

"No, you can go alone if you want. But you don't have to work overtime on this, Simonowitz."

"I don't mind," she replied.

"So, that's it for the day," said Bandman. "Call me at home if you find Bonner. If not, we'll try in the morning, and if she's still not there and hasn't called the hospital, we'll put a bulletin out for her."

"Okay," said Lydia. "Do you think we should lean a little more on the weeping widow tomorrow?"

"Absolutely, and I want to go back to the hospital and talk to the others that McBride worked with. I have a hunch that, unless one of the people we talked to today killed the guy—and I'm not discounting Ina Wolfman, far from it—they're telling the truth. And nobody down there is going to tell us what McBride was really like. We'll just get more of that, 'He was a brilliant physician,' stuff. If we want the real dope on the kind of guy McBride really was, we'll have to get it from the privates, not the generals."

Bandman and Simonowitz walked to the parking lot together and said good night. Lydia was tired and hungry. It was almost seven-thirty, and by the time she made a detour to Connecticut Avenue, where the nurse lived, and then drove to her own apartment in Glover Park, it would be after eight o'clock, and that was if Bonner wasn't home. Her stomach was growling with serious hunger, so she made a left at the next corner and headed for Tilden Street and into Rock Creek Park on Beach Drive.

Rush hour was almost over and she had the drive pretty much to herself. She enjoyed the ride, breathing in the relatively clear air through her window, looking forward to a thick corned beef sandwich.

The parking lot of the Parkway Deli wasn't full, so Lydia knew she wouldn't have to wait for a table. The rich aroma of deli food and the steamy warmth of the restaurant made her glad she'd let Alice Bonner wait an hour.

She polished off a huge sandwich and an order of fried onion rings and then stopped at the take-out counter for a piece of chocolate mousse cake for later. Back in her car, she retraced her path through the park, and fifteen minutes later pulled up in front of Alice Bonner's apartment building on upper Connecticut Avenue.

There was no doorman, so Lydia rang the buzzer next to the nameplate that said A. Bonner. There was no answer, so she rang again, this time leaning on the button for a few seconds. Finally, after a long time, a woman's voice said, "Yeah?"

"I'm looking for Alice Bonner," said Lydia.

"Who is it?" replied the voice, none too cordial.

"Are you Ms. Bonner?"

"Yes, who *is* it?"

"Detective Lydia Simonowitz of the Metropolitan Police. Would you let me in? I'd like to ask you a few questions."

"What about?"

"I think you'd rather we discussed this in private," said Lydia. "There are quite a few people out here listening."

There wasn't a soul in sight, but after a few more seconds the buzzer sounded and Lydia pushed open the door. She rang for the elevator and then, mindful of the chocolate cake in her car, climbed the two flights to Bonner's apartment.

The nurse was waiting in the hall just outside the apartment door. "I knew you'd get here sooner or later," she said.

"May I come in?" asked Lydia.

"Okay, but only for a few minutes. I don't have much to say. I didn't kill him. I know everyone thinks I did, but I didn't."

"Why does everyone think you did?"

"Because I had an affair with the bastard and then he dumped me, and everyone in the hospital knows about it. So they think I killed him out of unrequited passion or something like that."

"Will you tell me about your affair," said Lydia.

"No," said Alice. "I don't have to tell you that. That's private. It's my business. I didn't kill him, and that's all I have to say."

Lydia thought she probably had plenty more to say, but there was no way she could force the woman to talk without getting a warrant, and there were no grounds at all—yet—for issuing one. So Lydia had to content herself with one last try.

"Do you know who might have killed him?"

"No."

Lydia gave up. Bandman would have kept pressing, but she didn't know what to say. So she thanked Alice for her time, gave the nurse her card, and asked her to call if she thought of anything that might help the investigation. Fat chance that McBride's spurned lover would care to shed light on his murder investigation.

Back out on the sidewalk Lydia shivered in her light jacket; the night had turned cold. As she walked the few steps to her car, she noticed that the car in front of hers was different and had been parked so that its rear bumper was touching her front one.

"Inconsiderate bastard!" she mumbled to herself while checking how much room she had to the rear. It would take a lot of maneuvering, but she thought she could get out.

As she jockeyed her car from forward to reverse, gaining about an inch each time, she noticed the bumper sticker on the car in front: "Have you slugged your kid today?"

Lydia did a double take. It was *slugged*, not *hugged*. She felt a surge of depression. What kind of person would think such a thing, let alone advertise it? Then she noticed the small decal in the lower left rear window: National Rifle Association Member. She grunted with exertion and disgust and wondered if the next child-abuse case she investigated would belong to the man who owned this car.

5

AMANDA WAS DREAMING. She was in a lake being dragged alongside a motorboat, held fast at the waist by a restraining strap. The motor was loud at her side, and the water lapped against her head and sloshed into her ear. Although she was held fast, tied to the boat, she was not afraid, just uncomfortable, and she wondered when she would be untied and allowed to swim free.

The sensation of water seeping into her ear grew more and more annoying, and as wakefulness pushed the dream away into the night, which was still not over, Amanda became aware of Shadow, who was licking her ear and pushing her wet nose in among the strands of hair, purring thunderously. Ken's arm was tight around her, and as she hovered on the edge before sinking back into sleep, she imprinted the moment on her memory so that she would always have it to draw around herself whenever she needed it.

Shadow stopped licking, came under the covers, and curled up against Amanda's naked breasts, still purring. Amanda put her arm around the pudgy animal and stroked her as she felt the rise and fall of her husband's chest against her back.

The next time she woke, Shadow was sitting on the windowsill watching the leaves fall, and Ken was no longer asleep. In fact, he was doing things to indicate that he was indeed wide awake. She turned toward him and looked at his blue eyes watching her.

If eyes are the mirror of a man's soul, then Ken James's eyes opened into the soul of a man who wanted to remain utterly private. The clear blues reflected nothing more than curiosity and interest. They wanted to know everything but gave away nothing.

Now the eyes were soft and friendly, open wide, watching Amanda's reaction to what the hands were doing.

No words passed between them, but she continued to watch him watching her, and even when she was holding him tight inside her and her own eyes were closed against the onslaught of the coming tidal wave, she could feel him watching her.

As she let herself be buffeted about on roaring waves, even as she was washed gasping and panting onto the safety of the shore, his eyes were on her. They closed only after he knew she was safe on the beach, and he allowed himself the pleasure of his own ride on the waves.

Later, as they sat across from each other in the sunny kitchen, Ken crunching cereal, Amanda spooning up boysen-berry yogurt, she said, "No alarm clocks tomorrow, okay?"

He smiled at her. "You didn't hear any alarms go off this morning, did you?"

"No, I didn't," she had to admit. "You have your own biological alarm—fueled by hormones!"

They laughed as he got up to pour them each a second cup of coffee.

"We're not going anywhere tonight, are we?" Ken asked anxiously.

They tried to keep Friday nights clear of all social engage-ments. It was their pleasure, as it had been since long before they were married, to be only in each other's company on Friday evening.

"No, of course not, it's Friday," she replied. "I'll stop for groceries on the way home. Do you have any special dinner requests?"

"Do you think we could have one last meal cooked on the grill?" he asked.

"Listen, if you want to freeze your buns off cooking outdoors, I'd love one more charcoal meal. I'll get some of those good Italian sausages at Snider's."

She put her coffee cup in the sink, kissed Ken lightly on his forehead, and said, "I've got to run. That night nurse who wouldn't open Mrs. Lambrusco's windows is probably in my office right now, and I'm going to have to do something about Alice Bonner. Ugh. And Townsend wants to see me—at my earliest convenience, he said. I'm sure it's about what happened on Tuesday."

"Aren't the police handling that?" asked Ken.

"The police? God, do you think it's come to that? Do you think they'll get us all for criminal negligence?"

"Amanda, are we talking about the same thing? Wasn't McBride killed on Tuesday?"

She breathed a sigh of relief. "I wasn't even thinking about McBride," she said. "It's that idiot, Barbara Morrison, the one who accidentally killed a patient, that Townsend wants to talk about."

"Oh," said Ken, not knowing what else to say. He knew how guilty Amanda felt about the incident and how angry she was at the nurse. "It wasn't your fault," he said. "Try to remember that."

"You sound just like Glen," she replied testily. "I *know* it wasn't my fault. I'm not the one who walked off and forgot all about his fluids, but I'm *responsible* for all the nursing care of every patient in that hospital. Why doesn't anyone understand that?" Tears threatened again.

"I understand responsibility, honey," he said. "After all, I run a pretty big company. But if you're going to do this job without getting sick over it, you're going to have to learn the difference between overall corporate responsibility and personal culpability for the actions of a single worker over which you have no direct control. If you can't learn that, you can't be an effective executive. And you can't cry in front of your boss."

Amanda smiled and hugged her husband. "Thanks, sweet love. That's why I have you—to smear mascara all over your shirt!"

Upstairs, repairing her eye makeup while Ken changed his shirt, Amanda thought about what he had said. It made sense. It didn't make her feel any better about the patient who had died, but it gave her a starting point for what she would say to Townsend.

"Thanks for the good advice," she said as she put the milk pitcher in the refrigerator.

"You'll do the right thing," said Ken. "And tonight we'll solve the murder."

She smiled, kissed him again, and said, "Bye, sweet love."

Amanda was thoughtful as she drove to work. This was going to be one hell of a day. In addition to dealing with Townsend on the Barbara Morrison fiasco, she had another problem: whether to tell the police about what Eddie had said yesterday. Last night, after the catered dinner and with a bottle of champagne fizzing around in her head, Amanda had told Ken about McBride's murder, what Eddie had confessed to her that afternoon, and the conclusion she had come to on the way to the airport.

"Don't worry about the police finding out that you can't die from a scalpel in the trachea," said Ken. "They've figured that out for themselves by now. I'd rethink your decision, though, about keeping Eddie's secret. I know he's your friend and you feel loyal to him, but what if he did it? You'd be obstructing justice, withholding evidence, or some such."

"I don't think I'm withholding evidence," replied Amanda, "because what he told me isn't *evidence*. And I don't think I'm obstructing justice because Eddie said he didn't do it. If I knew he did it, and then I didn't tell the police, that'd be another story."

"Suit yourself," said Ken, who, after hearing the story, didn't seem particularly interested in the murder. He had met McBride a few times, had seen nothing but the man's surface charm, and even at that, knew him only slightly. It didn't seem to have much more of an impact on him than a newspaper article on the murder of a total stranger.

"But," Ken added, "I'd hate to see you mixed up in this any more than necessary."

Now, following her usual route to the hospital, Amanda thought about last evening's conversation and was annoyed at Ken's apparent lack of interest and his suggestion that she break Eddie's confidence.

Now, be honest, she told herself. You really are tempted to tell the detectives about Eddie. You think he did it!

I do not, she contradicted herself. I have no idea who killed McBride, so I wasn't lying to the police.

But that was then—before Eddie spilled his guts, thought the Amanda who agreed with her husband. Everything's changed now.

Even if Eddie hadn't done it, he had a strong motive, and she felt she had an obligation to tell the police what she had found out since they questioned her the afternoon of the murder.

But she also had an obligation to the friendship, and as she locked her car and walked through the hospital parking lot to her office, she had no idea what she would do.

Doreen McClure was sitting in the outer office watching Louise type. She looked like a disgruntled baby.

It occurred to Amanda that this was no way to start a workday, although the way she and Ken had started *their* day had been very fine indeed and put her in a generous mood.

"Would you like a cup of coffee?" she said to Doreen. "I apologize for being late. You'll be paid for the overtime."

Doreen looked surprised at the promise of extra money, but she refused coffee and settled into a chair with her arms across her chest, looking ready to take a bite out of Amanda.

The staff nurse refused to understand why anyone, let alone someone with a tracheostomy, would want to sleep with the window open.

"It's not up to you to pass judgment on patients' sleeping habits," said Amanda. "It's your job to see that they sleep comfortably in any way they choose as long as it doesn't endanger them or anyone else. That's what you're paid to do."

Doreen shrugged and said, "I do the best I can."

"In this case your best wasn't good enough. Would you like to transfer to days or evenings?" asked Amanda.

"No," was the curt reply.

"Would you like to resign?"

That brought a surprised look. "Why did you ask that?" said Doreen.

"Because you don't seem happy working here—and because although I can't fire you for this infraction, I'm not happy having you work here. You don't seem to agree with J.F.K.'s policy of treating patients as they want and need to be treated, so if you'd like to resign, we can work out a settlement right now," said Amanda. She *wanted* this woman to resign. She wanted every single nurse in the hospital to quit on the spot so they'd have to transfer the patients somewhere else and lock the place up. Then she could go home and read novels and not have to think about who would screw up next.

"But I need this job," replied the nurse, more subdued now.

"Then please start using some common sense and behave like a professional nurse."

Amanda stood up, indicating that the bawling-out was over. She was tired of this spoiled, petulant young woman and couldn't wait to catch her in another infraction so she could fire her. "You'll receive a letter summarizing this meeting. Understand that it represents an official warning. If you make another mistake you'll be fired. Think it over, and if you believe I've been unfair, come to me to discuss it."

She went to the door and opened it, resisting the urge to kick the girl in the butt on her way out.

Amanda barely had time for a trip to the john before she was due in the hospital's boardroom, the most pleasant place in the hospital—except for Leo McBride's office, she thought.

Half the seats were already filled, and she wasn't the last to arrive. David Townsend, who had called this emergency Friday-morning meeting, would be the last one in. He liked to make entrances, and Amanda had the impression that if he thought he could get away with it, he would ask everyone to stand when he came into the room. Pompous ass! she thought even as she recognized how well he ran the hospital. It was the best place she had ever worked in, and she appreciated Townsend's administrative style, if not his personal one.

He let Amanda run the nursing department her way; he left her alone and always would unless she went over the budget or created trouble for the hospital—like she was doing now. And if that happened too many times, there would be no bawlings-out and no crabbing and carping behind her back to other department heads. She would simply be fired.

Amanda liked that. She always knew where David Townsend stood—which was more than she could say for some of her colleagues, many of whom enjoyed what she called "rearview bloodletting."

She sat about a third of the way down from the head of the polished mahogany table and looked around appreciatively at the handsome room. This was wood paneling at its finest, she knew, and the dark red carpet on the floor was pure wool—no synthetics for the board of directors of J.F.K. Memorial Hospital—and the portraits of past medical directors were done by first-rate artists. The water pitchers between each two chairs were silver, and the glasses were lead crystal.

Amanda relaxed in the deep leather armchair and almost expected to see bearers, dressed in nothing but loincloths, bringing in a dozen sacrificial virgins.

Her reverie was interrupted by the simultaneous banging of a gavel (when a discreet throat clearing would have been sufficient) and the last-minute entrance of Eddie Silverman.

She saw him look around the table for her, and when their eyes met, she winked, but he looked away without giving her an answering smile. She thought perhaps he hadn't really seen her, so she stared at him for a while to get his attention, but he refused to acknowledge her. What was going on?

". . . staff of John F. Kennedy Memorial Hospital deeply regrets the brutal slaying of our esteemed colleague . . . blah, blah, blah . . . cooperate fully with the police in their efforts to apprehend . . . blah, blah."

Mark Sullivan, the hospital's public relations director, was reading the statement he had given to the press on Wednesday afternoon. It was beautifully written, with all the right platitudes, and it said nothing.

"Well done, Mark," said Townsend. "What's been going on since then?"

"Actually, not much," replied the former journalist. "Everyone in my office was questioned by the police. The hospital's official comment to the press is basically 'no comment.' You know—we can't interfere with or comment on an ongoing investigation—that sort of thing."

"What about the funeral?" asked Townsend.

"It's going to be at Caldwell's on Saturday—time to be announced. The hospital sent flowers to Mrs. McBride, and we'll send a big splashy arrangement to the funeral. Then maybe a Leo McBride Memorial Fund of some sort . . ." Sullivan's voice trailed off as he ran out of ideas and waited for Townsend to provide some.

"There will be time enough for that later," said the administrator. "I want to concentrate now on presenting a united front to the police and press. Any thoughts on how to proceed?"

Amanda felt her face go hot and hoped no one could see her flush. She remembered what she had said to the detectives on Tuesday right after McBride had been killed. She was sure that if Townsend knew that she had told them what a bastard McBride was, she'd be out on the street in two seconds flat. She wondered whether a statement to the police was privileged information—like what you told your doctor. Amanda decided it probably wasn't and thought maybe she should call the woman detective. She seemed more sympathetic than Bender/Bonder.

What for? asked her conscience. To throw yourself on her mercy and ask that she forget about your sticking your foot in your mouth—as usual? You probably gave the police the juiciest information they had all day.

Amanda pushed the voice of conscience to the back of her mind and tuned in to the uncomfortable silence that had fallen on the conference table. It went on for a few long minutes until finally Jonathan Bernstein spoke.

"It seems to me that we don't have much choice in how we will proceed, David," he said. "The police are going to go about their business, and there's not much we can do about it. And unless someone in this room is a murderer, we don't need to think more about it. Leo's dead, and I guess some of us will miss him, but hell, I don't know why you're wasting our time like this. I have patients who need me."

"But the police haven't questioned everyone yet," said Townsend. "For instance, have you seen them?"

"No, but I'm sure it's just a matter of time," the surgeon replied dryly.

"Well, what are you planning to tell them?"

Bernstein didn't hide his annoyance. "What do you mean, what am I going to tell them? The truth, of course. I didn't know anything about it. I was in the O.R. What are you getting at, David?"

"I didn't mean to imply that you would tell them anything but the truth about the actual murder," replied Townsend somewhat testily. He was on the defensive now. "I mean, what are you going to say when they ask you about McBride, the man. They always do."

"They always do! How many murder investigations have you been involved in, David?"

Bernstein and Townsend were going at it again, and Amanda didn't know whether to be bored or amused. She had seen this scene played out so many times at department-head meetings that she could practically turn the pages of the script as they baited each other. In her mind's eye, she saw them as little boys throwing dirt at each other on the playground.

She had once described this image to Eddie, and they had laughed about it together. She looked across and down the table at him now, wanting to share the amusement, but he steadfastly refused to acknowledge her.

". . . see too many murder movies, David," Bernstein was saying. I don't think the police give a hoot in hell about what kind of person McBride was. They just want to get on with the business of catching the murderer."

"You're wrong," said Townsend, "but I don't want to argue with you about it. One of the reasons I called this meeting was to decide the kinds of things we ought to say about McBride and what's best kept within the hospital. What do you think?"

Again, a pall of silence descended on the department heads sitting at the long polished table with the portraits staring down at them. Amanda knew why they were reluctant to speak. These were people with a good deal of political savvy—they needed it in order to have worked their way up the administrative ladder—but they all had enough independence of spirit to resent being asked to tell a communal story to the police.

"David," she said, "if it were only us, *maybe* we could come to some agreement about what would be appropriate to say about McBride, although it would probably take us through the weekend to do it." She smiled to soften the harshness of the thought. "But that's all beside the point because it's *not* just us.

We have no idea who the police are going to talk to, and we can't write a script for every employee at J.F.K."

Townsend was no dummy; he saw Amanda's point immediately. "You're right," he said. "And I didn't mean to imply that we should in any way *lie* to the police or make it seem like we were all saying the same thing about McBride. But, people"—he paused for dramatic effect—"let's try to be discreet. Remember McBride has a family. Let's try not to embarrass them—or the hospital."

Mark Sullivan spoke again. "About the press—I've told you what the hospital's official comments are. We're not letting TV crews in the building, and the front desk and all the nurses' stations have instructions to be strict about asking for visitor's passes. But it's impossible to keep out every nosy reporter in this city, and they may lie in wait for you in the parking lot or call you at home. This murder has everyone titillated, and you can't blame the press for trying to get all the mileage they can out of it. I *urge* you to say nothing about the murder, but unfortunately it's a free country, and the hospital can't compel you to keep your mouths closed. So for God's sake, if you're going to talk to reporters, make sure the hospital comes up smelling like roses."

"Good point, Mark," said Townsend. "Amanda, will you make sure that the nurses are on the lookout for unauthorized visitors?"

"I'll see to it personally," she replied.

"Good. Does anyone have anything else to contribute?" More silence.

"Okay, then, thanks for your time," said the administrator. "Don't forget the infection-control meeting here Monday morning at eight-thirty sharp. The consultant is costing us a bundle, so no excuses. Everyone shows up. And remember, the watchword for the day is *discretion*."

The dozen or so people pushed their chairs back with a palpable sense of relief, and as Amanda was about to go over to Eddie, Ruth Sinclair, head of the dietary department and the only other woman on J.F.K.'s administrative staff, whispered to her, "Doesn't he make you feel like a kindergarten kid sometimes?"

Amanda smiled. "Nursery school!"

And then she looked up and saw Eddie walk out the door of the boardroom, practically at a trot. No doubt about it, he was avoiding her.

But David Townsend was coming straight for her. "Do you have a few minutes to talk now, Amanda?" he asked.

"Sure," she said. "Your place or mine?" Then she wanted to kick herself.

Great said her conscience. *Sarcasm! Just the appropriate response for a time like this! What the hell is the matter with you?*

But Townsend seemed not to notice the gaffe as they walked together to his office.

"Thanks for helping me out in there," he said. "I really appreciated it."

"It was my pleasure, David," Amanda replied. That was one of the things she liked about Townsend. He gave credit where it was due—even when he was about to haul you over the coals for something else.

"Okay," he said with a sigh. "Tell me exactly what happened."

Amanda took a deep breath; this would be the easy part. "Mr. Cottrell had had a gastric resection the day before," she began, "but you know how Dr. Lacey is . . . he tries not to put nasogastric tubes down because the patients hate them so much. Anyway, by the next morning the patient was doing real well and had progressed to sips of water every hour. He'd been out of bed three times and had even walked around the nurses' station once.

"Then his IV infiltrated, and Morrison pulled it out. She told the surgical intern, and he said he'd restart it. So far, so good. She wrote everything in the chart.

"About an hour later two medical students tried to restart the IV, but they couldn't find a vein, and they hated to keep sticking Mr. Cottrell. He *did* have pretty bad veins. So since he was allowed sips of water, they made him promise to keep drinking and left. So far, pretty good. I wouldn't have done that, but they're only medical students, and what do they know?

"Anyway, according to the students *and* Morrison, the students told her what they had done—or hadn't done, I guess—and said that the patient would be okay if he drank enough water. And they were going to advance him to full liquids that afternoon if everything kept going well.

"But now it gets kind of iffy because from here on out, no one documented anything—until it was too late. Morrison said she saw Mr. Cottrell drinking water, but she wasn't clear about how much or how often. He'd been getting seventy-five milligrams of Demerol every three hours or so, so I doubt he'd be awake much of the time, and when he was he probably didn't take more than a sip or two. Cold water probably doesn't feel too great splashing down into a stomach that's just been cut into."

Amanda paused and looked at Townsend, who was listening carefully without interruption, making a note occasionally. "The rest you know."

"I know it all too well," Townsend replied dryly. "What I didn't know was just how fast a grown person could get dehydrated. I thought that human beings could go for a lot longer than that without fluids."

"They can, David, if they're healthy to begin with, if they hadn't been refused anything by mouth since the night before surgery, if they haven't just been subjected to the trauma of a four-hour operation, and if their electrolytes—you know, all the body's chemicals—are in perfect balance," she replied.

"Mr. Cottrell wasn't in great shape when he walked in here. He even needed a potassium supplement the night before surgery. Morrison should have known that. She should have known that potassium is crucial in maintaining heart rhythm. She should have been on the lookout for something like this."

Townsend looked at Amanda levelly. "What would have been the right thing for her to do, Amanda?"

"The right thing would have been to either insist that the med students get that IV started, or if they really couldn't, to call the intern or resident and get it in. And in the meantime she should have *made* Mr. Cottrell drink. That's what's called 'forcing fluids,' and it's *completely* a nursing responsibility.

You don't need a doctor's order to do it, and it's elementary. You learn it practically from day one in nursing school."

Townsend knew all this. He had already had a general idea of the importance of fluid and electrolyte balance before this had happened—he knew more medicine than most people realized. But he had spoken with Bernstein and Lacey about it afterward and heard exactly what Amanda was telling him now. He appreciated the fact that she didn't try to weasel out of it and didn't try to blame it on the med students or God knew who else. But that didn't help the present situation. Honesty was fine, but it didn't keep the lawyers from swarming all over you with their fangs sharpened.

For a moment he felt a flash of gratitude to McBride's killer. The sensational murder had eclipsed everything, and now there would be no danger of Mr. Cottrell's death making the papers. You just never knew how families would react to things like this. Sometimes they went straight to the press—always after a trip to their lawyers, he thought with a grim smile.

Amanda wondered what he was thinking. The grimace that flashed across Townsend's face was weird. It was kind of a half smile, half expression of pain. She wondered if she should say something else.

"What could have been done to prevent it?" he asked.

Here comes the hard part, she thought, and took a deep breath. "I've been thinking about practically nothing else, David," she responded, "and to be honest, I don't think it could have been prevented."

His eyebrows shot up in surprise. "No, I didn't mean exactly that," she said when she realized how it sounded. "Of course, you can prevent negligence if you hire only people who are utterly and completely competent every single moment of the day. And I know that's the goal when people's lives are at stake—and that's what I shoot for, but I don't think it's possible.

"David, I do what I can when I hire nurses to check their references and use my judgment about who will work out well, but I'm not a prophet," she said, making an effort not to whine. "Last year, because of that flap about the nurse who had a forged license, I even started writing to schools to see if applicants really had graduated, and I check every single license with the District of Columbia to see if they're okay to practice. Do you know that Barbara Morrison had phenomenally high scores on her state board exams—higher than mine?"

Townsend sighed again. He supposed she was right, but that didn't erase the fact that the hospital was completely at fault. The legal department was braced for the onslaught they knew was coming.

"What do we do now?"

Another hard question. Amanda tried to appear confident as she replied. "There's not much we can do. I've already scheduled some in-service classes on fluids and electrolytes. It's mostly for show, but it can't hurt. Every nurse in the hospital knows what happened, and every one of them knows *exactly* who was at fault. There won't be any more fluid screwups for a long, long time."

"Good," said Townsend more sarcastically than he knew was necessary. But he didn't care how he sounded. Let Amanda Knight stew in her own fear for a while. She had a tendency to be too cocky, and he didn't mind taking her down a peg or two. But he also knew she was probably right; taking care of desperately sick people was a risky business.

Amanda went back into her office, refilled her coffee cup, pretended not to see the box of leftover doughnuts, and asked Louise to call Center Wing 4 and have Alice Bonner sent down as soon as she could reasonably leave the unit.

Then she sat at her desk and just shook, watching in detached amazement as her hands quivered and fluttered. She concentrated on taking long, slow breaths and tried not to think about the meeting with Townsend.

Gradually her heart slowed and her hands quieted enough so she could pick up the coffee cup, but it tasted bitter and sour. She knew that Townsend wouldn't rant and rave and scream invectives at her—that wasn't his style. But she didn't expect calm acceptance of everything she had to say. Maybe this is the calm before the storm, she thought. Maybe the ax is still going to fall.

Amanda was imagining herself kneeling on a scaffold in

eighteenth-century Paris, waiting for the guillotine to chop off her head, when she heard the soft knock on the door, and Alice Bonner walked in in her usual blaze of beauty. She smiled shyly and sat down in the chair that Amanda indicated.

Bonner was the most staggeringly beautiful woman Amanda had ever seen. It always took her a few seconds to come back to herself after absorbing the flash of shining jet black hair, worn loosely around her perfect face and framing huge bottle green eyes, fringed with heavy dark lashes.

"How are you feeling?" asked Amanda.

"I feel like a stupid jerk," Bonner replied, and burst into tears.

Amanda handed her a box of Kleenexes and waited for the short but intense storm to end.

"Aren't you being a little hard on yourself?" asked Amanda in a soft tone. She liked Alice and knew her to be a good nurse and an intelligent, warm person. Yes, she'd behaved stupidly, but at the age of twenty-four and with the looks of a movie star, that was to be expected.

"You're going to fire me, aren't you?" asked Bonner.

"I'm sorry to say that I have to," said Amanda, who really was sorry. "You pulled a big boner by not showing up for work and not calling to explain, and I have no choice. But no one else need know."

"I'm disgusted with myself; I usually don't behave this way."

"Do you want to tell me about it?" asked Amanda. Ordinarily she didn't get involved in the staff's personal lives, but this was different, and—admit it, she told herself—she was dying of curiosity.

Bonner laughed without mirth. "We weren't lovers in the sense that we loved each other. He came over to my apartment for sex about once a week, and I cooked a few dinners for him—he never once took me out—and we talked some, and that was about it.

"I knew all the time that he was a shit, that eventually he would dump me, and that he had no feelings for me at all."

"Then why . . . ?" asked Amanda.

"You want to know why someone who looks like me treats

herself so badly and allows herself to be crapped on by a toad like Leo McBride?"

"Well, yes," said Amanda. What the hell was she letting herself in for now? Didn't she have enough trouble of her own without getting involved in someone else's? But she had always been a sucker for a dramatic story.

"You're very nice looking," said Bonner, "but I bet people don't stop and gawk at you in the street. Before you were married, when you went out with a man, he probably didn't *stare* at you the whole time, never listening to a word you said, only biding his time till he could get you into the sack. Your women friends are happy to be seen with you because they don't always fade into the woodwork because everyone is always staring at you. Not everyone automatically assumes you're dumb as dishwater. Did you ever wonder why Elizabeth Taylor is so screwed up? It's because she's so beautiful and no one ever sees anything but her outer shell. No one ever wants to know what kind of *person* she is.

"So I never date, and I have no friends. When Leo came on to me, I let myself be flattered that a big important doctor wanted me. It didn't take long to realize that he was the same as the rest of them, only worse."

Amanda, who had had her share of trouble with men—and who had never once thought about Elizabeth Taylor's inner self—listened to this recitation of self-pity in astonishment. Who would have thought that so much beauty could produce such misery? Somehow, it wasn't convincing. Either Bonner was overdramatizing a period of loneliness and depression or she was wallowing in unhappiness because she didn't know how to make herself happy. Or she was trying to deflect attention away from the fact that she had killed McBride. After all, who had a better motive than Alice Bonner, spurned lover?

Eddie Silverman, said the voice she didn't always like to listen to.

Shut up, she told it. Aloud she said, "In what way was he worse than the others?"

"He was more of a user. All men exploit all women, but this guy was a champion."

There was the self-pity again in the refusal to acknowledge

that there were *some* men who treat women decently. Had Alice never met a nice guy?

"In what way did he exploit you? I mean, how was he especially terrible?"

Amanda wondered why she was pushing Bonner for these explanations. She could easily imagine how McBride treated women, and it wasn't a pretty picture. Why was she egging on this poor, sad woman who was about to lose her job?

"Let me tell you what he did to my sister-in-law," replied Alice. "She was feeling sick: kind of tired and feverish, and she couldn't get over it. She wanted to go to a doctor, but my brother was out of work and didn't have any insurance. So I asked Leo if he could recommend a doctor who wouldn't charge too much to examine her.

"He said he'd be happy to see her, and I said that Ruth wasn't asking for that kind of favor. But he insisted and told me to send her over to his office.

"It turned out that she was just anemic and needed iron. She thanked him and even planned to give him a little present in appreciation—nothing much, just a batch of cookies or something.

"Then she got his bill for two hundred dollars. Can you imagine anything so gross? He *knew* Bill wasn't working and they were having a tough time, yet he billed her. He tricked her—and me.

"He'll never have enough money to satisfy him, even though he has more than he can possibly spend. I don't understand that. I hated him for what he did."

"Yet you continued to sleep with him," said Amanda.

Bonner looked down at the floor for a few seconds. When she looked up, there were tears in her eyes. "It's amazing what a person will do out of loneliness and out of *wanting* so badly to be loved."

It was true. Amanda knew only too well how a woman could delude herself into believing that a few words of kindness and satisfying lovemaking could be mistaken for love and commitment. And she knew only too well the rage that could take its place when one was forced to give up that delusion. What she had to consider was whether Bonner acted on her rage and

killed the man who spurned her. That day up on the unit when
McBride humiliated her publicly showed how easily she could
lose her temper, but McBride wasn't killed in a fit of temper.
Or was he?

"Why didn't you come to work yesterday or at least call in
sick?" Amanda asked. She wanted to pull the conversation out
of the quicksand of emotionalism and back onto solid disci-
plinary ground.

Bonner sighed. "I couldn't face it. All Tuesday afternoon
people were staring at me, and some came over from other
units just to look. I suppose everyone thinks I did it. A few
even made comments about my getting back at Leo.

"My shift was over about three hours after we heard the
news, but it was about the worst three hours I've ever spent,
and I just couldn't face another whole day of it. So I took three
Valium that night, took the phone off the hook, and didn't set
the alarm. I didn't wake up until almost one in the afternoon.
And you know, no one from the hospital called to see if I was
all right. I guess they assumed that I ran away.

"I know how you feel about nurses being responsible, and I
don't blame you for firing me. I'd do the same in your position.
Actually, I'm not all that sorry. I couldn't keep working here
after all this."

Amanda saw her point. The raging gossip would die down
after a while, but Bonner would always be identified with
McBride's murder, and that was no way to spend forty hours
every week.

"You can continue working for two weeks," said Amanda.
"Or you can leave now and collect severance pay. The fact that
you were fired will never appear on a letter of reference from
this hospital or from me. You're a good nurse, Alice, and if I
were sick, I'd be grateful to have you take care of me."

Bonner knew that coming from Ms. Knight this was about
the highest compliment you could get, and she dissolved into
fresh tears.

"I didn't kill him, you know," said Bonner when she had
pulled herself together. "I hated his guts, but I didn't kill him."

This conversation was beginning to sound like the one she
had less than twenty-four hours ago with Eddie in that very

office. McBride seemed to have inspired an avalanche of negative passion from people who knew him well. Although, she thought to herself, at one time there must have been plenty of positive passion between *these* two.

Aloud she said, "No one is accusing you of killing Dr. McBride."

"Oh yes, they are," said Bonner bitterly. "You don't know what it's like up there."

She was wrong. Amanda could imagine it clearly: the cold stares, the furtive glances of curiosity, the conversations that stopped in midsentence when the object of the talk came near. The isolation in the locker room and cafeteria.

"But I *do* know," said Amanda. "It's not *that* long ago that I was a staff nurse and succumbed once to a very sexy attending physician who turned out to be much less discreet than any woman would want. He was a locker room braggart, in fact, and he made my life miserable for a while. So I do know what you're going through, and I don't envy you at all."

Bonner seemed grateful for Amanda's confession of a youthful mistake in picking lovers and said, "But it's not just the people here. The police think I did it. That woman detective came to see me last night."

"Well, it's logical that she would. You *did* have a special relationship with Dr. McBride, and your breakup was pretty spectacular."

Bonner sighed. "I know. You're right. But still, I hate having them think I did it.

"Listen, Ms. Knight, um . . ." She hesitated, embarrassed to say what was coming next.

Amanda again had an urge to bolt from the room, but she stayed in her chair and put what she hoped was a noncommittal smile on her face.

"When I pulled that stunt in the bathroom," continued Bonner, "and you had me down here on the carpet, I said some things I shouldn't have."

"I remember," replied Amanda dryly.

"Did you tell the police what I said?"

"No."

Bonner was visibly relieved, but Amanda knew what she would say next, and her stomach clenched.

"I'd really appreciate it if you wouldn't tell them. I was hurt and humiliated and didn't mean any of the things I said. You won't tell them, will you?"

Amanda felt little knife points of pain in her stomach and wondered dimly if she was getting an ulcer.

"I'll try to avoid it," she replied. "I won't volunteer anything, but if the police ask me direct questions, I won't lie for you. That's the best I can do. I'm sorry.

"Take the rest of the day to decide about how you want to leave," said Amanda. She'd had enough of this, and she wasn't at all convinced that Bonner didn't kill McBride. She could easily have slipped away from Center Wing 4 for the few moments it would take to slip the blade in.

"I've already decided," replied Bonner. "I'll finish today and take the time to look for a job."

"That seems like a smart thing to do," said Amanda. "You can count on me for a good reference." She stood up, indicating that the conversation was over, and hustled Bonner out the door.

The day was getting worse and worse, and the morning was barely half over. She went out to the coffeepot next to Louise's desk, refilled her cup, and sank her teeth into a jelly doughnut.

"Only five-year-olds need sweets to make up for horrid experiences," she said to Louise.

"Forty-year-olds need comfort, too," said Louise.

"Hey, don't rush me," said Amanda. "I still have two years left in my thirties."

"Well, it never hurts to practice," said her secretary.

6

EDDIE WAS ALMOST late to the meeting that morning because he had been in the men's room throwing up.

He thought he had handled himself well during the police questioning and was glad he hadn't said anything about the blackmail. Going down in the elevator, he permitted himself a sigh of relief when the nausea hit, and he crashed into the toilet stall not a moment to soon.

He had not heard a word of what David Townsend and the others were saying at the meeting. His mind was on the object of their concern and the interview with the two detectives. He knew they would question him sooner or later, but he wasn't prepared for the earliness of the hour or the suddenness with which they had loomed over him as he sat in the nurses' station going over lab reports from the day before.

"Dr. Edward Silverman?" the tall detective had asked.

The official form of address was ominous in the controlled frenzy of a busy medical unit at eight-fifteen in the morning. He knew immediately who they were, but he pretended not to. With a cheerfulness that sounded phony even to him, he said, "Always here to help!"

"I'm Lieutenant Paul Bandman of the Metropolitan Police, and this is Detective Lydia Simonowitz. We'd like a few words with you. Is there someplace private we can go?"

"We can use my office on the third floor," Eddie replied, and the three trooped down the stairs to the chief medical resident's office—more like a closet with a desk than a real office.

Eddie snatched a stack of medical journals off the chair and said, "I'll get another chair in a minute."

"Don't bother," said Bandman. "I'll stand."

Eddie sat at his desk and regretted it immediately because neither detective took the chair. Having to look up at them put him at a psychological disadvantage and made him feel vulnerable. He supposed they did that on purpose, but five years of being a physician didn't provide much opportunity to practice handing control over to others.

"We're investigating the murder of Dr. Leo McBride," said Bandman. "How well did you know him?"

"Very well—professionally," replied Eddie.

"What kind of man was he?"

"A brilliant physician. Really first rate," said Eddie. At least he could be honest about that.

Bandman looked disgusted, and Eddie felt a chill of fear.

"But what kind of *man* was he?" the detective repeated.

Eddie swallowed and felt the dry click in his throat that indicated a desperate need for a drink of water. He didn't miss the quick-as-a-flash glance that passed between the two police officers.

"I didn't know him socially at all. We didn't have that kind of relationship."

Detective Simonowitz spoke this time: "Even if you didn't socialize with him, Dr. Silverman, you worked with Leo McBride every day. You saw him under the most trying and stressful circumstances. You probably knew him as well as anyone in this hospital. Now, what kind of man was he?"

"He was a difficult man to get to know, but underneath it all he was a decent guy. I liked him. I'm going to miss him."

Bandman looked calmly at Eddie and said, "You're a liar."

"What do you mean I'm a liar! I didn't kill him."

"No one's accused you of killing McBride—yet," said Bandman in his soft, deadly voice. He was very conscious of the weight of the handcuffs hanging off the back of his belt.

"Then what do you think I'm lying about?" he asked, not hearing the whine in his voice.

"Why don't you tell us," said Lydia.

Eddie didn't know what to do. So he said he liked McBride.

So what? That couldn't be what they meant. What the hell did they want him to say? "I don't have anything to tell you," he said. "You're the one who wants to question *me*."

"Temper, temper!" said Lydia.

"Did you kill him?" asked Bandman suddenly.

"No, I didn't," replied Eddie. "Why would I want to kill him?" He knew they could see the sweat he felt on his forehead and upper lip.

"I don't know why," said Bandman. "But you hated his guts like everyone else, so suppose you tell us."

"I had no reason to," said Eddie. "And I didn't hate him. I worked with him all these years. I knew him very well. I told you, he was a nice guy." Eddie could hear the frantic tone in his voice and knew he was beginning to babble. He forced himself to stop talking.

Lydia changed direction suddenly. "When did you find out he was dead?"

This was it. There was no point in lying further. His lover, Donald, thought he ought to tell the truth, and Eddie could see the sense in that.

"Ed," he had said the other evening, "what are you going to do when they catch the killer if you lie? What are they going to think? Besides, you have no reason to lie."

Eddie made no reply, and Donald misinterpreted his silence.

"In what way do you look guilty? You went out for a walk. Big deal. The police aren't going to find out how much you hated McBride unless you tell them. Your friend Amanda is right. McBride didn't tell anyone he was blackmailing you."

But Donald had been wrong. These two detectives, neither one of whom had missed a flicker of his eyelashes, knew exactly how he had felt about McBride. But further lies were impractical. The police could easily find out he wasn't in the hospital.

"I found out the minute I came back," said Eddie, and he told them of the stroll through Georgetown and how he had found the place in an uproar when he returned.

"You must have been relieved," said Lydia softly.

That was when the first wave of nausea had rolled over him, and he thought he would puke all over the pile of back issues of the *New England Journal of Medicine*. The interrogation (that was how he had come to think of the interview from then on) had gone downhill from there, and by the time he had gotten up the courage to say he had to attend a meeting, he knew they didn't believe a word he said.

And that was why he couldn't look Amanda in the eye.

"That guy's hiding something," said Bandman. "Something big. Did you see the sweat pouring off him?"

"It was hard to miss," said Lydia. "But if he killed McBride, why would he admit to not having an alibi? He's had almost forty-eight hours to think one up, and he's smart enough to come up with something plausible."

"He thinks he's charming us with that cock-and-bull story about going out to admire gardens—and the baloney about McBride's basic decency. He thinks it'll make us go away and look elsewhere. But I want to know what else he's hiding, in addition to murder."

"So you think Silverman did it?" asked Lydia. She wasn't sure how Bandman had made the leap from one lie about how much the resident had liked the victim to making Silverman into a murder suspect. If they arrested everyone who lied to the police, there wouldn't be a soul left on the streets of Washington.

"How do I know?" asked Bandman. "I don't *know*, but I can tell you that I don't have any good feelings about the guy. There's something slimy about him, but that may be because of this other thing."

"What other thing?" she asked, feeling as though she'd missed something.

"The thing that he's hiding and I can't put my finger on."

"Paul, uh, um . . ."

"Out with it, kid. What's on your mind?"

"Eddie Silverman is gay," she said.

Bandman looked surprised. "Nah," he said, "he doesn't have any of the signs." Then he noticed that Lydia had the expression on her face that he was coming to know, the certain set of the chin that appeared when she was sure of something. So far her track record was damn good. "How do you know?" he asked.

"I don't know. I just know. Maybe it's single woman's radar. As him next time."

"I will," said Bandman. And he would. "Let's go lean on Alice Bonner a little."

Bonner was even less receptive to being questioned by two detectives in the middle of her workday than she was the night before, when Lydia had talked to her at home.

"I have nothing more to say," she repeated. "Do we have to talk right out here in the hall?"

"No, we can go elsewhere in the hospital—or down to the station house if you prefer," said Bandman. "Tell us about your relationship with Dr. McBride. I especially want to know about the breakup. It was a pretty dramatic scene, I hear."

"Who told you about that?" snapped Bonner, her eyes blazing with fury.

"It doesn't take much to set you off, does it?" added Bandman. "I can just picture you slugging the good doctor. Now, tell us what happened."

Alice cried as she stood with Bandman and Simonowitz in the utility room next to the bedpan flusher. She told the police about her affair with Leo McBride without minimizing her rage and humiliation, and since the whole hospital knew everything anyway, she saw no reason to prevaricate about what had happened at the end.

"I'm glad he's dead," she said. "I know you probably think I killed him. I didn't, but I'm glad he's dead. He got what was coming to him."

Then her green eyes flashed again with anger. "If you want to arrest me, go ahead, but I have sick people to take care of."

Bandman and Simonowitz looked at the swinging door through which Bonner had just stormed.

"She sure has the moxie to do it," said Bandman.

The last time Lydia had heard anyone use the word *moxie*, was when Jimmy Cagney had said it just a month or so ago on her VCR. She thought it was sweet to hear it from Bandman now, and she felt a wave of affection for him. "And she has a surefire motive. Even in the movies, the woman scorned is a prime suspect," she said.

"And so is the wife who's going to inherit pots of money."

"And so is the man who's hiding a deep, dark secret."

The two detectives grinned at each other. This was getting good. A rich and famous doctor, a barrel full of suspects . . . a good, solid intellectual challenge. It was shaping up to be a winning case—all except for the parade of nurses who brought a steady stream of full bedpans to be flushed in the hopper.

"Let's get out of here," said Bandman, wrinkling his nose. He glanced at his watch and said, "That meeting ought to be breaking up any time now. We still have to talk to the surgeon, what's his name, the chief."

"Jonathan Bernstein," said Lydia.

"Right. And I want to find out more about Ina Wolfman, so I think we need to pay a little call on her husband. And then back to the chief nurse, what's-her-name Knight. I think she may know more than she's letting on. She hated McBride, too."

"Who didn't?" asked Lydia.

"Dr. Silverman," said Bandman. "But he's lying through his teeth. McBride must have been a real charmer." He was silent for a moment, thinking about someone so terrible that everyone who knew him well wished him dead. And one of those people made the wish come true.

"Let's split up for the rest of the morning. I'll take a trip out to NIH to see Wolfman, you talk to Bernstein, we'll grab a bite at that deli across the street, and then we'll go to see Knight."

"See you in about an hour or so," said Lydia as she pushed both buttons on the elevator. Down to the parking lot for Bandman and up to the operating room suite for herself.

Amanda worked for an hour on the budget, the part of her job she hated most—except for firing people like Alice Bonner—and then decided to go to the cafeteria for lunch. She had paged Eddie earlier to go to Giovanni's, but he had said he was too busy to eat. There was a coolness, a distance in his voice that Amanda found puzzling. That, combined with his avoidance of her this morning at the meeting, raised her suspicions to fever pitch. Perhaps he had a guilty conscience because he killed McBride, and now he couldn't face her.

Oh, cut it out, she told herself. You're imagining things, and you're annoyed at having to go to McBride's funeral in the middle of a Saturday afternoon. And face it, you've never been good at disciplining people. You've had a rotten morning, you're guilty about eating the doughnut, and now all you can have for lunch is a cup of plain yogurt and black coffee.

Amanda's mood blackened with each step she took, and by the time she had paid for her yogurt and coffee, she was in a real funk. Then, when she saw Eddie at *their* table eating lunch with Alice Bonner, she wanted to throw the tray at both of them. They were engaged in conversation, their heads close together, their faces serious. They looked like conspirators, planning something. Had they done it together?

For God's sake! said the voice of logic. They barely know each other. She was screwing McBride, and Eddie must have known about it. Everyone else did; you can't keep a thing like that secret for more than five minutes in a hospital. He hated McBride and would have felt contempt for anyone low enough to climb in the sack with the bastard.

Amanda acknowledged what the logical part of her mind told her, but she also knew enough that affairs of the heart (or regions lower down) were not governed by rationality, and there was no reason why the two of them couldn't have compared notes on what a shit McBride had been and agreed to help each other kill him—each for different reasons. One could have acted as lookout while the other stuck in the scalpel.

Oh, grow up and eat your yogurt, said the voice again. Who do you think you are, Nancy Drew?

Amanda had no one to eat with. She couldn't sit with a group of staff nurses because it made them uncomfortable to have the boss at their table, especially with all the trouble that had been going on lately. She hated to eat with doctors because all they ever talked about was medicine. She could eat with the nursing supervisors, but none were around; nor were any of the other department heads. So she found an empty table, put some saccharin in her coffee, and opened the carton of yogurt.

Why had Eddie lied about being too busy to eat? Was he avoiding her? He had seen her come into the cafeteria, had given her the briefest possible flick of the eye, and then had returned his attention to Alice. Did he look guilty, or was that her imagination, too? If he didn't kill McBride, was he sorry now that he had confided in her yesterday? Was he having doubts about trusting her?

She felt guilty again, as if Eddie knew she had contemplated spilling his beans to the police. She wouldn't—she hoped—but she *had* considered it.

She looked down at her tray in surprise. The yogurt carton and coffee cup were empty. She had been so lost in thought that she had eaten without realizing it—and without tasting anything. Disgusted with herself, she went back to her office.

"That was an awfully short lunch," said Louise.

"I've been pigging out a lot lately, so I could only have yogurt, and that doesn't take long," said Amanda. "I'm still starving. Maybe if I go out for a walk, the fresh air will take my mind off food."

Amanda found the heavy sweater that she had brought to the hospital last winter when the heating system had failed and staff and patients shivered through three days of repair work. She crossed Foxhall Road and strolled through one of Washington's most affluent neighborhoods.

Georgetown was home to wealthy lawyers (which in this city were as common as the fat squirrels now preparing for winter), physicians, lobbyists (who were almost as plentiful as lawyers), well-connected and highly paid newspeople, politicians, White House aides, and housefuls of young people who worked at lowly jobs in the halls of power and packed themselves into group houses, willing to put up with discomfort in order to have a "good" address.

She breathed deeply of the air that was reasonably fresh along streets that didn't have much midday motor traffic and thought about the events of the morning. Amanda realized she'd have to spend some time this afternoon with the head nurses to juggle staff now that Bonner and Morrison were gone. They wouldn't be pleased to be so shorthanded, and for that matter neither was she. The more rushed and frantic the nurses were, the more likely they would be to make mistakes. She would have to mollify them with promises of a quick replacement. And then she'd have to keep that promise. Even as she strolled past the elegant houses and beautifully tended gardens, Louise was setting up interviews with nurses whose applications and résumés stuffed several manilla folders, but how the hell was she going to be able to predict who would pull a stupid stunt like Barbara Morrison and who would be as good as Alice Bonner?

Amanda felt sick when she thought about the variety of ways one could screw up nursing care; leaving someone to dehydrate after surgery was only the beginning. There were hundreds of medications that could be mixed up or given to the wrong patient. There were patients themselves who could be mixed up and treated the wrong way. The equipment that nurses used was so complicated now that it was easy to use it without knowing if it was working properly or not. There were side rails to forget to put up so patients could roll out of bed, and there were doctors' orders written on charts not to notice. There was food that could be given to patients who weren't supposed to have any, and there were call bells that could be placed just out of reach so a patient could quietly bleed to death without being able to summon help.

How did she know that the next nurse she hired—one with a straight-A average and references that made her seem like the Messiah—wouldn't commit one of these atrocities?

You don't, said the voice of practicality.

Great, she thought. So it'll be my ass in the sling, too.

Yup, said the voice. But your ass is the competitive one. It's the one that wanted to sit in the top-job chair, not drag on the floor at the end of ten straight days of taking care of sick and dying people. Do you want to go back to that? Amanda shuddered.

Okay, then, don't complain about all the responsibility.

"I'll complain if I want to, dammit," Amanda muttered as she started back toward the hospital.

While Amanda was strolling the streets of Georgetown, just as Eddie had said he had done two days before, Bandman and Simonowitz were sitting on a bench at a bus stop in front of the hospital, their lunch spread out between them, an elderly woman laden with plastic shopping bags glaring at them as she leaned against the bus stop sign.

Lydia had been waiting outside Giovanni's when Bandman returned from the NIH.

"It's mobbed in there," she said. "And anyway, it's all hospital people. We wouldn't be able to talk. How about getting take-out and sitting on a bench?"

"So, how did it go with Bernstein?" asked Bandman between bites of his Italian hoagie.

"Actually, it turned out to be more interesting than I thought it would. I found him in the doctors' lounge—the place is disgusting; they don't even throw their coffee cups away— dictating his operations for the morning. He made me wait until he'd finished.

"Then we talked a little about McBride. It was refreshing to hear from someone who really didn't hate the guy. He said he and McBride never had anything to do with each other socially, and only rarely did they consult about a patient. Often they didn't speak to each other for weeks at a time.

"The interesting thing, though, was that he said that everyone in the hospital saw the two as rivals for Miller's job. Apparently the old guy is going to retire at the end of next year."

"And not a moment too soon. He's pretty fogged in," said Bandman.

Lydia smiled. "Anyway, Bernstein said that he didn't want to be medical director because all he cares about is surgery, and if he got 'kicked downstairs,' as he put it, he wouldn't be able to operate as much. But he didn't want McBride to get the job, either, so he let everyone think what they wanted about the rivalry."

"Do you believe him?" asked Bandman.

"Actually, I do. I was listening to him when he dictated the operations; he was totally engrossed. The building could have blown up and he wouldn't have heard it. I think he's telling the truth when he says he's interested only in surgery.

"And he has a good alibi. He says he was in the operating room at the time of the murder. He didn't finish his cases— that's what they call them: 'cases'—until after noon on

Tuesday. I still have to talk to the nurses and technicians who were in the O.R. with him, but if his story checks out, I think we can scratch him as a suspect."

"A real workaholic, huh? I've never understood that," said Bandman. "I can't figure out why some people don't want to do anything but work all the time."

He shook his head, as if nonplussed by the people he came in contact with, and stared out across the street, looking at nothing, squinting a little in the bright sunshine. Lydia remained quiet, not wanting to interrupt his reverie.

After a few minutes he blinked and said, "I had a strange half hour. Wolfman is an odd duck."

"Tell me," said Lydia.

"Well, first of all, I wasn't allowed to go into his office; he had to come out to see me. Apparently there are security restrictions in the lab where he works. God only knows what they're doing there. Probably torturing rabbits or something.

"In any event, Wolfman was *not* happy to see me. He said he hardly knew the man and didn't seem to have any reaction to the murder at all."

Bandman was silent again, remembering the strangely sterile interview.

"The man is dead now. I just want to forget about him," Wolfman had said in response to Bandman's question about whether he had felt the same way about McBride that his wife did.

"But *we* can't forget, Mr. Wolfman. We have to find out who killed him. Do you have any idea who that might be?"

"No. And it's *Dr.* Wolfman."

"I'm sorry, Doctor. How long had you known McBride?"

"As long as my wife worked for him."

"And in what capacity did you know him?"

"Capacity? What do you mean 'capacity'?" demanded Wolfman, the anger starting to show now.

"Your wife said you were his patient."

"She had no right to say that. No right at all."

"What was wrong with you, Dr. Wolfman, that only Dr. Leo McBride could cure? What serious illness did you have that made all the other doctors give up on you?"

There was a long silence, during which Wolfman seemed to be sorting through a choice of responses. Finally he made up his mind.

"My medical problems are my business," he said in a less angry voice. "I'm better now. I'm grateful to Dr. McBride, but he's dead, so I don't have to be grateful anymore. Now, if you'll excuse me," he said, getting up and opening the door, "I have no other information for you."

"So what do you make of that?" asked Lydia when Bandman had finished the story.

"Not much, at least on the face of it. McBride took care of the guy once a long time ago; he's the husband of McBride's secretary, and that's about it."

Again, Bandman stared off into space, and again Lydia waited.

"But still . . . ," Bandman mused aloud, "what could have been so wrong with him that he doesn't want to talk about it? It wasn't cancer, and now he's completely cured—a real mystery disease. And why is he being so uncooperative? His reluctance to spend more than a second and a half with a police officer reminds me more of the scum down in Anacostia than a nice middle-class scientist, and a government worker at that.

"I can't stand people hiding things from me. It comes with the territory. You'll see!"

"Should we run a background check on him?" asked Lydia.

"It couldn't hurt," replied Bandman, and Lydia made a note to do it when they got back to the office.

They gathered up the sandwich papers and soda cups and Lydia threw them into the freshly painted blue-and-white litter can at the bus stop.

"Boy, the city sure takes care of Georgetown," she said. "You know, two years ago, they took away the can at my corner—to repair it, they said—and never brought it back. I knocked myself out to get another one—I even went down to the sanitation department one day *in uniform*, and they acted like I was nuts!"

"Come on, Lydia, you know it takes an act of Congress—

literally—to get anything done in this city. Let's go see Amanda Knight."

As Amanda walked back through the front door of the hospital, she felt depressed and weighed down by what Eddie Silverman and Alice Bonner had told her. Either one *might* be a murderer, although neither seemed like the type. But what kind of person would kill another? She supposed that anyone could kill if severely provoked, and these two had grade-A motives. A woman scorned and the victim of blackmail. She didn't see how she could *not* tell the police what she knew.

And she wasn't looking forward to going to McBride's funeral the next day. She didn't *have* to, but when David Townsend had come into her office after the morning's meeting to tell her the time and place, he assumed she would be there. And so she would. It wasn't worth aggravating him over an hour of her time, even though the weatherman promised a glorious autumn Saturday.

Amanda turned the corner of the corridor and opened the door to her outer office. Sitting in chairs near Louise's desk were the two detectives.

Shit, she thought. I do *not* want to deal with these two again.

But she managed a smile and said, "Hello, officers. Waiting for me?"

Who else would they be waiting for, you jerk? said the voice that was always so damn reasonable. Monty Hall to show them what's behind Door Number One?

"Ms. Knight, we need to ask you just a few more questions," said Bandman.

"Just give me one minute to make a phone call," she replied. "And I'll be right with you."

The detectives smiled and said nothing when she shut the door behind her. She dialed Glen's private office number with her fingers crossed. "Make her be in," she prayed. "Don't let her be out to lunch."

"Glencora Rodman," sang the familiar voice on the third ring.

"It's me," Amanda hissed.

"Well, speak up. I can't hear you. You sound like you're in a tunnel."

"I can't talk any louder. The cops are outside my door right this minute. They want to talk to me again. I just want to know if you're free tomorrow morning. I *have* to talk to you."

"Sure. What do you want to do?"

"I'll call you back when they leave. We'll decide then. Bye." Amanda hung up without waiting to hear the questions she knew Glen would fire at her.

Amanda walked to the door and said to Louise, "Would you ask all the head nurses except obstetrics and pediatrics to be here at two-thirty for a very short meeting?"

To Bandman and Simonowitz she said, "Please come in. As you heard, I can't give you too much time."

She indicated that they should sit on the couch, and she took a chair opposite. Then she thought that maybe she should have stayed behind her desk to signify that this was official business. Amanda often had trouble deciding where to seat people. She knew that the game of office musical chairs had political significance, but she was at a loss when playing power politics. It all seemed so childish to her, but Ken said it was important to understand. He was good at playing political games. Corporate soap operas, she called them.

". . . not certain how he died," Bandman was saying.

"I'm sorry," said Amanda. "Would you repeat that?"

Wow, thought Lydia. This must be some cool, self-assured cookie to be wool-gathering while two police detectives sit in her office on a murder investigation. Lydia didn't know whether to be impressed or on her guard.

"I said," repeated Bandman, "that we've gotten the coroner's report and we're not certain how Dr. McBride died, and we wondered if you can shed some light on it."

Amanda looked at them, puzzled. What kind of question was this from the police?

"I don't mean to be rude," she said, "but if your pathologists don't know the cause of death, how would I?"

"You were one of the first on the scene. Did you see anything, hear anything, smell anything that might give us a clue? Frankly," said Bandman in his softest voice, "we're stuck, and we need all the help we can get."

Amanda was intrigued—and more than a little charmed by this rumpled, obviously nice man who seemed to be having a hard time.

"All I saw was the scalpel sticking out of his throat," she replied. "But by now everyone knows that it didn't kill him. And you don't know what did? Maybe he had a heart attack or a stroke or something," she said. "Although on second thought, that isn't very likely."

"Why not?" asked Bandman.

"Because of the expression on his face," said Amanda, now looking at the mental photograph she had taken in that first shocking instant of discovery. "If he'd had a heart attack, he would have registered pain. Heart attacks hurt terribly, you know. If he'd had a stroke, he would have had another expression on his face. It's hard to describe—sometimes a sort of blankness or a distortion of the features, depending on the part of the brain that was affected. But Dr. McBride just looked mildly surprised—as if he couldn't quite believe that this was happening. Maybe that doesn't make much sense, but you asked for my impressions."

"It makes perfect sense," said Lydia, speaking for the first time. "Because he didn't die of a heart attack or stroke. There was no evidence of anything like that. But," she paused, perhaps for dramatic effect, "did you know that he had liver cancer?"

"No kidding!" said Amanda. "So *that's* what was wrong with him."

"What do you mean? Did you know he was ill?" asked Bandman.

"No, I didn't *know* anything was wrong. He wouldn't have confided in me. But I sensed that he wasn't his usual self. He seemed to have less energy, less . . . I don't know . . . interest in his usual things. But I didn't think much about it. But *liver cancer*, that's heavy-duty stuff. I wonder how he kept it hidden. You're pretty sick with liver cancer. Was he being treated?"

"He kept it hidden by covering the jaundice with pancake

makeup, and yes, he was getting what I think you medical people call 'aggressive therapy.' He had enough cancer drugs in him to float a battleship."

"Pancake makeup!" said Amanda. "That's just typical of McBride. Keep up appearances even though you're falling apart underneath.

"I never heard even a hint of rumor," she continued. "So he must have kept it a secret from everyone. Where was he being treated?"

"We don't know," said Lydia. "That's one of the reasons we're here. We'd like you to find out if he was treated here."

Amanda remained silent.

"We want you to look through the medical files to get background on McBride," said Bandman.

"Oh, you'd have to go to Medical Records for that," said Amanda. "I can tell you where they are, but I don't think they'll help you. Patient confidentiality and all that."

"Yes, we know," said Bandman dryly. "We've tried."

"Well, you can't blame them," she said. "Did you try the administrator or Dr. Miller?"

"We've asked everyone. You're our last hope," said Lydia.

"Why me? What makes you think *I'd* commit a serious breach of medical ethics?" Amanda was angry now. "Do I look like someone who would do something like that?"

Bandman and Simonowitz said nothing. They simply waited in silence.

Amanda rose to the bait. "Oh," she said in her most sarcastic voice, "just because I said I didn't like McBride the other day, you think I'd go into the computer files to spy on his private business. You have a hell of a nerve!"

Bandman fixed her with a level gaze. "Well, would you?"

"I would not!"

"No harm in asking, is there?" said Bandman pleasantly.

That took Amanda aback. There *was* no harm in asking. Her mother always told her to ask for what she wanted. If she was denied, she would be no worse off than if she had not asked. But more often than not, she'd get what she wanted. It was good advice.

She smiled and said with no trace of her former anger, "No

harm at all. But I can't do it. I'm sorry. I'd really like to help you."

Bandman shrugged, apparently accepting her refusal. "Well, then, is there *anything* else you can tell us? Who were his enemies? Who had a grudge against him? Who had a motive to kill him?"

Amanda looked down at her hands. This was it. This was the time she had to make a decision about whether to betray her friend and former employee. She believed Bandman when he said they were stuck. If they didn't know *how* McBride died, and they didn't know who had a motive to kill him, they didn't know much. And she, Amanda Knight, was in a position to at least get them started.

"There's nothing I can tell you," she said.

Bandman glanced at Lydia and then turned back to Amanda, who didn't miss the look that passed between the two detectives.

"Does that mean you know or suspect something and can't or won't tell us, or does it mean that you have no pertinent information at all?" asked Bandman.

"Wait!" he said as Amanda opened her mouth to speak. "Before you say anything, let me remind you that if you do have information, if you do know something—even if you only suspect something—and if what you know or suspect leads to the arrest and conviction of a murderer, and if you don't tell us now, you *could* be held liable as an accessory after the fact."

Amanda was miserable. She didn't know if Bandman was telling the truth, exaggerating a remote possibility, or bluffing. These two detectives knew she was holding back, and if they were even remotely perceptive, they would see she was struggling with her conscience. The silence in her office was deafening, and Amanda was uncomfortably hot in her corduroy blazer.

"I'm sorry," she said. "I really wish I could help you. I didn't like Dr. McBride. What I said about him the other day was indiscreet and I regret saying it, but it's true. And there really is nothing I can tell you."

No one said anything for a time. Bandman just stared at her sadly like a teacher disappointed in a promising pupil. He was giving her another chance to tell what she knew. She said nothing even though it took all her willpower to keep her mouth shut. She was sweating.

"Okay," he said finally, "never mind about that. Tell us about Ina Wolfman and her husband Frank."

Amanda was relieved. This was far less dangerous ground. She said she had heard that Ina had been questioned and was very upset, and then told the police what she and Ina had talked about. "She seems worried that you're so interested in her husband. Why are you?" asked Amanda. "They didn't even know each other."

Bandman blinked. "Who didn't know whom?"

"McBride and Mr. Wolfman," she replied.

"What makes you say that?" asked Lydia. She and Bandman were both on full alert now.

"Ina told me. That's why she was so puzzled about why you asked about her husband. She said they had never met. And he never said anything about having met McBride," replied Amanda, curious about their interest in Frank Wolfman. "What's he got to do with all this?"

"We ask the questions, Ms. Knight," said Bandman politely. "Tell us everything you know about Ina Wolfman and in what capacity you know her husband."

"I don't know much. She was probably a good secretary, protective of her boss and all that. I hardly ever saw her. And yesterday was the first time I'd ever laid eyes on her husband. Until this minute I didn't know that he knew McBride."

"What makes you think they knew each other?" asked Lydia.

"From the things you've just said," she replied. "Ina told you one thing and me another, and we both noticed it at the same time."

This woman was no dummy, thought Bandman. Maybe his poker face wasn't as successful as he thought. He decided to admit as much.

"What do you make of that, Ms. Knight?" he asked.

"I don't know," she said. "But I'd sure as hell be suspicious."

"Suspicious enough to tell us what you're holding back?" he asked.

Amanda flushed with embarrassment. "I wish I could help you. I really do. As I said, I didn't like McBride, but I don't want to see his killer get off scot-free. But there's nothing more I can say."

"If you change your mind and want to help, call me," said Bandman coldly, handing Amanda his card.

He turned to leave, as did Simonowitz. On the way out she too gave Amanda a card, but she smiled and said, "My home phone's on the back. Call anytime—day or night."

Amanda closed the door behind them and burst into tears, but as she was mopping her eyes, her mind was racing. Why had Ina lied to the police—or to her? Did McBride and her husband really know each other, and if so, how? What could they possibly have in common? Should she talk to Ina again? But what if Ina didn't know that her husband knew McBride? Could Ina or her husband have had anything to do with McBride's murder? Those two nebbishy people? What in the hell was going on here?

That evening Eddie and Donald were in their kitchen fixing dinner. The kitchen would have been the envy of a professional chef and had every piece of equipment anyone could ever want—right down to the fish poacher and asparagus steamer. Copper pots, all polished to a high gleam, hung from the ceiling, and there was enough counter space to prepare a banquet. The two men worked in silence, each sipping occasionally from a glass of white wine. Suddenly Eddie cried out.

"Shit!" He dropped the skillet he was holding and ran to the sink to hold his hand under cold water. "Ice cubes, quick!" he said to Donald, who got two out of the freezer and handed them to Eddie.

"Not like that, stupid. Put a lot in a big bowl. Hurry up!"

Donald did as Eddie directed, saying nothing, his lips tight with annoyance, watching as Eddie filled the bowl with cold water and plunged his hand into the icy liquid. He saw tears in his lover's eyes and assumed the burn was really bad.

"Let me see it, Ed," he said. "Do you want me to take you to the emergency room?" He reached for Eddie's hand.

But Eddie jerked out of Donald's grasp. "Leave me alone, it's nothing."

"If it's nothing, why are you making such a big deal out of it? Come on, let me see. Besides, your hand's going to freeze. You don't have to be a doctor to see that!"

Eddie took his hand, which hurt more from the cold now than the burn, out of the basin and put it into Donald's outstretched one. There was nothing there except an overall redness that even now was fading to natural flesh color. The lovers stood motionless together, hand in hand in the kitchen, the half-prepared meal forgotten.

Donald led Eddie to the living room, sat close to him on the couch, and said, "Now, tell me everything."

It took almost an hour to tell the story, starting with the blackmail and ending with lunch today with Alice Bonner. He left nothing out, and when he described how he had crouched like a cornered rat in the men's room, puking his guts out, he began to cry.

Donald held his lover gently in his arms, but his face had the expression of a mightily worried man. Could Eddie have done it?

He waited until Eddie had stopped crying and blown his nose and then asked, "What did you and Alice talk about at lunch?"

"Oh, I don't know, this and that," replied Eddie.

"I didn't know you were friendly with her," said Donald. "You never mentioned her before. I thought you usually ate with Amanda."

"For Christ's sake, Donald, can't I eat lunch with someone different for a change? I'm starting to get tired of Amanda. People in the hospital are talking."

Now Donald was really worried. Eddie was crazy about Amanda; she was his favorite person at the hospital and was the only one he'd miss when he finished his residency, and he never before gave a damn about what the grapevine had him and Amanda doing after hours. He even thought it was funny. And this blackmail business. Why hadn't Eddie told him about it?

"Why didn't you tell me about the blackmail, Ed? We could have thought of a way to stop it."

"Short of resorting to murder, you mean," said Eddie in an uncharacteristically sarcastic tone.

"I didn't say that."

"No, but you were thinking it."

"I was not."

"Yes, you were. You think I murdered McBride just to get him off my back," said Eddie, his voice rising and taking on a slightly hysterical note.

Again, the two men stared at each other, this time the mood in the room black and ugly with self-pity and suspicion.

"Well, did you?"

"You fucker," screamed Eddie. "You goddamn lousy son of a . . ."

The phone rang.

They let it ring six times, seven times . . . all the while staring at each other in shocked silence.

The phone rang on, and finally Donald got up to answer it.

"Oh, hi, Amanda," he said in response to the voice on the other end, watching Eddie shake his head to indicate that he didn't want to talk to her.

"No, I'm sorry, he isn't here. I think he went to the gym, but I'll tell him you called."

Donald said good-bye to Amanda and went to the coat closet and put on his jacket.

"I'm going out to get something to eat, Ed," he said. "And then I may go to a movie. I need to be away from you for a few hours. When I get back, I want you to tell me the truth about everything that happened. You owe me that. And I want an apology for the way you just behaved. No, not now," he said in response to Eddie's interruption. "You think about this for a while and make up your mind what you want to do. If you're falsely accused, I'll back you all the way. If you killed him, we're finished right now."

Donald walked out the door, shutting it gently behind him. Eddie slumped on the couch and groaned with misery.

7

CICELY MCBRIDE SAT quietly in the stretch limousine that Caldwell's Funeral Home had sent to fetch her. Several people had offered to drive her to Leo's funeral, but she thought it would be appropriate to ride alone to his last opportunity to be the center of attention. Besides, she was sick of talking to people, and the surprise visit this morning from the two detectives had shaken her. She needed this time to compose herself.

"How can you possibly want to question me on the very day of my husband's funeral?" she said just a few hours ago to that tacky detective and his girl Friday or whatever she was.

"Mrs. McBride, with all due respect for your loss, don't start that again—please," he had said.

Cicely decided to stop acting. It wasn't going over well, and in truth her life was a lot better without Leo. It didn't take more than a day or two for the difference to become apparent. Oh, there was an advantage to being married to someone like Leo McBride, but in Washington there are lots of Leo McBrides. Some are doctors, most are lawyers, a few are politicians and diplomats, even fewer are media people—and all of them provided the same social and economic advantages.

She would wait a year or two before taking another Leo to the altar. Now, as soon as his will went through probate, she would have enough money for her very special needs to last for a while, and being a newly widowed woman was not necessarily a social inconvenience. If she stayed single for too long, the invitations would dwindle, but Cicely had no intention of doing that. She would use this time to look around for another suitably rich and well-placed husband to share her home and her social activities, but not her *life*.

But first, she had to get these damn detectives off her back.

"Very well, come in," she said, none too graciously. "But I can only give you a few minutes."

Bandman settled himself comfortably in a chair and then said without preamble, "Did you know your husband was dying of liver cancer?"

"What?" she asked in a tone that verged on a shriek. "He was *murdered*. You told me that yourself."

"Calm down, Mrs. McBride. Your husb—"

"Calm down! Calm down! First you tell me he's murdered, his throat slashed. Now you say he died of cancer. What's going on here?" She had a hysterical note in her voice, but Lydia didn't think it rang true. She glanced over at Bandman, who was wearing one of his inscrutable expressions, so Lydia mentally shrugged.

I'm imagining things, she thought. Nevertheless she got up and sat next to Cicely on the couch, putting her hand on the widow's arm, gripping tightly. "Listen to me," she said in the same voice that had worked so well with Ina Wolfman. "Calm down and listen to me."

Cicely turned her head and blinked.

"Your husband *was* murdered. His throat was not slashed. We told you that someone stabbed him in the trachea, the windpipe, with a scalpel, but he didn't bleed to death. We told you all that, but you were upset at the time—"

"Well, of course I was upset!" said Cicely, her voice rising again. "Wouldn't you be upset if your husband was murdered?"

Lydia pressed her fingers hard into the smooth flesh again. "Yes, I'd be upset. I'd be devastated. But I'd want to help the police catch whoever did it. And I'd cooperate with them so they could do their job."

Bandman watched Lydia work on Cicely. She talked to the woman as if to a five-year-old who'd hurt herself and needed to be calmed down so her mother could put on the iodine and bandage. But Cicely McBride was no baby. He decided to let her finish the questioning, jumping in only if she forgot something.

Cicely, sipping the scotch that Caldwell's had so thought-fully provided in the small bar in the back of the limo, now remembered how she had behaved when the woman detective had told her that Leo had had cancer. Did she carry on too much? Did they really believe that a woman could not know that her husband was turning a lovely shade of yellow right in front of her eyes? Did they believe that he had hidden such a thing from her, that she never noticed that her own husband was months, maybe only weeks, away from death? What did the detectives think would make Leo go to such great lengths to hide it from her? From everyone?

She felt angry at Leo for making her share the details of her intimate relationships with these two strangers. It was humil-iating, and once again she felt a wave of relief that he was gone forever. They had asked where Leo had been treated, who his doctor was, and for once she could tell the truth. She didn't know, and she saw their disbelief. How could the man's own wife not have known?

"Mrs. McBride, I know this is a delicate subject," said Lydia, "but liver cancer has some outward effects. He was very, very jaundiced. You know what that means, don't you?"

"Of course I know what it means," she had snapped. "I'm a doctor's wife. I *was* a doctor's wife." Her head went down in what she hoped was a moment of genuine sadness.

"Didn't you notice how ill he looked? Didn't you notice that his face, his eyes, were very yellow?"

Cicely sighed. "My husband and I had separate bedrooms. We had not been, uh, intimate, for many years. I never saw him nude."

For a moment Bandman and Simonowitz thought she would cry—real tears this time—but then anger flashed across her face.

"If you want to talk to someone who saw him naked, go get that bitch Alice Bonner—and practically every other nurse at the hospital."

Cicely now regretted that outburst. She should have just

played the grieving widow and kept her rage to herself. She
knew she had fallen for the sympathetic cop trick, just as she
was positive now that Seth Morgan had tricked her on
Thursday night. She'd made a fool of herself and had wasted
$2,500 in the bargain.

That evening after Leo's family had gone back to their hotel
after a tense, uncomfortable dinner, Cicely soaked for a long
time in a tubful of hot, fragrant water. She sank down so her
entire body was underwater, closed her eyes, inhaled the
perfumed steam, and let her mind float off.

The trip to the caterer in the afternoon had been fun,
although she had to remember to keep her face suitably somber
and not act as if this were just another of her many parties. The
funeral was to be at two o'clock, so she and the caterer had
settled on tea food: a variety of sandwiches and cakes with tea,
coffee, sherry, and a full bar set up discreetly in the far corner
of the living room. As usual, she ordered a far more elaborate
spread than was necessary, and if the caterer thought it was a
little too stylish for a post-funeral reception, he said nothing.

She could relax now until her next public appearance on
Saturday afternoon, but relaxation didn't come as easily as it
should. She added more hot water to the tub and tried to
concentrate on loosening the muscles that would soon be under
Seth's control. Usually when she took her pre-massage bath,
the combination of the warm water lapping gently between her
thighs and thoughts of how the massage would end made her
right hand sneak down beneath her belly and relieve the
quickly mounting tension that gathered there—just to take the
edge off, she told herself. Just so she could relax fully under
Seth's hands and not appear so anxious and needy.

But this evening her thoughts were on a body other than her
own: one enshrouded in a white sheet that slid forward on its
morgue slab from a drawer that looked remarkably like an
ordinary office filing cabinet. An extra-large cabinet.

His face looked rested, perhaps a little surprised, but he
often looked that way when he spoke to her. He looked that
way the last time she had seen him alive. When the morgue
attendant opened the drawer, Cicely stared at Leo long and

hard. He was different somehow. There was something changed about him, and it wasn't just the small wound at the base of his throat. He looked like Leo but yet not like Leo.

Now, drying and perfuming her body, Cicely couldn't put her finger on what it was. She had no reason to, really. Cicely had never seen death before. She had never looked at a corpse, so she had no way of understanding that although the features remain the same in death, the face changes. She would never understand it. For the rest of her life, though, whenever she thought about her husband in his death throes or lying on that morgue slab, she would wonder about it.

She dressed in a silk teddy and then put on white crepe lounging pajamas with a single heavy gold chain around her neck. When she was fully dressed, she opened the small safe in the wall of her bedroom that contained some of her jewelry and the white powder that had come to mean so much more than the flashing stones and creamy pearls in their velvet-lined cases. She removed the plastic bag and tiny sterling silver spoon, and with practiced motions, prepared and inhaled a hefty dose of the drug that gave her the courage to do the things she oughtn't do. Then she went down to the living room to wait for Seth.

Cicely opened the door almost before the peal of the bell had faded, and Seth put the case containing his portable massage table and various lotions and toys on the floor. Right away he saw how nervous she was, and he hoped the favor she would ask was big enough to make her add significantly to his collection of presidential portraits. He also hoped she wouldn't ask the impossible. Seth was neither a risk taker nor foolhardy.

"Thank God you're here," she said, taking his hand and leading him toward the couch. "I need you to do something for me. It's a favor, and I'd be *ever* so grateful if you'd accommodate me . . . just this once. Can I get you a drink?"

Her voice took on a girlish, wheedling tone that disgusted Seth, and there was nothing he wanted to do less that sit around for an evening drinking with Cicely McBride. Even though he refused the drink, he smiled and said, "There's not much I wouldn't do for you, Cicely. Let's get you started on your treatment. You look tense as a cat. Come on," he said, opening his bag and setting up the padded table. "Get those lovely things off and hop up here. Lie on your tummy."

He didn't want to look at her face.

When she was naked, he began massaging her upper thighs instead of starting on her back as he usually did. He knew that as he stroked and kneaded her thighs and buttocks, her legs would part, and her vulnerability would increase as her need became more intense.

"You're wound up very tight, Cicely," he said in his most soothing voice. "You really need me."

"I need you in more ways than one," she replied, her voice beginning to betray her physical *and* mental anxiety.

"I know you do."

"Seth, I need you to tell the police that you were giving me a massage the morning Leo was killed."

His hands stopped in midstroke. Cicely McBride needing an alibi was *not* what he had expected. So she *did* kill her husband!

Seth thought fast. "Wow, Cicely, that's pretty serious stuff. I'd be an accessory to murder. That's a felony."

"But I didn't kill him," she said. "The police think I did, but I didn't."

Bullshit, thought Seth. But he kept his voice neutral and friendly. "I believe you, Cicely, if you say so, but why do you need an alibi?"

"I can't tell you."

Seth was silent. He stepped away from the table and began to towel the oil off his hands, thinking about how he could make Cicely's predicament work for him. His instincts told him that Cicely didn't have it in her to plan a murder, let alone act it out. But she was up to *something*, something definitely no good. Maybe she was screwing someone she shouldn't be screwing. Maybe she was even working for the Russians. In this town everyone was spying on someone. Then again, whatever she had been doing couldn't be as serious as murdering someone like Leo McBride, and *no one* needed an alibi unless they were guilty as sin.

Seth decided to take the risk, but he needed more control over her if he was going to lie to the police. That is, *if* he had to lie. The more he thought about it, the more he realized that there was no reason for him to be officially involved in the investigation. Why should the police question *him*?

"Look, Cicely," he said in a patient voice, just a shade away from patronizing, "you're asking me to jeopardize my whole life, to risk being charged with a felony. And you won't even tell me why. I'd love to accommodate you, babe, but you understand . . . I just can't. I really wish I could."

Cicely turned over and got off the massage table. Not bothering to cover her naked body, she walked to a small antique desk and took a cream-colored envelope from the drawer. She handed it to him and said, "Please, Seth, I really need your help."

He noted the genuine desperation in her voice and thought that perhaps he had underestimated her. Maybe she *was* up to committing a murder. He looked inside the envelope and found two pictures of Grover Cleveland—he had a great affection for old Grover—and one of William McKinley. Twenty-five hundred dollars for a lie he might never have to tell.

"Two things, Cicely," he said, pocketing the envelope. "I won't perjure myself, and if I find out that *you've* been lying to *me*, the deal's off. Now, how about the rest of your treatment?"

Suddenly Cicely felt old and tired and conscious of her nakedness. She quickly got into her clothes and said, "Do you mind, Seth, if we call it a night? The last two days have been a strain for me, and I think I ought to just go to bed."

"I understand, of course, Cicely," he replied. "Sleep well and don't worry about a thing. I'll see you Monday for our regular appointment."

But they both knew she'd cancel the appointment, and as Seth walked out the door, it was understood that there would be no more appointments.

Now, riding to her husband's funeral in the back of a limousine, she sighed when she thought about how much she'd miss those massages. She'd have to find someone else, and there was no guarantee that the new man would have Seth's talent.

She hoped Seth would keep his word, but there was no

guarantee of that, either. She couldn't exactly sue him for breach of contract if he didn't. Cicely was certain now that the detectives, especially that Bandman, would keep digging and digging until they were satisfied, no matter how many people he hurt in the process. No matter how many lives he ruined. He'd been so insistent this morning.

"Look, Mrs. McBride," he'd said. "I'll be candid with you. I don't know who killed your husband. Personally I think it could have been you just as easily as anyone—you had the best motive—and I don't think you liked him any more than anyone else. But we don't have proof yet, and on the off chance that you *didn't* do it, I'd appreciate your help. Can you shed any light—any at all—on who might have wanted him dead?"

Cicely realized now that she had said the wrong thing. He had given her a perfect opportunity to deflect suspicion from herself, but she had behaved badly. "I would think that's your job, Lieutenant," she'd replied.

Bandman was disgusted. "We're doing our job, Mrs. McBride," he said through obviously clenched teeth. "But we don't know your husband. You did. You know his friends, his associates, who might have had a grudge against him. Help us, please."

Cicely had softened a little. "Lieutenant, I'm trying to make it clear to you that my husband and I were married, but we weren't close. We haven't been for many years. We went to parties together, and I know his social acquaintances—I ought to, I provided them. I know a few of his professional associates, but I had nothing to do with his practice or his patients. We led separate lives, for the most part. Can you understand that?"

Bandman ignored her last question. "About ten or twelve years ago your husband treated a man named Frank Wolfman, his secretary's husband. What can you tell us about that?"

"Nothing," she replied. "I just told you, I know nothing about his practice."

"But Wolfman was more than just an ordinary patient. Didn't he mention the fact that his secretary's husband was ill? The man works for the NIH. Try to remember."

"The name isn't at all familiar," she had responded.

"What about the name Ed Silverman?"

"He worked with my husband. He's a resident at the hospital. Why?"

"How is it that you know that name?"

"Because he was here on Labor Day. We give a party every year for the residents and some of the nurses and other hospital staff."

"Did he bring his wife?"

"He isn't married."

"Did he bring a date?"

"Dr. Silverman wouldn't dare bring *his* type of date to this house," she said with disdain.

"Oh?"

Bandman was silent, waiting for Cicely to elaborate. Finally she held out her hand and flipped it up and down in a limp-wristed motion. "You know," she said, "he's that way."

"Gay?" asked Bandman.

"Yes, if you really must be so specific."

"Specifics are important in a murder investigation," he replied. "How do you know that Dr. Silverman is gay?"

"My husband told me."

"I thought you and he didn't discuss his professional associates."

"This was different."

"In what way?"

"What do you mean, 'in what way'?" she asked, exasperated now.

"In what way was Dr. Silverman's professional association different from the others? Because he's gay, or for another reason? And how did your husband know he's gay?"

"I don't know how he knew, and we didn't discuss it at length. He just mentioned it in passing once, and we never discussed it again. No one's supposed to care anymore about that sort of thing, are they?"

"But you do," said Bandman. "And obviously your husband did, too."

This time she said nothing—because she really didn't know anything else about Eddie Silverman and because she wanted to get Bandman and his partner out of the house.

"Where were you, Mrs. McBride, at the time of your husband's death?"

The suddenness of the question threw her into momentary confusion, and it took her a second or two to remember what she had said on Tuesday. She was sure that the detectives had noticed her hesitation, but there was nothing she could do about it now. She had repeated her previous story about getting up late and reading magazines. It sounded plausible, it's what she really did practically every morning, but she could see that they didn't believe her.

But it was out of the question to tell the truth.

8

AMANDA WAS POURING hot coffee into a Thermos bottle when the doorbell rang.

"Hi," she said to Glencora. "New sweater? It's pretty."

"No, it's last year's. I just don't wear it much. How many times do I go on cross-country bike trips? Are you packing the ice axes? It's freezing out there!"

Amanda laughed. "It'll warm up. But I'm bringing a Thermos of coffee. Do you want a cup now?"

"No, thanks," said Glen as the two women walked back to the kitchen, where Ken was rinsing the breakfast dishes and putting them in the dishwasher.

They greeted each other with minimal enthusiasm, and Ken excused himself a few moments later. He kissed Amanda and said, "I may go to the office this afternoon if I can't get a tennis game. Then again, I may take a nap."

Amanda stroked his cheek. "Either one is better than going to a funeral! But we'll be back in about two hours. I can't send McBride off into the great beyond in jeans and sneakers. I have to come home to change."

"Okay. Well, have a nice bike ride, you two, and be careful of the traffic."

Ken went into his study, and Amanda and Glen went out the back door where Amanda's bike stood where she had left it an hour ago. It was gleaming in the bright sunshine, two months' worth of garage dust wiped off earlier.

Glen took her bicycle off the car rack, and the two set off down the street, turning into Bradley Boulevard toward Great

Falls Park on the Potomac. They rode along the wide bike path for a while in companionable silence, enjoying the beauty of the morning and nodding a greeting to joggers.

"Thanks for making me do this," said Glen. "It's really nice out here. But I'm afraid my lungs won't know how to handle all this fresh air! Now, tell me everything. Don't leave out a single detail."

"Okay, but you have to promise that you won't tell a soul. Seriously, Glen, I really mean it," she said even before Glencora could give her word. "It's important. You'll see why."

"I promise," said Glen, "but can I ask you a favor? When the whole thing is over and they catch the killer, I want to write an article about it for the magazine. I won't mention your name if you don't want me to, but I need the inside stuff from you. Okay?"

"Okay, it's a deal," said Amanda, and the friends smiled conspiratorially at each other.

Amanda told her everything: she described Bandman and Simonowitz, repeated her conversations with Eddie Silverman and Alice Bonner, and told her friend how she'd lied to the police about not knowing anything. It was good to tell the whole story to a sympathetic listener.

"When the detectives left my office yesterday, Glen, I was so mad at myself and so frustrated that I sat there crying like a damn baby. I could hardly get through the rest of the afternoon. Thank God it's the weekend because I don't think I could function at work another day."

"Of course you could," said her friend. "If you had to, you would. But you don't have to today, so relax and let's figure out who did it."

"Oh God, that's what Ken said yesterday morning when I left for work. He said we were going to solve the murder at dinner. He was just joking, but then when he asked how my day went, I cried again."

"Good old blue eyes. Did he at least bring you a present from Japan?" asked Glen, who didn't really like Ken. She thought he was a cold fish and not quite good enough for Amanda. "He'd better take you to the Bahamas when this is all over."

"The Bahamas! He's ready to have me committed," said Amanda. "He thinks I'm crazy for getting so involved in this, for caring so much. He knows how much I disliked McBride, so he assumes I'm glad he's dead and will think no more about it. That's what he'd do."

"Well, why *do* you care so much?" asked Glen, who already knew the answer.

Amanda stared at her. "How can you ask that? Aren't you just dying of curiosity? Don't you just *have* to know what happened? I mean, my God, Glen, the whole thing is so *bizarre*. And do you want to know something else? Something really strange? Ina Wolfman, of all the little pip-squeak people, lied to the police. Or else she lied to me about her husband and McBride knowing each other."

"Hmmm," said Glencora. "I see what you mean. Listen, Amanda, I'm with you. I just didn't want you to take what Ken thinks to heart too much. I know you love him, and I suppose he has good qualities, but you have to admit he's a little *removed* when it comes to things like this."

"Glen, I know he appears cold to you. He *doesn't* get emotional about things. But he cares about me, he lets himself relax with me, and he trusts me. He's come a long way in the ten years since we met him in Italy. Last week I even caught him petting Shadow, although he was embarrassed when he knew that I saw him."

"A man who's scared to give affection to a cat because people will think he's a sissy? Come on, Amanda, that's a man with ego problems."

"Glen, you promised. We have an agreement. . . ."

"I know," said Glencora. "I'm sorry. I won't trash him ever again. I'll even be nice to him!"

But Glencora would continue to take little digs at her husband, and the thing was, everything she said was true. But everything Amanda said in his defense was also true.

Take the matter of bringing her a present from Japan. He had asked when he left if there was something she had especially wanted.

"How about black pearls?" he had suggested.

"To tell you the truth, I'd much rather have a strand of coral beads . . . about this long," she had said, indicating on her chest the size of necklace she'd like. "Kind of a medium coral color," she'd added.

Ken had brought her a necklace of black pearls—much too short. Amanda was sure they'd cost more than the coral, but it annoyed her that he hadn't listened to her preference and then seemed disappointed that she wasn't wildly excited with the gift. But she believed him when he said he'd gone from store to store to find just the right gift. Kindhearted, decent, loving Ken—who had almost no notion of how to find out and then do what other people wanted.

"Let's run down the suspects," said Glen. "Do you have any idea who did it?"

"I don't have any proof of anything, but Eddie Silverman and Alice Bonner have awfully strong motives. But what bothers me as much as *who* did it is *how* it was done.

"McBride didn't die of the stabbing, but if the murderer didn't want to kill him, why did he bother to stick a knife in his throat? Besides, he stuck it in only once. He didn't slash or gash or do anything messy. There was practically no blood. You know what it feels like to me, Glen, and I know this is a weird gut reaction: I have the feeling that the murderer didn't *want* to kill McBride . . . that he just wanted to warn him or scare him or something."

"You're right, it *is* weird," replied Glencora. "But let's not eliminate it. Some people send threatening letters, and some make anonymous phone calls. Our guy sticks a scalpel in his victim's throat. So what you're saying is, there are really two people involved: one who wanted to scare McBride and the one who wanted to—and did—kill him. Do you think they're the same person?"

"I don't know," replied Amanda. "It all hinges on motive, doesn't it? Why would anyone want to stab a person, in the *throat* no less, unless he wanted to kill him? Maybe the guy *intended* to kill McBride but didn't know how to do it. In that case there's only one person."

"But McBride didn't die of the stab wound," pointed out Glencora. "And if his secretary, what's her face . . ."

"Ina," replied Amanda.

"Right. If Ina was gone to the storeroom only for a few minutes, and if that small a stab wound wouldn't be fatal, especially as he didn't lose much blood, then how in the hell did he die?"

"Aha!" said Amanda. "That's the sixty-four-thousand-dollar question. It has to be poison. Either an incredibly slow-acting poison that would have had its final effect at exactly the time of the stabbing, which is too coincidental for words, or an incredibly fast-acting poison that took effect at the time of the stabbing."

"I vote for the latter," said Glen, "although why would you need to use two killing methods at the same time when one good one would do. The guy sounds like a woman who wants to screw when she's ovulating and *really* doesn't want to get pregnant!"

Glen and Amanda laughed uproariously, remembering all the times they'd commiserated with each other over just that very problem. "I love you, Glen," said Amanda. "You always put things into such good perspective."

"Okay, let's concentrate on who did it," said Glencora. First, the wife. First is *always* the wife. What's she like?"

"It's hard to tell," said Amanda. "When I first met her, I thought she was a real bimbo and about ten years old emotionally. But the more I saw her—which wasn't all that much—I thought there may be more to her."

"How old is she really?" asked Glencora.

"Midforties and resenting every day that passes," said Amanda. "I think she behaves like a kid because she thinks it's cute and people will believe she's younger than she is.

"She's irritating as hell, and she's certainly not the intellect of the Western world. But for some reason I feel sorry for her. She seems so pathetic and useless, and I always have the feeling that she'd really like to do something with her life. But maybe that's only wishful thinking on my part. You know how I hate useless people.

"She's such a *type*. You know, money marrying money, a husband and wife having nothing in common but their love of consumer goods. People who have too much money for their own good. I wonder if she and McBride were even in love with each other when they got married.

"No, scratch that," she continued, musing out loud. "*She* was in love with *him*. He was a good-looking guy; he must've been a knockout when he was younger. And a world-class doctor—presidents and kings as patients—you can sniff out that kind of potential even before it happens. It's exciting, all that power. She was in love with him, all right.

"But I'm not so sure about him. He was an opportunistic bastard, knew a good catch when he saw one, took advantage of her family money to set himself up in practice, didn't have to bother being a junior partner and work his way up, got patients from her friends, went to all the right parties, charmed the gold out of everyone's back teeth, and used his medical brilliance to good advantage.

"If he was in love with his wife at the beginning, it faded fast, as soon as that first blast of sex wore off (I'll bet she was a virgin when they got married), and he just kind of tolerated her as a good-looking possession and a kind of jazzed-up housekeeper/hostess."

Glencora asked, "How do you know all that?"

"I don't *know* any of it," she replied. "You know how I just babble on and make up stories about people, figure them out from the way they look or little behavior clues they send out without realizing it."

"Okay, even if every word of that is true, did she murder her husband?" asked Glencora. "You make her sound like a spoiled brat."

"That's *exactly* the way to describe her," said Amanda.

"But is she spoiled enough to throw a really big temper tantrum—one with a knife or a vial of poison in her hand—to get what she wants? Or to get rid of what she doesn't want? Is she smart enough to pull off a murder this sophisticated? Does she have the nerve?"

"Maybe, if she had enough motive," replied Amanda. "It certainly couldn't be for money. She has practically all the money in the world. But maybe she finally got terminally pissed off about all his other women. McBride wasn't exactly Danny Discreet about his affairs, but hospital scuttlebutt says he thought he was getting away with it. But if we knew every time he unzipped his fly, then the whole medical community knew. And probably his wife knew. And it wasn't even so bad that he wanted to go to bed with every woman who wasn't tied down, although it got kind of disgusting after a while. It was his arrogance about it all—as though women were put there just for his pleasure. Look how mad I'm getting just talking about it. Can you imagine how Cicely must have felt?"

"If he were *my* husband," said Glen, "I wouldn't stab him in the *throat*! So we've got Cicely at the top of the list for motive but near the bottom for method. If she was going to stab him, she should have done it at home with a kitchen knife.

"Does Cicely have an alibi for the time of death? Does she *really* have all the money she needs? Maybe she needs his insurance and inheritance? Maybe she has some heavy expenses that her husband didn't know about."

"I don't know the answer to any of those questions. Cicely and I are not exactly bosom buddies."

"You're going to have to think of a way to find out that stuff," said Glencora. "Now, what about the two with the great motives?"

"I've told you everything I know. Either—or neither—could have done it. Eddie has the best motive. I mean he had the most to lose if McBride told the whole world he was gay. On the other hand, the blackmail could have gone on forever, maybe even escalated after Eddie got out into private practice and started making real money. Maybe he felt he just had to put a stop to it. But this way was so amateurish. And he, and Bonner too, knew he wouldn't be *killing*. It's the *method* that's got us stumped, Glen, and there's nothing we can do until we find out how he died."

"So let's find out," said her friend.

"But, Glen, if the police don't know, how should I?"

"Good question. You'll just have to think of something."

"Sure, just like that!" Amanda snapped her fingers. "But I'm sick of talking about McBride. I need your advice about something else. Ken and I think it's time to give a big party. When should we do it? New Year's Eve or Valentine's Day?"

"One thing before we talk about parties—and I *love* to talk about parties," said Glencora. "If McBride was blackmailing Eddie, why couldn't he have been blackmailing someone else? And that would give someone else a motive to knock him off."

"Oh great," replied Amanda. "Just what we need; another suspect. But you're right. He could have been collecting dirty money from lots of people. But who? And why? Why would a man like McBride make a second career out of blackmail?"

"You said he was a real shit," replied Glencora.

"But not a stupid one. I can see him hating Eddie enough to do it as a kind of spur-of-the-moment thing. But blackmail on a grand scale? No, it wouldn't have been his style."

"But murder isn't in the style of anyone you know . . . unless there's a lot you're not telling me!" said Glen.

Amanda sighed. "Well, that just goes to show that no one ever knows what anyone else is capable of."

Glen saw that her friend was growing morose, so she changed the subject. They seemed to have exhausted all the possibilities, anyway. "On to the party. Valentine's Day, definitely. Everyone does New Year's, and anyway the caterers are all booked by now," said Glen.

"Caterers. I've never had a catered party. I wouldn't know how to hire one," said Amanda, who had cooked for three days, and taken two to recover, from the party she'd given six years ago, when she'd bought her little house on Highland Drive.

"Well, that's why you asked for my advice. Can we have a cup of that coffee now? And then we need to look around for the john."

"Sure," said Amanda. "But I wouldn't mind finding the bathroom first."

They finally reached the park, which ran for several miles along the river. They could hear the roar of the waterfall in the distance and the shouts of a ball game nearby. They rode in that direction, assuming there would be bathrooms nearby.

Sure enough, they saw the familiar brown Park Service building on the other side of a large parking lot and rode toward it.

"We have to go in shifts," said Amanda. "Otherwise someone will rip off our bikes."

Glen rolled her eyes in disgust at the perfidy of human nature as her friend disappeared through the door. "How was it?" she asked when Amanda emerged.

"Not bad, considering," said Amanda. "Not as bad as it will be later. At least there's toilet paper!"

"Let's find a place by the river," said Glen, and the two women spent twenty minutes sitting on a huge rock watching the water rush by below, talking of inconsequential matters, happy and utterly comfortable in each other's company.

Amanda looked at her watch. "I have to go. It wouldn't do to be late to this. Half of VIP Washington will probably be there. By the way, do you want to come with me? You could write it up for *Style and Sense*."

"No, thanks, I think I'll pass. We don't acknowledge death. Too depressing for our readers."

Driving to Caldwell's under a sky rapidly darkening with stormclouds, Amanda thought about the morning with Glen and wondered if her friend was egging her on to get more involved in the murder just so she could have firsthand information for *Style and Sense*.

Nah, she wouldn't do that to me, she thought.

Why wouldn't she? asked the voice she sometimes didn't like listening to. She's a journalist and they'll do practically anything to get a story.

But she's my friend.

So is Eddie Silverman your friend. And he *killed* someone.

We don't know that for sure, thought Amanda, her heart sinking.

Yes, we do. We know it in our guts.

By the time she arrived at the funeral home, it had started to rain, but she saw a car pull out of a parking space only a few steps from the front door. She wouldn't have to get her new shoes wet.

Most of Amanda's funeral experiences had been with her own family. They were usually highly emotional affairs. Everyone talked to everyone else. Tears flowed freely, and sometimes laughter broke out as people remembered funny things about the one who had died.

Now, walking into the hushed, tense, wood-paneled room designed to resemble a church, Amanda felt intimidated and wasn't sure what to do. She hung back to watch others, and then followed a group of people to a short receiving line next to the casket. Cicely and their son Robert were there, as well as a man who looked like McBride and was probably his brother. The other woman must be McBride's sister-in-law.

Amanda glanced quickly at the casket and was relieved to see that it was closed. Once, several years ago, she had been to the wake of the mother of one of her fellow supervisors, and when she went up to the casket to pay her respects, she was shocked to see that the corpse had her eyeglasses on. And then, before Amanda could ward it off, she was seized by wave after wave of hysterical laughter that welled up from the same place that also gave rise to uncontrollable panic. For what seemed like hours, she stood staring at those ridiculous glasses, wondering what the corpse would see when she got to where she was going, her shoulders shaking until the fury subsided.

Please, God. Don't let me make an ass out of myself here, she prayed.

It was going to be all right, though. She felt calm as she pressed Cicely's hand and murmured a few soothing phrases. The widow seemed serene and very much in control of herself, almost as if she were giving a tea party rather than playing the principal mourner at her husband's funeral.

Amanda was pressed forward by the growing crowd of people behind her. She expressed her sympathy to the others and nodded to Townsend, who probably checked her off on his mental list of hospital employees. Those who showed up would score a brownie point; those who didn't would be remembered.

Amanda started down the aisle and wiggled her fingers in greeting to people she knew. Jonathan Bernstein was sitting in the third row with his wife, and she would have slid in next to them, but they suddenly moved over to make room for someone coming in from the other end of the row.

So she took a seat in the row immediately behind them and turned her attention to those now looking for seats, noticing what the women were wearing and watching the expression on people's faces. Most of them didn't have much expression—they could have been rush-hour commuters on Metro.

Some of the faces were instantly familiar, though; for instance, the secretary of state and the vice president. McBride played in the big leagues.

She was roused from her reverie by a soft voice asking, "Do all these Secret Service guys make you feel secure?"

She turned to see Lydia Simonowitz sitting next to her. "Hi!" she said. "Do you always come to the victim's funeral?"

"Actually this is my first one," said Lydia. "To tell you the truth, this is my first murder case. I just got promoted to detective, but Lieutenant Bandman believes in going to funerals. He thinks it gives you a feel for the victim, the kind of person he was. But he had something else to do today, so I'm on my own.

"How come you're here?" she asked. "I thought you didn't like the deceased. McBride, I mean."

"I didn't, but Mr. Townsend, the administrator, made noises like he expected all the department heads to show up, and I didn't think it was worth butting heads with him about it. I'm not in a position right now to risk annoying him."

"Speaking of getting people annoyed," said Amanda, "I really want to apologize for yesterday afternoon. I can't grant your request, but I didn't have to be so snooty about it."

"That's all right. You're about a thousand times more polite than—"

Lydia was interrupted by a blast of organ music that startled them both, and a minister walked in from a door hidden in the wood paneling. He approached the pulpit, and the funeral began.

There were a few hymns, a eulogy from some official in the American Medical Association, and a ten-minute sermon about McBride's contribution to medicine. Everything that was said was absolutely true; McBride *had* been a brilliant physician, but Amanda was more interested in what was not said. No one mentioned that he had been a devoted husband and father, no one said that his friends would be bereft without him, no one talked about his acts of charity or good works. It was a service entirely without feeling—totally befitting the star.

The whole thing took less than an hour, and as the congregants stood while the pallbearers carried the coffin out to the waiting hearse, Amanda said to Lydia in a low voice, "Who am I a thousand times more polite than?"

Lydia seemed confused. "Oh, did I say that? I guess I must have been talking of the type of people we usually deal with. Not nearly so high toned."

Amanda didn't believe her. Lydia had been on the verge of naming a person, but during the service she must have thought better of it. Amanda wanted to know who it had been: Eddie, Cicely, Alice Bonner, Frank Wolfman (she knew Ina would be too intimidated by the police to be less than polite), someone she didn't know about?

Lydia wondered why Amanda was so curious. She'd obviously been thinking about it during the funeral. In fact, Lydia believed that Amanda thought about Leo McBride's death a good deal. She obviously knew something she wasn't telling, and she appeared to feel guilty about it.

Neither woman was at the funeral in a strictly official capacity, although neither *would* be there if they had not had a working connection with the man who was safely tucked into the hearse for his last ride on earth. Lydia acted on an impulse.

"Would you like to get a cup of coffee?" she asked.

Amanda was surprised—and pleased. "Yes, that would be nice. Where would you like to go?"

"Actually, now that I think about it, how about going someplace nice for tea? It's a good day for it."

They were standing in the doorway of the funeral home, and although it had not yet started to rain seriously, the sky was black, and the wind whipped the dry leaves around in an unpleasant, menacing way.

"What a great idea," said Amanda. "How about the Grand Hotel, or is that too far out of the way?"

"No, it's fine," said Lydia. "At least they have indoor parking."

"Good, I'll meet you by the front door."

Amanda drove through the gathering gloom, deliberately not thinking of what she and Lydia would talk about. Instead she decided what to wear to the party this evening. Then, as they had done for the past few days, her thoughts strayed to the predicament she was in. Why couldn't the nurses use the brains God gave them and stop screwing up? Barbara Morrison had made the worst mistake, but there had been plenty of others. Just two weeks earlier, there had been a serious medication error, and the very next day a patient's surgery had to be canceled because the nurses let her eat breakfast that morning. Amanda shuddered when she thought about the disaster *that* could have been if the patient herself hadn't said something.

The patients aren't supposed to be saving their own lives, she thought grimly. That's what they come to us for.

The nurses are no worse than the other fuckups at J.F.K., said the voice that sometimes sympathized.

But that's not the point. I know that all hospital personnel are getting worse and worse, but I can worry only about the nurses.

What was *wrong* with them? Didn't they care? Didn't they understand that nursing was *not* the same as being a clerk in a department store? It wasn't just a job; it was a matter of entering into a relationship of duty and obligation with people whose very lives depended on how they interpreted that obligation.

Amanda understood very well how frustrating and difficult it was to be a hospital nurse, especially now when the patients were sicker than ever. Their insurance companies didn't let them stay a minute longer than was necessary, and not many people could afford to shell out the thousand dollars a day it cost to stay at a private hospital such as J.F.K. Memorial.

Even you don't want to do it anymore, she admitted to herself. If you weren't in the front office wearing nice clothes instead of a white uniform, you'd be out of nursing like a flash. So how do you expect anyone else to get any satisfaction out of it?

Amanda sighed again. It was true. The amount of satisfaction one could derive from making a real difference in someone's recovery was minimal compared to the administrative and other kinds of crap that nurses had to put up with.

But that's not the point, either, she thought angrily. If they hate their jobs, then they should quit—or go up the ladder like

I did. But if they're going to do what they're doing, then dammit, they should do it right.

She sighed again. There didn't seem to be much she could do about it now, and anyway she had arrived at 24th and M Street, N.W. Lydia was already waiting for her in the lobby.

"Did you have your siren on all the way?" Amanda asked.

Lydia laughed. "I'm driving my own car today, but I worked in this precinct for a while and know all the back roads."

They walked upstairs to the corner of the upper lobby, where tea was served, basking in the elegance of the hotel and the softness of the love seats on which they sat facing each other.

"This was a wonderful idea," said Amanda. "I haven't been here before. Have you?"

"No," Lydia replied, and then couldn't think of anything else to say.

The two women stared at each other for a moment, acutely uncomfortable, each perhaps regretting the decision to meet like this. What popped out of Amanda's mouth next was as much of a surprise to her as to Lydia.

In a deep mock growl she said, "Okay, sister, tell me who I'm more polite than or I'm going to have to use my fingernail puller-outer on you!"

There was a second of stunned surprise, then both women burst out laughing, and Lydia said, "I confess! You're more polite than Cicely McBride. She's done nothing but give us a hard time. She's a real bitch, and if you ever tell anyone I said that, I'll use *my* fingernail puller-outer on *you*!"

They laughed again, and both women knew it would be okay now and relaxed and enjoyed each other's company, sipping hot fragrant tea and spreading Devon cream and raspberry jam on rich scones.

They talked at first about the murder, but only in the most general way, because that was what they had in common. After a while they talked of themselves. They both had a fondness for Chuck Mangione's and Claude Bolling's jazz, and neither had patience for the current glut of movies about the sexual awakening of adolescents.

"Being a teenager was so awful that I hate to remember it,

let alone pay good money to watch someone else go through it," said Lydia.

Amanda agreed. Both women had spent most of their adolescent years with only one parent, and each was an only child. They agreed, also, that early loneliness had been significant in shaping their attitudes and feelings.

They were beginning to warm to the subject when the waiter came by and asked if everything was all right. Amanda assured him that they were content and then said, "I hate it when they interrupt a conversation. If everything wasn't all right, I'd let them know. It's so intrusive."

Lydia said nothing. Waiters everywhere did that, and she had long since learned to tune them out. Amanda had overreacted to his innocuous question and now seemed to be falling into a morose mood.

"Is anything wrong?" asked Lydia.

"Yes, there is," said Amanda. "I lied to you and Lieutenant Bandman yesterday."

Lydia's expression barely changed. "I know. Do you want to talk about it now?"

"You knew I was lying?" asked Amanda.

"That's why they promoted me to detective," she said.

Amanda smiled, but she felt a deep sadness as she said, "I have no proof of anything, but I've had two conversations in the past two days that you should know about. But before I tell you what they are, I want you to know that I'm betraying one of my closest friends and am breaking the confidence of a former employee. I'm not doing this lightly, and frankly, I feel like an absolute shit."

Lydia still said nothing; she simply sat forward in her chair and listened to what Amanda had to say.

9

AMANDA AWOKE TO the soft rustle of the newspaper and the aroma of fresh coffee. It was the latter that finally penetrated the mists of sleep, but she kept her eyes closed for a few minutes, conscious of Ken's leg resting against her thigh, savoring the deliciousness of the long, empty Sunday ahead.

Shadow, who lay on her chest, began to purr. The cat knew Amanda was awake even though her eyes were still closed. She opened them and found the huge yellow ones staring into her own.

She rolled onto her side, gently shoving Shadow onto the down comforter and sliding her hand up her husband's leg.

"Well, good morning," said Ken, smiling. "I thought you were going to sleep all day."

The clock read 8:37; he had probably been up for at least an hour, judging by the pile of already-read sections of the newspaper. Ken didn't believe in wasting a lot of time sleeping.

Amanda growled a little and padded to the bathroom to brush her teeth and wake herself up. When she returned to bed there was a steaming cup of coffee on her night table, and she took a few sips and inhaled the fragrant steam before she felt able to speak. Putting an electric coffeepot in the bedroom had been one of their best ideas.

"Good morning to you, too," she said as cheerfully as she could. Amanda was not a morning person.

She pulled the stack of newspaper sections toward herself, and she and Ken read in silence for a while. It didn't take her

132

long to get through the paper because it seemed that one day's news was much the same as the next, and there was little that she considered real news.

Today's pickings were slimmer than usual, and Amanda felt restless and anxious to do something physical. Down in the kitchen, opening a can of cat food and looking out at the leaves blowing around the yard, she decided what to do.

"I'm going to play Dolly Domestic today," she said to Ken as she got back into bed next to him, carrying a tray of orange juice and bagels smeared with cream cheese and piled with smoked salmon.

"And what does Dolly Darling have planned?" he asked.

"I'm going to bake bread, make a nice thick stew for supper, and in between all that I'm going to pull out all the dead crap in the garden. It looks like hell."

"I was thinking the same thing about the yard," he said. "We'll do that together when I get back from tennis. Do we have enough trash bags?"

"I bought some the other day when I went to the store. When are you playing?"

"Noon," he replied. "I'll grab some lunch with the guys. Do you want to go to the movies after supper?"

"Let's see how we feel then," she said, polishing off the last of her bagel and getting out of bed.

She put on a pair of blue jeans and a red cotton sweater and went down to the kitchen, leaving Ken surrounded by sections of the *Washington Post* and the *New York Times,* which would soon be supplanted by his briefcase.

Amanda opened cupboards getting out the things she needed to bake bread and making sure she had all the stew ingredients. These bursts of domesticity were rare, but she enjoyed them when they happened. It was pleasant to spend time in the cheerful kitchen, listening to Mozart, kneading dough, setting it in a bowl to rise, browning the beef for stew, and leafing through her cookbooks to find something interesting for dessert.

She liked these quiet times with just the two of them in the house and no one from the outside world to disturb them. But today thoughts of McBride's murder intruded on her peace.

Be honest, said the voice that always tried to force her to be. It's getting under your skin. You think about it all the time. More than you should—more than you think about your job. And if you keep on like this, pretty soon you won't have a job to think about. She had betrayed one of her best friends as well as a former employee, and she was disgusted with herself for that. It was the police's job to find out who had killed McBride and she didn't *have* to help them. But on the other hand, what if either Eddie or Alice Bonner had done it? Wouldn't catching them be easier now that she had revealed their motives? She kneaded the bread dough and went over every word of her conversations with Bandman and Simonowitz, and then with Lydia alone after the funeral the day before. They needed her help, and she had refused to give it, getting on her moral high horse about divulging confidential medical information, but then she revealed two intensely private conversations. But there was a reason beyond pure medical ethics that she wouldn't help the detectives get the medical records that they wanted. Suddenly she knew what that reason was and made a decision. She waited until Ken had driven off to his tennis game, punched down the risen dough, quickly shaped it into loaves, and put it in pans for the second rising. She raced upstairs, washed the flour smudges off her face, changed to a warmer sweater, and backed her Honda out the driveway.

At noon on Sunday the hospital lobby was just beginning to fill with visitors, but the administrative wing was quiet, almost eerie. She let herself into her office, closed the door, and booted up the computer.

If anyone was going to read those records, she would. She was just about to enter her password to get into the file of stored records, when she stopped. She had no real business doing this, even if she was the director of nursing. And for reasons she wasn't quite sure of, she didn't want anyone to know she had been in the computer files. It was easy to trace who had logged in and out of medical records because all password use was permanently recorded. She wanted no questions asked about why she had sneaked into the hospital on Sunday morning to look into medical files that were none of her business.

But she couldn't do a thing without a password, and they were all secret. Even Louise didn't know hers, and she knew no one else's. Amanda sat frustrated in front of the computer monitor, the cursor blinking steadily, waiting for a command. How was she going to get in?

If Ken were here, he could probably figure out some way to set up a system by which a random combination of letters and numbers would soon come up with *someone's* password. Then she sat up straight and said out loud, "But they're not random." She remembered the day she had chosen her own.

"We prefer that people pick their own words," Charley Boston, the head of Medical Records, had said. "That way they're not as likely to forget them."

"Do you mean I can choose any word I want?" Amanda had asked.

"As long as no one else has picked it first," Charley replied. "And as long as it doesn't have more than eight digits— numbers or letters in any combination. Most people pick their birthday or their children's names or their street or something like that so it's easy to remember."

Amanda had chosen Beatrice, her mother's name.

"Don't forget it," said Charley as she left his office, "because the computer will give you only three chances to get it right. That's to prevent someone from sitting down with a dictionary trying words until one fits. After you've given the third wrong password, the computer will end the program, and you'll be out of luck. And we're not allowed to give out passwords on the phone. You either have to come down here in person or put in a written request."

Amanda was impressed. "You seem to have all the safety checks in place," she said.

"Oh sure," Charley had said with a grin. "Until some whiz kid beats the system and we have to start all over again."

Now Amanda wanted to beat the system, but she felt as much like a whiz kid as a three-star general.

"Okay," she said to herself. "Think this through. You picked your mother's name because Charley suggested that you choose someone or something close. So what was McBride's mother's name?"

Amanda had decided to use Leo McBride's password because it seemed safer than guessing anyone else's. And it also seemed fittingly macabre.

She didn't know McBride's mother's name—or his father's. His son was named Robert, but Amanda passed that up as too common. Surely someone else would have chosen it. She couldn't imagine him using his wife's name, and he had no pets. She didn't know his birthday, but she could look up the name of his street. Baser Lane, it said in the phone book, so Amanda typed in BASER in the space indicated by the blinking cursor.

Instantly the words INCORRECT PASSWORD appeared on the screen, and again the cursor flashed patiently.

"Now think," she said to herself. "What meant something to him?"

Money and medicine. That was what had interested Leo McBride, but it was from the latter category that McBride would choose a word.

Amanda stared off at nothing, thinking of nothing, trying to make her mind a blank. Suddenly she blinked. Of course that was it! She was staring at her bookcase and there, side by side, in fat, dignified glory, were McBride's three texts: *Principles and Practices of Internal Medicine, The Internist* and *The Theory and Practice of Internal Medicine*. The common word jumped out at her immediately, and she typed INTERNAL into the computer.

The computer hummed, and her heart pounded. She'd done it! But immediately she was disappointed: the words PASSWORD CANCELED flashed on the screen.

Damn! They're quick down there, she thought, annoyed and admiring at the same time.

She wondered how soon after word of McBride's death had reached Medical Records they canceled his access. And why would they be so fast with the delete key? Dead men didn't need passwords. Had other people done what Amanda was trying now? Were there safeguards built into the program that Charley hadn't mentioned?

Amanda still didn't want to use her own password, so she decided to try Eddie's. She felt only a minor twinge of guilt when she restarted the program. She typed in Eddie's name, the date and time, and when the computer asked for her password, she held her breath and typed DONALD, his lover's name.

It worked. She was in. She was certain she wouldn't find the first record she was looking for, and sure enough when she asked for McBride, Leonard, the computer came up empty. She didn't think he would be treated at his own hospital—not if he wanted to keep his cancer a secret.

But when she entered Wolfman, Frank, the computer told her there was no record for him, either. That surprised her, so she tried Wolfman, Francis. Nothing. Wolfman, Franklin. Nothing.

She went through every first name beginning with F she could think of and tried a variety of spellings of Wolfman. Each time the monitor remained frustratingly empty.

Perhaps she was doing something wrong to the computer. So she typed in Knight, Amanda, and instantly the screen filled with information about the time, five years ago, that she'd spilled a cup of boiling water all over her hand and was treated in the emergency room for second-degree burns.

She looked at her hand now as it rested on the computer keyboard. Not a trace of the ugly, fiery tissue or the huge, thin-skinned blisters that had popped out within ten minutes of the accident. She'd been bandaged for weeks, during which time she'd submitted to almost daily debridement of the dead skin as it sloughed off. The pain had been incredible, and she'd been terribly handicapped by the mountainous white bandage. But her hand was perfect now: no scarring and, most important, no crippling of her fingers.

She shuddered as she recalled the horror of that accident and quickly wiped her record from the screen, going once more through the variations of Frank Wolfman that she had tried before. Still nothing.

She sat in front of the computer, frustrated and annoyed. Why are you doing this? asked the voice that always had to know the reason for everything. Amanda didn't know how to reply. What difference did it make where McBride was treated? He would have been dead of the disease in a month or so anyway if someone hadn't been so impatient. Her head snapped up. "That's it! Whoever was treating him killed him."

Who else would have constant access to his veins? There was no sign of a struggle in the office; McBride hadn't resisted whatever had been done to him. He had calmly put his arm out for the dose of chemotherapy and had no reason to believe that this time it wasn't a cancer-killing drug that was being injected. This time it was a Leo-killing drug.

If that's true—and I have to admit that it sounds plausible, said the voice who *did* give credit where it was due, then who did it?

Good question, thought Amanda grimly. We're right back at square one. But not exactly. It had to be someone local. An oncologist wasn't going to come down from Sloan-Kettering in New York or even from Johns Hopkins in Baltimore to slide a needle into a patient's vein a few times a week, even for a spoiled and demanding Leo McBride. So it had to be a Washingtonian.

Amanda could understand why McBride wouldn't want to be seen going regularly into the office of a cancer specialist, but why would he risk having such a doctor come to him here? Why wouldn't he have the treatments at home?

But what if it was a doctor who had business in McBride's office anyway? asked the voice that was getting excited as the pieces fell into place. It had to have been someone with easy access to chemotherapeutic drugs, so that eliminates surgeons and orthopedists and gynecologists. It had to be someone from the Department of Medicine.

It had to be someone who was obligated to cure him and needed to kill him.

Amanda felt sick and dizzy as she realized who that one person had to be: the friend who was no longer her friend. She glared at the computer as though it had been the machine's fault that Eddie felt driven to kill McBride. Then she turned it off, put on her jacket, and picked up her car keys from where she had thrown them on her desk.

While Amanda had been staring at the computer screen, unbeknownst to her, Bandman and Simonowitz were again questioning Eddie Silverman.

He looked terrible and knew it. Ever since Donald had left him weeping on the couch Friday night, he had thought of nothing but the trouble he was in. He'd been on call all weekend and couldn't concentrate on work. Twice he had made mistakes that he knew about, and he shuddered to think how many times he had screwed up without knowing it. They were crammed into his tiny office again, but this time they were all standing. He at least had the presence of mind to refuse to sit down.

"Dr. Silverman, what were you doing Wednesday a little before noon?" asked Bandman.

"I told you," he said, "I went out for a walk."

"Is that something you usually do?"

"No."

"Why that day?"

"I don't know," said Eddie. "I just had an urge to get some air."

"Did that urge have anything to do with the fact that Dr. McBride had called you a damned idiot in front of half the hospital not two hours before?"

"And," added Lydia, "in those two hours did you stew in your own anger and then go downstairs and stick a knife in his throat?"

"No," said Eddie. "I didn't kill him. I swear I didn't kill him. How can I prove that I didn't?"

"We don't think you can," said Bandman.

All of a sudden Eddie seemed to deflate. He slumped against the wall, and for a moment the two detectives thought he would faint. Instead, he looked at them and asked, "Are you going to arrest me?"

"I wish we could," said Bandman. "Believe me, I wish we could. But you'd be out on bail in an hour, so it seems a waste of taxpayer money to go to all the trouble of booking you. But I wouldn't leave town if I were you."

"Look, Dr. Silverman," said Lydia in a placating tone, "by the way, can I call you Ed?"

"No," he said angrily.

For the first time in two days he felt a little relief. They had no evidence at all. If they did, he would have been arrested. They were bluffing.

"Look," said Lydia, "you know that things don't look good for you. You hated McBride, he humiliated you publicly not two hours before he was murdered, and you were—in an amazing coincidence—out of the hospital just wandering the streets of Georgetown, and you can't come up with a single person who can attest to having seen you.

"What would you think if you were in our shoes?"

She had a point, but he still thought it would be okay. "Dr. Silverman, are you a homosexual?" asked Bandman.

Eddie's head snapped up as though he had been struck. That damn Amanda! The two men stared at each other, and Eddie tried furiously to get his blank, frozen mind to function again. Bandman watched what was going on behind the young doctor's eyes, knowing that Lydia was right.

Bandman didn't like this part of his job. It wasn't that he objected to making suspects sweat; that was, after all, the only way to get any information out of most of them. And it was up front. He'd ask questions; he'd ask *hard* questions; he'd ask them over and over again; he'd question a suspect six times a day if he had to; he'd *exhaust* a suspect with questioning if he had to. But it was all out in the open. This wasn't. This was sneaky, and he didn't like it. But he did it anyway.

"I asked you a question, Dr. Silverman. Are you a homosexual?"

Eddie's brain cells clicked on again. "That's none of your business," he said.

"So that means you are," said Bandman. "If you weren't, you would have denied it."

Eddie flushed. "You can think what you want, Officer, but unless my sex life has something to do with McBride's murder, you don't have any right to the information."

"Oh, it has something to do with the murder, all right," said Bandman. To himself he said, but I'll be damned if I know what.

Eddie thought that Bandman must have given some subliminal signal to his partner because immediately Lydia said in her calm, soothing voice, "Let's leave that alone for now, Dr.

Silverman. Let's even assume that you're innocent. Who do you think killed McBride?"

"Alice Bonner," he said without a moment's hesitation.

"Did she tell you that at lunch Friday?" asked Lydia.

"How did you know we had lunch together?" he asked, genuinely surprised.

"That's why they call us *detectives*, Doctor," she said with a sweet smile. "We find things out. What did the two of you talk about at lunch?"

"Nothing much, this and that."

The police didn't believe that any more than Donald did. It stank with the rottenness of the lie that it was, and Eddie knew he'd have to come up with something better.

"Why are you accusing her of murder, Dr. Silverman?" asked Bandman.

"I'm not accusing her," said Eddie. "You asked me who I think did it, and I think she did."

"Why?"

Eddie just shrugged. He wished he'd kept his mouth shut. Accusing Alice wouldn't help him. He knew that, even as her name popped unbidden out of his mouth.

"How many times have you eaten lunch with her before Friday?"

"None," he replied. He should have lied, he thought. He should have told them he ate with her occasionally. Then it would be her word against his.

"Why all of a sudden two days after a man you both detested is murdered? Why are the two prime suspects huddled together over hospital lunch trays? Why, Dr. Silverman?" Bandman pressed hard.

"Is it illegal to eat lunch with a nurse? I eat with Amanda Knight all the time. I eat with lots of nurses all the time."

"But never Alice Bonner," said Bandman. "Someone like her must scare the bejesus out of someone like you."

That got Eddie pissed off, and Bandman saw that it was useless to have gone off on that tack—this time.

"I'm sick of this," said Eddie. "It's not illegal to be gay in the District of Columbia. If you want to arrest me for murder, go ahead. But I'm not answering any more questions. I'm tired. I've been on call all weekend, and I need to get some sleep."

He held the door to his office open, indicating that he wanted them to leave. But his heart was thudding with fear. They *could* arrest him if they wanted to, and now he thought he had pushed them into it.

But he was safe for now. "Somehow I don't think there will be any rest for the wicked today," said Bandman on his way out. "I'd look in the Yellow Pages under defense attorneys if I were you," he added.

Eddie said nothing, but his face hardened momentarily into hatred. It was as if his features turned to stone, and Bandman didn't miss it.

"So now we know what he was hiding," said Lydia.

"Yeah," replied Bandman, looking as though he might cry. Lydia couldn't figure it out. The detective hadn't leaned on him all *that* hard, and it *was* beginning to look as though they had their man—although proving it would be another story.

"I hate doing things like that," said Bandman morosely. "I hate bringing things into investigations that don't belong there. Murder isn't gay or straight or black or white or Jewish or Christian. It's wrong. It's evil. It's stupid. But it doesn't have a religion or a race or sexual predilections. Silverman either did it or he didn't. If he did, he ought to hang for it. But he doesn't deserve to be harassed because he's gay."

Lydia didn't know what to say. She was surprised to hear something like that from a detective with a reputation for unerring instincts about suspects. She didn't agree with Bandman entirely, although she supposed he was right in theory. The trouble was that people didn't conform to other people's theories about them. But this was not the time to begin a philosophical discussion about how far the police could go in questioning suspects. She changed the subject.

"Frank Wolfman checks out okay," she said. "He has no rap sheet."

Bandman looked at her as if pulling himself back from far away. "I knew he wouldn't."

+   +   +

Amanda locked her office and walked down the corridor, feeling elated and miserable at the same time, when she saw Jonathan Bernstein coming toward her.

"Hi, Jonathan," she said. "I almost didn't recognize you with clothes on."

He looked flustered and immediately turned bright red, turning his head to see if anyone had heard. Poor man, she thought. He had absolutely no sense of humor. She put her hand on his arm, which threw him into a fresh fit of embarrassment, and said, "Relax, Jonathan. I meant real clothes instead of surgical scrubs."

"Oh," he said, obviously relieved. "I thought you meant . . ." His voice trailed off. "I don't know what I meant; I mean I don't know what you meant. Oh, hell."

The guy was really in a dither. Amanda had never seen him so distracted and confused. But he was such a social zero, such a nerd, that Amanda couldn't resist taking a little dig. She kept her hand on his arm, tightening her grip a little.

"Are you saying I *might* recognize you with no clothes on?" As soon as she saw his face, Amanda was sorry she had embarrassed him. He looked like a trapped rabbit. She'd never seen him this way before and wondered what was wrong. He was probably often in the hospital on Sundays to see patients, but it was unusual to see him in the administrative office corridor on weekdays, let alone a weekend when most doctors just looked in on patients and got out of the hospital as fast as they could. She said as much to him.

"Amanda, this McBride thing has me going crazy. I think the police think I killed him."

"Did you?" she asked.

He looked horrified. "Of course not," he practically shouted. "I was in the O.R. the whole time."

"So then what are you getting so upset for?" she asked. "That's about as airtight an alibi as you can have."

"But the police questioned me on Friday."

"They've talked to me *twice*," she said. "It's just routine." So she lied a little. With her it wasn't totally routine, but

Jonathan looked like such a basket case that she wanted to calm him down.

"I don't think so, Amanda. They talked to the O.R. nurses, too. It seems that I finished my last case about ten minutes before Ina found McBride dead."

"So?"

"So that means I could have had time to sneak down, kill McBride, and get back up there before anyone missed me. At least that's what the police think."

"Did they actually say that? Did they come out and accuse you?"

"Well, no, not exactly."

Bernstein looked so miserable that Amanda began to feel sorry for him. She also sensed an opportunity for herself.

"Jonathan, come on into my office for a minute. I want to ask you something, and I don't want to do it here, where the walls have ears."

Once inside her office with the door closed, she told Jonathan what the police had told her about McBride's liver cancer. "Did you know about it?" she asked.

"I do now," he said. "Because the police told me the same thing. Did they tell you about the pancake makeup and contact lenses?"

"Yes. Isn't it weird? Why do you suppose he went to such great lengths to hide the cancer? Where was he getting treated?" asked Amanda.

"I have no idea. It could have been any oncologist in the city. It doesn't matter now, anyway."

"You're right," said Amanda, "But I wonder why he was hiding it. I wonder," she mused aloud, "if it was just male ego. He didn't want to appear weak and sick in front of his colleagues. And he *certainly* wouldn't have gotten the promotion if anyone knew about the cancer."

"If he was as far gone as the police said he was, he wouldn't have lived to enjoy it even if he got it," said Bernstein. "And anyway, Amanda, that business about male ego is silly. No one would hide a fatal illness just out of vanity."

Amanda said nothing. Apparently Bernstein didn't understand the first thing about human nature, especially the male variety. "Living to enjoy it wasn't the point with McBride, I think," she said. "*Getting* it was everything. Seeing you and everyone else *not* get it was the point."

Again Bernstein looked skeptical, and again Amanda was convinced that his understanding of people didn't go beyond the state of their organs and blood vessels.

"Listen, Jonathan, I've got to run. I've got yard work to do before it gets dark. Don't worry about the police. They're having a hard time figuring out who killed McBride and are barking up every tree in the forest."

The surgeon still looked unhappy, but she could tell that he didn't know anything more than he said he did, and she didn't want to waste time listening to his fear. She said nothing about her talk with Lydia yesterday.

Amanda drove home, sorry she had gone to the hospital, sorry she had made the discovery about Eddie.

Don't you think you're letting your imagination run away with you? asked the voice. And have you stopped to think that the reason you couldn't find Frank Wolfman in the computer is that Ina was telling the truth? He and McBride never knew each other. There was no mysterious disease.

Then why did she tell the police about it? Why did she lie to them—or to me?

Good question, admitted the voice that didn't have everything figured out, after all. Let's forget it for a while and go home and attend to your husband and try to make up for the stunt you pulled last night.

Amanda grinned as she remembered what had made Ken so mad. She had gone to the dinner party given by the lobbyist who wanted something from Congress and needed Ken's help as a favor to her husband. She had made it clear when they got married that she was not going to play corporate wife and would not participate in his business activities that masqueraded as social functions. This was one of those functions, but she had agreed to go because he had asked nicely and because she wanted to spend Saturday night with her husband.

While they were dressing, she had wrapped her arms around him and said, "Don't forget that you owe me one. I didn't make you go to McBride's funeral this afternoon!"

"And I'm grateful," he said. "How do you think you'll want to collect the debt?" he asked.

She just chuckled and said, "I'll put my thinking cap on and surprise you!"

They had driven to the party, happy in each other's company, and had driven most of the way home in frozen silence. She knew she had embarrassed him, but the woman was such a dumb cluck and so pretentious that Amanda had not been able to resist putting her down.

"What a lovely dress," Arlene Derringer had said. She was the wife of one of the tycoons, and Amanda had met her a few times before and knew her to be about as boring as one could be and still be alive.

"Thank you," said Amanda. "Yours is simply smashing."

"Whose is it?" asked Mrs. Derringer.

"Huh?" said Amanda, although she knew exactly what the woman meant.

"Whose dress is it?"

Amanda saw Ken watching her and listening to the exchange. She looked at his face and could read nothing there. She winked at him but received no answering smile. He was warning her not to do it. She tried. She really tried.

"That color is just perfect for you," she said to Mrs. Derringer in an attempt to deflect what she knew was coming.

"Thank you, but I'm dying to know whose dress that is you're wearing."

"It's mine," said Amanda. "It was hanging in my closet, so I guess it's mine."

She saw Ken roll his eyes and the host put his hand over his mouth to keep from laughing. Everyone knew about Arlene Derringer's one-track mind.

"No, I mean who made it?"

Amanda knew perfectly well what she meant, but the woman was too dumb to know she was having her leg pulled.

"Who made it?" asked Amanda, all innocence. "Probably a few exploited, half-starved Korean women."

The host laughed outright, and Ken walked away, this time with plenty of expression on his face.

Mrs. Derringer looked confused, and Amanda felt guilty for taking advantage of her.

"I'm sorry," she said. "I didn't mean to tease you. It's not a designer dress—just a plain old thing off the rack at Woodie's."

Ken had barely spoken to her on the ride home, and when he did it was clipped and formal. She felt herself getting angry, too. He was treating her as if she needed to be punished, and she resented that. He was making a big deal over a little teasing and she said as much.

"These people are important to me, Amanda, and I can't have you insulting them."

"In the first place," she said, "*they* are courting *you*. Try to remember who had dinner at whose house. In the second place, everyone but you and Mrs. Derringer thought it was funny, and she's too dumb to know the difference. And in the third place"—her voice was heating up with righteous indignation now—"you knew when you married me that I'm a smart ass. You were attracted to that quality when you met me, and you still are. You're attracted to my ass, too," she added.

He softened a little. "I know I'm rigid," he said. "I know you were just joking. But . . . Hey, what are you doing?" he asked.

"I'm unbuttoning your shirt to see what it's stuffed with," she said.

This time he laughed and drew her close to him on the seat of the car, and only a short while later she thought of several very creative ways to collect her debt.

Eddie walked into the house late Sunday evening, so tired he could barely see straight. He hadn't gotten more than three hours' sleep from the time he had walked into J.F.K. Memorial early Saturday morning until now. And he had to be back at eight-thirty tomorrow for that damn infection-control meeting. On the way home he had hoped that Donald would be out. He was too tired, too frightened to deal with his lover's suspicions tonight. Maybe tomorrow, maybe next week. Maybe never. No luck. He heard the beat of rock music as he unlocked the door. It was well past the dinner hour, but when Eddie went to the kitchen for a glass of milk, he found Donald eating a hamburger and salad at the kitchen table, a book propped up next to his plate.

"Hi," said Donald. "Rough weekend? You look like hell."

"Thanks," said Eddie sarcastically. "It's always nice to have support from the home front."

Donald looked at his lover, blinked once, and went back to his book. He wasn't going to take that crap. He meant the remark to be sympathetic and Ed had completely misinterpreted it.

"I'm sorry," Eddie said. "The weekend was one of the worst ever. We had another code who didn't make it. And the police are hounding me."

Donald did not ask how it had gone with the police, and to avoid thinking about what he knew that meant, Eddie went over in his mind once more the three cardiac arrests of the past few days: the gut-wrenching effort to save the patients, the amount of drugs and electric current pumped into them to restart their hearts, the absolute futility of the effort much of the time, the monumental expense to the family or insurance companies. The patient this morning had been a woman, only forty-eight years old, who was dying of cancer. He had gotten to know her well, and knew that she had made peace with her pain and had finally accepted the inevitability of her death. But she had never asked to be left alone when the end came. She had never signed a living will, so the hospital had no choice but to try to shock her back to a few more days of pain and living decay. That's what hospitals were for, weren't they? But he now thought of the guilt he had felt as he applied the defibrillator paddles to her chest. He thought about how the two other doctors and nurses in the room were unable to look at each other. What they were doing was wrong, he thought. They all thought that, but they had no choice. They were bound to save lives, no matter how miserable, no matter how pain wracked.

Eddie began to cry. For what they had done to that woman this morning. For the ruined relationship with Donald. For allowing himself to be consumed by hate. For the irrevocable path he had chosen. For being so goddamn fucking tired.

Once again Donald led his lover to the couch. "We have to talk, Ed," he said. "Things can't go on like this."

"I know," said Eddie. "We will, I promise. But not now, Donald. Please not now."

"Yes, now. I have to know where I stand."

"Where *you* stand!" screeched Eddie, and Donald could see that his lover was coming apart. "Don't you ever think about anyone but yourself? I'm the one who's in this thing up to my neck and all you can think about is your own hide."

Donald had had enough. "Why shouldn't I think of myself?" he asked, angry now, too. "You seem to be a lost cause. Did you think of me when you stuck a knife in that bastard? Did you bother to tell me he was blackmailing you? All this time, all these months you were changing right before my eyes, when you stopped being my funny, lovable, smart, nice Ed. All the time I thought it was me. I thought you didn't love me anymore, that you didn't care about me.

"I wanted to talk to you about it, but you always seemed so tired and so upset about work. I decided to be considerate, to let you have your space, to work it out yourself. I thought you were worried about finding a place in a practice. I hoped it would be okay again when residency was over. I never thought about anybody *but* you," said Donald. "But now," he said, "now when I know the truth, you bet your sweet ass I'm thinking about myself, for a change. Why shouldn't I?"

Eddie said nothing. There was nothing to say. Silently he got up from the couch, went upstairs to the bedroom, and dialed Alice Bonner's number. He let it ring ten times and then gave up. "Out dancing on McBride's grave," he muttered to himself as he flopped onto the bed and closed his eyes.

Alice Bonner was not dancing on McBride's grave. She wasn't moving. Next to her body, sprawled on the bed, was an empty pill bottle and an overturned glass. On the night table was a half-empty bottle of vodka. The little plastic drugstore vial was labeled Valium, 10 mg. The prescribing physician was Leo McBride.

✦ ✦   10   ✦ ✦

"GOOD MORNING, LOUISE," said Amanda. "Did you have a nice weekend?"

"I did, thank you," replied the secretary. "And you?"

"Wonderful, thanks."

Amanda's weekend would have been better if she hadn't spent so much of it worrying, not only about which nurse would kill or maim the next patient—and the creative way she might choose to do it—but also about McBride's murder. On the way to work it occurred to her that if she could solve the murder, she could score brownie points with Townsend and he'd be less apt to fire her the next time there was a screwup.

One thing had nothing to do with the other, but it never hurt to fantasize. Besides, she *was* spending an awful lot of time thinking about McBride.

Admit it, she told herself, you want to catch the killer so that Eddie will be off the hook.

That's all very well and good, but you know damn well that not only is Eddie *on* the hook, he deserves to be. Why don't you butt out? Do you really want to be the one to prove he did it?

He didn't do it, Amanda insisted.

Yes, he did, and you know it. How else do you explain the way he's been behaving lately—especially since Wednesday?

But if he's guilty, why did he come to me the very next day and tell me that he didn't have an alibi, let alone admit that McBride had been blackmailing him so I'd be sure to notice that he had a good motive?

He wants to enlist your sympathy, to throw you off the scent.

Jesus, what am I, a bloodhound? Amanda asked the voice that knew just how nosy she was.

You might as well be. And while you're at it, get yourself a deerstalker hat. It'd look cute on you!

Oh, go to hell, she thought, laughing in spite of her sadness.

Louise followed Amanda into her office. "I have some news for you before you go off to the infection-control meeting," she said. "It's not good."

"Oh God," said Amanda. "Go ahead."

"Alice Bonner was brought into the emergency room last night. She tried to kill herself."

Amanda felt stopped in her tracks, her face frozen into a mask of disbelief. "Oh my God," she said. "Over being fired?"

"I don't know any of the details, Amanda. I just know that she took Valium and booze and almost succeeded. A friend of hers got worried and had the janitor in her apartment building break the door down. The friend said she worked here, didn't know she had been let go."

"How is she?" asked Amanda. "Is she conscious?"

"Just barely, I think. She's in I.C.U.," said Louise. "I'm sorry I had to be the bearer of such bad news first thing Monday morning."

"Don't be sorry," said Amanda. "I'm glad you told me. I'll go up to see her later. I just can't imagine anyone wanting to kill herself over being fired from a job when another will be so easy to get."

"Maybe it had something to do with McBride," said Louise. "Maybe she really loved him and couldn't live without him."

Maybe, thought Amanda. Then again, people kill themselves out of guilt—like after they've murdered someone.

Amanda sat at her desk for a long time, thinking about Alice and suicide, wondering what went through the beautiful nurse's mind just before she lost consciousness. She wondered if Alice looked as gorgeous near death as she did in life. She wondered what she looked like now, lying in the intensive care unit, hooked up to machines, maybe a ventilator, probably a urinary catheter, certainly intravenous lines. Her lips were probably dry and caked, her eyelids puffy, the backs of her hands maybe black and blue from . . .

The intercom buzzed. "Only five minutes till the meeting," said Louise.

"Thanks," said Amanda, shaking herself out of her morbid gloom. "I'm coming."

She gathered up a pad of yellow lined paper and the manilla folder that contained her budget proposal. She could work on it during the infection-control meeting. A whole morning of bacteria, viruses, and disgusting parasites was a bit much, and writing columns of figures could be disguised as taking notes.

However, it wasn't fifteen minutes before she realized that not only could she do the budget during the meeting, she could probably knock off a novel, so little did the consultant's talk deviate from the copious outlines and notes he had prepared and distributed.

J.F.K. Memorial had been having a problem with infections lately, and that was troublesome. It was bad enough that people came into the hospital sick; it was inexcusable that they should get sicker while they were there, especially if it was the hospital's fault. There was even a special name for the problem: nosocomial infections, those that originated in the hospital. It was embarrassing, it was dangerous, and one day it would result in a lawsuit or, at the very least, trouble with the Joint Commission on the Accreditation of Healthcare Organizations and the District of Columbia licensing board.

So Townsend had responded the way he usually did: he hired a consultant. And now the boardroom was packed not only with department heads but supervisors and staff representatives. There were four people from nursing there besides Amanda: three supervisors, one from each shift, and the president of the staff nurses' association. They all sat together.

The man droned on about things that should have been common sense to anyone working in a hospital: wash your hands, cover your mouth and nose when you sneeze, stay home if you're contagious, don't put the dirty bedpans next to the clean ones, if you contaminate a piece of sterile equipment, ditch it.

Only he wasn't saying it that way. He was using sixty-four-dollar words when two-dollar ones would do. Apparently he thought that at the price the hospital was paying him, he had to sound erudite. Amanda thought he just sounded pompous.

She glanced through the packet of materials and saw that not only was there a complete outline of this guy's talk, there were also reprints from leading journals about controlling hospital infections. She could read everything at her leisure, work up a plan of attack for the nursing department, meet with the head nurses and supervisors, and revise their current infection-control policy. Saralynn Baker, who worked a few evenings a week, had spent a year on a fellowship at the Johns Hopkins School of Hygiene, learning all about epidemics. Amanda would have dinner with her one day later in the week and pick her brain.

Now that she had decided what she would contribute to lowering J.F.K.'s high infection rate, she felt free to let her mind wander, and when she did, it homed in on murder. Eddie had not returned her call, although he must have known it was important. They hardly ever called each other at home. And now Alice Bonner had tried to kill herself. Did the police know about it? Should she call Lydia?

The hell with it, she thought. Let the police figure stuff out for themselves. I've done my bit.

At the coffee break she looked around for Eddie but didn't see him, and afterward she vowed to concentrate on what the consultant was saying. After all, she didn't know everything, and there was the off chance that he might say something useful.

He didn't, and from the palpable sigh of relief that swept down the conference table when the ordeal was over, she wasn't the only one to feel that Townsend had just dumped some big bucks down the bedpan hopper. But at least the article reprints would save her a lot of time in the library.

As she was gathering her papers together, she saw Townsend coming toward her with a grim, determined look on his face. "I need to see you in my office, Amanda—now."

Her heart lurched. *Now* what?

Townsend didn't spend his usual two minutes on small talk before he got down to it, and his face was deadly serious.

"Barbara Morrison called me today. It seems she was refused a job at Little River Hospital because you gave her a bad reference."

Amanda waited for him to finish, but he just sat and stared murderously at her. What response did he expect? She tried to be as noncommittal as she could.

"Yes?"

"Amanda, for God's sake, you know our policy!" Townsend was really mad. "We *never* give bad references. If the legal department finds out about this, they'll have my head."

Amanda couldn't believe what he was saying.

"David," she said through clenched teeth, not caring that he saw how angry she was. This was real cause for anger. "Are you saying that I'm supposed to give a good reference to a nurse who killed—*killed*, David—a patient because of stupidity, laziness, and goddamn criminal negligence? Are you *really* saying that, David? Because if you are . . ."

"Wait a minute, Amanda," he said in his most soothing voice. "She's gone from here. She's not our problem anymore. But she *could* be if we go around bad-mouthing her. She could sue us for libel. And, Amanda"—he was downright patronizing now—"don't you think we have enough legal problems as it is with this episode?"

When Amanda got really angry, she felt dizzy. Right now the room was spinning as though it would never stop.

Ken had taught her a trick that served two purposes: it controlled the dizziness and prevented her from giving in to the rage. She put her hand on the edge of the desk and pressed down as hard as she could while she stared intently at the painting on the wall behind Townsend. She inhaled and exhaled three times slowly. The intense concentration worked; the room steadied and she felt less enraged—but far from calm.

"David, I'm going to say something that you're not going to like, but I really mean it. I'm angry—really tearing mad—but this is not said in the heat of anger. I mean it.

"Barbara Morrison killed that patient as surely as someone killed Leo McBride. The intent may have been different, but the result was the same. She has to be punished as much as McBride's murderer does. And I'm going to see to it that she is. I'm going to get in touch with the D.C. licensing people and do my best to see that she never practices nursing again.

"And as far as references are concerned, I will continue to tell whoever asks *exactly* what happened. It's true she's not J.F.K.'s problem anymore. But she's nursing's problem. She's a menace to the profession—to the whole damn healthcare system. I refuse to have her future screwups on my conscience.

"I feel strongly about this, David, as strong as I've ever felt about anything. If you can't see it my way, let me know, and I'll resign."

There was dead silence. Amanda felt literally sick at the thought of losing her job, but behind the nausea lay the absolute calm of knowing she was doing the right thing. She waited and watched and knew that he knew she wouldn't budge.

But he tried. "Amanda, I'm sure we can work this out. I don't expect you to say that Morrison is a wonderful nurse, but—"

"No, David. Not this time. I don't agree with the hospital's policy of always giving a good reference. I never have. It only encourages mediocrity and rotten performance. But I've never disobeyed the policy. I've kind of weaseled my way around it a few times and let people read between the lines." She smiled and noticed a flicker of reciprocal feeling on Townsend's face. That gave her hope.

"But this time I can't do it. I won't do it." She sighed and searched his face, but it had returned to its usual passivity. Executive neutral, she called it.

"David, I don't want to resign. I like it here. You're a good boss, and I think that basically we have the best nursing care anyplace in the area. You know that. But I don't have a choice this time. It's a matter of principle—important principle."

She stood up. "Let me know your decision," she said, and left his office.

Don't run, she said to herself. Pretend the place is on fire. Don't panic. Don't run, but get the hell out of here as fast as you can.

When she had driven a few blocks into the quiet streets of

Georgetown, she found a cul-de-sac, turned off the motor, and sobbed for fifteen minutes.

When Amanda got back to her office, she felt better. In fact, she felt fine. She hated the thought of losing her job, but J.F.K. wasn't the only hospital in Washington, and Townsend would give her a fantastic reference. Besides, she was pretty sure she had called his bluff. He couldn't take the chance of not knowing how she would explain suddenly leaving a job she liked and was good at.

There were two applicants for Alice's old job to see before lunch, but since the first one hadn't arrived yet, she called the I.C.U. and found that Alice was only semiconscious and was not making much sense when she was awake.

"Is she going to make it?" she asked Frances Flannery, the charge nurse.

"Yeah, but there's no telling what she'll have between her ears when she finally wakes up," said Frances. "She did a good job on herself. This was no empty gesture, Amanda. If you like, I'll call you if she wakes up a little."

"I'd appreciate that, thanks," said Amanda.

"How was the infection guy?" asked Frances.

"He knows his stuff, but he didn't say anything we don't already know. I think nursing's problem is a matter of implementation, not ignorance—at least in the I.C.U.," she replied.

"You hit the nail on the head," said Frances, who ran the best intensive care unit Amanda had ever seen. She had a good crew of nurses doing one of the hardest jobs in the hospital, and Amanda had never seen a breach of sterile technique behind the swinging doors that opened into the weird world over which Frances Flannery presided.

Frances's nurses never screwed up, and that was generally true of intensive care units everywhere. Maybe it had to do with the constant stress and tension. Maybe it was being on edge all the time, waiting for the inevitable crises—for the monitor alarms that were always going off. Maybe they felt that if they let their guard down for an instant, it would be all over.

Maybe I ought to throw myself on Frances's mercy, she

thought. Maybe I can run the whole hospital like she runs the I.C.U.

"Think about how we can be even squeakier clean, and I'll get everyone together later this week or early next," said Amanda. "And let's just the two of us have lunch sometime soon."

"I'd like that," said Frances.

"Take special care of Alice. She's had a rough time."

As soon as Amanda said that, she realized she shouldn't have. It was undiplomatic. It made it seem as though Frances and the other nurses didn't take equally good care of everyone.

"I will, Amanda. And . . . I hope I'm not stepping out of line here . . ."

"Of course you're not," said Amanda, who hated it when people prefaced their remarks with something like that. It always meant that they were about to.

"What Alice did was *not* your fault," said Frances.

Amanda was silent for a moment, not knowing how to respond. The remark went way out into foul territory, but Frances thought she was being kind and thoughtful.

"I know it wasn't my fault, but I appreciate the concern," she finally said, hoping that every nurse in the hospital didn't feel the way Frances obviously did.

She still had a few minutes before the first interview, but instead of letting herself sink into gloomy thoughts over Alice, she took a fresh pad of paper and drew a line down the center. She chewed the inside of her cheek and soon came up with a list.

SUSPECTS	STRENGTH OF SUSPICION
Eddie Silverman	9-1/2
Alice Bonner	9
Cicely McBride	7 (? more)
Jonathan Bernstein	3

She wasn't sure why she thought Cicely might rate more than a seven, probably because Lydia had spilled the beans that she was unwilling to say where she was at the time of the murder, and because Glen had said that you always have to suspect the wife, especially the wife of someone like Leo McBride. Amanda didn't think Cicely had the nerve to commit a murder, but the jails were filled with violent people who didn't bother to think too much about what they were doing. If the murderer had thought things through carefully, he or she wouldn't have done it in a busy hospital where anyone might walk into McBride's office at any time. There was only one way out, so there was an enormous risk of someone seeing the killer enter or leave. Cicely may indeed have taken a risk like that, thinking that no one would consider it unusual for her to be in her husband's office.

The phone rang. It was Eddie. "If you're not too mad at me, could we go to Giovanni's for lunch?"

"Sure we can, Eddie. And I'm more puzzled than angry. I don't understand why you've been behaving so badly."

"I apologize, Amanda," he said. "I feel terrible about it, but let me explain at lunch, okay?"

"Okay," she said. "I have two interviews before I can eat. I'll page you when I'm ready."

Amanda hung up the phone and interviewed the two nurses. One came in chewing gum and had bloodred fingernails that looked like lethal weapons. She didn't have a ghost of a chance, and Amanda told her so.

The other had possibilities. She seemed smart and eager but had been out of college only since May and already wanted to leave her first job. She said the working conditions were terrible but wouldn't elaborate, and that made Amanda nervous. What was going on at Sacred Heart that this nurse wouldn't encounter here? Whatever it was, why wouldn't she talk about it, and why couldn't she cope with it?

"How would you feel if I called your head nurse and director of nursing for a reference?" asked Amanda.

"Oh, I don't think I'd want you to do that," replied the young nurse, Irene Ramirez.

"Well, then, how can I find out if you're good at your job?"

Ramirez looked blank. "I don't know. I never thought of that. I *am* good."

"You may very well be," replied Amanda, making up her

mind to scratch her from the list of contenders. "But I need an opinion other than yours."

"I went to a very good nursing school," said Ramirez.

"That counts for practically nothing," said Amanda. "Almost anyone can get through nursing school these days. I taught at a university with an excellent reputation for a number of years, and I know what goes into educating nurses. Not much of practical use, believe me. It's what you do out in the world of work that counts. It's how you function in the real world of taking care of sick, hospitalized people that interests me. If you can't do that, then I don't want you working at J.F.K. Memorial."

Ramirez stared at Amanda through remarkably huge eyes that reminded her of Alice's. Apparently this had never occurred to her before, and she didn't know what to say.

Amanda stood up. "Look," she said, "if you change your mind about my calling for references, let me know. Otherwise, I can't consider you for a position on our staff."

That would be the end of that one, she thought. She said as much to Eddie as they crossed the street and entered the fragrant delicatessen.

"It's not that I mind that they're beginners," she said. "One can always learn. What *really* bothers me is that they have no common sense. They don't seem to know how to *think*."

"Doctors are the same way," said Eddie. "And they have these monumental egos to complicate things—especially when they first get out of med school and think they know everything, when in fact, they don't know diddly."

"But you weren't like that," she said.

"But I'm a rare and precious creature," he replied with a smile.

"Well, precious, grab that empty table, and I'll get our lunch," said Amanda.

Amanda set the tray with their sandwiches and drinks on the table, and for the next few minutes, they concentrated on eating.

But after a few bites Eddie said, "I want to explain why I've been behaving like such a crazy man."

Amanda looked at him expectantly. She wanted to tell him

to think nothing of it, to say, "It's okay, Eddie, we all get in bad moods." She wanted to be done with it and get back to being friends, but this couldn't be brushed off, so she said nothing.

"As soon as I left your office on Thursday," he began, "I was sorry I had said what I did. Not that I told you about me"—here he lowered his voice to a whisper and looked around to make sure no one had heard—"but that I told you about the blackmail. Not only do I feel like a dope for submitting and not having the guts to tell McBride to go to hell, but now you probably think I killed him. I feel as though your opinion of me has gone down about a thousand notches.

"And what's more, the police have been grilling me. They think I did it, and they're out to get me. I'm scared shitless. I don't have an alibi, I had a perfect motive, and you hear stories all the time of the wrong man being tried and convicted and spending the rest of his life in prison."

"Did you do it?" she asked. "Did you kill McBride?"

"Boy, you sure don't pull any punches, do you?" he asked. "I thought we were friends."

"Did you?"

"No."

"Look me in the eye when you say it."

"I didn't kill him."

A lie. He looked straight at her, all friendly innocence, and she wanted to jam the sandwich down his throat.

"You don't believe me, do you?" he asked.

Now it was her turn to avoid his gaze. "You don't pull any punches yourself," she said, her attempt at lightening the atmosphere falling flat.

"Do you believe me?" Hard, insistent this time.

"No."

Eddie said nothing. There was nothing to say. He simply got up slowly and walked from the restaurant.

At dinner that evening Ken said, "You're awfully quiet, Amanda. Do you feel okay?"

"No, I feel terrible."

An expression of concern puckered his handsome face. "What's wrong? Do you want me to call a doctor?"

"No, sweetheart. It's not that kind of terrible. I feel awful about Alice Bonner and about Eddie."

She had told him about the nurse's suicide attempt and her lunch with Eddie. He had said all the right things, but she knew he didn't understand. She also knew that he thought she was crazy to get involved in something that was essentially none of her business. Now he tried to reassure her again, but she could tell that he had lost interest in the subject. "Honey, why don't you let the police take care of this? That's their job. I know you like to be in the middle of things, but this is eating you up inside. It's not worth it."

"That's not the point, Ken," she said, a little impatient with his failure to understand her. "The point is that I like Alice. She's a good nurse and, believe me, it's not easy to find competent nurses these days. Not only am I annoyed at having had to fire her, I'm sad that she felt she had to die over this.

"And if she did it for the reason I think, I'm sorry that she murdered McBride. I'm sorry to see that *any* woman would get so involved with such a sleazebag to the point that she couldn't live without him—and didn't want him to live without her. I'm sad that she was so weak."

"I thought you believe that your friend Eddie killed him," said Ken, genuinely puzzled.

"I do."

"But how could they both . . . ?"

"I don't know," she said, raising her voice until it sounded shrill even to herself. "You make it all sound so logical. I don't know what to think. All I know is that I feel terrible.

"I need a hug," she said. "Do you know anyone who could give me one?"

They stood wrapped in each other's arms for a long time, their eyes closed. She felt herself begin to relax in her husband's embrace and wished they were in bed under the warm comforter so she could let herself slide off into sleep. She felt too exhausted and drained even to finish dinner.

Ken too seemed to go off into a dreamlike state; she could feel it in his breathing. God, I could stay like this forever, she thought when all of a sudden they heard the clink of silverware on china.

"Goddamn that monster," said Ken as he clapped his hands loudly and Shadow jumped off the table, a piece of chicken in her mouth. "And she stole it from *my* plate!"

Amanda had to laugh. Ken always had perfectly well behaved dogs who responded to his every command. Cats were a new experience in living companions, and his attempts at disciplining Shadow, who, like all her species, just laughed at all attempts to do so, were comical exercises in human frustration.

"Poor baby," Amanda crooned, cutting a piece of her own chicken and feeding it to him. "Poor starving, put-upon corporate executive with a terribly miserable existence." She kissed him on the neck and bit his earlobe, keeping up a running commentary that became more and more erotic, until he pulled her down on his lap and she straddled him.

Two minutes ago, when he had shooed Shadow off the table, sex was the farthest thing from her mind, but now as she sat facing him, feeling his mounting excitement beneath her spread legs, she felt a rush of passion, of uncontrollable lust, wash over her, and she bent her face to his, parted his lips with her tongue, and gave herself over to rapidly mounting desire.

Eddie and Donald were doing something much less fun than what Amanda and Ken were doing.

"Look me straight in the eye and tell me you didn't murder McBride," said Donald.

This was the second time in less than a few hours that someone important to him had made that request, and again Eddie complied. "Does that make a difference?" he asked. "Do you believe me now?"

"Yes."

"Well, I don't believe you. I don't believe that you believe me. I think you think I did it," said Eddie.

"So where does that leave us?"

Eddie noticed Donald's glaring omissions. There were no protestations of faith in his innocence, no declarations of support, no offers to help. "It leaves us in a very bad position," he said. "It leaves us in a relationship that has no foundation of trust. It leaves me feeling as though you never trusted me, if you think I'm capable of killing someone."

Donald sighed heavily. "I don't know if you did it or not," he said. "I know, though, that *everyone*, me included, is capable of murder. I know you're a doctor; I know you're dedicated to healing. I know how squeamish you are when it comes to killing anything, even spiders and roaches. But I don't know that you didn't kill McBride. I'm sorry, Ed. I wish I could lie to you and pat you on the shoulder and tell you that everything will be okay. But I'm not sure it will."

Donald paused, seeming to think about what he had to say next. Then he took a deep breath. "The police came to my office today."

"What?" shrieked Eddie.

Finally Donald touched his lover. "Cool it, Ed. Do you want to hear what they said, or do you want to get hysterical?"

"Both," said Eddie, but he relaxed under Donald's hand and said in a defeated, resigned voice, "Go ahead."

"They wanted to know if I thought you had a motive for killing Dr. McBride, and I told them it was none of their business."

Eddie hung his head and closed his eyes. "That was the wrong answer, Donald." He paused. "How come they came to you? How did they find out we're lovers?"

"I don't know," replied Donald. "How do the police find out anything? And why was it the wrong answer? What was I supposed to say? You *do* have a motive. At least I didn't tell them that. You ought to be grateful for that."

"Grateful!" screamed Eddie, his voice exploding into venomous rage. "Grateful! You shit! You fucking shit! You're going to send me to the gas chamber, and you expect me to be grateful. Fuck you. Just fuck yourself to death."

He wrenched free of Donald's hand, still on his arm, and leaped to his feet, breathing heavily, his face suffused with rage. He stood over his lover wanting to kill him, wanting to punch and kick and scratch and bite and slap. His hands tightened into fists, and it was then that Donald felt real fear.

$$+ + \quad 11 \quad + +$$

AMANDA STOOD UNDER the shower, letting the water beat down on her back, thinking about last night. She felt herself blush.

Good God, she thought. Fucking at the dinner table. What a brazen hussy!

But she smiled through the blush, remembering how she and Ken had enjoyed the spontaneous burst of passion, how he had held on to the edge of the table to keep the chair from tipping over backward.

And when she had gotten home from visiting Alice, she was horny again. She had been consumed by wave after wave of lust that Ken could hardly keep up with.

"I don't know where that all came from," she gasped when she was finally satisfied. But she did know. It came from the nearness of death, and it happened every time.

She remembered when her favorite aunt had died. That was the most powerful it had ever been. She was in graduate school then, and when she came home from the funeral, she called a man she was dating and treated him to a night of the most frenzied sex he had ever had. It also happened when patients she especially liked died, although in those cases the urge wasn't as strong.

It had frightened her for a long time because it seemed so inappropriate, so unseemly to take off mourning clothes and hop into the sack.

"But, Amanda," a psychiatrist had said, "it's natural to want to reaffirm the fact that you're alive when you've just witnessed the evidence that you won't always be. And what more life-affirming thing is there than sex? What else makes you feel more alive?"

It had seemed like a rational explanation then, and she had accepted it. Now she understood it to be much more than that. It was what Dr. Schneider had said, but it was also the ultimate closeness, the physical contact, the feel of her own living flesh responding to her most elemental needs. It was good.

She turned off the shower, and as she dried her hair, put on her makeup, and got dressed, she thought about Alice Bonner.

After finishing her so deliciously interrupted dinner, she had gone to the hospital and taken the elevator up to the fifth-floor intensive care unit. Alice was lying there as Amanda had imagined. There was, thank goodness, no ventilator, which meant that Alice was breathing well on her own. But she had an intravenous line running into a vein on the back of her hand, and a plastic bag of urine hung from the bottom of the bed. Amanda looked at it and saw with satisfaction that the drip of urine was steady and plentiful. At least she hadn't damaged her kidneys.

She sat on a chair next to the bed and said, "Alice, can you hear me?"

The beautiful nurse opened her eyes. "Yes," she said.

"How are you feeling?" asked Amanda.

"Okay."

"Is there anything I can get for you?"

"No, thanks."

This was *not* the same Alice Bonner who had spilled her guts in Amanda's office Friday morning. The change was striking, but Amanda couldn't tell if it was emotional, physiological, or a little of each.

The charge nurse whom Amanda spoke to when she first came into the unit said that the neurologist had found no evidence of brain damage, and Amanda could see for herself that the large, dark eyes were clear and alert. Alice's *brain* seemed fine—but her *mind* might be a different story.

"Do you want to talk about anything?" Amanda asked. She felt increasingly uncomfortable, as if she were an intruder.

"No."

"Did you kill Leo McBride?"

Instantly Amanda's conscience bawled her out. How *could* you? How can you be so insensitive? Alice made no reply. She simply stared at Amanda out of those incredible eyes that were now swimming in tears.

"Well, did you?" asked Amanda again.

"Leave me alone," she muttered, and turned her head away.

She doesn't want you around, said the voice that sometimes had to point out the obvious. She can't face you, so leave her be.

So Amanda had left and gone home to make more love with her husband. Now, driving to work this morning, she was more confused than ever. Did Alice or Eddie do it? They both *acted* guilty. Or did someone else . . . like Cicely McBride? What was her role in all this?

Even as Amanda was thinking about her, Cicely was becoming increasingly worried. The police were hounding her.

They had been back yesterday afternoon, again demanding to know where she was while Leo was being murdered. She obviously couldn't tell them, so she maintained the story about being home alone. And just as obviously they didn't believe her.

"I've been a police officer for twenty-two years, Mrs. McBride," said Lieutenant Bandman. "Fifteen of them as a detective, and I've investigated everything from first-degree murder to the theft of a pair of earrings. I know when someone is lying. And you're lying now."

"Look, Lieutenant—"

"No, you look," interrupted Bandman, "even Simonowitz here thinks you're lying, and she's not nearly as cynical as I am."

Cicely glanced over at Lydia, who put a regretful expression on her face, as if to say, "I want to believe you, Mrs. McBride, but I just can't," and nodded sadly.

"I think you killed your husband. I'm not sure yet how you did it, but you did it. My guess is that you went to the hospital that morning—after all, no one would think twice about seeing McBride's wife going into her husband's office—and slipped a scalpel into his throat."

"But you said—"

"Let me finish, Mrs. McBride. I know I said that the scalpel didn't kill him. That's true. The *scalpel* didn't do it. It was the poison that you put on the blade that did it."

"That's ridiculous. I don't know anything about poison. I told you, I never left the—"

"And I told *you* not to interrupt," said Bandman, very low, very grim. "I'm going to get a court order to exhume your husband's body, and the medical examiner is going to tear it apart—cell by cell if he has to—and we're going to find that poison.

"You had the best of motives: a woman scorned, to borrow a phrase from old Willie the Bard. You knew about some of your husband's lovers, Mrs. McBride, but by no means all of them. We've done quite a bit of checking around, and I'm sorry to be so crude, but the great doctor went after anything in skirts. If he were a woman, people would call him a nymphomaniac. My father had a nasty expression for what your husband was: a whoremaster."

Cicely sprang up from the couch, her face suffused with rage and humiliation. In a flash she stood in front of Bandman's chair, and he caught her wrist just as it swung forward to strike his face.

He gripped her wrist hard enough to hurt, hard enough to leave red marks, until he felt her muscles relax and she capitulated.

"Assaulting a police officer is not an easy rap to beat, Mrs. McBride. Now, sit down and tell me where you were last Tuesday."

Bandman was wrong about one thing. She *did* know about Leo's sex life, every dirty detail, and she took a kind of grim satisfaction in keeping score. She knew every time he started an affair with a new woman, and she knew when it was over. They were always over very quickly. Sometimes she even made a point of meeting the women, and sometimes she didn't have to became she already knew them. Some of the women took it badly when the great Leo McBride dumped them—she knew what Alice Bonner had done less than an hour after she had done it—and some were philosophical about it. But few refused him.

But her little victory over Lieutenant Bandman wouldn't help her now. She still couldn't tell the truth, and she didn't trust Seth Morgan, but she had to use him as an alibi on the off chance that he would keep his word. If he didn't, she was in worse trouble than if she had stuck to the story that she had been home alone. It occurred to her that she might be arrested, and wondered if she should get a lawyer. Wouldn't that look suspicious?

"Okay, Mrs. McBride. Have it your way," said Bandman in a resigned, sad voice. "You're making my job harder, and it seems a waste of taxpayer money, but Simonowitz and I will start questioning every one of your friends, relatives, and acquaintances. Eventually someone will tell us something about your whereabouts. We're very stubborn and persistent."

"And," said Lydia, speaking for the first time, "this is my first murder case, and it'd be a big feather in my cap if I could be in on solving it. Catching the killer of Dr. Leo McBride would go a long way toward my getting another promotion."

Cicely made a decision then. She told them about the massage at Seth Morgan's "studio," and when they asked why she had been reluctant to say so in the first place, she hemmed and hawed and stammered and blushed and couldn't find the words.

"Oh, I get it now," said Bandman, "a massage parlor for women. Well, well, equal opportunity has finally come of age."

Now, thinking about it on the following Tuesday morning, Cicely was outraged once again at the disgusting Lieutenant Bandman, making that snide remark, enjoying her embarrassment. Then she wondered if she had made an error. Bandman would not have given the massage another thought—that is, if he believed her and if Seth had come through for her—if she hadn't acted like a schoolgirl.

If she hadn't lost her temper, he wouldn't have attached any sexual significance to it. He was sophisticated enough to know that rich ladies had massages the way they had designer clothes, expensive haircuts, and fur coats. It was nothing remarkable. If only she hadn't given in to their badgering. Maybe she *ought* to get a lawyer. At least he'd prevent her from making a fool of herself again.

She couldn't tell if the detectives had believed her story. Probably not, judging from the way she had been behaving. She had lied so much that even *she* wouldn't believe her now. She was dying to know what Seth had said and was positive the police had spoken to him by now, although he hadn't returned the four or five messages she'd left on his machine.

Cicely decided not to take any more chances. There was no way she was going to spend the rest of her life locked up in some dirty jail cell after she had gone to so much trouble. So she reached toward the phone and dialed the number she had committed to memory a long time ago.

Amanda had two hours to go before the monthly department heads meeting, so she filled her coffee cup from the pot near Louise's desk and settled down to read the packet of materials she had gotten at the infection-control meeting the day before.

There were so many pathogenic microbes floating around that when one thought about it, it seemed almost impossible to protect patients from becoming infected by at least some of them. There were *Streptococcus* and *Staphylococcus*, the ubiquitous *E. coli*, and about a zillion different viruses. In fact, short of putting all patients, visitors, staff, and every object that came in contact with them through the huge walk-in steam autoclaves, there was no way to banish all microorganisms.

"But we can at least give the patients a fighting chance," she mumbled as she opened the thick loose-leaf notebook to the section on infection-control policies and began to draft notes for changes and improvements. She wrote down what occurred to her immediately and then decided to let it simmer for a while in her brain. She'd talk to Saralynn Baker and get more ideas.

Then, in the last half hour before the meeting, she leafed through some of the reprints of journal articles. Most of them were what she expected: retrospective studies of nosocomial infections, not much of practical value as far as nursing was concerned. But she'd read them all eventually, just in case.

She was about to stuff them into her briefcase when the one

on the bottom of the pile caught her interest. It was about a microorganism she had never heard of: aflatoxins.

What do you know she thought glumly, a new bug to worry about.

But aflatoxin turned out not to be bug, but a mold that grew on corn and peanuts. As she read more of the article, she found that it was a scientific report from the Department of Agriculture to the Food and Drug Administration about acceptable levels of these toxins in food. She saw quickly that it had nothing to do with hospital infections and was about to toss it into the wastebasket when she changed her mind and put it in the folder along with the rest.

Amanda slipped into a seat next to Ruth Sinclair, the head of the dietary department, at the board table. This morning they were going to talk about plans for the snowstorms that occasionally paralyzed the nation's capital.

"We can't keep meeting like this," said Ruth.

"I know," said Amanda. "I've about had it with meetings, too. But I think this will be short."

"I know what my department is going to do if it snows," said Ruth.

"What?"

"Let the patients starve."

Amanda snorted with laughter. "At least give them IV fluids!"

"Okay," conceded Ruth. "But only two flavors: rutabaga and squash."

Amanda pulled the aflatoxin article out of her folder. "Did you get this in your packet yesterday?"

"No, but it looks fascinating," said Ruth with disgust as her eye ran down the first few paragraphs.

Amanda shrugged. "He probably put it in by mistake."

She was right about the meeting. It was mercifully short, and she was back in her office in less than a half hour. Then for reasons she didn't understand—and didn't bother to question—she turned on her computer and logged onto Medline, the National Library of Medicine's computerized index service.

The computer asked her if she wanted books or journal articles; she indicated the latter. Then it asked her to type in her request in plain language. AFLATOXINS, she typed. The machine hummed for a few seconds and then told her that there were more than 8,000 citations.

"Jesus," she said. "All this about something I've never heard of till now. And this doesn't count the books written about it and the chapters in other books."

Luckily she knew how to work the computer system so she could narrow down the choices. She asked for the citations in English and decided to go back only ten years, even though the FDA had been involved for more than twenty.

Even so, the computer told her there were several hundred articles written about this toxin, which, she was beginning to see, wasn't as obscure as she had thought.

Amanda decided to scroll through the citations and look at some of the titles. In the world of scientific and medical publishing, you could tell by the title exactly what the article was about—and for this she was grateful. She found titles such as "New Action Level for Aflatoxins," "Aflatoxin Control: Past and Present," "Regulation of Mycotoxins in Food" (Amanda looked up *mycotoxin* in her medical dictionary and found that it was a poison derived from mold; mycology is the study of molds), and "Aflatoxin as a Cause of Primary Liver-Cell Cancer in the United States: A Probability Study."

There was enough reading here for weeks, but she didn't know what she was looking for because she wasn't sure *why* she was looking. She went back to the beginning and selected a few of the more intriguing titles and requested the computer to print out the abstracts for her. As she waited for the printer to finish, she continued to scroll through the titles, not paying full attention.

Amanda tore the paper off the printer and stuffed it in her pocket. "I'll be in the library if you need me," she said to Louise. There was no one in the medical library at that hour of the morning, and Amanda had free access to the bound volumes of medical journals. She took the computer printout from her pocket and pulled some of the big books off the shelves. She noted that most of the articles on the printout referred her to journals more esoteric than the ones J.F.K. Memorial subscribed to. If she wanted them, she'd have to go to the National Library of Medicine a few miles up Wisconsin Avenue.

As Amanda read, she took a few notes, but it soon became clear that aflatoxins were an agricultural, not a medical, problem. If the Department of Agriculture found that a batch of produce was adulterated by more than twenty parts per billion of aflatoxins, then it was considered unfit for either human or animal consumption.

This is one hell of a poison, she thought.

In fact, all the articles said in no uncertain terms that aflatoxins were the most potent carcinogens known to man, and in countries where people ate a lot of aflatoxin-contaminated food, the incidence of liver cancer was unusually high.

Liver cancer!

There it was again. Liver cancer was rare enough for Amanda to be surprised to come across it twice in one week. She took a big medical reference book off the shelf and found that it constituted only 2.5 percent of all cancers in the United States. In comparison, lung cancer is between 15 and 30 percent, cancer of the pancreas is 5 percent of all malignancies, and cancer of the prostate is 17 percent of all cancers in men.

Amanda read further and confirmed that not only is liver cancer extremely rare (although it strikes more men than women), Leo McBride was a highly unlikely candidate—unless he was hiding a lot more than the disease.

Primary cell carcinoma of the liver, she read, is most common in people who have had cirrhosis of the liver and/or chronic hepatitis B. And right there in the sixteenth edition of *Cecil's Textbook of Medicine*, a redoubtable text if ever there was one, she found the following in the very first paragraph of the section on liver cancer:

"Epidemiologic evidence has also suggested a link between hepatocellular carcinoma and ingestion of aflatoxins, mycotoxins produced by *Aspergillus flavus*, a mold that can grow in warm, moist areas and contaminate peanuts and stored grains."

So either McBride was the victim of a rare fluke, or he got the disease in one of three ways: as a result of cirrhosis, which is common in alcoholics and almost never seen in anyone else; from chronic infection with hepatitis B, most often seen in promiscuous male homosexuals; or from aflatoxin poisoning, which since 1965 is almost impossible in the United States.

McBride couldn't have been an alcoholic. He was surrounded every day by sharp medical eyes, and someone would have noticed. He *could* have secretly been a promiscuous homosexual (and would have felt guilty about it and thus needed to blackmail Eddie for that very reason), but it was unlikely that he had chronic hepatitis B. Someone would have caught on. Although, Amanda had to admit, no one seemed to know about his liver cancer.

Amanda closed the books and sat at the library table chewing her pencil. What did she know now that she didn't know before? What did all this mean? Nothing, really. She didn't *know* a thing, but she was surrounded by coincidences too strong to brush aside.

She went back to her office and called a man she had dated until she had fallen so in love with Ken that the possibility of other romantic liaisons had been obliterated.

"Well, well, Amanda Knight! What a treat to hear your voice!" said Roland Armstrong. "How have you been? Changed your mind about the big-time corporate executive and want to fall back into my arms?" he asked.

"I've been very well," she said. "And so is my marriage. I don't want to fall into your arms, but I *would* like to have lunch with you—strictly business," she said in a hurry so he wouldn't get any ideas.

"Strictly business, eh?" said Roland skeptically. "Are you going into the virus business? Don't you have enough germs over there in that hospital of yours?"

Roland Armstrong was a noted and much-published research virologist at Johns Hopkins University in Baltimore and had been one of the people responsible for proving the connection between one of the herpes viruses and cervical cancer. Amanda had met him many years ago when she was a graduate student in women's studies, and she had interviewed him for a paper on cervical cancer. She had no idea now what that paper was about.

"Yes, thanks. We have plenty of germs—more than we know what to do with. What I want to talk about is something else, but I can't discuss it on the phone. Are you free for lunch tomorrow? I don't mind driving to Baltimore."

"Sure, come on up. Meet me at Ikaros on Eastern Avenue at noon. Do you remember where it is?"

"How could I forget?" she asked, smiling. "How many bowls of egg-and-lemon soup did we scarf down there?"

"Not nearly enough," he said. "I'll see you tomorrow."

Amanda ate lunch in the hospital cafeteria with Ruth Sinclair and two nursing supervisors and spent the rest of the afternoon touring the hospital. She did this periodically without notifying anyone first. It was the only way she could tell what kind of care the nurses were really giving the patients.

If she and the quality-control people went over the charts of discharged patients, they saw *what* had been done for patients—how many injections, how many bed baths, how many enemas—but they couldn't tell *how* these things had been done. Did the nurses smile? Did they do everything they could to make the patients comfortable? Did they answer call bells within thirty seconds?

That last was Amanda's strict rule, one the nurses hated. They thought it was unreasonable, and she had a hard time convincing them that she meant it. One day during a head nurses' meeting she had gotten exasperated.

"Close your eyes," she had told them. "I mean it," she said when they looked at her in puzzlement.

They complied, although she could feel their resistance. "Now, imagine that you're home with your husband or lover or mother or someone you care about, and that someone has just collapsed and is writhing on the floor in agony. Now, I want you in your mind to dial nine-one-one to get help. On my signal, raise your hand when you think thirty seconds have passed, and all the time you're listening to the phone ring, watch the one you love gasp in pain and beg for help."

She had said, "Now," and watched their faces. Most were

Great! Thanks a lot, thought Amanda. I finally went a whole fifteen minutes without thinking about my ultimatum to Townsend. I'm *so* glad you reminded me.

The thought that she might not have the opportunity much longer made Amanda slide out of the snack bar booth and take the elevator up to the operating room suite. She found Dr. Jack Durango in his office with his feet on the desk, his eyes drooping over a medical journal.

"Hi, Amanda," said the chief of anesthesiology. "Long time no see."

"Hi, Jack."

"Sit down. Want a cup of coffee?"

Amanda glanced at the pot on the windowsill and wrinkled her nose. "No, thanks, Jack. How long has it been since you washed that out?"

"Wash?" he asked incredulously. "Why would I wash it? I just made that coffee two days ago. It's strong stuff. In another day or so we can use it for skin preps!"

They laughed. Jack had a deliciously disgusting sense of humor.

"What can I do for you, Amanda? Want to take a fast nap?"

"Not the kind of nap *you* have in mind," she replied. Jack was famous for getting his patients down to phase IV anesthesia—a hair away from death, all muscles paralyzed, all systems slowed to the barest minimum—faster than anyone else in the hospital. If Amanda ever needed an operation, she wanted Jack Durango to be her gas passer.

"But I want to know how you could put someone into a really fast *permanent* nap."

That got his full attention. "Want to knock someone off?" he asked. "Am I allowed to know who?"

"Well, now that I've gotten rid of McBride, I thought I could take care of some of the others," she replied. Make a joke out of it and maybe he wouldn't ask too many questions. "I need something really fast and powerful."

"You've come to the right place," he said, and was off and running, describing the anesthesiologist's pharmacopeia of incredibly potent drugs without which modern surgery would be impossible.

There was Anectine, succinylcholine chloride, one of the most powerful skeletal muscle relaxants known. Only one milligram per kilogram of body weight of this superpotent drug was needed to stop the functioning of every voluntary muscle in the human body. Pavulon, pancuronium bromide, was just as good; even better because it took only about a hundredth as much to have the same effect. Within forty-five seconds all neuromuscular control was knocked out—a giant body black-out that took the administration of yet other drugs to reverse.

If all the O.R. personnel decided to take even a short coffee break after a patient had been given enough Anectine or Pavulon to suppress neuromuscular reactions when the surgeon began carving him up, it would be curtains. These drugs were powerfully fast and dangerous and were to be used only by skilled anesthesiologists, and then only after a patient had been put to sleep. Either one would be a perfect murder weapon in the hands of a person who knew how to use it.

"Then we have something in a different class, but even more effective in its own way," said Jack. He sounded like a salesperson in ladies' lingerie discussing the structural differences in brassieres. He was so thoroughly engrossed in describing the arsenal that he had forgotten that it was *people* killing they were talking about.

"Fentanyl is newer than some of the others and it lends itself easily to manufacturing analogs, like sufentanyl and lofentanyl, which is why it's so popular as a recreational drug."

"*Recreational?*" screeched Amanda. "Isn't it an anesthetic?"

"Yeah," replied Jack. "But you know druggies. They'll take anything to get a fast rush."

He explained that fentanyl, a fast-acting anesthetic, is a hundred times as strong as morphine and the analogs are about 3,000 times as strong. "It's not botanically based, like codeine and heroin and morphine, Amanda," he said, "so that makes it much more pure—and much more addictive, because it has a bigger wallop. You get *real* high *real* fast."

"And could a big enough dose kill you *real* fast?" she asked.

"Dead as a doornail," he replied, grinning. "Stiff as a carp."

+   +   +

Amanda drove home through the gathering twilight thinking about what Jack had told her. The killer *could* have used one of those drugs on McBride. It would have been fast, neat and efficient. He would have had to have access to them, though. She flashed back to her conversation with Jonathan Bernstein on Sunday. Maybe he *should* be worried about the few minutes' discrepancy between the time he actually finished his cases and the time he said he did.

Amanda, if he did it, why would he tell you that the police were suspicious? asked the voice that always had to make things come out right.

For the same reason that Eddie told me, she thought. To deflect suspicion by disarming me. Maybe everyone sees me as their nice Aunt Sadie whom they can moan to and not have things come slamming back at them.

Well, they're wrong this time, aren't they? asked the voice grimly as Amanda thought about McBride. The hospital wasn't the same without him—no more "you won't believe what the bastard did this time" stories. Although the medicine practiced at J.F.K. Memorial was as good, a certain edge had gone off, leaving the residents and attending physicians more relaxed than they should be. The hospital would get fewer VIP patients, and that would hurt revenue and eat into its glossy image. Perhaps McBride as a person wouldn't be missed, but his presence as a medical force would.

But still, that was no reason to get involved in his murder investigation. Why was she planning to chase up to Baltimore in the middle of a workday on the strength of only the faintest hunch? And why couldn't she stop thinking that there was a connection between McBride's death and aflatoxins?

Don't forget, she reminded herself, he didn't *die* of liver cancer. He just had it. And where on earth would McBride have eaten contaminated peanuts?

Well, that's why you're going investigating tomorrow, said the voice of practicality. Because you're a nosy busybody. You ought to learn to mind your own business.

You mind *your* own business, she said as she pulled the car into the driveway.

12

AMANDA FOUND A parking space only a block away from the Greek restaurant in Baltimore and checked her hair and makeup in the rearview mirror before getting out of the car. She knew she looked good in a speckled brown tweed skirt, the soft blue cashmere cowl-neck sweater that gave her a look of sweet vulnerability, and a brown corduroy blazer with an old-fashioned brooch pinned to the lapel.

She fed the meter and walked toward the restaurant, waving to Roland, who was coming from the opposite direction.

"You look great," they said in unison, and then laughed as sparks of electricity flew between their hands clasped in greeting.

"The same old electricity!" Again they spoke as one, and again they laughed.

Amanda made a sweeping bow and held out her hand, indicating that the floor was his.

"It's good to see you," Roland said. "I've missed you."

She thought fast. She didn't want this to turn into a lunch filled with reminiscences, and she didn't want him to think she was interested in starting something with him. Although his blond, bearded good looks were not lost on her—and she didn't miss the eyes that swept approvingly over her—she knew Roland's tendency to turn maudlin, and wanted to avoid that.

She decided to ignore the last remark. "Let's eat," she said. "I'm starving. Then I want to pick your brain about something."

They gave their order to the waiter, and Amanda sipped a cup of thick Greek coffee.

"But first," said Roland, "tell me how you are. Really."

He wanted to hear that she was miserably unhappy with Ken, that she was sorry she had broken off their relationship, and that she missed him as much as he obviously missed her.

"I'm fine, Roland. In fact, I'm terrific. I like my job, even though it's a pain in the ass sometimes . . . and I love my husband even though *he's* a pain in the ass sometimes. I'm happy. Are you?"

"I guess so," he replied with a sigh. "I have everything I say I want. My grant was renewed for another five years. I'm dating two nice women. Martha had a litter of beautiful pups, and I'm going to breed her again in the spring. So I'm happy." He smiled.

Amanda didn't believe him, but she didn't want to go on a soul-searching trip with him. They had been down that road too many times, and she no longer cared.

"Good, I'm glad," she said, spooning up the rich egg-and-lemon soup. "Now . . . here's what I need to talk to you about. First, can I count on you not to tell a soul about this?"

"Cross my heart and hope to die," he said, and she knew he meant it.

"You know that Leo McBride was murdered, don't you?"

"I think I heard it on the news," he replied. "Last week, wasn't it? I didn't pay much attention. You know how I am."

"I do indeed," she replied dryly. "Anyway . . ." Her voice turned brisk as she told him everything. There was no reason not to. Roland listened attentively, eating mechanically and probably not tasting any of it. But she could see he was interested. There was nothing Roland loved so much as an intellectual puzzle, and he had great intuition, as do all first-rate scientists.

"I have this incredibly strong feeling that aflatoxins are involved somehow. I don't see how McBride got liver cancer any other way. But I can't figure out how he was exposed to it."

"Did he travel a lot to places that don't do much about food and water inspection?"

"I don't think so," she said. "They had a house on Martha's Vineyard or Nantucket—I always get the two confused—and they went there for a month or so in the summer. McBride wasn't too interested in expanding his cultural horizons."

"Did he do any research work? Did he spend time in labs?"

"Not that I know of," she said. "By the way," she added, her little red flag of intuition flapping wildly in the breeze of an improbable idea, "could you synthesize aflatoxins in a lab? I mean, I know the mold grows on corn and peanuts and stuff in the field, but could you make a synthetic aflatoxin in a lab?"

"That's not really the point, Amanda," Roland explained. "You don't need to make a synthetic substitute. You can grow the stuff anywhere that conditions are favorable. And in a lab you can *make* the conditions favorable. You don't need a field of crops to do it. Depending on how much you want, a few petri dishes would do the trick."

"How exactly could you do that?" she asked, her excitement mounting.

"It's easy for someone who knows what he's doing. You just take some growth medium, say polished rice for example, and then you sterilize it."

"You mean just plain old, ordinary rice?"

"Yep, right off the supermarket shelf," replied Roland. "But you'd have to sterilize it first so it doesn't get contaminated with stuff you don't want. Then you mix it with water, usually half and half, add the mold culture, keep it in a sterile environment at around room temperature or a little warmer—I don't know the exact temperature—and let it grow. In five or six days you have a nice little mold garden going."

"But how do you get the original mold culture to get it started?" she asked.

"You buy it."

"But surely not at the supermarket?"

"No, but not far from it. Just about any large scientific-supply company has a good selection of molds. The one you're talking about, *A. flavus*, might not be quite as common, but you just look through the supply-company catalogs until you find out who sells it."

"Can just anybody buy it?" she asked. She was incredulous at how easy this sounded.

"Well, probably not anybody off the street. But most any

scientist who works for a reasonably reputable lab. And I suppose anyone else who wants to buy it under the table. I don't know the regulations on this, Amanda, but there may be something about getting a permit to buy some of these potentially toxic things. But any big institution would have all the right documents. That is, *if* one needed a permit."

Amanda thought for a minute. She hadn't tasted much of her meal, either. "Okay," she said, "so now you have this glob of mold growing in your petri dishes. How do you convert it to aflatoxins?"

"It's not really a matter of conversion. Aflatoxin is a metabolite—you know what a metabolite is, Amanda. It's a product of a substance that has been chemically changed by a living organism. So aflatoxin is a kind of by-product of this mold. And by the way, there are lots of different types of aflatoxins, some more dangerous than others, I think. I don't know too much about this, Amanda. I'm a virus man, myself. But if you want to know more, I can give you the name of someone to call."

"You're doing great," she said. "So how do you make the mold produce a metabolite?"

"You don't make it. It does it by itself. That's like saying, how do you make us digest this lunch? We just do it because that's what we do. *A. flavus* makes aflatoxin because that's what *it* does."

"Then how can you get the aflatoxins out? Or separate them, or whatever?"

"If you really want all the fine details, you'd have to talk to a chemist, but what you want to do is extraction or separation chemistry. That is, you want to get the essential fractions out of this mess. There are a lot of ways. You can crystallize it or filter it, I guess, but the easiest, I think—now remember, Amanda, I'm not a chemist."

"That's okay," she said. "Just keep talking." She was scribbling furiously on a small notepad as Roland talked.

"I think the easiest method is some type of chromatography."

"Huh?"

"Chromatography is a separation process; actually there are

several different types, but they're all based on the principle
that you want to redistribute the molecules of a mixture—say
the *A. flavus* mold—so that one type of molecule is separated
from all the rest. And you keep doing this in sequence so that
eventually the mixture is separated into all its molecular
components."

"So it's like passing the mixture through increasingly fine
filters?" she asked, completely at a loss.

"No, because we're not talking only about the size of
molecules, but their shape, and how tightly packed together
they are. The process depends on types of molecules. You have
to dissolve the mixture in a solvent. I don't know what the
mold is soluble in, maybe chloroform or alcohol. Again, you'll
have to ask a chemist. Then the solvent will *ad*sorb a type of
molecule, which will separate it from the rest of the mixture.

"You can also do it by mixing the whole mass in a solvent,
whatever one is appropriate, and then heat it until it boils, and
extract the crude *A. flavus* from the mold mass by passing it
through filter paper and then centrifuging it. Then you mix it
with an adsorbent material—whatever aflatoxins will adhere
to— and get it out that way. Are you catching any of this?"

"Sort of," she said. "I understand enough to know that it can
be done in a lab. How complicated is all this?"

"Oh, for an experienced chemist, it's a breeze." Roland
snapped his fingers for emphasis. "You need the right equipment, of course, but chromatography is real basic—like giving
shots for a nurse."

"Is it dangerous?"

"Well, they're called afla*toxins* for a reason. They're poisons. But having said that, don't think they're poisons like
cyanide or arsenic. Those are chemicals; these are toxins:
they're live things. *Salmonella* and *Clostridium botulinum* are
also toxins, and you know what they can do. Toxins can kill
you, all right, but they're not chemicals."

"How much aflatoxin can kill you?" she asked.

"I have no idea. You'd have to look up drug studies and see
what the LD-50 is for animals. And you'd have no way of
knowing that it would be the same in humans."

Amanda knew that LD-50 was the dose at which half the

experimental animals died when given a chemical or biological. Thus do researchers begin to understand what a substance can do. LD-50 trials are among the first in a long series of experiments in the search for a new drug, and of course, just because an animal didn't die, it doesn't mean the substance is free of side effects, some of which can be about as bad as death itself.

Years of painstaking research on animals, and then humans, followed the establishment of a lethal dose, but since aflatoxins weren't intended as drugs—their "purpose" was the exact opposite of therapeutic—there would be no controlled studies to show the effects of aflatoxin poisoning in humans. Science can't ask people to submit to poisoning just to see what will happen.

Amanda remembered from the little reading she had done yesterday morning that there seemed to be some controversy in the scientific community about the correlation between liver cancer in laboratory rats and the same disease found in humans exposed to aflatoxins. The rats were subjects of controlled scientific experiments, and the people were subjects of observation of past events. It was like comparing apples and oranges.

"Give a guess," she said to Roland. "Is it a highly toxic substance or sort of medium toxic?"

"Well, I'd think that the purer the extract, the more dangerous it is. If you're working with it in a laboratory, you'd want to have good ventilation, and you'd want to be real careful about how you handled it."

"What else can you tell me?" she asked.

"You've just about picked my brain clean," he said. "Now, if it was viruses you wanted to discuss, well, we could stay here for days. Then maybe we could go back to my apartment and exchange some."

Uh, oh. They were sliding onto dangerous ground. "Roland, why can't you accept that I'm married to Ken? I *like* being married to him, and I don't intend to cheat on him. Now, stop this."

"I'm sorry, Amanda. I really am. It's just that you look so delicious today. So, tell me. How's your job?"

They talked for a while about this and that, and when the check came Amanda grabbed for it.

"It's my treat," she said. "It's the least I can do after I forced you to talk about something as disgusting as mold during lunch."

They shook hands on the sidewalk, and on the spur of the moment, she reached up and pecked him on the cheek. "Thank you," she said. "You're a good man, Roland. And believe me, there aren't many around."

It was almost two-thirty in the afternoon when Amanda got back to her office. She glanced through her telephone messages, saw nothing urgent, and sat at her desk staring off into space. She still wasn't sure why she had gone to Baltimore to ask Roland about aflatoxins. Neither was she sure what they had to do with McBride's death. She knew only that there was a connection there somewhere. His liver cancer was no coincidence.

Suddenly she snapped back to attention, picked up the phone, and dialed the National Institutes of Health.

"Will you connect me with the employee locator, please," Amanda said.

"Who do you want to find?" said the voice.

"Dr. Frank Wolfman."

There was a pause during which Amanda heard the muted click of computer keys. "His number is four nine six, five five five five."

"Thank you," said Amanda, and then dialed Frank's number. Her heart speeded up, and she prayed that *he* wouldn't answer the phone. She wanted whoever did answer to say his name and the name of the department. "Cellular biology, Sally speaking," said a voice that sounded as though it came from a fourteen-year-old.

"Would you be good enough to give me the name of the head of the department and the address, please," said Amanda.

"Who are you and why do you want to know?" demanded the voice that seemed to age ten years in two seconds.

"My name is Ludmilla Wantanova (where had *that* name come from?) and I want to write a letter to the director.

Wouldn't it be rude to address him as 'Hey, you'?" said Amanda in her most businesslike, severe tone.

"His name is Dr. Frank Wolfman, but you can't speak to him now, he's in a meeting."

So, she thought. He's the big wheel.

"His mailing address, please."

"Just address it to Building Eighty-seven, NIH, Bethesda, Maryland two-oh-two-oh-five," she said.

That was exactly the information Amanda wanted, and she thanked the secretary and hung up. Then she called back fifteen minutes later, hoping she would get another voice. If she got Sally again, she'd hang up and try later. But this time a man answered.

"Dr. Wolfman's office, please," she said.

When another woman answered, Amanda said, "Will you give me Dr. Wolfman's office number, please. This is Federal Express, and we have a rush package for him."

"Just bring it to Building Eighty-seven," she said without hesitation.

"I have to get the office number for the driver," said Amanda.

"This is a secure building, and he can't go beyond the reception area anyway, so all he has to know is Building Eighty-seven," said the secretary.

"Okay, but our driver makes rounds until six o'clock," said Amanda. "Will there be someone there until then to receive the package?"

"Well, the secretaries go home at four-thirty, but Dr. Wolfman usually stays late. Tell the driver to ring the buzzer on the office door, and he'll hear it. The lab is secure, so the driver can't come in, but Dr. Wolfman can come out."

Amanda was enjoying her Federal Express persona, so she went on. "A secure lab?" she said, with just the slightest trace of concern in her voice. "What does that mean? Is this going to be dangerous for our driver?"

"Oh, no. It just means that you need a security code to enter. That's why I said to ring."

Amanda decided, just for the fun of it, to see how far she could push this woman for information.

"Well, if you don't mind my asking," she said, "don't you people do medical stuff over there? How come you need all that security?"

"Sometimes we work with microorganisms that are potentially dangerous, so we use containment labs."

"What are microorganisms?" asked Amanda as innocently as she could.

"They're germs. Look, I have another call waiting," said the woman. "Just tell the driver to ring the buzzer. I'll tell Dr. Wolfman to be expecting him."

Amanda had had very little in mind when she picked up the phone to call the NIH, but now she had a firm plan. She looked at her watch. It was twenty after four—plenty of time if she put a move on. She grabbed her purse, slipped into her jacket, and wished a good afternoon to Louise, who was getting ready to go home, too.

She and Ken lived in Bethesda, about two miles from the NIH, so she had time to go home and change her clothes. She would drive by the house first to see if Ken's car was in the driveway. If he was home already, she'd go directly to the institute. She wanted to look less feminine, more businesslike, when she met Wolfman.

The driveway was empty, so she raced upstairs, ignoring Shadow's pleas for something to eat.

"You still have food in your bowl," she said as she hugged the cat. "And anyway I'm not really home yet."

Once dressed in her most tailored black suit and white blouse, she drove the short distance to the federally funded medical research institute, probably the premier institution of its kind in the world.

Amanda had no idea where Building 87 was on the campus that sprawled over a few hundred parklike acres. She slowed her car at the sight of the first person in a white lab coat and asked for directions. The woman told her how to get there but said, "They won't let you in. It's a secure building."

Amanda knew that the NIH worked with some pretty scary bugs, but she was under the impression that most of the classified, dangerous research was done at Fort Detrick, about thirty miles up Interstate 270 in Frederick, Maryland. Fort

Detrick had been the center for germ warfare research until long after World War II, and they were well equipped to handle dangerous microbes.

But when she pulled into the small parking lot behind Building 87, she could see right away that this building was designed for any kind of diabolical experimentation that the human mind could dream up. It was made of cinder blocks and had no windows. She set her parking brake, turned off the ignition, and sat for a while, screwing up enough courage to go in. She noticed that the back door looked a lot like the heavy steel doors that banks have on their vaults.

She thought about backing her car out of the lot and driving home. They're never going to let me in here anyway, she thought. And even if they do, I'll probably have to take a disinfectant shower and scrub with a steel brush before I leave.

And you don't have a clear idea of why you're poking your nose where it doesn't belong, anyway, added the voice that was always nattering on about details. You don't know what you're going to say if you *do* see him.

I'll worry about that when the time comes, thought Amanda as she got out of the car and walked around to the front entrance, which she was surprised to see was an ordinary government-issue door with Building 87 stenciled in black paint.

She walked in and found herself in a small reception area that contained three desks, complete with computer terminals, files, pens and pencils in cups, and pictures of smiling families. All very ordinary, all very unmenacing. And empty.

There was not a soul in sight, so Amanda walked to the rear of the reception room, toward another ordinary door. She looked for the buzzer but saw only a piece of masking tape. She knocked on the door and waited awhile, but no one came, so she knocked again. Still nothing.

With her fingernail she peeled back the tape to reveal the buzzer beneath. As she was about to touch her finger to it, she stopped and tried the doorknob instead. It turned easily in her hand, so she opened it cautiously and stepped into the twenty-first century.

"Holy shit, Toto," she said to no one, "we sure as hell aren't in Kansas anymore!"

The door clicked closed behind her, and Amanda heard the lock catch. Immediately she knew she had made a mistake and grasped the knob to let herself out. It was locked.

She noticed the absence of a keyhole in the knob or on the door. On the wall just to the right of the doorjamb, however, was a keypad of numbers—a coded security system. The same type of keypad was mounted on the wall opposite on a small steel plate.

The steel plate was set into walls made entirely of glass stretching the entire length of the corridor. On the other side of the glass walls was a huge room, which Amanda recognized instantly as a laminar-flow room.

Naylor-Noyes Corporation had several laminar-flow rooms in which they put together the most sensitive parts of their computers, and Ken had once taken Amanda on a tour of one of them. The key to the success of the room was the circulation of air. All air flowing into the room was triple filtered, and all air flowing out was not recirculated. The purpose was to make the room as free of microorganisms as possible.

The people who worked in the room at Naylor-Noyes wore protective garments; sometimes just white head and body coveralls and shoe booties, and sometimes what appeared to be space suits and helmets with independent breathing apparatuses, depending on what was being manufactured.

Here the purpose must have been serious indeed, because Amanda could see one space-suited figure, complete with helmet, backpack, and breathing hoses, working against a wall to the right. His hands were thrust through two holes cut into the wall.

Attached to the holes were clumsy-looking gloves, and at the ends of these were long, pincerlike instruments for grasping objects.

Three sides of the room were appropriated for these sets of holes, and in all but the one that was occupied, Amanda could see empty gloves dangling unused on the other side of the glass wall. Beyond the glove holes were racks of test tubes and other containers. She was sure that whatever was in those test tubes was nothing she'd want to snuggle up with.

"Holy shit," Amanda said again, and had an immediate urge to hold her breath until she got out of there. *If* she got out.

She watched the space cadet for a few minutes. He appeared to be giving injections to eggs with a long, incredibly thin needle. He picked up each egg with one set of pincers and with the other set slid the needle into the egg. Never once did he break an egg, either with the pincers or the needle. Whatever was in that syringe must have been highly dangerous. She'd heard that some of the stuff NIH messed around with was so potent that it could kill all the people for miles around if any of it were accidentally released into the atmosphere.

She looked up then and noticed klaxon horns and red warning lights in the corridor and the laminar-flow room. There were red buttons every few feet along the wall that said EMERGENCY LEAK, and right next to them were chains that looked like those on old-fashioned toilets. But when her eye followed the chains up to the storage tanks, she saw stenciled on them a chemical formula—and it was *not* H_2O.

Amanda felt as though she had wandered onto the set of one of those movies about military command posts under mountains that controlled enough nuclear missiles to blow up the world. She was scared, but she made no move to try the door again.

What are you so scared of? she asked herself. That's not just ordinary glass you see in front of you. It's several panes thick, and anyway the nasty germs aren't in the room, they're behind yet more thick glass. So you can keep breathing.

But you're not supposed to be here, the more cautious self said.

So what are they going to do, arrest me?

They could, couldn't they?

If they wanted to be so damn careful, why don't they keep their doors locked and hire guards?

Well, that's a good ques—

Oh, shit. You're in for it now, she thought as the space cadet turned and saw her. Be cool, she warned herself. You're a taxpayer.

That's the stupidest thing you've ever—

"Who are you? How did you get in here?" The voice boomed out of unseen loudspeakers and reverberated up and down the corridor like a physical assault.

Amanda jumped and her heart lurched and then raced madly.

"Oh, it's you," he said, none too pleasantly, as he came over toward Amanda's side of the glass.

"I'm looking for Frank Wolfman," she said. "Are you he?" The face mask distorted the man's features, and she had seen Wolfman only briefly that one time in McBride's office.

"Press the button so I can hear you," said the voice. He gestured toward the keypad of numbers.

"Well, I can hear *you*," she said, her finger on the button. "You don't have to shout at me. Are you Dr. Wolfman?"

"Yes. What do you want? And how did you get in here?"

"I walked in through that door," she said.

"That door is always locked," Wolfman replied.

"Not this time it wasn't," said Amanda, much more confidently than she felt. She did not add that the door was locked now, and she was trapped here in this glass-and-cinder-block corridor.

Wolfman said nothing for a few beats. Obviously someone had screwed up on security. He spoke again, this time his voice a little quieter and more reasonable.

"What do you want? You're not supposed to be in here. This is a secure building."

Amanda felt her heart slowing and her confidence returning. "Well, someone made a mistake, didn't they? It doesn't seem all that secure to me. If I can get in, anyone can."

"Look," Wolfman said, now in a normal tone of voice, "just tell me what you want, and we can both go home."

"I was thinking about Dr. McBride and how he died, and what was wrong with him before he died, and wondering if, uh, perhaps you could give me some help and answer a few ques—"

"Who the hell do you think you are, coming in here, asking me questions? McBride's death is none of my concern. Get out!"

"Look, Mr. Wolfman . . . . I'm sorry, Dr. Wolfman,"

Amanda said in her most soothing tone. "I'm just trying to help. I want to know who killed Dr. McBride as much as you do."

"I don't give a flying fuck who killed that bastard," said Wolfman. "Now, get out before I personally throw you out!"

So he *did* know McBride. But why was Wolfman in such a rage? So she didn't call first for an appointment. The breach of etiquette wasn't *that* big a deal. He should be annoyed but not on the verge of apoplexy. Amanda's radar was on full red alert now.

"The police have been nosing around asking questions," she said. "They've been nagging your wife, and now they're nagging me. She said you were a patient of McBride's, and they want to know what was wrong with you.

"Oh, I didn't come to ask you that," she continued hurriedly as she noticed him getting ready to interrupt her again. "I wouldn't pry into your private affairs, but there is something else I wanted to talk to you about, and I thought because you're a scientist . . . well, maybe you could help me."

"I don't give a damn what you thought, Ms. Knight. All you rich bitches are the same. You think you can run roughshod over the rest of us and use us as your whipping boys. Well, you're wrong. I told the police and I'm telling you: my knowing McBride is none of your goddamn business. Now, get out of here. This time I mean it." He turned and started to walk away.

"Why did your wife lie to the police?"

Wolfman whirled around to face her, his eyes open wide behind the thick plastic face plate, but he said nothing.

"She killed him, didn't she?"

This time there was no reaction at all. He continued to walk across the great empty room. Amanda yelled at him and pounded on the thick glass wall, but she knew he couldn't hear her.

Then she was alone.

At that moment Ina Wolfman was being confronted with the same lie as her husband, but she was reacting far differently.

"Mrs. Wolfman," said Lydia as patiently as she could, "we

have all afternoon. In fact, we have all evening and all night and all of tomorrow to wait for you to stop crying. But if you want to get rid of us so you can go home and cook dinner for your husband, stop it this instant and answer our questions."

The minute Lydia mentioned home and cooking and her husband, Ina's sobs intensified, and Lydia bore down.

"Look, I don't know what's going on between you and your husband. We're police officers, not marriage counselors, but whatever part of it affects our investigation, we want to know about. Now, I'm going to ask you again—very slowly and clearly, so there'll be no mistake: why did you lie about your husband knowing McBride?"

"I didn't lie," she said, breaking into fresh paroxysms of sobbing.

Lydia was sick of it. "Turn off that goddamn faucet. It's not doing you any good. Save it for your husband."

"Oh God," moaned Ina. "Oh, sweet Jesus." But she made an effort to control herself.

"I didn't lie," she said. "I swear I didn't. How can I make you believe me? You've *got* to believe me!"

"The thing is," said Lydia later, "I believe her. At least I believe that she believes it. It may not be true, but she's telling the only truth she knows."

"Wolfman and McBride knew each other, all right," said Bandman. "But I'll be damned if I know how."

13

AMANDA TURNED AROUND and tried the door through which she had entered; it was locked tight. She rattled the knob in frustration and anger. Nothing. She yelled and banged on the door, which she now saw was made of heavy steel. Still nothing.

At one end of the corridor was a solid wall of cinder block. At the other end was another door that looked like one used on a bank vault—securely locked. Next to it was yet another keypad of numbers. Again, in frustration, she pressed all the numbers. Then she thought about air—all those movies where bank robbers accidentally let the vault door swing shut and were trapped all night and died of suffocation. But this was a big space with thousands of cubic feet of air.

But how long will it last? she asked herself. How many cubic feet of air does the average person breathe in an hour?

About the same as a stupid person—which you are, said the self that was always pointing out the obvious.

Oh, shut up. Let's get out of here, and then we can worry about being stupid.

But let's keep calm, okay?

Okay, she replied. We won't cry because that uses up too much oxygen, and we *certainly* won't get hysterical because we have to keep our act together so we can think.

Then why are tears rolling down your cheeks right now? Stop it!

Amanda drew a deep, shaky breath. Okay. I've stopped. I'm calm. Let's think this through. There are two doors, both locked, both controlled by a security code. So that's one possible escape route. I'll start pressing combinations of numbers at random until I find the right one.

Are you nuts? Do you have any idea how many possible combinations there are? You don't even know how many digits are in the code. It's probably four, but who knows? In a place like this, it could be all ten. You'd need one of Ken's super computers to figure it out.

Okay, okay. But at least it'd give me something to do if I'm locked in here forever.

You won't be here forever. Only until tomorrow morning.

Oh, God, I'll have to stay in here all night. Ken will be so worried. There's no bathroom. "I'll pee in my pants," she moaned.

Well, at least he'll call the police, and maybe they'll see your car outside.

Why would the police come here? No one knows I'm here. And why would they search for me at all? You have to be gone for twenty-four hours before you're counted as a missing person.

But Ken will pull strings. Hey! You're starting to cry again. You promised you wouldn't.

Screw promises, she thought as she slid down the wall and sat on the cold tile floor. But the tears that threatened to spill over didn't, and she got down to serious thinking about how to escape. She knew she could always hit the emergency button, which must be connected to some central security office, but that would bring the research community's equivalent of a S.W.A.T. team, as well as every single policeman in Montgomery County. It might even make the papers if it was a slow news day and if the reporter monitoring the police band decided that a false alarm at NIH would make an amusing story. Then, of course, some enterprising investigative type would do a long series about the lack of security in our nation's medical research labs, and she would be mentioned in every single story as the woman who simply walked into a secure building—like the security guard who noticed the break-in at the Watergate—that started the whole affair. She'd be a laughingstock forever.

Don't you think you're getting a little carried away with yourself? asked the voice sarcastically.

I suppose so, Amanda thought. But you know damn well that all hell will break loose if I hit that red button.

You're right. So let's think of another way out. How about smashing the glass?

With what, my dainty little fist? Or maybe the sledgehammer I have tucked away in my purse? Christ, I have to pee!

At the far end of the corridor where the steel door was, Amanda heard a scratching sound.

Rats! she thought immediately.

Jerk, said the other voice again, how would a rat get in here? There's someone at the door.

Amanda scrambled to her feet just in time to see the huge door swing open, and a blast of cold October air rushed in.

A man was standing silhouetted in the doorway, and she rushed past him into the parking lot, where she stood trembling and gulping in great gobs of air. Her car was parked not ten feet away, just where she'd left it.

"I thought I told you to get out of here," said Frank Wolfman.

She looked at him closely. His facial expression didn't match the harshness of his voice. His eyes were no longer penetrating and menacing; in fact, they seemed distracted and far away. He had a pinched, drawn expression, and his body stance was not that of someone in full authority. His shoulders were hunched forward, and he didn't seem to be standing firmly upright.

Amanda sensed all this rather than fully seeing it, but her quick impression was enough to give her the courage to take an aggressive position.

"I couldn't very well get out because you had me locked in. Holding me against my will, I think the police would call it. And another thing—don't you ever, *ever* call me a bitch again."

Then, scarcely believing her good fortune at having been freed from that futuristic prison, she turned her back, stalked to her car, found her keys without fumbling, and drove out of the parking lot.

Don't think now. Don't think about anything, she said to herself. Just find a bathroom fast.

She screeched into the Exxon station a block down on Wisconsin Avenue and made it to the ladies' room in the nick of time. And as she sat in the filthy stall with the crude, unimaginative graffiti on the walls, she realized there was no toilet paper. *That* did it. Amanda burst into wild sobs. She cried for a long time, until she had gotten rid of all the fear and anger. And then, still gulping and hiccuping, she found a pack of tissues in her purse and pulled herself together.

"Hey, are you all right in there?" called a voice through the door.

"I'm fine, thank you," she said with as much dignity as she could muster as she opened the door to let the woman into the bathroom. "But if people are going to deface private property, at least they could spell it right!"

Amanda laughed as she waited for the light to change at Wilson Lane. The woman must have thought she was completely nuts, sobbing like a banshee because people couldn't spell.

Well, at least she'll have a story to tell at dinner tonight, she thought, and began to plan her own evening meal.

Ken hadn't come home yet, so she changed into a corduroy skirt and a blue-and-white denim blouse. While she started dinner she thought about what had just happened.

That she had done a stupid thing was a given, but how was she to know that Wolfman would become so enraged? What the hell was he so mad about? He had acted all out of proportion to the occasion.

Amanda was positive now that Frank Wolfman knew Leo McBride, but she didn't think the two were doctor and patient. Did Wolfman kill McBride? Or did he give him liver cancer? Could he have been making aflatoxins—or extracting them or whatever—at NIH? Wolfman worked in, and was head of, a department called cellular biology. She didn't think they worked on molds there. Bacteria and viruses were more like it. But molds are made of cells, too, as are all living things. It was a secure government building; they could do whatever they pleased in there. If Wolfman was guilty of murder, *why* would he kill McBride? You don't know anything about their relationship, and you're not going to find out, said old practical-voice again. One is dead, and the other isn't about to tell, so why don't you just forget it? Besides, wouldn't you be royally pissed off if some stranger came to your office and asked questions that were none of his business?

Yes, I would, Amanda silently replied. But he didn't give me a chance to ask anything. For all he knew I could have been there for a weather forecast. He could have at least waited to see what I wanted before he freaked out like that. And why did Ina tell the police that McBride cured her husband of something dreadful? Frank was obviously working on something far more pernicious than aflatoxins when she walked in on him. You didn't need to wear a space suit and breathe purified air for metabolites of mold, no matter how toxic.

So there *was* no connection. Maybe she was jumping to conclusions and he was innocent, although he didn't act like an innocent man.

Maybe he's just a grouch, said the skeptic in her.

Locking someone in a building is taking "grouchy" to its outermost limits, don't you think?

He didn't lock you in there, said the skeptic. You locked yourself in accidentally. *He* got you out. If he hadn't come back, you would have been in there all night, and you wouldn't have been very dainty when you were found in the morning.

You're right.

Of course I'm right, said the skeptic. And another thing, let's say that Wolfman *was* making aflatoxins. Maybe he was doing it on his own time, which was why he stayed late. Remember the woman on the phone said he usually stays till six o'clock or so—when the secretaries and the people out front leave at four-thirty.

Hey! I never thought of that, thought Amanda.

But even if he did, continued the skeptic, everyone who worked in the lab would know. He'd have no way of hiding it. You saw the place. It's like a fishbowl. And you'd better believe that every single container of every single thing they have there is labeled *very* carefully. So how would he hide a big blob of mold culture?

So, okay, he couldn't.

Why don't you just admit the truth. Frank Wolfman had nothing to do with McBride's death. He's just a weird guy. Maybe he and McBride played the horses together. Whatever it was is not only irrelevant, it's none of your damn business. You're just grasping at straws because you can't face the fact that Eddie Silverman did it.

You have to admit, it's hard to swallow, Amanda considered.

It is. But you've faced worse before in your life.

Just then the garage door opened, and Ken was home. He kissed her on the back of the neck and said what husbands all over the world have been saying since the beginning of time: "What's for supper?"

"Thin gruel and dry crusts of bread," she replied.

"Great! My favorites. Any interesting mail or calls?"

The simplicity of the domestic conversation was such a relief after the terror of being locked in that cold, germ-filled building that Amanda felt tears welling up again. She turned toward the stove, hoping that Ken's latest installment of the great corporate soap opera would last long enough for her to pull herself together.

When she finally turned around, she sniffed and said, "Onions."

Sometimes Ken's not noticing nuances of mood came in handy.

"Do you have work to do tonight?" he asked.

"I really should go back to the hospital. I haven't done late rounds in ages. But I won't leave till about eleven o'clock, so we can have a nice, leisurely dinner, and then I'll tuck you in before I leave."

Ken smiled. "I'm not sure I can last until eleven. I'm pooped."

Later she drove to the hospital and parked at the curb in front of Giovanni's. The hospital lot was too spooky at this hour. She took the elevator directly to Doreen McClure's unit and walked to the nurses' station. What she saw there filled her with both rage and elation.

McClure was sitting at the head nurse's desk, head down on her arms, fast asleep. The intercom master control board that connected to the patient's rooms was lit up like a Christmas tree, indicating requests for a nurse.

Amanda stood quietly for a moment, watching the nurse sleep, her palm itching to slap McClure silly. Then she reached out and flipped the toggle switch next to one of the indicator lights and said in a loud voice, "May I help you?"

McClure's head snapped up. Her expression of recognition and certain doom was one that Amanda would always treasure. Amanda spoke to the patient through the intercom as she watched McClure scramble to pull herself together.

"Get whoever is in three-sixteen on a bedpan," said Amanda. "And then come back and help me answer the rest of these lights."

The other staff nurse came out of a patient's room, and together she and Amanda got the requests sorted out. When McClure returned, Amanda took her into the utility room, and there among the emergency oxygen tanks, the shelves of sterile supplies, and the crash cart, Amanda fired her.

"I want you out of this hospital so fast that you make smoke."

"You have no right to do this to me," said the nurse. "I can sue you."

"I have every right. And I am doing it. Now get out, or do you want me to call security?"

"All right, I'll go, but you'll hear from me."

"I can't wait," said Amanda sarcastically. "Now get out." The nurse banged out through the swinging door, and Amanda helped the remaining nurse take care of the patients until the replacement showed up an hour later.

She forced herself to squelch the anger and outrage as she helped give injections for pain, get people on and off bedpans, and check dressings and intravenous drips, and by the time she was ready to leave, she felt as calm as she pretended to be. Doing the simple, helpful things that sick people need to have done soothed her.

As Amanda waited for the elevator, which she noted was no

faster or more efficient at night than during the day, Deborah, the other nurse, came up to thank Amanda.

"This has been going on for a long time," she said. "I'm glad you finally caught her."

Amanda got angry all over again. "Do you mean that Ms. McClure had been sleeping on duty for a long time and no one said anything?"

"Yeah."

"Why?"

"Well, you just can't turn in one of your colleagues," said the nurse defensively.

"You bet your sweet nursing license you can," said Amanda. "And further, if something had happened to a patient because of Ms. McClure's negligence, and if you had known about it and said nothing, *you* would have been a party to it and thus equally culpable. Think about that the next time you turn a blind eye when a nurse puts a patient in jeopardy. Consider this an official warning."

Amanda stepped into the elevator that she had been holding open with her foot and waved good night to the nurse.

"Dumb jerks," she muttered to herself. "Stupid idiots."

As she drove through the quiet streets of Georgetown and upper northwest Washington, she thought once again about how she could cut down on the recent spate of stupidity and dereliction of duty. It didn't help to know that other hospitals had far worse problems. It didn't help to know that nursing had changed drastically in the past two decades, that service to the sick was no longer the primary goal. And it didn't help to know that the problem pervaded all of American society.

By the time she got to the redbrick house in Bethesda with the graceful white columns and black wood shutters, she felt thoroughly defeated, glad she had fired McClure on the spot, but despairing of ever solving the larger problem. She knew the firing would be the hottest piece of hospital gossip for a week, and maybe the message would sink in . . . for a while.

She had left the lights on for herself downstairs, but their bedroom was dark. Ken was asleep, so she pulled her Honda into the driveway next to Ken's big dark green Saab 9000 and closed the door as quietly as she could.

She locked the car and walked along the brightly lit path to the back door when she stopped in her tracks. Beyond the pool of light she heard a rustle in the rhododendron bushes.

She listened for a while, sensing the cartilage on her ears grow rigid. This is what happens to dogs and cats, she thought. Their ears perk up when they hear something in the night.

She heard nothing more. It had probably been her imagination anyway, so she continued toward the house, smiling as she thought of herself as a puppy with its ears up, its whiskers tense.

The rustling again! This time louder and closer.

She stopped, her heart pounding in fear, all senses on full alert. A deep, loud menacing warning, more like an animal's growl than a human voice, came from the rhododendron:

"Death will come soon!"

Amanda opened her mouth and screamed and screamed and screamed. She was rooted to the spot and kept screaming until Ken banged open the back door and ran to her.

"There's someone in the bushes," she said.

He grabbed a long-handled three-pronged gardening claw that was leaning next to the door and headed in the direction she pointed, calling over his shoulder, "Call the police!"

Three minutes after she had panted their address into the phone a police car drove into the yard, followed by two others. Four officers ran into the bushes where Ken had disappeared, and two others looked around the rest of the property. Strong searchlight beams pierced the darkness, and the red and blue lights from the top of the police cars made a monotonous flashing pattern on the house. For no reason at all she remembered that those lights were nicknamed gumball machines.

Ken and the officers emerged from the rhododendron and approached her, and once again she was questioned by police.

She told them what she had heard, all except the death threat.

Tell them, dummy, the voice of practicality hissed.

And then they'd ask me why I was getting death threats, and I'd have to tell them about my little escapade at NIH this afternoon. Then I'd be in real deep shit.

You are asking for trouble, said the wiser self.

I'm sure you're right. Now leave me alone, she said to herself. I'll work this out.

"Did you see anything?" she asked the policeman, one of the biggest men she had ever seen. Her fear melted away at the sight of his huge blue-suited presence, and she had to restrain herself from asking him to stand guard in front of their bedroom door all night. "Well, ma'am, it's the strangest thing," he said. "We saw a few footprints, but they aren't like anything I've ever seen before. They're like boots—really big boots with sort of tire treads on the bottom. We're calling for the lab guys now to take a cast of them. Not that we're likely to catch the guy, ma'am, even though two cars are out patrolling for him right now."

It was only then that Amanda noticed that there was only one police car left in the driveway.

"It's just that the prints are so strange that I'm sure the lab boys would love to get a look at them. But whoever he is, he's not on your property anymore."

Amanda was shivering now, and Ken looked cold without a jacket. He said, "Well, come in, officers, and wait inside until your other people get here."

They accepted the offer, and Amanda put the kettle on for tea. Amanda, Ken, and the two officers talked awkwardly in the kitchen while they waited. The hot tea did its job, and she stopped shaking and thought longingly of the bottle of Valium in the medicine chest, kept for emergencies.

This qualifies, said the voice that passed judgment.

Thanks, she replied sarcastically.

My pleasure. Take two. You've been very brave. Stupid, but brave.

"Hey, Biff," said the big policeman's partner. "I just thought of what those prints remind me of. Remember when Armstrong and the other guy landed on the moon and they kind of clumped around in those space suits? Those kind of boots."

Frank Wolfman!

Amanda let out a low moan, and the three men looked at her strangely.

"Are you okay, honey?" asked Ken.

"Yes, I'm fine. It just seems funny to think of a spaceman walking around in our bushes." She giggled.

She giggled again and knew she was going out of control. She dashed out of the room and made it up to the bedroom before collapsing on the bed in hysterical sobs. Ken was right behind her, and he held her close until the storm of crying was over and she lay in his arms hiccuping and sniffing.

Later, after Ken had locked the house and the policemen had finished their work, they sat together in the Jacuzzi, leaning against the back of the tub. Amanda snuggled close to him, safe in the protective circle of his arms. She closed her eyes and thought of nothing.

At first the swirling water was relaxing; then along with Ken's insistent stroking and probing, it started to act as an erotic addition to what his hands were doing.

"Ken, sweet love, I'm too tired. I don't think I can."

"Shhh," he said. "Don't do anything. Don't move. Let me do everything. Let me take away the fright."

And he did.

Then, afterward, as they lay snuggled together under the big comforter with Shadow pressed close against her, Amanda felt safe and warm and happy.

But she knew the fear would be back.

14

BANDMAN WAS IN a bad mood and Lydia didn't know if she should leave him alone, pretend nothing was wrong, or try to jolly him out of it.

Actually, she didn't feel too terrific, either—for the same reason. They were stuck. They didn't know who killed McBride, and time was passing quickly.

"It's not that we have *no* idea," said Bandman morosely. "We have too many. And now Ms. Knight comes up with this craziness that Frank Wolfman gave McBride liver cancer!"

Lydia had called Amanda early that morning. "Are you all right?" she had asked.

"Sure. Why wouldn't I be?" Amanda replied.

"I heard about your prowler last night," said Lydia.

Amanda was impressed. "I had no idea that police communications were so efficient," she said.

"Well, actually, they aren't. Ordinarily I wouldn't know about it. You don't live in the District of Columbia police jurisdiction, but I know a Montgomery County detective who works in your precinct, and he called me. It was mentioned in morning roll call, and he made the association with the McBride thing. You must have been scared. Any idea who it was?"

Amanda was almost positive that she knew exactly who it was, but if she said as much to Lydia, she'd have to explain how she knew, and that would mean going into the whole NIH episode.

"No," she said. "Did you hear about the odd-looking boots, though?"

"I did," said Lydia, "but I don't know any more about them than you do. Unless . . . you know more about them than I do."

It was obvious that Lydia didn't believe her, so she decided to make a joke of it.

"Ken and I finally cleaned up the yard on Sunday. It looks so pristine without all those dead summer flowers that maybe someone thought it was the surface of the moon!"

The remark fell flat. "Umm," said Lydia, "well, if you think of who it might be, give us a call."

"Oh, I will," said Amanda, feeling stupid and mean spirited for lying to Lydia, who not only knew she was lying but deserved to be told the truth because she was working hard at her job—and Amanda wasn't making it any easier.

"Well, actually, there is something I want to talk to you about."

"Oh?" replied Lydia, her voice brightening.

"Don't get excited. It's very farfetched and probably nothing, but it's been on my mind."

"We'll be right over," said Lydia.

"Would you mind terribly waiting until lunchtime—if you can stand hospital food. Believe me, it's not an emergency, and I'm swamped with work. Would one o'clock be okay? The cafeteria is a lot less crowded then."

"We'll be in your office at one," said Lydia.

The two detectives were exactly on time, and the three walked to the cafeteria. Amanda said, "I'd recommend the salad bar. It's the least depressing thing."

Lydia took her advice, but Bandman bought a hot meal of "mystery meat," overcooked carrots with all the vitamin A steamed out, and some hashed-brown potatoes that actually didn't look bad.

Amanda took a long slurp of Diet Coke, mixed the dressing into her salad, and said, "I know you're going to think this is completely crazy, but I think Frank Wolfman gave McBride liver cancer."

Both Bandman and Lydia tried to keep their faces expressionless. The former had better success, but he was the one who spoke first.

"About a thousand questions just occurred to me, Ms. Knight, not the least of which is: How do you *give* someone cancer?"

Amanda explained about aflatoxins: how she had read the article that the infection-control consultant had left in her folder accidentally, how she had gone to the library to do more research, how the connection between the mold poison and liver cancer had just popped out at her, and how she had learned that it was relatively easy to make in the laboratory. She said nothing about her trip to Baltimore. And she certainly said nothing of her misadventure at Building 87.

When she had told her story, she sat forward expectantly, waiting. For what? For Bandman to slap his forehead and say, "Of course! Why didn't *I* think of that? Thank you, Ms. Knight. The Metropolitan Police Department is profoundly grateful to you for solving this crime, and the mayor is going to give you a medal"?

What happened was that both detectives sat silently, looking at her quizzically, probably thinking she had gone right around the bend. Bandman chewed slowly and deliberately and stirred a disgusting amount of sugar into his coffee.

Finally he said, "Let's assume you're onto something. I doubt that you are, but let's just assume. First, *why* would Wolfman do something like that? What's his motive? Second, *how* would he manage to make these poisons without other people finding out? I've been to his lab, Ms. Knight. It's all made out of glass. Everyone can see what everyone else is doing. And he certainly couldn't smuggle them out. We were told it's a secure building, and it sure looked secure to us. Third, *even if* he had a motive *and* an opportunity, how would he get the poison into McBride? From what you've said, liver cancer results from a long-term cumulative effect of these poisons. Fourth, why didn't the medical examiner find any evidence of it?"

These were the questions Amanda had been asking herself over and over, but now, put to her bluntly from someone else—a professional detective, at that—they formed an impenetrable intellectual barrier, and she realized how silly she'd been. Her whole game of amateur sleuth now seemed childish and potentially destructive, and she resolved to drop the whole thing.

"You're right, Lieutenant Bandman," she said. "It's completely implausible, and I'm sorry to have gotten you down here on a wild goose chase. I guess I read too many murder mysteries. I'm not Miss Marple, and I apologize for wasting your time."

He had been embarrassed then. "Ms. Knight, don't be so hard on yourself. I'm not saying that Frank Wolfman *couldn't* have killed McBride, as you think he did. All I'm saying is that it's a long shot—a very long shot. But because something isn't probable doesn't mean it isn't possible. And I will *not* dismiss your suggestion out of hand. If I did, I wouldn't be a very good police officer, would I? Besides, if we hadn't come down here, I wouldn't have had the chance to sample this delicious cuisine."

Ms. Knight had smiled. "I warned you about the food. Actually, you can't blame it on JFK Memorial. The hospital has a food-service contract with Intercontinental. No hospital of any size runs its own kitchen anymore; it's much too expensive."

"Intercontinental? The airline?" Lydia has asked. "Do you mean I'm eating airplane food?"

"Well, we like to think that when you fly Intercontinental, you're eating hospital food!"

The three had laughed, and Amanda said, "Want to hear another loony theory?"

"Sure, why not?" replied Bandman.

Amanda described how whoever had been treating McBride substituted poison for the anti-cancer drugs. "That would explain the absence of a struggle. McBride would have had nothing to fear. The track marks were already in his arm. The killer could have used a very fast-acting neuromuscular paralytic drug that's metabolized so fast that by the time anyone got around to doing an autopsy, there would be no trace left."

"Great minds run along the same track, Ms. Knight," said Bandman. "Lydia and I have been giving lots of thought to poison, but we hadn't thought of your theory. We were going more along the lines of a poisoned scalpel."

"Ms. Knight, if what you describe is what happened," chimed in Lydia, "and it does sound plausible—why would the killer bother with a scalpel?"

"I don't know," Amanda admitted. "For effect? For a very macabre effect?"

"How dramatic," said Bandman sarcastically. "And who, Ms. Knight, has a flair for the dramatic?"

Amanda sat miserably, head down, looking at her plate. She couldn't bring herself to say the name.

"Your very good friend, Ms. Knight. Your friends who lives in the overdone town house on Corcoran Street with his architect lover."

Amanda was near tears again as she lifted her head and faced Bandman. "Maybe it was Jonathan Bernstein," she said, grasping at straws. "After all, he's a surgeon. Eddie never goes near the O.R."

Lydia put her hand on Amanda's arm. "It wasn't Bernstein, Amanda. You know it wasn't."

"I know. It's just that . . . Eddie . . . how could he? He's such a sweet person. We've been friends for so long. I don't understand how he could . . ." Her voice trailed off. There was nothing more to say.

The silence at the cafeteria table thickened. Amanda seemed swamped by unhappiness, Bandman was lost in thought, and Lydia wanted to get going. The trouble was, she didn't know where.

On an impulse she said, "Amanda, come with me to the morgue. We can talk to the M.E. and you can tell him what you told us. I admit that I think the aflatoxins thing sounds pretty far out, but your other theory, well . . ."

Lydia saw Bandman staring incredulously at her, but she avoided his gaze and decided to deal with the reprimand later. Somehow this seemed like the right thing to do. Besides, it couldn't hurt. Nothing went on in a morgue that this woman hadn't seen hundreds of times before. She was a nurse, after all.

Amanda seemed to brighten. "I'd like that," she said. "Give me ten minutes to do some things in the office. Where are you parked? I'll meet you there."

+   +   +

Lydia drove the unmarked police car, grateful for the light early-afternoon traffic. The morgue was located on the grounds of the District of Columbia General Hospital, which shared acreage with the district jail, at the opposite corner of the city—both geographically and in every other way—from J.F.K. Memorial.

"I want to tell you again that I feel like a complete jerk," said Amanda. "I know I've gotten carried away with this murder, and I'm not sure why. Please don't think it's because I have no confidence in the police, because obviously Lieutenant Bandman is the best, and you're on your way to being the best.

"I'm puzzled myself about why I've become so obsessed about it. And I'm forced to admit that I *am* obsessed. You and my best friend, Glencora Rodman—you two would like each other—are the only ones who know how much I think about McBride and his murderer."

"Not your husband?" asked Lydia.

"In the beginning he knew I was curious, but basically he thinks I ought to mind my own business.

"Uh, Lydia, I uh, um . . . I know who was prowling around our bushes last night. Frank Wolfman."

"You'd better tell me everything, Amanda. I mean it. *Everything*."

This time Amanda held nothing back about what had happened between her and Frank Wolfman.

"He could have done it, Lydia, but there's no real reason for me to think so. And it's not just because I don't want it to be Eddie. But I'm going to mind my own business from now on. No more playing detective, sneaking around where I don't belong."

"Good," said Lydia. "I was kind of hoping that we've been starting a friendship, and I'd hate to see you get bopped on the head by a mad scientist before we get to know each other better."

Amanda smiled. She was glad Lydia had said that because she too liked the police detective and looked forward to making a new friend.

Lydia took her time driving down Massachusetts Avenue, and the two women admired the lovely embassy buildings.

"Have you ever been to an embassy party?" asked Lydia.

"No, but I'd love to," said Amanda. "I'd probably have a lousy time because I'm not good at that kind of cocktail-party chatter, but it would be fun to get dressed up in something really spectacular, drink champagne that someone else paid for, and meet famous people."

She laughed. "It's silly, I guess, and I know that all the famous people would be just politicians. But still, I'd like to be invited. It's one of those experiences you'd like to have—just once."

"Yeah," said Lydia. She was distracted by what Amanda had just told her.

"Amanda," she said, "when we get there, tell the M.E.—his name is Sal Mateo, by the way, and he's a real nice guy—everything you told Paul and me, but don't expect any great revelations. They're pretty thorough down there, and if they didn't find poison the first time, it's not likely they'll find it now."

"But it's not impossible," said Amanda. "Maybe they didn't look for it in the right place. If it's a biological toxin, it may not show up the way a chemical poison would."

She described what Roland Armstrong had told her about chromatography. "Maybe finding aflatoxins is basically the same as extracting them. That is, you can't extract them if you can't find them, and you can't find them if you don't use the right tests."

"Anything's possible," replied Lydia. "But I don't want you to get your hopes up that we're going to solve the mystery this afternoon. And another thing: *even if* the M.E. finds McBride's tissues loaded with aflatoxins, that doesn't *prove* anything. It doesn't mean it was the murder weapon, and it doesn't mean that Frank Wolfman got them into McBride. It just means that somehow, somewhere, McBride was exposed to or afflicted with, or whatever you say, this poison. Don't forget, we haven't even established a cause of death yet.

"Also, Amanda, you have to understand that in police work we deal with evidence, not hunches. Oh I know, hunches and intuition are important," she said as Amanda was about to protest. "And I know that Paul has a strong feeling about Ed Silverman—and about Cicely McBride, too, but don't tell him I told you that. But these feelings can only steer you in the right direction. Then you have to have evidence. There are only two ways to get a murder conviction: either the killer has to confess—and there are so many restrictions now on the kinds of confessions that are admissible in court that sometimes even a confession doesn't hold water. Or you can gather enough hard evidence that the D.A. can make a case. And as you know, even that doesn't always work. Juries are unpredictable animals.

"And another thing," she went on, "in police work there's a saying that if you want to catch a murderer, you have to have motive, opportunity, and means."

"Milk of magnesia," said Amanda.

"What?" said Lydia, turning her head and blinking in confusion.

"I didn't mean to be flip. Motive, opportunity, and means is M-O-M. That's the medical nickname for milk of magnesia," explained Amanda.

Lydia laughed. "Well, sometimes we *do* have to wade through a lot of shit! But what I mean is that people don't kill other people for no reason. And they have to have been *able* to do it. I mean, it's no good pinning a shooting on a guy who was in China, even if he hated the victim's guts, and everyone knew that he did. And you can't pin a shooting on him if he had no gun. Of course, a lot of this is hard to prove."

"Like, maybe he had a gun but threw it in the ocean. And maybe *he* was in China, but he paid someone to do the actual killing," said Amanda.

"Exactly," said Lydia. "So even if McBride is loaded to the gills with aflatoxins, there's nothing to tie it to Wolfman."

"But will you try?"

"Yes, we will. When you went back to your office, Paul told me that he's going over to NIH and lean on Wolfman a little this afternoon."

"Good," said Amanda. She was glad that the police were

finally taking her seriously, but at almost the same moment, she realized her predicament.

"Uh-oh," she said.

"Uh-oh is right," replied Lydia. "Did you and Wolfman talk at all about aflatoxins? Does he have any reason to think that you suspect him of poisoning McBride?"

Amanda thought carefully. "No, he only thinks that I'm curious about his connection with McBride."

"I'm worried that Wolfman might really come after you now."

"Nah," said Amanda much more confidently than she felt. "He only wants to scare me. He's like a flasher. They just want to show off their cocks, not actually *do* anything with them."

Lydia decided not to explode that myth just now. But if Wolfman *was* guilty, Amanda could be in serious jeopardy.

"I want you to have police protection," said Lydia. "Let me assign an officer to stay with you."

Amanda was horrified. To be followed all over the place by a policeman. No way!

"It's not necessary, Lydia," she said. "I appreciate your concern. I really do. I think it's sweet."

"It's not *sweet* Amanda. I'm worried about you."

"You don't have to worry," said Amanda, who wasn't totally convinced of that. "I promise I'll go right home from work today. I have no plans tonight. Ken and I are going to negotiate a guest list for our first really big party—so save Valentine's Day. Do you have a honey?"

"There's someone I'm dating, and I'll tell you all about him sometime, but I don't want you to change the subject. I can't force you to put yourself under our protection, all I can do is urge you. I won't nag, but anytime you want to change your mind, call me. Do you have both my numbers?"

"I do," said Amanda. "And I thank you. Now tell me about your honey."

Lydia laughed. "After we finish at the morgue. And after I ask you one more question—a big question: What makes you think Frank Wolfman murdered McBride? What was his motive?"

"That's *the* question, Lydia, and I wish I knew the answer.

At first I was just curious about why Ina lied about his knowing McBride. But then, when he went wild on Monday afternoon, I just got real suspicious. His anger was all out of proportion to my asking things that are none of my business. Combine that with what I know about aflatoxins and McBride's liver cancer, and I just got this irresistible sense that he could have done it. I can't imagine what his motive is. If you find out, will you let me know?"

"Believe me, Amanda," said Lydia dryly, "you'll be the first to know—just to get you off the case!"

They continued down Massachusetts Avenue, past some of the most expensive condos in the district, around construction for the new Metro Rail Green Line, and then past the huge Romanesque building that housed Union Station.

"Last summer one day," said Lydia, pointing to the station, "I parked at a meter there when I met my mother, who was visiting from New York. Right there in the fountain I saw a man taking a shower. His clothes were neatly folded on the pavement next to two plastic shopping bags that held everything he owned. He had stripped down to his underpants and was soaping himself with a sliver of soap that he probably scavenged from somewhere.

"I stood next to my car for a few minutes and watched him. Then I looked for the uniformed cops who hang around the station and saw three of them way over by the cab stand. The man was committing a misdemeanor and had to be taken out of the fountain even if he wasn't arrested for vagrancy. I didn't want to keep my mother waiting, so I decided to tell one of the uniforms and let them deal with it.

"I had to walk around the fountain to get to the station, and as I got close to him, the man said, 'Good morning, miss. Beautiful day, isn't it?' Real cheerful.

"I didn't know what to say. He spoke as pleasantly as if he were waiting in line at the bank, not taking a shower in a public fountain in one of the most public and exposed places in the city. I was intending to have the guy arrested, or at least chased away, but he was so smiley and cheerful that I felt kind of stopped in my tracks.

"We had a really nice conversation. He told me that this was the best fountain in the city because the water splashed down from just the right height, and the water in which he stood was neither too deep nor too shallow. He had apparently done a lot of research.

" 'It's important to keep clean, don't you think?' he said. 'Some of the guys I stay with never wash, but I believe in maintaining my usual habits whenever I can.'

"So I told him I agreed with him and said to enjoy the shower.

"I had just broken up with a guy and was feeling really down and depressed, but when I saw this vagrant, I felt guilty about missing Morty, thinking that I was in a lot of pain over it, when here was this homeless man being so cheerful. I felt as though I didn't have a right to be unhappy."

"Well, I don't know if you could call unhappiness a right," replied Amanda, "but how did seeing him affect your sense of loss? The two things are entirely different; not having a home is not the same as not having a boyfriend. Being a vagrant is not within your sphere of possibilities. Breaking up with a boyfriend is, and we all operate within a kind of narrow range of experiences, and it's hard to compare one kind with another. It's like comparing the beggars on the street in India with people living in the projects just a mile from here. It's not the same kind of poverty at all."

"You're right, of course," said Lydia. "On an intellectual level or in theory. But I still felt as though that man was a thousand times worse off than I was, and I was grateful to have as much as I have."

"But that's different," replied Amanda. "Being glad of what you have is not the same as feeling guilty for being unhappy because someone else has less."

"We'll have to talk more about this, but enough philosophizing for now," said Lydia. "We're almost there. Have you ever been in a city morgue?"

"No, but it must be the same as a hospital one," replied Amanda, who had spent all of a minute and a half in a morgue since she had been a student nurse. She had felt queasy then and all she had actually seen that day was scrupulously scrubbed and disinfected stainless-steel post-mortem tables with not a corpse in sight.

They found a spot in the third row of the hospital parking lot and walked toward a locked side entrance labeled Employees Only. They rang the bell, and Amanda noticed that next to the door was what looked like a garage door—to let the hearses and ambulances in and out, she supposed.

One of the dieners, the morgue assistants who help with autopsies, sometimes making the first gaping incision for the pathologist, let them in after Lydia showed him her shield.

"Dr. Mateo is expecting us," she said.

The two women walked into the spacious, sunny main room of the D.C. Morgue, and Amanda's first impression was that of a major disaster; a train wreck, maybe, with disemboweled bodies strewn everywhere.

Four autopsies were in progress. Four torsos were laid open. The red of the bloody tissue and organs contrasted with the death pallor of the skin of the cadavers that lay stretched out on the gleaming tables. The windows high up on the wall let in bright sunshine, which fell in yellow ribbons on the grisly scene and created a surrealistic effect that seemed to make the bodies come alive and the pathologists and dieners turn into wax mannequins.

Each cadaver was attended by a green-suited pathologist who wore a large plastic apron over surgical scrubs. The doctors cut apart the bodies, examining organs and tissues, sometimes throwing whole organs into the scale that hung above each table. Sometimes they took snippets of tissue and put them in bottles half-filled with liquid fixative, sometimes they tossed parts aside, and sometimes they threw them down the drain at the bottom of each autopsy table, which Amanda noticed was connected to a pipe that led to God knew where.

And the smell: the thick smell of blood, the sweet rottenness of tissue that had begun to decompose at the moment of death, and the stench of fecal material from open bowels. Amanda heard Lydia's voice from a great distance and dimly felt the pressure of her hand on her arm.

"Are you all right?" she asked.

Lydia gave her arm a little tug, and Amanda was able to uproot herself from where she stood.

"Yes, fine," she replied. Her voice, too, was far away, and to make matters worse, she wasn't even sure it was her own. Nothing was real anymore except those obscene forms lying on the tables and the smell that engulfed her.

Amanda summoned all her willpower and walked with Lydia to the last autopsy table, where Dr. Salvadore Mateo, chief medical examiner for the District of Columbia, had his gloved hands deep in the belly of one of the scrawniest men Lydia had ever seen.

"Hi, Sal," said Lydia. "Whatcha been into lately?"

"Ho, ho, where have I heard that before?" the pathologist asked as he turned to greet his visitors.

Amanda had the impression of a great gorilla, so tall, hairy, and overpowering was Mateo as he shifted the huge cigar to the side of his mouth and grinned at them.

His smile turned to an expression of concern as he noted the color of Amanda's face. She was a goner if he ever saw one, and he had seen plenty of goners. He estimated that it would be no more than a minute before she crumpled, and he saw that Lydia had realized it as well and was ready to make the catch.

But he revealed none of this as Lydia introduced them: "Sal, this is Amanda Knight, who has some theories about how Leo McBride died."

"And this is Salvadore Mateo, the Dean of Death."

Amanda opened her mouth to acknowledge the introduction, but what came out was, "I lied. I'm not okay."

And then there was blackness. She didn't remember feeling faint or falling. Her lights just went out, and when she woke, she was lying on her side on a stretcher in a small office. There was someone dressed in green leaning at the foot of the stretcher, talking to Lydia. She guessed it was Mateo. As her eyes focused she became aware of a small metal basin touching her cheek, and the very next moment she had reason to be glad it was there.

As soon as she had relieved herself of lunch, the cheerful, bearded face hovered over her, whisked the basin to a sink in the corner, and then looked at her once again through the deepest, softest brown eyes she had ever seen. She knew at once that she was recovering; she definitely was feeling the full effect of those eyes.

Mateo's hand slid under her back, and he said, "Sit up. You won't feel as dizzy."

He was right. As soon as she was vertical, her head cleared enough to ask, "If you'll show me where the ladies' room is, I'll splash some water on my face and be back in a second."

"Are you okay to go alone?" inquired Mateo. He could see that she was fine because her face was a healthy flesh color, and the light dusting of blusher didn't stand out like two garish blotches the way it had a few minutes ago. The dark brown hair was a little damp with the sweat that had felt cold and clammy as he carried her to the stretcher that the morgue attendants kept handy for this very purpose.

Mateo was trained to be a careful observer, and he couldn't help carrying the habit out of the morgue into real life. Now he noticed the steadiness of her gaze through clear green eyes that were shining with intelligence and wit. She was dressed beautifully and expensively, and he wondered how she could afford such clothes on a nurses' salary. Even the big guns in nursing were way underpaid. But Lydia would give him the full scoop later.

"I'm fine, thanks," Amanda said, and kept her composure until she was safely behind the door of the toilet stall. Only then did she allow herself to relax and wait for her trembling arms and legs to quiet themselves. She leaned to the side and pressed her cheek against the cool steel of the partition, then closed her eyes, opened her mouth, and breathed. Her stomach heaved again as the bloody scene flashed in front of her eyes.

Don't look at it, she said to herself. Think about the beach. Think about the hot sun soaking into you. Think about running into the ocean to cool off.

The deep breathing helped, and soon she felt steady enough to get up and wash her face without looking at it, comb her hair, which was still damp at the scalp, and rinse her mouth as best she could. Then she pasted a smile on her face and went back to the others. Mateo had a cup of hot tea ready for her.

"Are you sure you're not an angel of mercy instead of a

pathologist?" she asked as she sipped gratefully at the fragrant liquid. Immediately her stomach stopped playing bumper cars with whatever was next to it, and she felt the final layer of gauze lift from her mind.

"Ms. Knight, you are the eleven thousand four hundred sixty-seventh person to have taken a dive in my morgue—and most of them have been men!"

She smiled her thanks, this time a real smile, and the three of them began to talk in earnest.

Back in the car with Lydia, she said, "God, I'm starving. What a waste of a perfectly good lunch!"

Lydia laughed and said, "What did you think of Sal?"

"He's one of the most attractive men I've seen in a long time. *Very* appealing—except for the cigar. And he seems like a nice guy, too."

"He is appealing, and he *is* a nice guy," said Lydia with a smile and a self-satisfied look. "And the cigar is only for the morgue. He doesn't smoke it any other time."

"He's your honey!" said Amanda

"He sure is. And I think I lucked out this time," said Lydia.

If it had been Glen sitting next to her in the car, Amanda would have peppered her with questions, but she didn't know Lydia well enough for that, so she simply wished her well with the romance.

Lydia dropped Amanda off at J.F.K. Memorial's emergency entrance and said, "Don't forget—if you change your mind about protection, call me. And, Amanda," she said, putting her hand on Amanda's arm, "*please* don't do anything foolish."

"I won't. I promise," said Amanda. "And you won't forget to let me know the minute Sal finds out anything, will you?"

Lydia assured her that she would not forget, and the women bade each other farewell. Amanda walked through the hospital to her office, half-disappointed that the trip to the morgue had not been more conclusive and half-jubilant over Sal Mateo's attitude. He had taken her seriously, and they'd had a long talk about aflatoxins as a carcinogen.

"You're right about the causes of liver cancer," he had said, "but the chances of any American ingesting enough aflatoxins over time to cause liver cancer are so remote as to be virtually impossible.

"I will send some liver tissue, blood, and other tissues to the chemistry lab, though, and ask them to look specifically for aflatoxins," Mateo promised, "but there are hundreds of other carcinogens in this world, and the D.A. would never be able to prove that this was what had done the trick. Right, Lydia?"

"He wouldn't even bother to try. The defense would tear him apart in no time flat," replied Lydia.

"So are you saying that it's possible that Frank Wolfman could get away with murder?" asked Amanda.

"I don't think he did it," said Lydia as gently as she could.

"Then why are you so anxious for me to have police protection? What makes you think he's so dangerous and unpredictable?"

"Because of what you told me," said Lydia. "And I said I don't *think* he did it. I don't *know* that he's innocent. And what's more"—she paused for emphasis—"we don't even— technically, anyway—have a murder here. All we have is attempted murder because we don't have a provable cause of death and we don't have a murder weapon."

"So we have to find out exactly how McBride died in addition to who killed him. And we do that in one of two ways: either we find out how and look for someone with those means or we find out who and then figure out how."

And, thought Amanda as she sat down behind her desk, no one seems to be very close to doing either.

15

YOU KNOW, YOU'RE one of the biggest jerks ever to have drawn breath, said the voice of sanity. This is completely crazy. You told the police what you thought; now let them take care of it. That's why God made police departments: to investigate murders—and to take risks.

But they think I'm crazy, said Amanda.

I can't imagine why, said the voice sarcastically. Besides, you're scared shitless.

Well, *he* doesn't have to know that, replied Amanda. Oh, hell, they're working on the street.

Her conscience was right as usual. She *was* crazy to be here. She *should* leave all this up to the police now that she had dumped her suspicions in their lap. But her good intentions didn't last, and now Amanda was in Arlington, Virginia, just across the Potomac River from Washington, at the corner of Frank Wolfman's street. But as she put her turn signal on, she saw that the way was blocked by orange-and-white wooden construction horses topped with blinking amber lights that signaled road work. The unmistakable smell of fresh asphalt pierced the cold October night.

It was a little before eight o'clock in the evening, but the neighborhood was pitch black. Only one streetlight glowed at the intersection, and the only other illumination came from the few houses that had porch lights on.

Amanda parked the bright red Accord, which looked deep purple under the mercury light, illegally close to the intersection. But the neighborhood was quiet, and Courthouse Road was filled with cars that couldn't drive onto the newly paved Linden Lane, so she didn't worry about a ticket.

She locked the car and walked up Wolfman's street, thankful for the sidewalk. The minute she left the corner, the dark closed in on her, and she felt spooked even though she was in the middle of a prosperous-looking suburban development that hadn't been there five years before.

She couldn't understand why the residents didn't demand better lighting. Don't these people ever go out at night? she wondered.

She continued slowly up the sidewalk, her rubber-soled Docksiders making no noise on the pavement. She was dressed in blue jeans, a dark hunter green turtleneck sweater, and an old navy blue pea jacket that she had bought at an Army-Navy outlet about twenty years ago.

Not a very smart way to dress for a dark night on a dark street, said the voice of practicality. You look like a cat burglar.

So how was I supposed to know I'd have to hike through gloom? she responded testily. Besides, I have my heart socks on. They'll protect me.

Her socks were bright red wool with white hearts woven into them. Ken had given them to her for Valentine's Day last year. She had given him a white toothbrush emblazoned with red hearts. Later that night, when Amanda had come out of the shower, Ken was sitting up in bed reading a novel, and Shadow was curled up on her pillow—wearing a diamond bracelet around her neck.

It had been an uncharacteristically romantic gesture, and the thought of it warmed her now. She smiled as she imagined her husband playing his usual tennis game at this very moment. She loved to see him in shorts. He had the most beautiful legs.

Just get this over with, she said to herself, and you can go home and look at those legs all you want.

She found the Wolfmans' house, which was dark except for a dim light in one of the downstairs rooms. There were no cars in the driveway, so she couldn't tell if anyone was home. She paused at the bottom of the driveway and looked around. There was no one on the street.

The garage was not attached to the house, so she walked

silently and unobserved up the driveway and around the
garage. She saw nothing. The door was closed, and there
weren't even any garden tools lying about.

Amanda walked back down the driveway, intending to
return to her car. But again she stopped at the foot of the
driveway.

Don't do it, said the voice. You came on a wild goose chase.
Now admit it and go home. What did you expect to find,
anyway? Dr. Frankenstein's laboratory complete with bubbling
cauldrons? And, it added, sounding exactly like her mother, be
grateful you weren't arrested for trespassing.

I know, I know, thought Amanda. I'll go in a minute. I just
want to look at one more thing.

She went up the front walk, mounted the two steps, and
stood at the front door. Behind the sheer curtained window
where the light was she heard Wolfman's voice.

"You stupid cunt!" he shouted. "I told you not to . . ."

The rest was garbled. Maybe he had turned his back or
moved. Amanda wasn't certain what to do. She had obviously
come upon a domestic quarrel.

Leave, said the voice of reason. This is none of your
business. Just get out. Go home and admire your husband's
legs.

I'll stay just a second more. I want to hear what he's so mad
about. And what kind of man calls his wife a cunt?

A real shithead, that's who. A man you don't want to mess
with.

But Amanda didn't leave. She craned her neck and looked in
the window. Wolfman was walking around waving his arms,
gesticulating, and shouting.

"I told you to do it my way, but no, you had to . . ."

He moved away again, and Amanda stepped to the edge of
the broad cement stoop, which was two steps above the level
of the front walk. The small roof extension that covered the
stoop was held up by two wooden beams, and attached to one
of them was a metal downspout that led from the gutter above.

Amanda hung on to one of the beams with one hand and
leaned out over the edge of the stoop for a better view of what
was going on in the living room. She held her other arm out a

few inches for balance. The voice of reason was quiet for once. It had most likely given up in disgust in the face of such ludicrous and foolhardy behavior.

What Amanda saw made her gasp.

Wolfman had a gun in his hand, and he was alternately waving it around in the air and pointing it at Ina, who sat cowering on the couch. He continued to yell obscenities at his wife, but Amanda had heard enough. She would get the hell out of there and call the police from a neighbor's.

But she had leaned farther over the edge than she thought, and as she flailed her right arm for support, her left hand slipped off the beam and she lost her balance. She grabbed frantically for something more solid than air and felt a surge of relief as she made contact with the metal downspout.

With her heart pounding wildly, she pulled herself upright. She had almost regained her balance when the downspout ripped away from both the gutter above and the beam to which it was insecurely anchored. She tumbled into the azalea bushes with a resounding crash, thinking nothing more practical than, these damn new houses are built like shit.

She came to rest wedged between two azaleas and only had time to note that the ground had been freshly mulched when the front door was yanked open and bright light spilled out into the night, clearly illuminating Amanda's ridiculous position.

Wolfman stared down at her and she returned his gaze, and for a moment that seemed like forever, neither one spoke.

"You!" he said in a hoarse stage whisper. "Get up!"

As Amanda struggled to her feet, she saw that Wolfman looked around to see if anyone had heard the commotion, and feeling reassured that it had gone unnoticed, he pointed the gun at Amanda.

Whenever she saw a movie or television program in which someone was threatened with a gun, she wondered what she would feel like if it were to happen to her. Amanda was sure she would be paralyzed with fear and would not be able to think straight.

Thinking *straight*, she now knew, was not the problem. Thinking at all was. Her brain had turned completely to ice; she could actually feel the coldness inside her head.

So this is where the expression "icy fear" comes from, she thought.

Don't tell anyone, said the voice she should have listened to all along, but you're thinking. Just do what he tells you for now, and we'll get out of this somehow.

As Amanda got to her feet, Frank grabbed her roughly by the wrist and hauled her up onto the stoop. "Get in the house," he snarled, keeping a tight grip on her wrist and shoving the gun into her side. It hurt.

He slammed the door shut and threw the bolt, and in the split second that she was free of his hands and his attention was turned to securing the door, Amanda regretted not taking Ken's advice to learn judo.

"Women should know how to protect themselves, honey," he had said. "I'd feel a lot better if you'd take a course."

"You're right," she had replied. "Maybe next year when I have more time. For now I'll just scream. The police always say that a woman's best weapon is her lungs."

A fat lot of good my lungs are going to do me now, she said to herself as Frank dragged her to the couch and flung her down next to Ina, who was weeping. She looked as if she had been crying for a long time and was not about to stop.

"What are you doing here, cunt?" asked Frank.

"Which cunt are you addressing?" asked Amanda sarcastically.

Instantly, the voice of reason snapped, Stupid, don't make him ang—

The blow to her face sounded like a gunshot as the crack of flesh against flesh rang in her brain. For the briefest instant she thought she *had* been shot even though she could see that the hand that hit her was not the one holding the gun. A wave of fear flooded her system with adrenaline, and as it receded, serious nausea took its place. The only thing that prevented her from splashing leftover beef stew on the blue carpet was the severity of the pain in her face.

These successive physiologic reactions to the physical assault lasted less than a minute; then she was left limp and trembling on the couch with only a dull ache on the side of her face.

Ina was crying with renewed vigor, and Frank stood in the middle of the living room on the hideously bright blue carpet, staring at the two women.

"Shut up, Ina," he said. "Can't you ever do anything but cry?"

"Frank, I told you this would come to no good. I told you all you'd get was trouble. And now look what's happened."

"Shut up, bitch. You're in this, too. You're the one who gave him the stuff. You didn't think it was such a bad idea when we started. You wanted him to suffer as much as I did. And now you want to turn us in. How stupid do you think I am? Do you think in a million years that I'd let you do that to me?"

The puzzle was starting to fall together, and even though part of Amanda's mind was trying to figure out an escape plan, the other part saw clearly that it had been Ina Wolfman who had given McBride the poison that her husband had supplied. She must have been doing it for years and that was why she stayed on working for McBride.

"You were never McBride's patient, were you?" Amanda said to Wolfman.

"Shut up, cunt," replied Frank.

Being called a cunt with such mindless frequency was almost as bad as being held at gunpoint by a man who was obviously half-mad with rage and confusion. But she said nothing this time and looked around the living room to see if there was anything she could use as either a way to escape or overpower Wolfman.

Overpower! Don't even think it, said old practical-voice again. See the gun? *That's* power, and don't you dare mess around with it. If anything's going to get you out of this—and it's not likely that anything will—it'll have to be your brain, so start using it!

There were only two ways out of the living room: the way she had come in: a solid door, now securely bolted, and an archway leading to the dining room beyond. She could easily crash through any of the four large windows *if* there wasn't the little matter of the gun—which she could now see had a silencer on it. She recognized it from the movies.

There was no escape.

Maybe she could talk her way out of it. She'd often heard it said that women could sometimes convince an attacker not to rape them if they remained calm and said the right things. But Wolfman didn't seem to be much in the mood for conversation, and Ina was going to be no help at all.

"Dr. Wolfman," she said very softly and tentatively.

He said nothing, but he heard her and stopped pacing the length of the couch and looked at her. She took his silence as permission to speak.

Still in her softest voice she asked, "Why did you hate Dr. McBride so much? What did he do to you?"

It was Ina who spoke: "He wouldn't leave us alone. Frank made one mistake, and he never let—"

"Shut up, shut up, shut up, shut up, shut up, shut up!" roared Wolfman, completely out of control. He screamed invectives at his wife while his features contorted and his face turned almost purple.

Fear clawed at Amanda once again, but even so, it occurred to her that he might have a stroke and she wished mightily for that. It also occurred to her that now that Wolfman was out of control, she might spring off the couch and take away his gun.

Don't move! said the voice of instinct. This is a madman. Turn yourself into a statue. Don't move a muscle. Just hold still until he exhausts himself.

Amanda obeyed her instincts, but Ina Wolfman either didn't have them or didn't listen to them. She began to plead with her husband again.

"Frank, listen to me. We can stop now. We've done what we set out to do. You always said you didn't care if you had to pay in the end as long as you took care of that man and made him suffer. Frank, please."

Frank Wolfman stood stock-still. He was as silent and motionless as stone.

There was a measure of time, Amanda didn't know how much, when she knew it would happen, yet it couldn't happen because things like this don't happen to people like her.

Even as he raised his arm and she heard the click of the safety catch being released, there was a measure of time in which she believed it wouldn't happen because it *couldn't* happen.

Then, when she knew it would happen, even as she saw the gun with its long, ugly snout being raised, there was a measure of time in which she thought it wouldn't happen because she wasn't ready for it to happen.

There was a measure of time, it seemed like a very long time, in which she felt an overwhelming sense of grief; a raging, all-consuming grief that was herself grieving for herself.

Then, when she heard the quiet, almost dignified *pffft* of the firing mechanism, there was a measure of time in which she permitted herself to take leave of herself, even though she knew she was still alive. If she were not, she would not have heard the gunshot.

Then, immediately afterward, there was a time in which she was able to tell herself that she didn't know what the warm, sticky fluid was that covered her face and hair and soaked into her pea jacket. She also managed to avoid recognizing the pieces of blood-smeared gray-white tissue. She knew that the sharp, hard fragments were bone shards, but in that measure of time she refused to know where they had come from.

There was also a time, although it was fast drawing to a close, that Amanda could believe that Ina Wolfman was going to be all right because the hand that had fallen into her lap was still twitching.

Amanda looked at Frank Wolfman, but he was so far away that it was as if she were looking through the wrong end of a telescope. He stood at the end of an impossibly long tunnel, yet she could see his face clearly. The rage was gone; his features were no longer contorted with madness. It had all gone to his eyes, which stared at the body of his wife without focusing on her.

Amanda was very cold, and she slowly became aware that her jeans were wet in the crotch.

I wet my pants, she thought. I hope it soaks their couch. I hope I ruined the fabric. He deserves to have his couch ruined, it's so ugly.

She found Frank Wolfman guilty of having an ugly couch.

Silly. But it was enough for now. It was enough because now she could acknowledge that something had happened; something bad enough to have made her pee in her pants, and bad enough to feel angry that someone could buy a couch that ugly.

She knew that very soon she would have to acknowledge a far deeper anger, and she would have to face the obscenity of the dead woman beside her on the couch.

She could feel the protective shock wearing off, and already she wanted it back.

"Get up," he said, but she made no move. The voice had come from so far away that she couldn't be sure she had heard it. And anyway, there was a hand and arm in her lap weighing her down—a soft white hand, even now turning pink from the blood that collected there because the pump that forced it back up had stopped.

"Get up," he said again. This time the voice seemed to boom out from all around the room, as it had when she faced him through the glass in Building 87. It pressed in on her from all sides, and she sprang to her feet, shoving the lifeless arm out of the way.

"Turn around and look at her," the voice ordered.

There was no possible way she could do that. He ought to have known that. But she did, of course, because the booming voice was overwhelmingly compelling. She turned around and looked at what had once been Leo McBride's secretary.

Amanda breathed a sigh of relief. It wasn't as bad as she thought it would be. It wasn't as if the bullet had disfigured Ina's face. It had simply removed it—and most of the front of her head as well. So she could think of it as the stump of an amputation, and that made it all right.

Lots of people had amputations. It was something you could get used to.

The relief lifted her spirits, and she felt a moment of elation that escalated to wild happiness. It wasn't that bad! Thank God it wasn't a death, after all—just an amputation. Amanda was so grateful, so happy.

She laughed aloud in wild, exuberant joy. She laughed again, and then she couldn't stop laughing. What a riot this was turning out to be!

Ina Wolfman had always had a peevish, mousy face, so her husband simply amputated it. How clever he was! It was so much cheaper and faster than plastic surgery. Why hadn't other people thought of it?

Amanda chuckled and guffawed, bending over and straightening up in her exuberance. But the laughter was coming from the wrong place. It surrounded her, controlled her. It made the rest of her urine run down her thighs. It consumed her.

NURSE LAUGHS HERSELF TO DEATH

"Amanda Jane Knight, 38, Director of Nursing at the John F. Kennedy Memorial Hospital in Washington, D.C., died Friday of laughter after witnessing a facial amputation. It is believed to be the first such death. . . ."

The splash of icy water in Amanda's face ended the obituary composition. It ended the laughter, and for an instant she thought it had ended her life.

Wolfman dragged her into the kitchen by her wrist, and now she stood before him, her face and hair dripping wet, the crotch of her jeans clammy with cooling urine, and her mind her own again.

"Listen to me, bitch," said Wolfman. "I want you to do exactly what I tell you. If you make a sound, if you do a single thing to attract attention, if you don't follow every order instantly, you'll look like old Ina in there. Understand?"

Amanda nodded.

"Say it!" he commanded.

"I understand," she whispered.

"Dry your hair and wipe your face."

As she took the dish towel that smelled like spaghetti sauce, and rubbed it over her dark hair, trying not to think about what she was wiping off her face, she forced herself to assess the situation. It was clear that he planned to kill her. He *had* to kill her now. She could accept the logic of that, and strangely enough, knowing the outcome didn't throw her into a panic. What made her nervous was not knowing how and when it would happen. He could blow her apart at any moment, and she wanted to be prepared.

If he was going to blow you apart, he would have done it by now, said the voice of reason.

Yes, but why didn't he? What does he have in store?

Your hysteria scared him. He wants you calm, neat, and presentable. He wants you to obey orders. That means you might come in contact with other people. That means you're going somewhere.

"Where are we going?" she asked Wolfman.

"Don't ask questions, bitch, just do as you're told. Where's your car?"

"At the corner."

"All right, we're going to walk down there. I'll be behind you, and you know what I've got in my hand. You've seen what it can do. If you scream, if you open your mouth, if you do *anything* to attract attention, you're dead. Understand?"

"I understand," she said.

They left the house by the kitchen door and walked down the driveway and onto the sidewalk. He was right beside and slightly behind her, just as he said he would be. She thought about screaming or breaking into a run and heading for a house across the street with all the lights blazing. Would he really shoot?

Are you kidding? asked the voice of logic. You saw what he did to his wife—his own *wife*. Just keep walking.

But this may be my only chance.

If you scream, who do you think is going to hear you? It's cold out. Everyone has the windows closed. Besides, even if someone heard, what good would it do? This is Washington, the city where no one takes responsibility for anything. No one wants to get involved. Just keep walking.

Amanda kept on along the sidewalk, cursing her indecision, realizing it would be foolhardy to challenge him, but knowing that time was running out.

They turned the corner onto Courthouse Road, and Wolfman said, "Stop," when they came to a light blue Chevrolet. He unlocked the driver's side door and said, "Get in."

She slid behind the wheel, and he locked her in and walked

around the front of the car. Immediately she put her hand on the horn button and pressed hard. The suburban silence was shattered, and Frank Wolfman's shocked face was frozen in horror as he stared at her through the windshield.

What was Morse code for S.O.S? Three long, three short, three long. Or was it the other way around?

Who cares? Just keep honking, said the voice.

But it was too late. In a flash Wolfman had the passenger door open and yanked her hand off the steering wheel. Then he grasped both her wrists with one hand, and with the other he slashed the gun butt across her cheek.

She felt the bone structure on the side of her face give way. It simply crumpled like a paper cup, and the pain was so overpowering and intense that at first she didn't recognize it as pain. Mercifully, her mind dimmed again, and when it cleared, there was no mistaking what she felt. The pain raced around her head, whistling and screaming, like an amusement park ride run amok.

Okay, so now you know he means business, said the voice. Now you'll do everything he says. You'll ignore your pain because that's the only way you can deal with it. He's telling you something. Pay attention.

Amanda blinked back the tears and looked at Wolfman through one eye. The other had swollen shut, and she wondered desperately if it had been blinded. Perhaps bone fragments . . .

"Turn the key and drive," he said.

"Let me wipe the blood off," she said. It was pouring out of her cut flesh, and she was afraid she wouldn't be able to stop the bleeding.

In a gesture so puzzling that she couldn't comprehend it, Wolfman reached into his pocket, brought forth a clean white handkerchief, and tenderly pressed it to her cheek.

"Thank you," she said, and although the pressure of the handkerchief made the pain ricochet around her head at an even more dizzying speed, she had to stop the bleeding.

"Start the car and drive where I tell you," said Wolfman in the most even tone she had heard from him all evening.

She glanced at her watch. Not quite eight-thirty. Only about a half hour had passed since she had left her car on the corner of Courthouse Road and Linden Lane. Ken would just now be working up a sweat, nowhere near ready to go home. And even after he arrived home at nine-thirty or so, he wouldn't begin to worry about her for another hour or so.

As they drove through the quiet streets of suburban Washington, the only sounds in the car were Wolfman's occasional orders. When they turned onto the George Washington Parkway and headed away from the city, Amanda thought she knew where they were going.

"Where did you get the aflatoxins?" she asked.

His reaction was almost as violent as it had been when she honked the horn. He grabbed her upper arm, yanking it so painfully that she thought it would separate at the shoulder. The car swerved to the right across another lane of traffic, in which there was no other car at the moment, and onto the shoulder. It was only when Wolfman had instinctively loosened his grip, seeing where they were headed, that Amanda could regain control and prevent the car from crashing through the trees and into the river beyond.

"How do you know about that?" he asked in a voice that was almost a bark.

Amanda's heart was pounding in fright from the near crash; the pain in her head was so bad that she didn't see how she could remain conscious much longer—and she was angry. She was enraged.

"I figured it out. And I want to tell you right now that if you touch me or hurt me one more time I'm going to kill us both. I'm going to drive this car into the next cement overpass, and there's nothing you can do about it. You're going to kill me anyway, and I want you to leave me alone until you do. *I do not want you to hurt me again.*"

Where was this resolve coming from? How was her voice so steady when her entire being was on the edge of . . . what?

She was approaching death, that much she knew, but she couldn't *feel* it. She couldn't feel anything but anger and the pain in her head and shoulder.

Don't think about it. Don't think about anything, said the voice very softly now. There was no trace of the usual sarcasm.

It was calm, even soothing. Just keep driving. Keep alert. Pay attention to everything. Stay conscious. I don't think he'll try to hurt you again. You shocked him and scared him, and now he isn't sure if he believes you about driving into a wall.

"What do you mean, you figured it out?" asked Wolfman. "I want to know."

"Well, go ahead and want. I'm not going to tell you."

"You're right about dying. You are going to die. I have to kill you, you know. I regret it. I really do. I tried to warn you the other day not to get mixed up in all this, but you're a stubborn bitch, aren't you?"

"Don't call me bitch," said Amanda. "I told you not to. And I notice that you don't seem to have much regret about killing your wife. You blew her away, just like that. And if you regret having to kill me so much, don't do it. Just let me out here. Maybe you can blame the murder on someone else, and you'll get away with it. Say it was an intruder."

"Oh sure," said Wolfman. "And what are you going to say to whoever picks you up on the road? How are you going to explain your face?"

Amanda started to hope; she continued without even thinking about what she was saying. "We'll make up a story together," she babbled. "We can pull off the side of the road right now and get our stories straight. I'll stick to mine, I promise. We can say I was in your house—we'll think of a reason—and the intruder came in and killed Ina and then forced us both into your car, and he let me off here, and, and . . . ."

Her voice trailed off. Wolfman was laughing at her preposterous attempt to save herself. "Go toward Maryland," he said as they approached the end of the parkway and merged into the beltway.

He's not going to *let* you go, said the voice, practical once again. *If* you get out of this alive, it'll be because you saved yourself. He has to kill you, Amanda, so tell him about the aflatoxins. I don't know why you should, just do it and don't question it.

So Amanda told Frank Wolfman about the infection-control conference, her library research (she said nothing about Roland

Armstrong; why get him killed as well?), and the association she made with the toxin and liver cancer.

"So you see," she concluded, "if I can figure it out, other people can, too—like the police. They already know that I think you did it. Do you really expect to get away with this?"

"Yes, I do. There's no way anyone can *prove* I did it. The only people who know are you and Ina, and I've already solved half of *that* problem."

"But they'll still get you for Ina's murder—and mine," she said.

"Don't count on it," he replied. "Now shut up."

Amanda obeyed. There didn't seem to be anything else to say. She wondered remotely how he planned to cover his tracks, but she didn't care enough to ask. In fact, she didn't care about anything, and that worried her.

Maybe I'm losing my mind, she thought. Maybe I've had brain damage. Even *that* didn't concern her as it should. Just concentrate on the moment, she told herself. Nothing else is important.

"Get off at Old Georgetown," said Wolfman. "Do you know how to get into NIH from there?" he asked.

She answered in the affirmative, and there was no further talk until they pulled in the parking lot behind Building 87. Wolfman got out of the car, locking the door behind him, and then went around to Amanda's side to open it. There was no question of her honking the horn now. She could scream when she got out, though. It wasn't *that* late, and NIH was loaded with workaholics who stayed in their laboratories till all hours. She would do that. He would hurt her again, but it was pointless not to try.

The door opened and he grabbed her wrist again and hauled her out of the car. The sudden change in position created a wave of nausea so overwhelming that the possibility of screaming was obliterated in an episode of vomiting so violent that she sank to her knees in the parking lot.

Wolfman had momentarily let go of her in his surprise, but now he clamped his hand on her arm and started to drag her on her knees toward the great steel bank vault door. Although she had finished vomiting, she was till retching and coughing, and she felt her consciousness fade as the pain in her head reached a pitch that she had not imagined could exist. She wasn't even aware of the muscles in her shoulders separating. She didn't feel the searing pain that was now spreading across her entire upper back.

She was glad she was going to pass out, and she waited to embrace the enveloping blackness.

But it never came to her rescue. She never lost consciousness. In fact, once Wolfman had dragged her to her feet and the terrible spasmodic retching had passed, she felt marginally better. The pain was still ricocheting around in her head, but she could tolerate it now.

As she opened her mouth to scream, Wolfman pushed her roughly into the cinder block corridor, where she had been trapped so short a time ago. This time there would be no escape—unless she could reach one of the emergency buttons. This time she would welcome the biological S.W.A.T team. She would welcome a platoon of Marines.

She looked up and saw one of the buttons only about three or four steps away, and as she tensed her muscles to rip her arm out of Wolfman's grasp, he unlocked a door, shoved her into a pitch black room, and slammed and locked the door behind him.

+ + 16 + +

AMANDA STUMBLED TO a halt in pitch blackness so complete and enveloping that she thought she would suffocate.

She had no idea how big the room was, and she felt disoriented and dizzy. Instinctively she put her hand out to steady herself, but she felt nothing, so she cautiously took a few steps . . . and kept walking with her hand out in front of her like a blind woman until she came to a wall.

Amanda was pretty sure that she was at the wall opposite the door, but she could have gotten turned around in the confusion of being hurled into the room, so she walked along the wall, feeling for a light switch. When she had taken about a dozen steps, she banged her shin on something hard, and reached down to discover what felt like a wooden bench.

Still groping along the wall, she turned two corners until she found the switch. The sudden blaze of light hurt the one eye that was open and sent shafts of pain hurtling around her head again.

Never mind that now, she thought. Just sit down before you pass out.

Then she gave out a laugh that sounded more like a whimper, and said, "Pass out, hell. You're going to pass *on* soon."

And then, sitting on a wooden bench in an absolutely bare room made of cinder block, Amanda prepared to die.

Two years before she moved to Washington, when she lived in a Philadelphia apartment, she had come home one May

238

afternoon and found a fire raging out of control. It had started at the opposite end of the long building, but the high spring winds whipped it ever faster toward her apartment, and the firemen didn't seem to be having much of an effect.

She had gone in to rescue Shadow's predecessor, Thunder-Pussy, and then, standing in the parking lot, hugging her cat and watching the building burn, she had taken stock of her feelings.

"It's happening to you, Amanda," she had said to herself. "This time it's going to be *your* home on the eleven-o'clock news. Now, what is it that you're *really* attached to? Which of your possessions is truly irreplaceable?"

She had learned something good about herself that day. She would grieve over only a few things: her baby pictures, a tapestry that had taken a year to make, a few pieces of her mother's jewelry, and one or two other items of sentimental value. But she found that she was not emotionally attached to her stereo, her furniture, or her clothes. She was not despondent over the loss of her *things*.

Now, as she waited for Frank Wolfman to kill her, she looked at her life the same way. She was angry at the thought of dying. It was much too soon, especially now that she had learned to enjoy life, but she decided to concentrate on the good things she'd had: a childhood under the guidance of a remarkable mother, an adolescence that had taught her independence and resourcefulness even though it had been filled with pain, an education that had given her a career as well as . . .

The door burst open to reveal the now-familiar space-suited figure.

"Come on out, bitch," snarled Frank Wolfman in a voice made hollow and menacing by the speaking apparatus of the face mask.

All the calm philosophizing she had fortified herself with dissolved in a wave of the most intense fear Amanda had ever known. Arcing spasms clutched at her bowels; all her senses seemed to go on red alert, but at the same time went dull as adrenaline gushed into her bloodstream and forced her heart to race faster than it ever had before. The hair on her arms and at the back of her neck sprang upright, and her vision dimmed for an instant, but then cleared.

Her heart steadied, and her brain cleared. She didn't move. She never left her seat on the bench.

"I told you to come out of there," Wolfman said in a less menacing tone this time.

"Dr. Wolfman, I understand that you have to kill me," she said. How could she make her voice so steady when she was totally consumed by fear? she wondered. "But before you do, will you tell me *why* you killed McBride?"

There was a silence, punctuated only by the rasping sound of Wolfman's breathing through the air hoses. Amanda was aware that he must be wearing his space suite for a reason, and she was acutely conscious of her relative nakedness, even in the heavy pea jacket, now stained with Ina's blood. What was she breathing that he wanted to protect himself from?

The silence continued. "Please tell me," she said. "You have nothing to lose. I'm obviously not going to tell anyone, and I really want to know."

"He was a bastard," said Wolfman.

"That's it?" asked Amanda incredulously. "But that's no reason to kill someone. We all thought he was a bastard."

"It was his greed that did him in. He liked to humiliate people," said the space-suited figure.

Amanda didn't believe him. Unless Wolfman had some elaborate fantasy going that put him way beyond psychiatric help, there *had* to be more to it than that.

"Please tell me," she repeated, very softly this time. "We all hated him. He did awful things to people, especially someone very dear to me. Please tell me what he did to you that made you have to kill him."

Wolfman took two steps toward her, the ungainliness of the space suit making the advance seem especially threatening, and she involuntarily moved a few inches down the bench; her heart pounding once again. But to her surprise, he reached up and took off the helmet and sat down next to her.

He had aged twenty years since he had locked her into the room. His face was haggard and lined, and he looked exhausted. Frank Wolfman was an old, beaten man, and in that observation Amanda found renewed hope that she could save herself.

Only when he set the helmet down next to himself on the bench did she notice the flask of yellowish fluid he held in his hand. The flask was stoppered and sealed and had no label that she could see, but Amanda knew without a doubt that it contained the instrument of her death. It was against the accidental breakage of the flask that Wolfman had protected himself.

"Eleven years ago Leo McBride found out that I had been selling secrets to the Russians, and he'd been blackmailing me ever since."

Amanda said nothing, and Wolfman went on.

"Everyone in the scientific community knows that we do classified research here. Everyone knows that we're experimenting with biologics as an alternative to nuclear war." He laughed harshly. "Some alternative! This stuff"—he held the flask up, and the yellow liquid sloshed—"will make radiation sickness look like a bad cold if you inhale even a microgram."

He was silent again, perhaps contemplating the enormity of an all-out biological war, or perhaps the effect of one microgram. Amanda deliberately did not think about it.

"The Russians are doing the same thing. Everyone knows that, too. Sometimes we're ahead of them, sometimes they're ahead of us. It's all a big game, just like the nuclear arms race, except without the publicity." Again he laughed without mirth.

"The public," he said with utmost scorn, "those anti-nuke people out demonstrating like a bunch of college kids. They'd be *happy* to blow up the world if they knew what this stuff could do. And this isn't even the worst of it." He sighed in what seemed like resignation.

"When someone from the Russian embassy approached me a long time ago, I brushed him off. But he kept coming back, and each time he offered more money. So I thought, what the hell? Why not? It's not like I'm giving them something they wouldn't develop for themselves in a few years. And it wasn't like they didn't have stuff that was far worse than we had. It wasn't like I was *spying* for them or anything. Nobody was actually going to use the stuff; everyone knew it would be the end of the world. It was just a *game*, and they were willing to pay me to play.

"So I started selling them information, not very much, but enough to keep their own research on the right track. We had a drop point up in Gaithersburg—just like in the movies." Again there was that short, harsh laugh.

Amanda listened to the story, surprised at not being more surprised. Was it because she lived in Washington and assumed that half the people on the street were secret agents? Had she indeed read too many spy novels? Did life *really* imitate art?

She watched his face. Most of the menace and anger had gone out of it, but she knew that Wolfman was mercurial, and she warned herself not to be fooled by a momentary relaxation of his guard.

Nevertheless she began to think about how she could escape. It was no good trying to take away the flask. He would win a physical struggle, and even in the remote event that she could somehow overpower him, the danger of the flask breaking was too great.

There were no alarm buttons in this room; she had seen that as soon as she had turned on the lights. Was he planning to kill her here, or would he take her out into the corridor or into the laminar-flow room? Just a few minutes ago he had ordered her out of the room, so she thought he did not want her to die here. But why? This would be the perfect place for a murder. He could put his helmet back on, smash the flask against the wall or floor, and lock her in while he escaped out the bank vault door, protected from whatever vapors seeped under the door of this room.

She tried to think what he might have in store while his voice, now almost whining and petulant, went on.

"Then they started having me meet with their scientists, and that's when all the trouble began. This molecular biologist, and sometimes another guy who was a biochemist, would grill me about my work. They apparently weren't satisfied with what I had been giving them, and they wanted more and more information about lab procedures and experimental processes.

"We used to meet in various places far from Washington. Once we met at a restaurant in Charlottesville near the

University of Virginia. Once I flew to New York. Another time we hired a fishing boat in the Chesapeake Bay, and one day we met at a racetrack in Charles Town in West Virginia. I won thirty dollars in two races!"

He was silent again, this time for so long that Amanda was afraid he had changed his mind about telling where McBride came in.

"How did McBride find out?" she asked, again softly so as not to disturb whatever was going on in his mind.

"In the spring of 1977, March it was, I met one of the guys, Kosmirenko, the biologist, at a diner in Cherry Hill, New Jersey. Have you ever been to Cherry Hill, New Jersey, Ms. Knight?"

"As a matter of fact, I have," she said.

"Well, so has Leo McBride. He has a brother there, and that brother had a heart attack, and he went to visit him. And before he drove home, he got hungry and decided to stop for something to eat at a diner in Cherry Hill, New Jersey.

"I didn't know him then, of course. My wife had just started working for him a few months before, and I had met him only once, for a minute when I went to pick her up at the hospital when her car was in the shop. We shook hands and said hello and that was it.

"And I didn't know he was in the diner that day. But he saw me there. And then half a year later he went to a party at the Russian embassy. Have you ever been to a party at the Russian embassy, Ms. Knight?"

"No, Dr. Wolfman, I have never been invited to one."

"Well, neither have I. Ina and I aren't the type who get invited to embassy parties. Those people are happy to do business with me, but they don't ask me in through the front door.

"But the McBrides—oh, they go to embassy parties all the time. They've even been invited to the White House. Have you ever been to the White House, Ms. Knight?"

"No," she replied as softly as she could.

"Well, the McBrides have been to the White House."

He was quiet again, and Amanda was, of all things, getting bored. She knew the rest of the story even before he told it, and she wanted him to get on with it so they would walk out into the corridor. She had to get out of this room.

"Tell me about what happened at the embassy party," she said.

Wolfman snapped back from wherever his mind had been and continued: "Kosmirenko was there, and McBride recognized him immediately and put two and two together. He approached me the next day and started the blackmail.

"It wasn't very much money each time. Sometimes a hundred dollars, sometimes less. I guess he thought he couldn't squeeze out more than I earned. Or maybe it wasn't the money at all . . . God knows, he didn't need it," said Wolfman bitterly.

"Anyway, after about five years of it, I'd had enough and decided to kill him. But I didn't want to *just* kill him. I wanted to make him suffer the way he had made me suffer."

"Were you still giving sec—uh, talking to the Russians all this time?" asked Amanda.

"Oh no. As soon as I told them about the blackmail, *they* dumped me—just when I needed the extra money."

"What did you do with the money the Russians paid you?" she asked.

"I spent it. What do you think I did with it? Did you think I set up a secret Swiss bank account? How much do you think it was?"

How the hell should I know? thought Amanda. The Russians haven't exactly been lining up to buy nursing management secrets!

Aloud she said, "I don't know, Dr. Wolfman."

"Well, it wasn't much. I didn't get more than thirty-five thousand dollars altogether for all the things I gave them and all the times we talked." Again, his voice was bitter.

So you're a schmuck as well as a traitor, she thought, and at the same time she realized she had her wits about her once again. Her mind was completely clear; she was able to think around the pain in her head, which had even abated somewhat. She was still alive, and with the telling of this story, the tables had changed in some subtle way. Frank Wolfman still held all the physical advantage, but somehow the emotional and psychological advantage was hers now. She decided to try to increase that advantage.

"Tell me about making the aflatoxins," she said, putting a smooth coaxing tone in her voice.

"Oh that," said Wolfman in an almost offhand way. "I did it in my garage. It was simple. Any fool can grow a mold, and I just brought a few things home from the lab to extract the toxins."

He glanced over at Amanda's face for the first time since he had sat down. "You thought I did it here, didn't you? Dumb bitch! Did you think I'd make a murder weapon right here in front of everyone?"

Then, as if he were no longer interested in humiliating her, he averted his face and finished the story.

"I got Ina to give it to him a little at a time. When she brought him coffee, she'd put a few drops in. It was easy to put some in a sandwich when he would eat lunch at his desk." Again, he looked at her full in the face. "It's easy to kill someone if you use your head and plan it carefully.

"The hard part was living with Ina the whole time. She hated McBride as much as I did. Maybe even more because she worked for him and had to deal with him every day, but she didn't like the idea of killing him."

I can't imagine why, thought Amanda sarcastically.

"But she liked watching him get sicker and sicker," said Wolfman. "She liked knowing he had liver cancer. And she liked knowing that she was the only one who knew. It was she who made all his appointments at Sloan-Kettering for chemotherapy. It was she who helped him think up excuses for why he would be gone for a day or two at a time when he was getting treatment. It was she who suggested that he wear that glop on his face to hide the jaundice.

"Oh, she liked that part, all right. But she didn't like the *idea* that we were killing him, and she didn't like seeing herself as a murderer. So she talked me into killing him all at once.

"I thought it was a good idea, too. It was obvious that he didn't have much longer to live, that he would die soon of the cancer, and I didn't want any suspicion cast on me at all, even though we had stopped giving him the poison and I had gotten rid of all the evidence from my garage.

"So I killed him with Anectine. Ina waited for a day when he would be in his office alone at lunchtime and had no appointments scheduled, and then she called me. She went out to the storeroom, and if anyone had seen me enter or leave the office, it wouldn't have aroused suspicion, because I could always say I was looking for my wife."

"Anectine, how clever," said Amanda. "How much did you give him?"

"Two hundred milligrams," replied Wolfman. "It did the job in a hurry."

I'll bet it did, she thought. It did it almost instantly. If the usual dose took effect in less than a minute when injected directly into a vein, then the whopper that McBride had gotten must have taken effect in about fifteen or twenty seconds. Even so, that's a long time to hold down a struggling victim who must surely have known what was in store for him.

"How did you get it into his vein?" asked Amanda.

"It was easy. I went in and told him that I needed more time to get this month's payment to him. I made myself act real humble, and he loved it. He was actually pleasant to me, and we had a nice little conversation.

"Then when I went behind him—to admire his books, I said—he was positively gloating over me. Until the very end he never knew what was coming. Then I got him into an arm lock—it's not hard when you know what you're doing—and slipped the needle into his jugular. I just held him until he suffocated. He knew there was no escape. You see, I told him what was in the syringe."

Diabolical bastard, thought Amanda. Anyone who knows the drug knows its rapid, inexorable process. McBride, if he were smart, would have relaxed as much as possible to help the drug work fast because once it has been injected, there is no reversing it—unless specific other drugs are given. After the first few seconds he wouldn't have been able to move. No wonder there were no signs of a struggle.

Since Anectine doesn't affect consciousness, McBride would have felt himself die. He would have known, in those fifteen or twenty final seconds, what was happening to him. He would have felt his face and throat muscles relax into uselessness, and then his chest muscles and diaphragm would have become utterly flaccid, so much so that he could not even take a breath. He would have felt himself suffocate, and he would know that he'd be dead in less than a minute. Once the needle was in he never had a chance, and he would have known that.

"But what about the needle puncture?" Amanda asked. Unless the police knew something they weren't telling, or unless Sal Mateo had missed it, Amanda didn't understand how Wolfman had gotten the Anectine into McBride without leaving a telltale mark.

"I planned that ahead of time," said Wolfman, looking pleased with himself. "I used a needle that you'd never find in a hospital—one so thin that it can pierce single cells without destroying them. And then I stuck the scalpel in his windpipe for good measure—just to throw the police off the track. It was a nice touch, don't you think?"

"Fabulous," said Amanda dryly.

"You know what I regret most about the whole thing?" asked Wolfman.

"No. Tell me," she replied.

"I'm sorry that he never knew that *I* gave him the cancer, that I caused him to suffer the way he made me suffer. That's all. The rest I'm glad of."

Then he lapsed into morose silence and leaned back against the cinder block wall. Amanda stared at him in astonishment as he seemed to deflate. He still gripped the flask of yellow liquid, but he appeared otherwise relaxed, and when he closed his eyes, she made her move.

She sprang from the bench, bolted out the door, turned into the corridor, and smashed her hand into the first red emergency button she saw. In almost the same movement, she ran down to the end of the corridor where the steel bank vault door was and turned the handle.

Nothing happened.

She was not surprised that the door was locked, but it took a few seconds for the continuing silence to register completely.

No alarms clanged. No red lights flashed. No sirens pierced the stillness.

When she fully realized the futility of her escape attempt, she leaned back against the wall and slid down until she was sitting on the floor, holding her head in her hands, once again consumed by pain, fear, and grief.

She sat that way for what seemed like a long time—until she became aware of the space-suited figure looming above her. The helmet was back on, and this time he held a gun in his right hand as well as the flask in his left.

"Did you think I'd leave the alarms connected, you stupid bitch? Did you really think I'd just let you press a button and waltz out of here and ruin all my plans? What a dumb cunt you are. I disconnected everything. We're cut off; there's no one to help you."

It was not the fact that it was all over now and she really *was* going to die that made her so angry. It wasn't even that she should have known that he would turn off the alarms—and that it didn't make sense to think that he would let his guard down enough for her to run out of the room for help. It was that he kept calling her a bitch and a cunt—and a stupid one at that.

Amanda got to her feet and faced him. "I *told* you not to call me a bitch," she said, her eyes blazing, her voice full of venom. She had never before been this enraged, and the fact that it might be her last emotion made her even angrier. "I told you never to call me that again."

"Well, well, well, aren't we the brave little bitch," said Wolfman sarcastically. "Oh, *excuse me*. A brave little *woman*. Too bad no one will ever see your final perform—"

The noise and the voices came simultaneously. "What's going on in there?" asked a muffled voice, accompanied by banging and pounding on the bank vault door. "What happened in there?"

Amanda and Wolfman stared at each other in shock. Neither spoke, and the banging continued.

"Is anyone in there?" came the voice again. "What happened? Who pulled the alarm?"

Again the adversaries stared at each other. Still neither one spoke. Amanda tried to think, but she couldn't think of anything to think about. There was nothing she could do.

Wolfman was at a loss, too. He hadn't known about the fail-safe system on the alarm. If he smashed the flask, he risked killing himself as well as Amanda, but he couldn't stand there doing nothing forever.

The banging stopped, and Wolfman found his voice. "They can't risk coming in here," he said. "They can't open the door because if we've had a spill, they can't let it escape to the outside."

"That means you can't go out, either," said Amanda. "They'll be waiting for us. If you kill me in here, they'll catch you on the way out. If you break the flask, you'll die, too. Those portable air pockets are good only for so long. So we're both trapped.

"Put the flask back where you got it, take off that suit, open the door, and tell them it's all a mistake. It's the only sensible thing to do."

Wolfman could see the logic of what she said, but he was a long way away from clear thinking and saw only one way out. Grabbing Amanda from behind, he thrust the flask into her hand and said, "Here, this is your responsibility now. Drop it and everyone in three states will die."

Then, pressing the gun into her side with his right hand, he entered a code into the keypad near the door, waited for the click, and then turned the large handle that controlled the air lock and the two of them stepped outside.

"Keep back!" he shouted into the crowd of dozens of people in the parking lot. Amanda was blinded by the huge floodlights and stunned by the flashing red and blue lights of the police cars. Reality began to fade.

The crowd did his bidding, and Amanda felt a human wave moving away from her as she and Wolfman slowly walked forward and then stood still. She raised her hand to make sure that everyone could see what she was carrying, and from out of the crowd she heard a hysterical voice shriek, "Don't drop it!"

"I'm not going to drop it, you dope," she muttered, but not loud enough for anyone but Wolfman to hear.

He laughed his harsh, mirthless bark, and words came out of her mouth that she didn't know were in her head.

"I'm going now, Frank. Good-bye."

And with her free hand, she removed his arm from around her chest, only dimly aware of how easy it was, and stepped away from him.

She took two steps before she heard the *pfft*. She heard it just before—or maybe it was just after—she felt the searing icy hot glow in her side, and then she was flying through the air—flying away over the tops of the trees.

Light as a feather, she flew into the night sky, still holding the flask, higher and higher, way up beyond the people in the parking lot, up and up until she was no more than a dot in the heavens. And then the dot was gone.

✦✦ 17 ✦✦

AMANDA LAY IN in the intensive care unit at Sinai Hospital. She had been there for three days and couldn't seem to wake up. Nevertheless, she heard everything that went on even though it was all fuzzy and far away.

She slept most of the time, but when she was awake, she couldn't respond; she couldn't tell them that she heard them. But that was only remotely frustrating. For the most part, she was content to lie still and let them minister to her while she drifted in and out of consciousness.

At first she thought she would end up like a character in a horror movie—alive and alert but unable to communicate at all—where everyone thought you were in a coma but you really weren't. That led to thoughts of being buried alive and a few moments of panic until, with a huge effort of will, she moved her foot and hand.

She knew Wolfman had shot her because the ambulance attendants had called out, "Gunshot coming in!" when they wheeled her into the emergency room.

She knew that the wound had been frightfully bad, not by what the doctors and nurses had said, because she didn't remember the words, but because of the tone of controlled urgency and the speedy efficiency with which they had gotten her up to the operating room.

But she knew she would live because Eddie Silverman had told her so. He had pulled a chair up to her bed, slipped his hand into hers, and talked very slowly and quietly.

"You're alive, Amanda. You're not in a coma. Your EEG is

normal. You were shot in the chest, but you will recover. You lost three ribs and a lobe of your left lung. Your cheekbone was fractured, and you're going to need plastic surgery, but your eye was spared. There is nothing wrong with your eyes.

"Can you hear me Amanda? Squeeze my hand if you can hear me."

She did squeeze, but it was too late. By the time she had heard his request and gotten her hand muscles to obey, he had gone. She felt bad about that.

She also felt bad about Ken. He was there so often, talking to her, whispering sweet things, talking about their very private things. She wanted so much to tell him that she heard and appreciated and was sorry she was causing him so much pain. One day he sat by her bed, not talking, just smoothing her hair the way she loved, and she managed to smile a little, but she guessed he didn't see it because he began to cry.

She had never known him to cry like that before—in great gulping sobs as if he had fallen into bottomless despair. He cried for a long time, and she wished she could comfort him. When he left, he pressed his lips to hers for a long, long time, and she responded, but again it was too late. He left thinking she would never kiss him again, and she felt very bad indeed about that.

Time passed. She waked and listened, and then she slept. Sometimes there was pain, but it wasn't unduly bothersome. Mostly, she felt disconnected from her body, like the time one evening more than fifteen years ago when she had smoked too much marijuana at a party. She realized afterward that it had probably been laced with something nasty, but at the time her head floated above her shoulders, and all she could do was sit on the couch with a stupid smile on her face and watch the other guests. There was nothing for it but to wait for her head to sink gently back to her shoulders.

It was something like that now, and she would just have to wait until everything got connected again. In the meantime, it wasn't so bad. The nurses and doctors were kind and gentle, and the rhythmic humming and hissing of the respirators and other machines in the ICU were soothing. And as time went by, the voices and machine noises grew more distinct and seemed closer.

She started to move her arms and legs more, but she couldn't seem to open her eyes and wake up. Glen was allowed in to visit, as was Lydia. Both women cried, and Amanda felt bad about that, too.

If you feel so bad all the time, why don't you wake up and tell them you're okay? said her conscience.

It's so peaceful like this, she replied. I like to float. I like to go into the dark. Leave me alone. I don't want to deal with any of it now.

You don't want to deal with what happened at the end. You don't even want to *think* about what happened at the end.

Leave me alone. I mean it.

You're going to have to wake up sometime, and you're going to have to face the fact that you got Ina Wolfman killed. It doesn't matter that she was a murderer, it was your fault that her husband killed her. If you hadn't gone poking your nose where it didn't belong, she would still be alive.

I know that, said Amanda to her conscience. Don't you think I know that? Leave me alone and let me go back to sleep.

Okay, but you'll be sorry later.

Amanda didn't know how she could be any sorrier than she already was, and she let herself drift off again over the trees into the night sky, still holding the flask.

Eddie Silverman came to visit every day, usually two or three times. He had had many talks with the neurologists, who assured him that there was nothing physiologically wrong with Amanda. Her brain scans were all normal and her electroencephalogram showed no permanent damage.

"Then why is she still unconscious?" he asked in frustration. "Why won't she wake up?"

The neurologists shrugged. For some things they had no answers.

And then one evening, after she had been there a week, Eddie sat by Amanda's bedside and said, "Goddamn it, Amanda, wake up. I know you're okay in there. Wake up so we can talk. Wake up so I can tell you how sorry I am that I got you into this mess. I know you were trying to prove that I didn't do it, that I didn't kill McBride, and *you* ended up almost getting killed. *Please* wake up, Amanda. I miss you so much. I miss our friendship so much.

"Besides, your husband is going crazy. Your cat isn't eating right. We have to work things out between us. Now, open your eyes right this minute."

This time it didn't take forever for the smile to come. It wasn't a big smile, but it was there. This time the weights on her eyelids weren't insurmountably heavy. It was hard, but she dislodged them and blinked her eyes open.

Eddie Silverman burst into tears.

"Why is everyone always crying?" she asked in a half croak, half whisper.

Eddie didn't reply. He just kept his head on her shoulder and cried, soaking her hospital johnnie. And this time she made her muscles work in time to put her arm around him and pat his head.

"I'm okay now, Eddie," she said. "I'm okay. I'm awake now."

After that it got hard. The pain in her face and chest and shoulder blasted her fully conscious mind with its full force.

But the physical pain was nothing compared to the realization that she had been the instrument of death for another person. It helped only a little to know that Ina may eventually have been executed for her crime.

She felt no such remorse about Frank Wolfman's suicide. When Lydia and Bandman told her the full story of what the Montgomery County Police had told them about what happened in the parking lot of Building 87, she had simply shrugged at their description of how he had turned the gun on himself after removing his helmet.

"They told me that everyone was so concentrated on you, Amanda, getting that flask out of your hand before you hit the ground, that no one even noticed what Wolfman was doing until it was too late," said Bandman.

"Do you feel up to telling us what happened that evening?" asked Lydia.

She and Bandman had accompanied the county police who

had come to take her statement even before she was well enough to leave the I.C.U. She had been dreading telling the story, especially the part about Ina, but she told it from beginning to end, leaving out no details. She remembered everything and described how she had laughed and laughed after Wolfman had killed his wife. She even told them how she had thought it was an amputation.

Bandman had been so nice about it. "Amanda," he had said, "the mind is a wonderful thing. It protected you by tricking you into thinking that what had happened had not really happened. It allowed you to keep going, to save yourself."

"Yes, but—"

"But nothing," he interrupted. "You will have to allow yourself to heal. What you did was foolish. It was dangerous and impulsive, but you did *not* cause the death of Ina Wolfman, and if the flask *had* broken, you would not have been responsible."

"And, Amanda, Wolfman was feeding you a line of bullshit," added Lydia. "The stuff in the flask was some kind of cloned bacteria. Sal explained it to me, but I can't remember all the details. Wolfman and the others in that lab were trying to make it real toxic, and it would have done harm, maybe even killed some people *if* they had swallowed or inhaled a lot of it. But all the people in three states . . . nonsense."

"They don't work on the highly volatile, really dangerous stuff at the main NIH campus. It's in the middle of one of the richest suburbs in the country—right across the street from Bethesda Naval Hospital, where the President goes.

"They do all the creepy germ warfare stuff out in the desert or up in North Dakota or someplace like that. Not in the middle of Bethesda!"

"But I didn't know that at the time," said Amanda. "I believed him because I had no reason not to, and I knowingly endangered all those people."

"You walked away from him because you wanted to live," said Bandman. "What's so terrible about that? Besides, you held on to that flask for dear life. One of the county policemen told me they had to pry your fingers away, you were holding it so tightly. They were afraid it would break in your hand."

"So you turned out to be a heroine," said Lydia.

"Some heroine," said Amanda with a bitter laugh.

"Look," said Bandman, much more sternly than he intended and much more than he felt, "if you want to wallow in guilt and twist what happened to meet your own masochistic needs, suit yourself. I'm just telling you the facts. You did a dumb thing, but it wasn't a *wrong* thing."

Amanda and the detective stared at each other for a few moments before she smiled and said, "Lieutenant Bandman, you're a nice man."

Sal Mateo came in one afternoon after she had been transferred to a private room. He carried an armload of tulips. "Anytime you get tired of being a director of nursing, Ms. Knight, you can have a job in my morgue," he said. "McBride was loaded with aflatoxins."

"Please call me Amanda," she replied. "And I thought that when you found them, I would feel triumphant and would take a lot of pleasure in saying, 'I told you so.' But, it's funny. I don't feel much of anything. I knew they would be there, and they were there, and it all seems so matter-of-fact. But I don't think you'd want to hire someone who'd faint all over your corpses!"

"I have lots of cigars," he replied with a grin. "Cigar smoke is potent enough to drown out the most putrid smells. You'll see!"

They laughed, and then he said, "You know, Amanda, in a million years I wouldn't have thought of looking for aflatoxins. It's not exactly an ordinary murder weapon, and even if we had come across it by some fluke, there would be no way to prove that it had been used as an instrument of death.

"And Anectine and all the rest of those new anesthetics are metabolized so fast that they're gone by the time you start the autopsy. This isn't the first time that sophisticated drugs have been used as murder weapons, but usually there's other evidence that leads us to the killer. This time, though, we had nothing else. If Wolfman hadn't confessed, well . . ."

"He would have gotten away with murder," said Amanda.

"Yes, he would," replied Mateo. "And the thing that scares

me is that not only will someone else try it now—it's been all over the papers—but more and more people will try experimenting with weirder and weirder combinations of drugs for very un-nice reasons."

"It's a scary, un-nice world, isn't it, Sal?" she asked.

Even more than she dreaded telling the police what had happened between her and Frank Wolfman, Amanda dreaded confronting Eddie with her guilt about suspecting him.

"I knew you did, Amanda," he had said one evening. "And I can't blame you. When I look back on it, I have to admit that I did everything I could to look as suspicious as possible. I was stupid—an idiot. And I almost got you killed. I'll never forgive myself for that."

Amanda said to Eddie what Bandman had said to her, and the two friends smiled at each other as Amanda polished off the last crumb of the tuna-and-cheese sub that Eddie had brought from Giovanni's. "Thank you for not letting me starve on hospital food. I don't think I could get down another forkful of that tasteless shit. Even Ruth Sinclair has taken pity and cooked for me."

"Friends don't let friends eat hospital food," he said. "But if you *ever* do anything that stupid and dangerous again, I will positively wring your neck. I'm getting too old to endure that kind of worry and fear!"

"I still have two questions," she said, "and then we're not going to talk about this again. First, why did you and Alice have lunch together? And what about you and Donald? Are you two going to come out of this okay?"

Eddie sighed. "I'll answer the second one first. I hope we'll be okay. It was bad there for a while during the thick of it. We're still pretty angry at each other, but we decided to go into couples counseling to talk things out. We both *want* to get back on an even keel, so we're trying.

"And I'm not sure why I asked Alice to have lunch. I was scared. I didn't want to talk to you because I was so ashamed of what I had said and done. It occurred to me that the police would think she was a suspect, too, and I guess I just wanted to be with someone who understood. Or I had hoped would understand. She's actually kind of a silly twit. Nice but only about a quarter of an inch deep!"

"But she's a good nurse," said Amanda. "By the way, did you know that Donald sent me flowers?"

"No, I didn't," he replied. "That was nice of him."

On the evening that Lydia and Glen came to the hospital together, Amanda could see that they liked each other and were going to be friends. The three women chatted about nothing in particular. Amanda had had her plastic surgery and was learning to adjust to decreased lung capacity when she suddenly remembered Cicely McBride.

"Well, we put a tail on her," replied Lydia in answer to Amanda's question about what the widow had been doing when her husband was murdered. "Guess what we found out?"

"She really *was* getting her rocks off with Seth Morgan," said Glen.

"Wrong," said Lydia.

"Screwing the secretary of state," said Amanda.

"Wrong again. Give up?" asked Lydia with a wicked grin.

"We give up."

"She was buying cocaine from this sleazebag in Rockville. At least that's what we think she was doing. She still won't admit it."

"Cocaine!" said Amanda, trying not to disturb the stitches in her cheek.

"Rockville!" sputtered Glen. "Who buys cocaine in Rockville? Rockville is so . . . so . . . ."

"Boring," said Lydia. "But did you think Cicely McBride would put on a Halston dress and take her Jaguar to buy drugs from a street dealer in Anacostia? No woman in her right mind drives alone through Anacostia even in broad daylight."

"So what's going to happen to her?" asked Amanda. "Did you arrest her?"

"Yeah, we arrested her," said Lydia with disgust. "But she's got connections, and her lawyer made a deal with the D.A. They gave her immunity from prosecution, and she told what she knew about the man who sold the drugs, and of course he's in jail now.

"But Cicely got the best part of the deal because she wouldn't say who put her onto the Rockville guy. She didn't even know the dealer's real name. So she got off free, and whoever it was will find her and her society friends another nice, clean dealer. She said she was going to go into a drug-treatment program, but that'll last about two minutes."

The three women were silent for a minute, but Amanda saw Glen wink at Lydia.

"Come on, what's up?" she asked. "You two look awfully pleased with yourselves."

"Well," said Lydia, "uh, Seth Morgan sounded like kind of an interesting guy, so I thought I'd interview him about what he knew about the case. And then I bumped into Glen here one evening when we were both visiting you in the I.C.U. and we went out for a drink and I told her about Seth."

"And you made an appointment with him, didn't you, Glencora Rodman?" asked Amanda, even though she really didn't have to ask.

Glen rolled her eyes to the ceiling and smiled with remembered pleasure. "I thought I was having a series of epileptic seizures," she said. "I thought he was going to blow all my fuses. Afterward, I felt like Jell-O."

"That good, eh?" said Amanda. "And what are *you* grinning about, Detective Simonowitz?"

"Wouldn't it be selfish of me to keep secret the source of so much pleasure?" said Glen. "So I just casually mentioned to Lydia that if she had a spare hundred lying around . . ."

"She's blushing like crazy," said Amanda. "Tell me everything."

"Well," said Lydia," I couldn't very well use my own name. It's been in the papers enough lately. So I waited until a friend went out of town and I was taking care of her dog and plants—and then I called for an appointment."

"Well . . ." said Amanda.

"I didn't know a human being could have that many orgasms and live to tell the tale," she said. "The man has hands like . . ." She couldn't find words and sputtered to a stop, blushing furiously. "Please don't say anything to Sal or Paul or anyone, okay?"

"Are you kidding?" said Glen, and Amanda nodded agreement. Some secrets were so sacred that they hardly needed discussion. Glen and Amanda understood that, and so, apparently, did Lydia.

Amanda healed steadily and was cheered by a parade of visitors.

Alice Bonner brought a bottle of cologne and the news that she had gotten a job as head nurse at Potomac Medical Center.

"I'm so grateful to you for proving that I didn't kill Leo," she said.

"I'm glad you're happy," Amanda said dryly, "but I didn't exactly go out and get myself kidnapped and shot just to prove your innocence."

Did this woman think she was the center of everything that happened?

"I know you didn't, and I really didn't mean that," said Bonner, flustered now. "I'm sorry you're going to have a scar on your face," she said in an effort to be sympathetic. "How are you going to cope with it?"

"With makeup and time," replied Amanda. "Did you know that I lost a good part of my lung capacity and three ribs and I'll always have a problem with heavy exertion?"

"I did, and I'm sorry about that, too," said Bonner, but it was clear to her that the small, already healing facial scar was a much more serious wound. Perhaps incredibly beautiful women really *were* shallower than women with imperfections.

David Townsend was awkward but earnest. "He just wants me to hurry up and get back to work," she said to Ken. "And when I mentioned the business about giving Morrison a reference, he had the good grace to admit I was right. Maybe he gave in just because I got shot and he's feeling sorry for me, but I decided to take what I could get from him. And poor Dr. Miller. He's getting so fogged in, he can barely remember what happened. I had the feeling that someone told him he ought to come up to visit me."

"I think you ought to come home to visit me," said her husband. "I miss you. I reach out for you in the night and all I get is a fistful of cat hair."

"Well, there's no cat here now," said Amanda. "And if you reach out to me, I'd put my arms around you and do things that no cat would think of doing."

"Right here in the hospital?" asked Ken.

"Why not?" she asked. "Lovemaking is very therapeutic."

"Do you feel up to it?" he asked, having shoved a large armchair against the door and unknotting his tie as he came back to the bed.

"We'll go slowly," she replied. "But I can tell that *you're* certainly 'up' for it," she said as she got out of bed, pressed herself against him, and prevented him from talking any more because his lips were covered with her own.

They stood together like that for a long time, reveling in the joy of being fully in each other's arms again, inhaling the deliciousness of mounting passion, caressing and kissing and getting down to the practical business of undressing one another.

Three days later they repeated the act, only this time they were cuddled under their own down comforter with the gray cat perched on the dresser opposite, patiently waiting until she could jump back on the bed and her woman would put her arm around her, and the three of them would go to sleep in warm safety.

Epilogue

THE THREE WOMEN sat at Amanda's kitchen table. In the center of the table lay a large, flat white box with a few crusts in it, all that remained of a giant pizza. There were two empty wine bottles on the counter next to the sink plus another with only a few inches left in it.

The women were now working on dishes of heavenly hash ice cream. The cat had jumped onto the table to steal pizza crusts, and no one had told her to get down, so she ate her fill and now sat cleaning her whiskers.

Lydia and Glen were dressed in jeans and sweaters. Amanda wore her white terry cloth robe and smelled of perfumed massage oil.

None of them was sober. Even Shadow was a little drunk with happiness and tomato sauce.

"God, what pigs we are," said Glencora, smiling with contentment. She belched.

Lydia giggled. "My mother always told me that if you drink white wine you won't get as drunk."

"As drunk as a skunk," said Amanda.

The other two looked at her, waiting for her to go on.

"That's all I have to say," she said. "Did you expect some great witticism?" She giggled, too.

"After what happened to you tonight, we didn't expect you to stay awake this long," said Glen.

Amanda merely smiled a long, slow smile and blinked owlishly at her friends.

Three hours before, just after she flipped through the mail

and kicked off her shoes, the doorbell had rung. She looked through the peephole but didn't recognize the short dark-haired man who stood on the step, a large metal case at his side.

"Yes?" she asked. Ken was in Chicago for two days, so she was alone and not about to open the door to a stranger.

Just then the phone rang. It was Lydia.

"Let him in. It's okay," she said, and then hung up before Amanda could ask questions.

Amanda opened the door a crack, keeping her shoulder against it, just in case.

"I'm Seth Morgan," said the man. "Your friends have a gift for you." He handed her a sealed envelope, and Amanda closed the door while she tore it open and read the note in Glen's handwriting.

> Roses are red.
> Violets are blue.
> Let this man
> Put his magic fingers on you.
>
> Love and kisses,
> Glen and Lydia

She opened the door, her mouth twitching in a smile she was trying to suppress.

"The first week back at work is always pretty tense, and your friends thought you might enjoy a nice, relaxing massage."

He said this in a friendly, nonchalant manner—without any trace of a leer—but Amanda could think of no response. Apparently she didn't need one.

"Why don't I set up the massage table here, or wherever you prefer, while you get your things off. Come on back in just a robe." He smiled again and opened the metal case.

What the hell, thought Amanda as she climbed the stairs. I deserve this.

She was back in the living room in five minutes and saw that Seth had closed all the curtains and set up his equipment in a corner of the room near a lamp table, on which he had placed a few bottles and two clean white towels. A lamp at the opposite end of the room was turned on to its lowest wattage.

He smiled again, patted the table, and said, "Hop up."

She hesitated, self-conscious for a moment about the long scar that ran up her side, not to mention the fact that she was hardly accustomed to stripping naked in front of a total stranger.

What the hell, she thought again, and untied the sash of her robe. Seth took it from her, folded it neatly, and draped it over the back of a chair.

"Have you ever had a massage before?" he asked after she was settled comfortably on her stomach, her cheek resting on her crossed arms.

"Not a professional one," she said.

"Well, you just relax and enjoy this. I'm here for your pleasure, so don't hesitate to tell me what you'd like."

"Boy, when that man says he's there for your pleasure, he ain't just whistlin' Dixie," said Amanda, finally putting down her ice cream spoon. "I could feel my bones rattle inside my skin."

The three women shrieked with laughter as they each remembered their hour with Seth Morgan.

"But how did you know to call me just when he rang the bell?" asked Amanda of Lydia.

"Glen and I were at the end of your driveway in the police car, and we saw him ring your bell, so I got the dispatcher to patch me through to your phone," she replied.

"Then," said Glen, "we had enough time to drop the police car off at the station house, go get the pizza and ice cream, and drive over here."

"We saw Seth leave just as we got here," added Lydia.

"Thank you. Thank you. This was the most wonderful present I've ever had. Thank you for being such sweet friends. Thank you for giving us this delicious secret. I have to hug you both."

The three women stood together in the middle of the kitchen floor, their arms around each other, giggling drunkenly, while the cat watched them from where she sat on the counter, her yellow eyes huge with love and contentment.

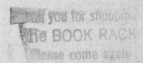